THE RiVER

THE RIVER
CRAIG A SMITH

The River by Craig A Smith

First published in the United Kingdom in 2025 by
Into Creative (Imprint: Into Books)

Paperback ISBN 978-1-7385149-3-9

Copyright ©Craig A Smith, 2025.

Craig A Smith has asserted his moral right to be
identified as the author of this work in accordance with the
Copyright, Designs and Patents Act, 1988.

All rights reserved. No part of this book may be reproduced,
stored or transmitted in any form or by any electronic,
mechanical or photocopying, recording or otherwise without
the express permission of the publishers, except by a reviewer
who may quote brief passages in a review.

A catalogue for this book is available from the British Library.

Cover design and typesetting by Stephen Cameron.

Typeset in Garamond.
Printed and bound by Bell & Bain Ltd, Scotland.

For sales and distribution, please contact:
stephen@intocreative.co.uk

Dedication

for the drifters

Acknowledgements

Massive thanks to George Paterson, Stephen Cameron, Jan Kilmurry, and the team at Into Books, for giving The River a home, and for cracking the whip when it came to trimming down the manuscript. It's a much better book for it. And has a lot less swearing.

Thanks to Claire Paterson Conrad at Janklow & Nesbit for her timely and enthusiastic assessment of the original manuscript at a time I really needed it.

For everyone who read my first novel, The Mile, thank you for keeping the wind in my sails and encouraging me to write another book. And a big thanks to Doug Johnstone for the beers and support.

Finally thanks to my wife Fiona and my (now grown-up) children Sophie and Riley, who offered advice and ideas throughout the sometimes painful process of creating a novel. They keep me keeping on, and if they can keep this up, who knows? There may even be a third book.

MONDAY

Lachlan sank into his second favourite chair and looked up at the clock mounted high on the magnolia wall. Twenty other ageing souls sat scattered around the room in various states of wakefulness, mostly oblivious to the clock's struggle. The second hand appeared to be frozen. After some time it jerked forward, before falling back again. The clock suggested four-thirty but it could have been any time, on any day, in any month.

Beyond the bay window the sun caught the tops of small waves breaking out in the Forth. Gulls swooped over the harbour. Behind it all the Bass Rock shimmered in the sun like a giant lump of quartz dropped into the sea.

Stella, one of the few people in the Seaview Care Home he had time for, rattled into the room with the tea trolley.

'The battery in that needs changing,' he said, pointing to the clock just as the second hand made another failed attempt at moving past the seven.

'So it does,' said Stella, pausing as she filled a china cup. 'I'll get it fixed.' She nodded towards another resident. 'I see Bob got to your chair first.'

Lachlan grunted, and looked again at the clock. The second hand was still failing to make the uphill journey. He knew how it felt. He focused on the figure seven, solid black on the cream clockface. The number that had haunted him these past few years. Seven ghosts had been visiting his dreams. Some pleasant, some not so much.

A noise at the window. A solitary magpie settled on the ledge. After a few seconds it took flight with a flap of wings. *One for sorrow...* A single feather drifted back down to the ledge.

Hello Mr Magpie how's your wife and family?...

He sipped his tea and his gaze fell again on the Bass Rock. Once a prison, now a bird sanctuary - the appearance of quartz a trick of the light, as sunlight shimmered over the shite of 100,000 gannets - it sat at the mouth of the Firth of Forth like a guardian, marking where the river met the sea.

ABERFOYLE 1950

This is where it began.

Lachlan hunkered by the loch and lowered his fingers into the cold black water.

'It's freezing Dad!'

He looked up, squinting into the sun. His father stood where the beach gave way to the trees, a silhouette topped by a plume of smoke spiralling into the blue.

'Lucky I'm not asking you to go for a swim then.'

Lachlan laughed and wiggled his fingers in the shallows. He grasped a slippery white pebble and lifted it from the water, examining its perfect smooth surface.

His father took a last draw and flicked his roll-up onto the rocky shore.

'We'll better be heading back son.'

'Can I keep this? For my collection?'

'That pebble? Well…' His father made a show of looking around. 'I suppose so, They'll not miss it.'

Lachlan smiled and tucked the stone into his pocket.

'So this is where it starts?'

His father hauled Lachlan over a dilapidated fence and onto a muddy path. They started back towards the main road, the sun at their backs casting long shadows ahead.

'The river? Aye, this is where it begins. The rain settles in the loch, and the river breaks away from it, then goes past our house, then Stirling, Edinburgh, and on to the sea.'

'Then where does it go?'

'Well, then it's part of the sea, so it can go anywhere in the world I suppose.'

Lachlan rubbed the pebble in his pocket and pondered this. Anywhere in the world. Imagine that? Water from his wee corner of Scotland. And it could go anywhere it liked. Amazing.

'So how does the loch not get empty?'

'Because it keeps filling up with all the rain from the hills.' They emerged onto the road. 'See, the water that makes it out to the sea? Well some of that evaporates - that means it floats into the sky in the heat of the sun - and turns into clouds, and they get blown about and some of them get so big that they can't hold onto all the water anymore. So it rains.'

'And the rain falls here?'

'The rain falls anywhere. The rain that fills our loch here might come from Venezuela, or Canada, or Iceland.'

'Or Timbuktu?'

'Or Timbuktu!' his father said with a chuckle. Lachlan loved to make him laugh, when his war-torn face creased into a smile and his frown momentarily lifted.

'You see son, it goes on forever, the water. It just keeps moving. It can't be destroyed.'

Lachlan kicked a fallen branch into the undergrowth. He looked up at his father, staring at the road ahead.

'Not even with an atomic bomb?'

'Come on, I told you to stop worrying about that.'

'But it happened in Japan, will the Russians not do it to us? They've got the bomb now. I heard it on the wireless.'

'I don't think they'd be that daft,' his father said, ruffling Lachlan's hair.

Lachlan pondered this then spotted a stone on the road. He decided to kick it, and if it stayed on the road Scotland wouldn't be annihilated by an atomic bomb. He swung a leg at it, and it bounced into the verge.

Best of three... he thought.

****

'Lachlan! Tea's ready!'

'Coming Mum,' he yelled. He dipped his paintbrush into the white paint and drew it across the pebble one last time - strengthening the white cross he'd carefully painted over the blue. He'd waited ages for the blue paint to dry, but he knew there was no point rushing it otherwise it'd all smear together. He examined his work - a perfect saltire.

The shelf above his bed held his other creations. His *flagstones*. Italy, France and Belgium had been easy enough but the Stars & Stripes of the USA had proven tricky. He didn't have anywhere near enough stars on it. He wondered if he should let the saltire dry then finish it off with a couple of red crosses to make a Union Jack, but he preferred it the way it was. Simple, and uncomplicated.

Anyway, this was Scotland, and that was Scotland's flag, and he didn't have any good reason for why he hadn't painted it first.

Stopping at the window on the top landing, he looked out at the garden. Morag, his neighbour, was playing down at the river. She had her skirt tucked into her knickers and was galumphing about with her wellies on. A fishing net on a stick of bamboo over her shoulder. The sun was casting the last of its light over Aberfoyle and he could just make out the tiny sparks of a thousand midges swarming in the air above the vegetable patch. If he ate his tea quick, he could maybe go out and play before bed. It wasn't a school night, after all. Sunday tomorrow, which meant church, but it also meant a lie-in and hot scones for breakfast.

At the kitchen table, head down, he held his breath while his father said grace.

'For what we are about to receive, may God have mercy on our souls.'

'Sandy!' laughed his mother. 'That's enough of that. Do it properly or you'll be getting bugger all.'

A more traditional version followed, and Lachlan started flattening his tatties with his fork, and shovelling mince on top. This was the only way to eat mince and tatties. Mum and Dad were just odd, taking wee bits of potato, then wee bits of mince. Where was the fun in that?

'So Lachlan, did you tell your mum what we did today?'

He wiped his chin clean on his sleeve. 'We went to the start of the river. I got another pebble for my collection.'

'What, away up at Loch Ard?' asked his mum.

'Aye Mum, we walked all the way.'

'Well you'll be ready for your tea then. Come on, eat it up and you can maybe go out for a wee bit before bed.'

He didn't need much encouragement. He loved Saturday nights because Saturday nights meant mince and tatties. The rest of the week he had to make do with home-made broth. Or the occasional bit of fish if his dad had been lucky. Sometimes his dad would catch his own, and sometimes he'd get a trout from someone at his work. Once he came back with a huge salmon that caused much heated discussion. Lachlan heard the phrase *no questions asked* and he came to the conclusion that it had been stolen somehow. His mum had mentioned *poaching* and Lachlan's only thought was that it'd be nicer fried in the pan.

He understood why they had the thing called rationing. He'd heard politicians on the wireless arguing about it. The Tories were saying rationing should end. His father would swear at the radio when they said this. Lachlan thought the Tories sounded alright, especially if it meant he'd be able to buy more than a wee poke of sweeties every month, but his dad seemed to think differently. One time he even threw his newspaper at the wireless and stormed out the house. Lachlan saw him minutes later furiously digging the vegetable patch, like there may have been buried treasure under there.

As it turned out, it looked like more people agreed with his father than with Lachlan, as Labour's election win that year meant Mr Atlee managed to keep his job. This seemed to please his father, although he'd heard him muttering to his mother that *his coat was on a shoogly nail*. Lachlan imagined Clement Atlee's big coat, hanging on the back of the door of his office in London, and every time Big Ben chimed the coat slipped a wee bit closer to the floor. He'd have thought, with all their money, and what with winning the war, that they could have put up a proper coat hook for him.

'I'm done!' he said, lining up his knife and fork at 6 o'clock on the plate. 'Can I go out to play?'

'Of course son,' smiled his mother. 'Away and see your wee pal. Me and your dad will get cleared up. Back in at 9 o'clock. I'll shout on you.'

****

'Lachlan McCormack,' giggled Morag from the river. 'Your face is filthy.'

'Och,' said Lachlan, licking the side of his hand and rubbing it over his mouth. 'It's gravy. Have you caught anything?'

'No,' said Morag, chucking her fishing net towards him. 'See if you have more luck.'

She made her way towards the shore with big sploshing strides, the water rolling over the top of her wellies.

Lachlan liked this about Morag. She wasn't like other girls at the school. She didn't make him play at dolls, or dressing up, or shops. She was more like a boy to be honest.

'Have you had your tea?' asked Lachlan.

'Aye, potatoes, onions and a wee bit of corned beef.' She belched and started laughing. Her face split with the huge grin that she seemed to be permanently trying to control. Like her face's natural state was to be smiling.

Lachlan stood for a moment, watching her, happy that she was his friend.

'Are you going to church tomorrow?' he asked, dipping the fishing net into the river.

'Suppose so,' said Morag. 'Can't miss old Whistlin' Willie now can we?'

It was Lachlan's turn to laugh, and soon they were sitting on the grassy bank mimicking the minister's gap-toothed delivery.

'It'ssss essssential that at timesssss like thissss we sssstudy the wis-sssdom of the sssscriptures,' Lachlan said, swooshing the net through the water.

'Remember the womensssss inssssstitute meetsssss every sssssecond Tuessssday,' giggled Morag.

'My dad says it's lucky he never mentions the Mississippi or the front three rows of the church would get soaked,' said Lachlan.

'*It's a load of rubbish*, is what my dad says,' said Morag. 'We only go because my mum insists on it.'

'Aye, I think I agree with him,' said Lachlan. 'Hey, me and my dad went up to the start of the river today. Have you been?'

'No, what's it like?'

'Up at the loch.' He pointed upriver. 'It doesn't spurt out of the ground like some rivers. The loch narrows, then it comes all the way past our houses, then Stirling and Edinburgh and it gets wider and wider, then goes away to the sea and it turns into rain and it falls on Timbuktu. Or anywhere really.'

'That's really interesting,' said Morag. She pretended to fall asleep by dropping her head to the grass and making loud snoring noises.

He watched her brown hair fall over her freckled face and he wanted to touch it, to move the hair away from her cheek. But he knew that would be odd, so he didn't. Instead he muttered, 'Well I thought it was.'

'Aye well you always were an odd boy.' She opened one eye and blew hair away from the side of her mouth. Sitting up, she quickly moved to pull down her sleeve, which had ridden up to her elbow. Lachlan just had time to spot a large bruise on her forearm.

'What happened to your arm?'

'Climbing the tree,' said Morag, pointing to the large oak that sat beside the river. 'Come on, I'll show you the best way up.'

****

'That's it, there,' said Morag.

Lachlan peered up through the branches. Morag was already perched far up the tree and he was gamely following, although his stomach was turning cartwheels. He put his foot where Morag indicated and grabbed the next branch.

'Hold it closer to the trunk, that's it. Now pull yourself up.'

He took a deep breath and hauled himself upwards, the branches scraping at his face and neck.

'Now what? How did you get up there from here?'

She was still a good six feet above him. Hunkered on a branch, he could see her knickers. She had no shame that girl.

'Now you need a wee jump. A leap of faith.'

'What do you mean?' Lachlan gulped, sounding slightly more nervous than he'd intended.

'If you stand on your tip toes and let yourself fall to the side here,' she pointed to another branch, just out of reach. 'You'll be able to grab that branch and swing your feet onto this one,' she indicated another bough, in an impossibly out-of-reach position. 'Trust me, it's easy.'

Lachlan gulped. A prickly heat spread over his back.

'Come on, you're not feart are you?'

'No, of course not. Give me a minute.' He adjusted his feet on the branch. 'Hang on, what was that?'

'What?' said Morag. 'Stop making excuses, come on.'

'Shhhh. My dad's shouting something, wait.'

'Oh Lachlan, my dad shouts all the time. Hurry up.'

He waited, but everything had gone quiet. Just the coo-coo from a wood pigeon and the chatter of some crows on the riverbank.

'Okay, here I go.'

He let go and for a moment felt like he was flying. Twenty feet up, he was holding on to nothing, just letting gravity move him where he had to be. Time stood still. He thought he heard a metallic clatter from his house. His parents were doing the dishes - they must have dropped a pan on the floor. After what seemed like an age, he felt his hands hit the branch. He grabbed it and swung his feet onto the next.

Morag cheered. 'Told you it was easy. Here.' She extended a hand and hauled Lachlan up.

With her help, he scrabbled up the trunk to her perch. There wasn't a lot of room up here, and they sat touching hips. Lachlan had nowhere to put his right arm, so awkwardly extended it behind Morag, resting it on her shoulder.

'Lachlan, what are you doing?' she frowned at him, while forcing that huge smile back down.

'I'm just… erm…'

'Lachlan!' Yelled from the kitchen window, his father. 'Lachlan. Get in here quick!'

****

He ran into the kitchen. His dad kneeled on the floor, the mince pot beside him. As he'd thought, it must have fallen while his father was drying it. But why was his mother lying on the floor too?

'What's happened?' Lachlan asked.

'It's your mum son, I don't know.' Panic in his father's voice. He never sounded like this. 'Go and get Doctor Black. Tell him it's urgent.'

Lachlan stepped closer. His mother lay ashen-faced. Her eyes closed, her mouth slightly open, with a line of spit running down her chin. Tears came to his eyes. 'Is she okay? Mum? Wake up!'

'Lachlan, go!' his father turned to him, eyes wide.

He ran faster than he'd ever ran before. His lungs bursting, his mouth dry like cold steel.

A minute later he reached the doctor's house and chapped the front door repeatedly. The blackened ring of the door-knocker squeaked each time he drew it back. Squeak. Bang. Squeak. Bang. These things would stick in his mind for a lifetime. The taste of metal. The stiffness of that black door-knocker and the slow footsteps from within. Within seconds of describing their predicament, Doctor Black, a trim man in his 50s with a walrus moustache, had grabbed a black leather case from the hallway and was rushing after Lachlan.

Lachlan skidded back into the kitchen. 'Dad, he's coming. He'll be here in a minute.'

'Good lad. Can you get a glass of water?'

Lachlan was relieved to see his mother sitting up, with her back against a cupboard. His father was holding her hand and mopping her brow with the tea towel.

'Is she okay?' Lachlan asked as he filled one of his dad's whisky tumblers.

'I don't know son. We'll have to wait for the doctor.'

His father took the glass and placed it to his mother's lips. Her eyes were open now but her face seemed lop-sided - like a painting that had been smudged down one side.

'Phoebe, come on love - drink this.' His father's voice was breaking up.

'What's happened Dad? I don't want Mum to die.'

'She'll be okay son. She's just had a wee turn, that's all.'

Moments later the doctor, red-faced and sweating, bustled into the kitchen.

'Lachlan why don't you go to your room and read your comics?' his father said, quietly. 'I'll need to tell the doctor what's happened.'

From his bedroom window, Lachlan saw his father hurry to the phone box. When he returned, all he could hear was the low rumble of Doctor Black's voice.

The ambulance arrived as night fell. He ventured onto the top landing just as his father called him downstairs.

The front door was open, and his mother was being wheeled out on a stretcher. Morag's mum stood in the kitchen, busying herself with the kettle.

'Morag's mum will look after you for a wee while son. We just need to take your mum into hospital in Stirling so she can get better.'

'Is she okay?' said Lachlan.

'She's going to be fine. Once she's had some medicine. Isn't that right doctor?'

Doctor Black nodded to Lachlan, but it didn't look like he was smiling behind that big moustache.

****

Lachlan sat by the river tearing clumps of grass and throwing them into the water. He didn't hear Morag approach.

'Hello Lachlan,' she said, quietly.

He turned to see her standing behind him, hands clasped in front of her.

'Hello,' was all he could say.

'I heard about your Mum. I'm… sorry. She'll be okay though won't she?'

'She's had a thing called a stroke.' Lachlan's eyes started welling up. It was a grey April day, the colour washed out of everything. It was difficult for Lachlan to imagine the sun ever shining again.

'My mum told me. She called it apo-something. Apoplectomy or something?'

'Apoplexy,' said Lachlan, taking no pride in the fact he'd learned a new word. 'It's the same thing, I think.'

'When will she get home?'

'We don't know. Soon I think. She's…' His voice trailed away and he turned to look at the river, not wanting Morag to see the tears starting to form. He knew his voice was breaking up but he took a deep breath and managed to say, 'She's not going to be the same though.'

He started tugging furiously at the grass. Throwing clump after clump into the river and watching them float downstream.

Morag sat beside him and drew her knees up to her chin.

'At least we didn't have to go to church today. Do you want to go fishing?' she asked.

'No.'

'Do you want to climb the tree again?'

Lachlan shook his head.

She leaned back and nestled her elbows into the grass. Lachlan turned away so all she could see was the back of his head. He wiped his face dry and cleared his throat.

'Do you want to go up to the start of the river?' he asked.

'Aye Lachlan, that would be fun.'

****

It was like going back in time. That's what Lachlan thought as they set off down the road, heading west into a fine drizzle that had just blown over the hills.

It was only yesterday he'd made the same trip with his father, and everything had been okay then. If he went back to the river's source, maybe things would get better. Maybe the new water that had filled the loch and was now making its way to its eastern edge would carry some good fortune towards his house. Some good luck from Venezuela. Or Canada. Or Timbuktu.

'Did you tell your mum and dad we'd be away for a while?' asked Lachlan.

'I told my mum. My dad's away out.'

'Oh,' said Lachlan. Morag's dad seemed to spend a lot of time out of the house.

Lachlan's father had returned at breakfast and spent some time explaining things. Lachlan's Auntie Jean from Stirling, his father's sister, would be with them soon. When she got here, his father would head back on the next bus to the hospital where he'd stay with Mum until she was better.

Lachlan had asked why this had happened to his mother, who hadn't done anything wrong, and was good, and healthy, and ate the apples from the garden that were supposed to keep the doctor away, but his father could only shrug and say *sometimes bad things happen to good folk son.*

This seemed like a huge injustice to Lachlan, but then his thoughts had turned to Hiroshima and Nagasaki, as they often did, and he thought of all the lives lost just six years ago. Those weren't all bad people. They were just families with children. Dead in an instant. His father didn't talk about the war much. As far as Lachlan could remember, his father had always been in Aberfoyle, but he knew he'd been in Holland, and France, and Belgium. He made bridges, that was all Lachlan knew. Had he killed anybody? *No*, his father always replied. *I just built bridges son. So we could get over the rivers and help as many people as possible.*

He was an engineer, but Lachlan preferred to think of him as a brave soldier, dodging gunfire and throwing grenades at Nazi tanks. Maybe he did that when he wasn't building bridges?

'How far is it?' asked Morag.

'Not too far, a couple of miles I think,' he said, although he had little concept of what this meant.

She smiled. 'Okay, what time will we get there?'

'I'm not sure,' said Lachlan. 'Anyway, do you have a watch? I don't.'

She laughed and said, 'No I just want to know how long it'll take!'

'Oh,' he said. 'Not long. Maybe an hour?'

This seemed to satisfy Morag. She'd perhaps thought they were heading off to the north pole or something.

They walked together, side by side, through the drizzle and along the empty road. The River Forth gurgled past them through the trees at the roadside, narrowing all the time as they approached its source. After half an hour, they heard a car approach from behind and stood at the side of the road to let it pass. Black with shiny chrome bumpers and bright red leather seats. A right toff driving it too. As it slowed to pass them Lachlan saw a mop of blonde hair in the back seat. A young boy, about his age. As the car accelerated down the road the boy turned to watch them from the rear window. He raised a hand and offered a solemn wave.

'Do you know who that was?' asked Morag.

'Looked like a Tory,' Lachlan said. Because that's the kind of thing his father would have said.

'That was the Laird, and his wee boy, from the big house up by the loch. He's the richest man in Scotland.'

'In the whole of Scotland?'

'Well, in this bit of Scotland anyway,' laughed Morag.

'Imagine being that rich you didn't have to walk anywhere,' said Lachlan.

'I like walking.'

'Me too,' said Lachlan. 'That wee boy looked quite sad though, don't you think?'

'He did a bit.'

'Does he have any pals? Where does he go to school? He doesn't come to ours.'

'No, he goes to a private school. Somewhere near Perth I think. He has to sleep there. Isn't even allowed to come home at night to see his mum and dad.'

Lachlan pondered this for a moment and said, 'Sounds like prison.'

'Aye, it does. I don't think I'd like that very much. I think his mum and dad are nice though. My mum used to work at their house, when she was younger. She was a kitchen girl.'

'What's that?' asked Lachlan, suddenly confronted by the image of his mum on the kitchen floor again.

'Not sure. Sort of like a slave I suppose. Except she was allowed to come home at night.'

'Sounds rubbish,' he said. He pondered this for a moment, then asked, 'What do you want to be when you're big?'

She turned her face to the sky and chewed the inside of her cheek. 'I'm not sure. Maybe an actress. Or an artist. Or a famous tree-climber. As long as I'm not a secretary, I'd hate to be stuck in an office all day.'

'Aye me too,' said Lachlan. 'It'd be like school. Forever.' He shuddered at the thought. They'd be back there tomorrow.

'What about you, what do you want to be? Do you want to work at the slate mine like our dads?'

'Maybe,' he said. 'I haven't really thought about it. I'm rubbish at football so I can't do that. I'm not very strong, so the slate mine probably wouldn't want me.' He shrugged. 'Maybe I'll be an explorer.' He grabbed a fallen branch from the road and waved it around, like he was fighting lions.

'That would be an excellent job,' Morag said, her smile breaking her face in two again.

'It would. And look, here's where we need go exploring.'

They left the road and turned down a narrower track into the trees, crossing the river over an old bridge. Its grey stone sides covered in damp green moss. The river was livelier here. Narrower. Bouncing over rocks and filling the forest with the sound of its youthful enthusiasm.

Morag grabbed his hand and said, 'Come on then, Mr Explorer. Where's the start of this river?'

****

They sat on the bank, just where the loch narrowed and the river began its long, slow journey to the North Sea. Morag munched on an apple she'd pulled from her pocket.

'Do you want a bite?' she asked, passing it to Lachlan.

He studied the apple and chose a fresh part to munch into.

'What's wrong with my slavers?' said Morag, looking indignant.

'Nothing,' said Lachlan. 'I mean, I don't know. I just didn't want my slavers going onto your bit.' He looked at the apple again and wiped around the part he'd bitten with his shirt cuff.

'Now it's all fluff, give it here you daftie.' Morag grabbed the apple and took a large bite, making sure Lachlan saw she'd bitten right over his teeth marks.

This made him blush. How could he feel so comfortable around Morag, but also so awkward? His back started itching.

'Well…' he said, changing the subject. 'Here we are. The start of the river.'

'Aye it's great,' said Morag. She shielded her eyes and gazed up the loch. 'So all this water ends up in the sea?'

'I think so. Well, most of it. Maybe some of it just swirls about and gets stuck here.'

'That's a shame.'

Lachlan thought about this. He looked at the side of the loch where algae grew. The water there was very still. A couple of flies buzzed over it, and the surface was busy with pond-skaters.

'It is,' he said. 'Like that bit there. Maybe that's stuck here forever?'

'It looks yucky,' said Morag, screwing her face up.

'I know. Maybe we should help it?' He grabbed his explorer stick. 'Come on.'

Lachlan beat a path through the long grass and leant towards the water, dipping the stick into the green gloop. He stirred it around the best he could but other than breaking the algae on the surface, he didn't seem to be moving much water. He pulled the stick out and reversed it. There were more twigs and leaves at that end and he was satisfied now that he was helping some of the water out of its trap.

'Okay, that should do it.'

Morag grabbed his arm and pulled him back towards dry land. She stood perfectly still as he awkwardly bumped into her. 'I thought you were going to fall in for a minute.'

Lachlan threw the stick down and wiped his hands on his shirt. He didn't know what to say so he said, 'That's that then!'

'What's what then?'

'That's that water away down the river. We saved it.'

'We did.'

Morag tucked her hair behind her ear and looked up into the grey sky. The drizzle had stopped, and there were a few patches of blue breaking through. They stepped back through the long grass, avoiding the nettles.

'Come on,' she said. 'School tomorrow. We'll better be getting home.'

****

'Okay Lachlan, I've made you a piece - it's in your bag,' Auntie Jean said, crouching to Lachlan's level and straightening his hair with a spit-covered hand. Jean always smelled of lavender. A friendly smell that suited her somehow. Lachlan squirmed and glanced up and down the road. There was nobody in sight, thankfully. Just another spring morning in his wee corner of Scotland. Birds singing, the river tinkling past, and the sun failing to break through the clouds. 'And here, you'll need this.' She reached around his head with a front-door key, tied to a bootlace, like an olympic medal. 'I'm away to see your mum and I won't be back until teatime. You can let yourself in.' She tucked the key under his shirt.

'Thanks Auntie Jean,' he beamed. The key cold against his skin.

With a hug, she waved him off. 'Don't you worry, your mum will be fine.'

He smiled and swung the front gate open. It clanged back on its spring and at that sound, Morag appeared at her front door. Lachlan knew the clatter of his gate was her signal to leave so they could walk to school together. He just managed to hear her say 'Bye,' as she pulled the door shut behind her. She usually bounced out the house in the morning, something wasn't right.

'Hello,' she said, looking at her shoes.

'What's the matter?' he said, hurrying alongside her. She seemed to be in an awful rush.

'Nothing,' said Morag with a sigh.

'I don't want to go to school either,' said Lachlan. 'Is that it?'

'Yes, I suppose so. It's too nice a day.'

'No it isn't.' He looked up at the grey blanket overhead. 'It's going to pour with rain, look.' He pointed to where the clouds were even greyer and thicker.

'No, it'll brighten up later. I'm pretty sure,' said Morag, tugging at the straps on her schoolbag, keeping a half-step ahead of him.

This was her approach to everything, Lachlan had come to realise. Whereas he'd always be looking at the grey clouds and the rain they'd surely bring, Morag would see beyond them to the blue sky that would follow.

****

Lachlan dozed as Mr Barclay scratched at the blackboard with his chalk while scratching at his backside with his free hand.

A grinning boy, Michael McLeod, glanced over at Lachlan. He pretended to sniff his fingers with a grimace and Lachlan let out an involuntary whoop.

Mr Barclay turned, the tails of his black jacket swinging out like the wings of a crow. 'Lachlan McCormack, do you have something you'd like to share?'

The class turned to face Lachlan. Fourteen faces of various shapes and sizes, all sharing the same gleeful expression at Lachlan's discomfort. Morag was staring out the window.

'No Mr Barclay, Sir.'

'Good. Keep your infantile expulsions to yourself. This here,' he tapped the blackboard, 'is of the utmost importance, so you'd be advised to pay attention. Now,' he scanned the room, looking for a victim. 'George Erskine - perhaps you can enlighten young Mr McCormack on today's topic?'

George straightened up and pushed his glasses up his nose. 'Yes sir. We are learning about William Shakespeare.'

'Correct,' boomed Mr Barclay. 'And who was William Shakespeare?'

'One of the greatest writers our country has ever known,' said

George, proudly. Although he was just parroting what Mr Barclay had written on the board.

'Correct. One of the greatest writers our country has ever known.' Mr Barclay tapped at his own words on the board. 'So, Lachlan, unless you want to spend your lunchtime writing that line a hundred times on this blackboard. I'd suggest you remain quiet.'

Lachlan mumbled, 'Sorry sir. But sir, what about Rabbie Burns? Isn't he the greatest writer our country has ever known?'

Mr Barclay smiled. 'Our country is Great Britain. Rabbie Burns may well be the greatest writer *Scotland* has produced, but you can't compare the two.'

'Why not sir?' Lachlan asked. 'Our country is Scotland is it not? Why not just say that William Shakespeare is the greatest writer *England* has ever known?' His brow furrowed. As did Mr Barclay's.

At that, the bell rang for lunch and Mr Barclay was saved any more awkward questions.

'Okay, straight to the gym hall after lunch,' Mr Barclay yelled over the rising din. 'Physical Education is as vitally important as the cerebral sort.'

As Lachlan passed, Mr Barclay ushered him aside and waited until the class had dispersed into the corridor.

'How's your mother Lachlan?' he asked.

'She's had a stroke sir,' Lachlan said. 'She's at the hospital in Stirling.'

Mr Barclay nodded. He placed a hand on Lachlan's shoulder and seemed to be at a loss for words. Something Lachlan had never witnessed in his four years of schooling. He nodded again and said, 'On you go then, I'll see you after lunch.'

'Yes sir,' said Lachlan. Then, 'Are you okay Sir?'

Mr Barclay sat on the edge of his desk, thought for a moment, then said, 'My sister had a stroke Lachlan. Just last year.'

Lachlan found the thought of Mr Barclay having a sister quite odd. He tried to picture a female version of Mr Barclay but it wasn't a pretty sight. 'And is she okay now sir? Did she get better?'

Mr Barclay had turned away, suddenly interested in straightening the paperwork on his desk. 'Away for your lunch Lachlan. I'll see you in the gym hall.'

****

'Right. Ten times round the hall. Go!' Mr Barclay blew a whistle and placed his hands on his hips.

Lachlan ran. His plimsolls squeaking on the polished wooden floor as he took the corners. Morag loped along at the rear of the pack and soon Lachlan had almost caught her up. Her pale arms were tight by her side, which with her white top and black shorts gave her the appearance of an unenthusiastic penguin.

By the third lap Lachlan was alongside her. He slowed to match her speed. 'What's the matter Morag? Why are you running like that?'

She cast him a sideways glance and said, 'Nothing, on you go, you'll be first.'

He broke away and soon Mr Barclay blew his whistle and the wheezing pack came to a halt.

'Okay, boys. Press ups. Ten. Girls, stand at the side and run on the spot.'

Lachlan could just about manage press-ups and counted them off slowly and surely. He looked across at Morag, she was usually at the centre of things but not today. She bounced from foot to foot at the periphery of the other girls. Outside, the sun broke through the clouds, like she said it would, and a shaft of yellow light illuminated her face. The dust motes in the hall danced in the glow, like the midges in his garden. She was usually like a sunflower, always turning her smiling face to the sun, but her mouth stayed closed in a tight line, her head down. Lachlan needed her to be happy. He had problems enough of his own.

'Beams!' shouted Mr Barclay. He'd pulled the wooden apparatus out from the side of the hall and stood back by the window. 'Two lines. Boys and girls. Onto the beam here. Jump off. Land properly. Go to the back of the queue. Ready? Go!'

Lachlan's turn came and he bounced up onto the beam, quickly tight-roped to the end, then jumped onto the mat with his arms in the air.

'Good Lachlan. Morag, go!' bawled Mr Barclay.

Lachlan walked back to the end of the line while Morag bounced onto the beam. She struggled momentarily, waving her arms out to regain her balance, and that's when he saw them. A cluster of bruises on her upper arms. Bigger than the one she'd got from climbing the tree. She made it to the other end and jumped off, keeping her arms low.

'Arms up when you dismount Morag. Like this.' Mr Barclay jumped into the air and threw his arms up, his top coming loose from his shorts revealing his wobbling gut. He glowered at the class, silencing the sniggers then added, 'Next time do it properly.'

Morag ran to the back of the queue. Her head down. She was avoiding Lachlan's gaze, and he thought he knew now where her smile had gone. He edged alongside her while Mr Barclay continued to bark instructions.

'I saw your arms Morag. The bruises. Is everything okay? Is your

Dad… he's not… is he hurting you?'

'No,' she whispered. 'It's nothing. I just banged them doing a cartwheel in the garden. Hit the wheelbarrow…'

'Okay,' said Lachlan, but he couldn't picture any sort of cartwheel that would have caused bruises like that.

'I don't really want to go home after school,' said Morag. 'Can we go play somewhere?'

'Aye sure,' said Lachlan, delighted at the prospect. 'What about Fairy Hill?'

****

They crossed the old stone bridge over the river and into the fields. It was now a fine afternoon. Warm and still, just as Morag had predicted.

'Should we tell somebody we're going? It'll take a wee while to get there,' said Lachlan, breaking the silence.

'Och no,' she said. 'My dad won't be home until six.'

'What about your mum?'

Morag snatched at a dandelion in passing and spun it in her hand until all the seeds were floating up into the sunlight. Normally she'd have blown it. What time is it in fairyland? She didn't seem in the mood.

'She's away for the day.'

Lachlan touched the door key hanging around his neck. He had a few hours of unsupervised freedom too, what better way to spend it than exploring with his best friend? He glanced at Morag, her mouth set in a firm line. Head lowered. This walk would do her good, and by the end of it, he was sure he'd know what the problem was.

After a few minutes they approached the town cemetery, behind a crumbling wall. Lachlan always crossed to the other side of the road at this point. He veered toward the opposite verge, kicking the long grass at the roadside.

Morag snorted. 'Fearty.' A faint grin appearing on her face, like the glow of the sun behind thinning clouds.

'I'm not feart,' said Lachlan.

'Aye you are,' said Morag. 'And if you're not, prove it.'

In an instant, she'd vaulted the wall and was standing among the gravestones.

Lachlan gulped as he clambered over the wall. He wasn't scared of the gravestones really. But he was scared of death, and he didn't really want to think about that sort of thing at the moment.

'Right, I'm here. Now what?' he said, with as much bravado as he could muster. He tried to keep as far from the headstones as possible, imagining all the bones underneath.

'Nothing, we just keep walking. Down to the old church.'

Lachlan looked ahead. The graveyard was split into the old and new. They were in the new section, for the recently interred. Beyond that were the crumbling old graves with their skull motifs and worn inscriptions, and the ruined old church. Just some walls now, the roof having caved in long ago. This was where the mad old Reverend Robert Kirk had delivered his sermons nearly two hundred years ago.

Everyone locally knew the story of the reverend and his book, *The Secret Commonwealth*. And everyone knew he'd died up on Fairy Hill, his body stolen by the fairies and replaced by a changeling. Lachlan's father joked that it wasn't so much the *fairies* he was interested in, as the *spirits*. He'd made a drinking motion with one hand and pointed to the bottle of whisky on the sideboard with the other. Lachlan was happy to take his father's interpretation of events as gospel rather than believe there were fairies on the edge of town that would steal you away in the night.

'Okay then,' he said. 'Let's go.'

They marched off through the headstones, Lachlan focusing on the church ahead.

'Oh, look here,' said Morag, stopping suddenly.

He glanced down at what looked like a fairly recent grave. The marble headstone gleaming, the inscription clear. Fresh flowers sprayed from an iron vase, embedded into the soft earth. The grass hadn't quite grown back over the grave, and Lachlan stepped back to make sure he wasn't standing over the earth where the coffin lay.

'What about it?' he said, looking back towards the church.

'The name Lachlan.'

Lachlan sighed and read the inscription: *Dorothy Barclay. 1904 - 1950. Daughter. Wife. Sister.*

'Barclay.' His heart sank. 'Do you think that's -'

'Mr Barclay's sister. My dad told me she'd been ill.'

'He told me that today. She'd had a...' Lachlan trailed off. He couldn't bring himself to say that she'd died of the same thing his mother was fighting to recover from.

Morag placed a hand on his shoulder. 'Come on you, let's get to Fairy Hill.' She led him back to the gate and onto the road.

He took a few breaths and wiped his eyes.

'I'm worried about my mum Morag,' he eventually said.

'I know. Me too.' She reached into her schoolbag and pulled out a red hair ribbon. With her teeth she tore this in two and passed one half to Lachlan. 'But we can ask the fairies to help.'

He smiled. 'Thanks Morag. You're a good pal.'

'I know,' she replied, and her smile returned - just briefly, but enough to fill Lachlan with a warmth that he still didn't quite understand, but that he'd soon grow to crave.

****

As they wound their way through the trees to the top of the hill, Morag's mood seemed to lighten. As if the further from home she got, the happier she became.

Lachlan too, felt unburdened for the first time all week. He grabbed a fallen branch from the ground and whacked at a few ferns in passing.

'Don't do that you ruffian,' said Morag. 'Especially not here. The fairies don't take kindly to their home being smashed up by snotty boys.'

'Sorry,' he said, tossing the branch into the bluebells and bracken. 'Do you believe in fairies then? My dad says the old reverend was just a drunk.'

'I do believe in fairies and they're going to damn you to hell for saying that Lachlan McCormack,' Morag's voice boomed through the trees. 'Why do you think all this is here?'

She gestured at the trees around them, each one had strips of fabric tied to the lower branches. Torn handkerchiefs, ribbons, even what looked like a smelly old sock dangled from a tree up ahead.

'Maybe all the people that did it were drunk too?' offered Lachlan.

'Lachlan, the fairies can cure things. You tie a ribbon to a tree and the fairies know you need help. These people can't all be wrong. Or drunk.'

Lachlan thought for a moment. He'd heard Morag's dad clattering home from the pub many a time, but his own dad didn't really drink that much. Or his mum. The pub in the village had its regulars, but for the most part, his wee village seemed like a sensible sort of place.

'Aye maybe,' he said. 'So where are we tying ours?'

Morag nodded ahead. 'There'.

Lachlan had feared she'd say that. The Minister's Pine sat alone in a clearing at the top of the hill. This was the tree believed to hold the infamous reverend's spirit, where the fairies had left the replica body as they dragged him into their underworld.

He slowed and took in the size of the tree, towering over its neighbours.

'Give me your ribbon. You'll need to give me a hand up,' said Morag. 'Go on,' she nodded at Lachlan's hands.

He handed her the ribbon, shuffled off his schoolbag and clasped his hands, bracing himself to take Morag's weight. In an instant, she'd placed one foot in his cupped hands and hopped up, grabbing onto the trunk. His nose was uncomfortably close to her private parts as she said, 'Give me a boost, come on!'

Lachlan wobbled momentarily. He wasn't exactly built for this, but with an almighty effort, he brought his hands up and propelled her upwards.

'Thanks!' she cried dangling by both hands from a branch.

Lachlan looked up then looked away again as he caught a glimpse of her knickers. Her legs were flailing against the trunk, looking for purchase. Eventually, she found a place to stick a toe and manage to scramble up, throwing herself over the branch.

He had never known anyone that could climb like Morag. He was convinced her family tree must have contained monkeys more recently than most. She stood now, on a higher branch, and called down to him. 'Okay this will do. I'm tying my ribbon on.'

'Who's ill in your family?' asked Lachlan.

'Doesn't matter,' she said. 'Now yours.' She pulled Lachlan's ribbon from her shirt pocket and tied it to a higher branch. 'Okay fairies. Make Lachlan's mum better, you hear me? He's a good boy and his mum's a good lady and she doesn't deserve to be unwell.'

'Thanks Morag,' he said.

'That's okay Lachlan, now catch me!' she cried.

He didn't have time to think. She bundled him into a bed of ferns and he would have laughed but for the fact she'd knocked all the wind out of him.

She grinned and ruffled Lachlan's hair as she climbed off his prone body. 'You'd make a good fireman.'

Lachlan just lay there, waiting for his lungs to work, but despite his pain this was the happiest he'd felt all week.

****

Morag's mood had brightened with their trip to Fairy Hill, but Lachlan still sensed something wasn't right. Her bruises weren't the result of a cartwheel-gone-wrong, he was sure of it. They approached the main road in the village and turned towards home.

He noticed her brow furrowing, as her pace slowed.

'So Morag, are you going to tell me what's the matter?'

She held Lachlan's gaze for a moment and with a sigh said, 'I'm not very happy at home just now, that's all.'

'Do you want to talk about it?'

She shook her head. Maybe it was better just to be her friend and let her sort it out herself? No, he'd be a strange sort of friend if he didn't keep trying. Morag had been a good friend to him today. He was sure their trip to Fairy Hill would give his mum and dad something to laugh about, if nothing else.

He was about to speak but stopped as Morag took a deep breath and stopped walking. She turned to Lachlan and said, 'Look if I tell you this, you have to promise not to tell anyone okay? I don't want anyone getting in trouble and I'm fine. You shouldn't worry about me, I'm made of tough stuff.'

'For a girl, you are, aye.'

She smiled at Lachlan's little dig, then continued. 'The bruises weren't because of a cartwheel.'

He nodded. They were passing a bench at the roadside so Lachlan sat down and indicated for Morag to join him. She straightened her skirt and dropped onto the bench with a sigh. The door of the pub opposite swung open and a man stumbled out, blinking into the sunlight. Lachlan had thought for a moment it was Morag's dad but remembered he'd be working at the quarry today.

'So, how did you get them?'

Morag started pulling at her fingers. Her head dropped and her hair fell over her face so he couldn't read her expression. Seconds later, her shoulders started jerking and he realised she was sobbing quietly.

'Morag,' he said. 'Is it your dad? Is your dad hitting you?'

Her shoulders heaved again and she buried her face in her hands.

He placed a hand on her shoulder and said, 'I know he's always in the pub. He goes there as soon as he has his tea and I hear him clattering in when I'm in my bed. He shouldn't be hitting you. We can go to the police if you want.'

'No!' Morag cried, through the tears. 'We can't go to the police. I'm fine. It's nothing, just a few bruises. I'm okay.'

He sat back on the bench. 'But what if he keeps doing it? He might really hurt you.'

'He won't,' said Morag, she was starting to control her tears now and wiped her face with her cardigan sleeve. She sat back and looked at Lachlan through tear-stained eyes. 'He won't hurt me, because it's not him that hits me.'

'Eh?'

Her face twisted. She looked like she was about to burst into tears again but instead took a deep breath and said, 'It's not my dad that hits me…' she gulped. 'It's my mum.'

Lachlan's mouth fell open. 'Your *mum*!?'

'That's why my dad goes to the pub all the time. I don't think they like each other very much. I said this to my mum one night and she grabbed me and shook me and told me never to say anything like that again.'

'But you did?'

'Yes, I said it again last night and she grabbed me again and dragged me up to bed. It was really sore. I was crying. She was crying. Then she fell down on her knees and started saying how sorry she was. Please don't tell anyone. I love my mum and I love my dad and I just want everyone to be happy.'

He wasn't sure what to make of this. On the one hand, he was glad it wasn't her drunk father who was hitting her. It seemed better that it was her mum, for some reason, but still left him feeling uneasy. He thought of his own mother, lying in hospital in Stirling then glanced towards the town clock. Five thirty. He'd better be getting home.

'I won't tell anyone I promise. It's our secret.' He stood, took Morag's hand, and hoisted her to her feet.

****

As they walked Lachlan felt for the key under his shirt. He pulled it over his head and grasped the key tightly.

'Latchkey kid,' said Morag. 'How grown up you are!'

Lachlan blushed, 'They'll be back soon. I was meant to let myself in but they don't need to know we were off exploring. Will your mum be home?'

'I don't think so,' said Morag. 'She left a key under the plant pot. She said she'd be home by six.'

'Well if you want to come out to play again, just chap my door.'

'I will.' Morag smiled and looked towards their homes. 'Isn't that your auntie?'

Lachlan squinted into the sun. She was right. His aunt must have come home early. Damn it. He'd be in trouble. She was talking to someone in the house though, who could that be?

'Oops, you're for it!' said Morag with a chuckle as she swung open her gate.

At the sound of the gate, Lachlan's aunt turned and saw him

sheepishly approach.

'Oh Lachlan!' she cried. 'Where have you been?'

'I was out playing with Morag, sorry.' He looked beyond her and saw that it was his father at the door. Something was wrong. He shouldn't be here. Time seemed to slow down.

'I was just coming out to look for you.'

As Lachlan approached she grabbed his hand. She looked funny. Her face was all puffy. He turned and looked at his father, who squatted to Lachlan's level and held out his arms.

'Come here son,' his father said. His voice quiet.

Lachlan walked into his arms. 'What's the matter Dad?'

His father buried Lachlan's head into his shoulder, grabbing it tightly and pulling him as close as he could. He seemed to be breathing in Lachlan's hair. Kissing his head. Rubbing his back and scalp.

'It's your mum Lachlan,' his father took a deep breath. 'She's dead son.'

****

Lachlan took a last look from his bedroom window. The bottom panes were still frosted from the night's chill but he'd cleared a space halfway up by breathing on the glass and rubbing a circle into the condensation with the cuff of his jumper.

He wasn't too keen on the jumper, truth be told. His Auntie Jean had bought it for his Christmas from a shop in Stirling and it still itched him terribly, even after two months. He hoped all the clothes shops in Stirling didn't sell itchy clothes like this because from tonight, he'd be calling Stirling home.

Still no sign of the removal van. Maybe he had time to say another cheerio to Morag? The hall was piled high with boxes and he had to shuffle sideways to get to the front door. He spotted one of the boxes from his room and lifted the flap, reached in and pocketed something from within. A gift for Morag. His dad was in the living room, shuffling the big brown sofa a little bit closer to the door.

'I'm just going through to Morag's,' Lachlan said, one hand on the front door handle.

'Aye sure son, listen out for the van though. Don't go too far.'

He skidded down the icy path and ran to Morag's door. He didn't have to knock as she'd heard the squeak of her gate and opened the door as he approached.

'Hello Lachlan,' she said with a smile. 'I suppose you've come to say cheerio?'

'Aye Morag, I suppose so.'

She stepped into the garden, grabbing his hand in passing. She led him to the gate then over the road.

'Where are we going?' he asked.

'Come on, we'll just go down to the river for a bit.'

'The van will be here soon,' he said, looking back over his shoulder.

'That's fine,' Morag said. 'I just want to get away from the house for a wee while.'

'I thought everything was okay now?' he asked. In the months since his mother's death Morag's mood had returned to normal. Her father hadn't been going to the pub so much, and things seemed to be happier in his neighbour's house.

'It is,' said Morag. 'Everything's fine now, look.' She hauled up the sleeves of her cardigan. 'See, no bruises.'

'Good, so why do we need to go to the river?'

'We don't Lachlan,' Morag flapped her arms up and down, exasperated. They arrived at the riverbank. Blocks of ice tumbled past in the shallows. Everything was crisp, fresh. The low sun cast a sharp light over the fields, highlighting every detail, every bump in the surface. There was a crackle in the air. 'I just want to say goodbye to you. Properly.'

'What do you mean? Prop-'. Before Lachlan could finish, Morag grabbed him and kissed him full on the lips. Just for a second, but in that second Lachlan felt like they would melt the snow and ice for miles. Like an atomic bomb blast, radiating outwards, but instead of destruction and ash and dust and collapsing buildings, the grass was turning green and flowers were springing up in concentric rings and fruit was bursting from the trees. All from this wee spot in the centre of Scotland, all the way to the sea.

'Lachlan? Lachlan?'

His vision returned and he realised Morag was staring at him, head cocked to one side with a smile like a slice of watermelon. 'Are you okay?' She laughed.

'I'm… erm… fine?' he managed. His tight-mouthed grin turned into a fully-toothed smile.

'Good,' said Morag. 'Because I think that's your removal van coming up the road.'

He heard the rumble of an engine in the distance. What a time to be leaving.

'I'll miss you Morag.'

'I'll miss you too Lachlan,' said Morag and she swung her arms around his neck, hugging him tight.

'Will we still be pals?'

'Of course we will. We'll always be pals. I don't think we'll ever leave Aberfoyle, so you'll know where to find me.'

'Aye, well I'll write to you when we're in Stirling. I can tell you about all the adventures I'm having in the big city.'

'You can. Although there's no Fairy Hill in Stirling.'

'No, suppose not. There's the river though. This one. Goes right through it.'

'I could send you a message in a bottle,' said Morag with a chuckle.

'Aye. I'll look out for it.'

'You won't be able to reply though. The river only flows one way,' said Morag, her brow furrowed.

Lachlan chewed his cheek. Then, remembering his gift for Morag, 'Oh, I've got something for you.' He reached into his pocket and pulled out his saltire stone. He thrust it towards her.

'Your Stone of Destiny?' laughed Morag. They'd been learning at school all about Scotland's ceremonial stone, and how it had been stolen from Westminster Abbey the previous Christmas. Some local folk even believed it was being hidden somewhere in Aberfoyle, but they were sworn to secrecy. Mr Barclay had tried to present this as being a terrible act of treachery against the King, but Lachlan and Morag had thought it was a splendid thing and had taken to re-enacting the theft in the playground using a broken corner of paving slab as the notorious contraband.

Morag took the stone and rubbed it with her thumb. 'Thanks Lachlan. This will always remind me of you. I'm sorry though. I don't have anything for you.'

'Oh don't worry,' said Lachlan, touching his lips and blushing.

Morag took a deep breath. She puffed it out into the freezing air just as the removal van arrived with a blast of its horn.

'Lachlan!' his father shouted from the front door.

'Coming Dad!'

'Well cheerio then,' said Morag. Her smile vanished.

'Bye Morag,' he said, blinking furiously. 'Are you coming back to the house?'

'I'll stay here for a bit.'

'Okay, well. I'll be seeing you.' He stepped backwards and turned away before she could see the tears that were beginning to spill down his cheeks.

'I hope so Lachlan.'

TUESDAY

Lachlan swallowed his painkillers, lay back on his bed, and surveyed the room. Yellowing walls, the same paint they'd used in the communal lounge; a worn easy chair; a cheap chest of drawers; a wardrobe with one door that didn't quite close; the door to his bathroom; and the window with his begonia on the ledge. He couldn't see the Bass Rock from his room, but it was there. Always there.

His gaze fell on the chest of drawers. His wedding photo had pride of place and he managed a thin smile at the memory. Beside it, a rare photo of a seven-year-old Lachlan with his mother and father - taken at the front door of their house in Aberfoyle. Black and white but taken on a sunny day - Lachlan's hands were shading his eyes and his mother's face was turned up to the sun. His father was wearing his usual white shirt, with one arm around his mother, and the other down by his side. A tell-tale line of smoke betraying the fact he had a roll-up in his right hand.

He scanned the newspaper. Police were seeking witnesses after another senseless murder; a random assault on a teenage boy returning from a night out. He dropped it to the floor and turned onto his side, wincing at the pain in his stomach, slightly duller now as the opiates found their way to his brain.

At the window, that solitary magpie landed on the ledge and peered through the glass. Lachlan's eyes were closed but he heard the tap-tap-tapping of its beak on the window frame as he drifted off to sleep.

STiRLiNG 1951

Lachlan sat at the small kitchen table and straightened his writing pad. He could hear his father cleaning out the fireplace in the living room, brushing last night's ashes into a sheet of newspaper. It would be one of the last fires until winter returned. Spring was here and the new house was becoming oppressively warm.

He licked the pencil tip and began.

Dear Morag

I hope you are well.

Well we've been in Stirling for a few months now and I have made some friends at school. Gerry is fat and funny and Johnny has curly hair and smokes.

My school is huge! There are lots more children here. My teacher is quite nice. She's called Mrs White. She's not too strict. Not like Mr Barclay.

Our house is funny. There are four houses in the block. Two at either side. We're downstairs and the Harpers are upstairs. I don't like them. They argue and he steals our coal.

We don't really see the people in the other two houses as their front doors are at the other end, but there's another old couple, and a mum with a baby.

The house is very modern. The outside of it is covered in tiny stones, some of them are quartz I think. It shines when it's sunny. It's quite nice but it's too warm. The garden is small. Just a patch of grass with a washing pole.

My bedroom is okay. It's not as big as my old one but it's very sunny. I have room for my books and my flagstone collection is on top of my chest of drawers. Do you still have the Scottish flag? I hope so!

There is lots to do in Stirling and it would be nice if you wanted to visit. Please write back to me.

Yours Sincerely

Lachlan

He read it back to himself. It wasn't all entirely true, but he thought it sounded upbeat. Morag didn't need to hear about his problems.

'What's that son? Applying for a job?' His father walked into the small kitchenette and filled a glass with water from the tap.

'It's a letter for Morag. Can I get a stamp?'

His father gulped down the water. Wiping his mouth, he said, 'Aye of course. You need to earn it though.' He opened a drawer and pulled out the ration book. 'You can go to the shops for me. Saturday treat. Mince and tatties.'

Lachlan was delighted to be given such responsibility. His father handed him the small, stapled booklet.

'Don't lose it!' he said. 'A pound of mince and an ounce of lard. Got that? Here's the money, there should be a penny or two in change.'

'Thanks. Is this not meant to be ending though?' He waved the ration book.

'Aye, if the Tories get their way. But folk are starving all over

Europe since the war and there's not enough food to go around. Those people need to eat too.'

Lachlan looked at the ration book, its cardboard cover creased and worn, and headed out the door.

****

'Hey, wee man, got a fag?'

Lachlan didn't turn around as the butcher's door closed behind him. He knew who it was without looking - Barry Turnbull had been the bane of his life since moving to Stirling - and he knew how this would end. His heart raced as he quickened his pace, gripping the brown paper bag he'd just collected from the butcher's.

Barry shouted - 'What's in the bag?'

Lachlan's gut lurched as he heard the footsteps quicken. 'Hey I'm talking to you. What's in the bag?'

He stopped and turned. There was no way he could outrun Barry, and he was resigned to what was coming next.

'It's just mince. My dad's waiting for me.' He turned quickly and indicated down the empty road. No cars. No people. Just a grim grey parade of harled houses separated by scrubby bits of grass.

Barry raised his head and made an exaggerated scan of the street. 'Is he? I can't see anybody. It's just you and me so hand over the bag and I'll maybe go easy on you.' He grinned, revealing a mouth like a vandalised graveyard. His pock-marked face contorted into what passed for joy in Barry's miserable existence.

Lachlan's mouth was dry. He could hear his heart pounding. 'This is our tea. My dad'll kill me if I lose it. So if you're going to batter me, just get on with it.'

Barry didn't need much persuading. Lachlan didn't even feel the blow to his face. He was flat on his back in an instant, his elbows taking the force of the fall. He brought his hand to his face - it came away warm and red. He tried to sit up and felt the blood flowing from his nose and onto his shirt. Barry picked up the bag then delivered a kick to Lachlan's arm that sent him sprawling again.

'Next time, just hand it over.' Barry spat on the pavement, just missing Lachlan.

He said nothing. He could feel the tears coming, along with the pain. His ears ringing as he spat blood onto the concrete. A brief flash of sunlight broke through the clouds and glinted off a pile of broken glass at the roadside, blinding him momentarily but he could make out the shape of Barry sauntering down the street, inspecting the contents of the bag. He heard him shout 'Maw, I've got a present for you!' as he approached his house. One of a block of four. The same as every house in this miserable scheme.

He forced himself to his feet and checked the damage. His hands scraped and bleeding, full of grit from the pavement. His elbows aching and seeping blood through his shirt. His face swollen and numb. He checked his nose - it didn't appear to be broken but was still issuing a stream of blood onto his lips. He spat again and was pleased to see no teeth falling out.

An old woman emerged from the newsagent's. She clattered her wheeled tartan shopping basket out behind her and headed with purpose towards Lachlan.

'What happened to you?' she asked, brightly.

'I got battered. He stole my mince,' sniffed Lachlan, gesturing towards the departing figure of his assailant.

'Aye well you need to toughen up son. Here.' She rummaged in her handbag and pulled out a handkerchief. 'Sort yourself out.'

'Thanks,' said Lachlan and wiped his nose with the perfumed cloth. It seemed like a terrible waste of a good hankie.

'You keep that, and get yourself home. You need to stand up and fight though son. You won't last two minutes here if you keep giving in to them.'

'I know,' nodded Lachlan. 'I've only been here for a couple of months. We came from Aberfoyle. Me and my dad. It was… different there.'

'Aye well you're not in Aberfoyle now.' She bustled past and carried on down the road, her trolley bouncing along behind her.

'You're right there,' muttered Lachlan. Gone were the trees, the fields, the sound of cattle braying and the gurgle of the river. And gone was Morag. In their place were row-upon-row of identical houses, newly planted grass that grew in sorry patches like a teenager's beard and Barry Bloody Turnbull. Above it all the castle brooded on its rock, silhouetted against a sky that seemed permanently grey.

****

'He what?!' Lachlan's father threw his paper down. 'And you did nothing? You just handed it over?'

Lachlan's brow creased and despite his efforts, his eyes began watering. 'I'm sorry Dad. There was nothing I could do.'

His father's shoulders slumped. 'Come here.'

Lachlan buried his head in his father's chest. Smoke and whisky. The reassuring smell of home. 'I hate it here. Can we not go back to Aberfoyle?'

He felt his father's hand ruffle his hair, 'No son, we can't go back.

You know why.'

'Because of Mum. I know. But why? I hate living here. I hate this house. I hate the folk upstairs. YOU hate the folk upstairs too.'

His father sat on the sagging brown settee - the same one Lachlan had cuddled in with both his parents up until last year. Lachlan hesitated for a moment, then joined him.

'Look son, we need to move on. We couldn't stay there. Not just because it made me sad, but my job, and everything else. Sometimes you have to make hard decisions. I've got my new job here at the coach-works and without that, I can't put food on the table or keep a roof over our heads. Do you understand? Stirling's a better place for a wee boy to grow up. You've made friends at school haven't you?'

Lachlan sniffed loudly and nodded, thinking of Gerry and Johnny. Luckily Barry was at the High School - a problem he'd have to deal with in a couple of years, but for now at least his daylight hours were relatively free from danger.

'Well there you go. I know you miss Aberfoyle. I do too, but there was nothing left for us there.'

Lachlan thought of Morag, but he knew his father was right. After they'd buried Lachlan's mum in the same little graveyard he and Morag had explored on their way to Fairy Hill last year, it was as if the last part of his father had disappeared and he'd been replaced by a replica. Like the fairies had stolen his soul. He'd started missing work, staying in bed all day. The smell of whisky filled the house. It wasn't long before a letter arrived telling him his services at the slate mine were no longer required. He didn't even seem bothered. Lachlan remembered him reading the letter and laughing. The first time he'd laughed in ages, but it didn't sound like a happy laugh. When there was a knock at the door one day, and Lachlan answered it to the flustered figure of Mr Finlay, their landlord, he'd thought little of it. But his father had started packing things in boxes that same day and Lachlan knew his time in their little house by the river was coming to an end.

'Right, there's still some soup left in the pot. We can have that for tea, and don't worry about Barry Turnbull. I'll sort that out.'

Lachlan wiped his tears as his father headed for the kitchenette. He heard a thump from upstairs, followed by shrieking and the sound of a door slamming. He'd never get used to having people living above him. It didn't seem right. He preferred his old bedroom with its wooden floors and draughty window. This house didn't have any draughts at least. If anything, it always seemed too warm. His father always had a good fire on the go, and it was Lachlan's job to run out to the concrete coal bunker to fill the bucket. One morning he'd spotted Mr Harper from upstairs helping himself to a shovel full of coal from Lachlan's bunker but he hadn't said anything. Mr Harper was a crooked skeleton of a man, who always had a roll-up cigarette hanging from his thin lips and seemed to spend his life arguing with his wife. As soon as the opportunity presented itself, Lachlan just filled his bucket from the Harper's bunker. *Two can play at that game.*

'Wash your face and hands,' his father shouted from the kitchenette. 'It'll be ready in a minute.'

Lachlan picked up his father's discarded newspaper and scanned the headline. KING OPENS FESTIVAL OF BRITAIN. Underneath the headline was a photograph of a slender, futuristic-looking tower shaped like a giant cigar. It appeared to float some distance from the ground. The caption read *"The Skylon, on the banks of the Thames, London"*. He looked out at the monochrome houses opposite, smoke belching from their chimneys into an overcast sky. London looked like a foreign country, or a city from the future on an alien planet.

He tossed the paper aside, then noticed a half-empty bottle of Bell's on the floor. Curiosity got the better of him, and he carefully took a burning swig from the bottle. He forced himself to swallow while screwing the lid back on. The moisture in his eyes seemed to dry up and for a moment he noticed the pain in his face had subsided.

Placing the bottle back on the carpet, he felt a strange numbness, and wondered if this was why his father seemed to love the stuff so much.

****

'Lachlan, wake up. Do you want to go fishing?' his father shouted from the hall. Lachlan had only been half asleep, the pain in his face keeping him awake.

They set off on what was an unusually sunny day. A few clouds high in the sky as they headed for the river. Most folk were still asleep and the only sounds were from the birds pecking away at scraps of food thrown from kitchen windows. The rumble of an engine and a repeated horn-blast - the bread van - was the only sign that they weren't completely alone in the world.

He looked up at his father, two fishing rods over his shoulder, like his rifle used to be, and his army satchel swinging by his side. Inside was yesterday's soup can, which had been washed out and was now full of worms he'd dug up in the garden, and a bundle of greaseproof paper containing two jam sandwiches. He hoped the bag wrapped around the worms was secure.

'Dad, why do you never talk about the war?'

His father looked down with a thin smile, thought for a moment, then said, 'I've told you son. I saw a lot of things I'm trying to forget. If I talk to you about it, I'd need to remember them again.'

'What sort of things? Like dead people?'

'Aye, I saw a lot of dead people.'

'What are they like?'

'They're the same as us I suppose, except they don't talk as much. Now wheesht. We're nearly there. Here, over this wall.'

Lachlan opened his arms and let his father hoist him up. As he turned, he spotted someone in the distance, hurrying down the road towards them. He ducked quickly behind the wall, putting his father between him and the approaching figure.

'What is it?' His father turned in the direction Lachlan was looking. 'Who's that?' Then, with a glance at Lachlan's face, a realisation. 'Is that the wee shite who battered you yesterday?'

'Uhuh,' said Lachlan. 'Come on Dad, let's go.'

'Aye,' said his father, but his back was to Lachlan and he seemed to be studying the figure of Barry Turnbull as he turned and headed along a side street.

'He's just a bully,' said Lachlan. 'Don't worry about it. I'll be fine.'

'You don't look fine. That's some black eye he's given you, and you're lucky you're not at the hospital today getting your nose fixed.'

Lachlan grabbed his father's hand and dragged him into the undergrowth.

****

Lachlan watched as his father tied a fat grey worm onto his hook, it squirmed as it was popped onto the barb.

'Do you want to try it yourself?' asked his father.

'Yuck, no thanks,' chuckled Lachlan as he took the rod from his father.

'Right, here. Stand like this.' Lachlan let himself be led as his father shuffled him into position near the bank and grabbed his arms from behind. He drew them back, pointing the rod into the trees at their back, then with a snap forced the rod forward, sending the line far into the river. The float bobbed on the surface as the hook sank into the slow, dark water.

'Okay, now wind it back a bit, like this.' He took Lachlan's hand and placed it on the reel handle. With a spin and a whirr, the line tightened and the float shifted back towards them slightly. 'That's good, leave it there.'

His father cast his own line and placed his rod on a Y-shaped stick he'd stuck in the ground. He fumbled in his pockets, pulled out his tobacco tin and started making a roll-up.

'What does that make you feel like?' asked Lachlan. He wiggled his rod, watching the red and white float bob up and down.

'Smoking? Nothing really, but it helps keep the midges away, and it stops me feeling rubbish from the last cigarette I had. I hope I never see you smoking.'

Lachlan gulped at the thought of his friend Johnny, who was ten years old and already smoking. 'I won't Dad. It smells rotten.'

'Aye, that's because it is.' He sparked a match and lit his roll-up, taking a deep drag and flicking the match into the river.

'So why don't you stop?' asked Lachlan.

'Sometimes we don't always do what's best for us.' He inspected the end of his cigarette and tapped ash onto the grass.

'Like moving to Stirling you mean?' said Lachlan, immediately regretting it.

His father sighed, blowing out a cloud of smoke that hung in the air.

'You see this water in front of you?'

'Uhuh,' said Lachlan, looking out as his float drifted slowly downriver.

'Well, you know this is the same river that ran past our old house?'

'The Forth, yes, of course.'

'Well what's different about it here?'

Lachlan looked puzzled, then said, 'It's bigger?'

'Aye, it's bigger. What else?'

'It's more bendy?' He looked upriver, back towards Aberfoyle and the river's source some twenty miles away but he could only see about a hundred yards of river before it disappeared in a long sweeping bend.

'Exactly, and why do you think that is?'

'Because it's bigger? So it's…' he thought of the word, '…heavier? It's not like at Aberfoyle where it was fast and not very deep.'

'That's it!' said his father with a smile. 'It's bigger. And it's slower because it's heavier. It's like us. Like me. Like you. It starts out wee and all excited, bouncing around, jumping over the rocks, and making a noise. By the time it gets here it's starting to lose all that, as it's gathering more water. Other wee rivers feed into it, and it has to carry all them too. It's growing up you see?'

'I think so,' said Lachlan. 'Why does it bend more though, why does it not just go in a straight line?'

'Because the ground here is very flat, look.' He waved an arm around, towards the hill of Abbey Craig topped with the stone tower of the Wallace Monument, and back towards the castle on its rock. 'Everything between the castle and the hills is flat as a pancake. So the river isn't forced in any one direction. It's looking for the path of least resistance. It's still a young river here, you could throw a stone to the other side easy enough, but it's winding this way and that because it's not sure where it's going yet. It's always moving towards the sea though, in tiny increments.'

'Tiny increments?' repeated Lachlan. He liked that. 'So it's just like me really. It doesn't know where it's going yet?'

'Exactly,' said his father as he leaned back onto his elbows. 'Now, do you want your jam piece?'

Lachlan grinned. 'As long as the worms didn't touch it.'

His father pulled the greaseproof bundle out of the bag and turned it a few times in his hands. 'I think we're safe.'

As Lachlan chewed he said, 'Dad, you know the old bridge down there?' He pointed towards the stone bridge crossing the river, just visible downstream.

'Stirling Bridge, of course I do. What about it?'

'Well do you know the first bridge, an even older one, is somewhere near here - where we're sitting?'

His father sat up, swallowing a mouthful of bread. 'No I didn't know that. How do you know about it?'

'I was reading about it. The Battle of Stirling Bridge. When William Wallace defeated the English in…' He looked up, chewing his cheek. '1297, I think. Ages ago anyway.'

'Aye, exactly son. Ages ago. Best forgotten about too. Are they teaching you that at school?'

'No. I read about it in a book I got from the library. William

Wallace hid his army up in the hills there. I suppose they thought this was a good place to fight because it's so flat. Anyway, the English army crossed the old wooden bridge, and then Wallace attacked.' He started swinging an imaginary broadsword around his head. 'We never get any Scottish history at school. It's all Oliver Cromwell and Shakespeare and stuff.'

His father's eyes narrowed into a smile, but he said nothing.

'Don't you think that's odd, Dad, that we don't get taught about our own history?'

His father shrugged. 'Well, it *is* your own history. You live in Britain. The United Kingdom. They're just teaching you the important stuff.'

Lachlan pondered this as he watched his float drift downriver. Something about it just didn't feel right, but he couldn't quite put his finger on it.

****

As the sun sank towards the distant hills, they gathered their things while swatting away the swarms of midges massed around the river bank.

'Ugh,' said Lachlan. 'I hate midges. Why do they always get worse at this time?' He spat as one of the tiny insects flew into his mouth.

'No idea Lachlan. I was an engineer. Not an entomologist.'

'An entowhatagist?'

'Someone who studies insects. Hurry up. I'm getting eaten alive.' He swatted at his neck and rolled his shirt sleeves down.

'Is that a job?' asked Lachlan.

'Of course,' said his father. 'It's a type of scientist. Why, do you like the sound of it?'

Lachlan screwed his face up. 'Nah, not really. Can't say I'm too keen on bugs. I don't really know what I want to be.'

'What about doing something with all that historical know-how?' He tapped Lachlan's head. 'You could work at the castle telling stories to tourists.'

'That sounds like fun. Do you like your job?'

'At the coach-works? It's okay I suppose. It's better than cutting slate anyway. I like fixing things, but I was never a clever wee thing like you. You could do anything you like, if you stick at it.'

Lachlan was both delighted and horrified at the thought of this. It was hard enough working out what he wanted on his play-piece sandwich, never mind choosing what he wanted to do for the rest of his life.

'You can change your mind though can't you? Like you did?' he asked.

'Aye of course you can. But you're better to stick at something you're good at,' said his father, as he shouldered his satchel.

'Okay,' Lachlan laughed. 'But I don't really know yet. I'm only ten Dad!'

'No rush son. But remember, you're like this river. Sooner or later you have to make up your mind, and make your way to the sea.'

Lachlan nodded and looked towards the far shore. The lowering sun was bringing out the detail in the landscape. The trees were bursting with fresh growth. Spring blossom caught the sun like confetti. The long grass swayed in the breeze and all around the only sound came from the birds. Chattering sparrows, the cooing of a wood pigeon, and the machine-gun chatter of a magpie. On top of Abbey Craig the Wallace Monument was turning a burnt orange.

'We didn't catch any fish Dad.'

'Ach fishing's not just about catching fish,' his father said.

He was about to question this when they heard a shout from the opposite shore. He turned to the source of the cry - a lady with a small brown dog was calling to them and gesturing towards the river bank, about forty yards upriver. She was clearly in distress.

His father cupped his ears and called, 'What is it?'

She said nothing, her hand clasped over her mouth now

'Come on son. She's maybe got another dog stuck in the river.'

They left their rods and bag by the shore and hurried through the nettles and the long grass.

'What's that?' said Lachlan, spotting something white, floating in the river.

His father stopped in his tracks, muttered something Lachlan couldn't hear, then hurried off towards the bank.

Lachlan followed, still unaware that everything that happened in the next minute would haunt him for decades.

His father ran into the river, quickly up to his knees but oblivious to the cold, and grabbed the thing in the water.

Lachlan had thought it was a bag, it seemed to balloon with air, but he quickly realised that this wasn't a discarded sack of rubbish. It was a man, floating face-down. He approached the shore slowly. 'Is he... okay Dad?'

His father didn't seem to hear him. Lachlan watched as he struggled to turn the figure face-up. He fell back into the water, soaking himself from head to foot. The woman on the far shore had followed them and her dog was now barking wildly, straining at its lead. Lachlan looked down again just as his father managed to turn the figure over. He met the gaze of a man of around his father's age. Mouth open. Hair matted against his skull. His skin grey and sagging. His eyes staring straight at Lachlan, unblinking. The eyes of a dead man.

Lachlan turned cold and fell to his knees. He closed his eyes tight but that staring face was still there, beyond his eyelids. Burning into his brain.

'Turn away Lachlan, don't look.' His father's voice seemed to come from somewhere else. Muffled and echoing around his head. Lachlan did as he asked and turned to look back at the trees and houses beyond. He heard his father pulling the body from the water and onto the bank. A magpie settled on a branch of a nearby tree and cackled a mad laugh. Lachlan concentrated on the bird. Its feathers glinting with a blue sheen in the dying light of the afternoon.

'Oh shit.' He sensed his father moving quickly behind him, leaping away from the body.

Despite himself, Lachlan turned to see the man lying about ten feet away. Facing away from him this time but it wasn't the man's face he was focusing on, it was the large blood stain on the side of his shirt. It looked like a map of Japan, snaking up his side. Within it were two darker red blotches like city markers. Hiroshima and Nagasaki.

His father moved between Lachlan and the body, obscuring his view. 'Come on,' he said. 'We need to get the police.'

****

His father pulled the heavy phone box door open and stepped inside. Lachlan stood on the pavement breathing heavily.

The rumble of a lorry's engine grew in volume as it approached then sped past. He sniffed the air, trying to regain his senses. He was beginning to enjoy the sweet smell of burning fuel. Petrol rationing had ended and this was a new sensation. He'd taken to waiting at junctions with Johnny and Gerry and sniffing the clouds of exhaust smoke belching from the waiting cars. It made them laugh. It was just something to do in a place where there was nothing to do.

The door swung open and his father stepped out. 'We've to wait here,' he said, reaching into his shirt pocket for his tobacco tin

'Had he been… killed… do you think? It didn't look like he'd just fallen in the river.'

His father said nothing.

In the distance, the sound of a bell ringing broke the silence. Lachlan watched as the police car approached. Its tall chrome radiator grill flanked by two round headlights - as if it was staring at them and sizing them up as it slowed to a halt.

Both doors swung open in unison and two uniformed policemen climbed out.

'Mr McCormack?' said the first, a tall man with a stern expression and lumpy skin.

'Sandy, aye,' said his father.

'I'm Sergeant Murray. This is PC Wilson. Climb in.' He opened the rear door of the car. 'It's down by the river?'

'Aye that's right.'

PC Wilson, slightly smaller and with a friendlier face, asked, 'Is there somewhere the boy can go? Is your wife at home?'

'No, he'll need to come with us.' His father bundled Lachlan into the back seat. He slipped across the brown leather to the far side. It smelled of pipe smoke and furniture polish.

A woman pushing a pram walked hurriedly past, glancing in at them. Was it the lady with the baby from the flat next door to theirs? He wasn't sure. His father pulled the door closed while the two policemen took their seats and set the bell ringing again.

A minute later they were parked by the river.

Sergeant Murray spoke to his father, while looking into the rear-view mirror. 'It's probably best that the boy stays here. Wilson will look after him.'

The doors closed with a clunk as Sergeant Murray and his father headed into the trees.

'So,' said PC Wilson, turning in his seat and resting an arm on the chair-back. 'Sounds like some fish you caught today eh?'

Lachlan smiled. He didn't want to think about the body.

'Can you tell me about it?'

Lachlan shrugged. 'We'd just finished fishing. Then a woman started shouting from the other side of the river.'

'A woman? What did she look like?'

'Just a woman with a dog. I don't know. A wee brown dog.'

'And the woman, was she old? Young? What was she wearing?'

'Just normal clothes,' said Lachlan. 'And not old. But not young.'

'Okay and what happened? Why was she shouting at you? Had your dad done something wrong?'

'No!' said Lachlan. 'She was shouting and pointing at the… the… man in the river. We were down nearer the bridge.' He pointed downriver towards their fishing spot.

'What happened to your face? That's some bruise you've got there.'

'I got battered yesterday, at the shops. He stole my mince.'

'Who did?'

Lachlan thought for a minute, then said, 'A boy, I don't know him. He's bigger than me though.'

PC Wilson nodded, 'And does he live around here?'

'Yes. I mean, I'm not sure. I don't know.'

The policeman stared at him, like he was trying to read his mind. Lachlan fidgeted in his seat, the leather squeaked under his backside. He could feel his back prickle with sweat.

'Okay then, that's fine. And the man in the river was here, just where they've gone into the trees?'

Lachlan looked out the car window, then began examining all the grubby fingerprints on the glass. 'Yes. He was floating near the bank and my dad pulled him out.'

'And what did the man look like. Did you recognise him?'

'No,' said Lachlan. He felt his stomach churn as the image of the dead man's face surfaced again. 'I think I'm going to be sick.'

He grabbed for the door release but it wouldn't open. He felt the bile rising in his throat as PC Wilson jumped from the car and released the door from outside but it was too late. He sprayed vomit down the back of the passenger seat then threw up again onto the pavement.

'I'm sorry,' said Lachlan wiping his mouth. 'When's my dad back?'

'Soon son. Here, out you come. Let's wipe this up.'

Lachlan stood shivering while PC Wilson took a rag from the boot and started hauling chunks of jam sandwich from the rear footwell.

'I'm sorry. I don't feel well.'

'That's okay. It's not everyday a wee boy sees something like this.' He threw the rag to the gutter and glanced towards the trees. 'Look, here's your dad.'

Lachlan and the sergeant were still talking as they approached. His father had retrieved their rods and his bag and to anyone passing it looked like he'd been caught fishing without a permit. Lachlan wasn't sure if his dad actually had a permit, but the police didn't seem too bothered about that right now.

'Right,' said Sergeant Murray. 'I'll secure the scene. PC Wilson will get you two home. If you could come into the station tomorrow Mr McCormack so we can take a formal statement, that'd be grand.'

'No problem,' said Lachlan's father.

'And Wilson, get back down here as soon as you can and see if this lot have anything to offer,' said Sergeant Murray, gesturing towards the houses opposite where several curtains appeared to be twitching in unison.

****

Lachlan had the table set for dinner when he heard his father's voice outside. He saw him talking to the lady with the baby from next door. He seemed to be laughing but she was standing back with a concerned expression. His father seemed very animated - he didn't usually use his hands this much when he was talking. She seemed to relax a bit and a smile came to her face.

He returned to setting the table, putting out the salt and pepper as he heard his father's key in the door.

'Hi Dad,' he called.

'Hello son.'

'What were you talking about with the lady from next door?'

'Well,' he slicked his hair back then opened the cupboard where the glasses were. He took down his whisky tumbler and pulled a bottle of Bell's from a brown paper bag. 'It was interesting.'

'She's never spoken to us before has she?' Lachlan said.

'No she hasn't. She didn't really want to speak there either to be honest.'

Lachlan waited for his father to elaborate.

'Remember she saw us getting into the police car yesterday?'

'Uhuh,' Lachlan said, and suddenly realised why she may have been unwilling to talk.

'Well I was just coming up the street there and she turned the corner in front of me. She took one look at me and practically ran away. I just asked her if everything was alright.'

'Did she think we were criminals?'

His father laughed, 'Aye, you could say that. See, the thing is, she'd been talking to people at the shops and she'd heard about the...' He took a swig of whisky. 'The... you know... the body.'

'Did she think you had something to do with it?'

His father nodded. 'Crazy eh? Just shows how quick folk are to judge.'

'Crazy,' said Lachlan. 'She seemed nice though.'

His father took another large mouthful of whisky and said, 'Aye, she is. Anyway, how was school?'

'Och, the usual. We're doing fractions. I can't do them.'

'Fractions? Easy. I'll show you after dinner. Sausage sandwich?'

Lachlan's second favourite dinner. 'Yup. Oh, did you go to the police station?'

'I did aye. Popped in during my lunch. That was interesting too.' He sparked the cooker to life and lay a few sausages on the grill. 'Spread some bread and I'll tell you about it.'

Lachlan removed four slices from the bread bin. He busied himself spreading a thin layer of butter on each as his father continued.

'Right, the thing is, the man hadn't been in the water that long. They can tell these things. They think he'd been in the river less than a day anyway, probably a lot less.'

'Is that important?' asked Lachlan.

'Well, aye, it is, because this helps them work out where and when he went into the water. It's not a fast flowing river, so they reckon he'd gone in not too far upriver from where we found him.'

'So do they think they'll find out who did it?'

'Who knows? They were out chapping doors and looking for witnesses - people who might have seen what happened.'

'Uhuh. We didn't see anything though did we? Just the woman with the dog?'

'Well… It just dawned on me on my way home from work. We did see somebody else that day didn't we?'

Lachlan thought for a moment. *Barry Turnbull.* He remembered ducking behind the wall as soon as he spotted him, while his dad took a long, hard look. The more he thought about it, the more he seemed to remember that Barry was almost running, or at least stumbling quickly down the road. And didn't he keep looking back over his shoulder?

'Barry Turnbull?'

His father raised his eyebrows and took another swig of whisky.

Lachlan placed the butter knife down. Could Barry have stabbed a man and thrown him in the river? He touched his cheek, still numb from Saturday's punch, and thought that he could.

'We should tell the police,' said Lachlan.

His father checked the sausages under the grill, then said, 'Aye, I think you're right.' He turned the grill off. 'We can have these later. Come on.'

****

It took half an hour to walk into town and Lachlan was delighted to see the blue "Police" sign above the station door up ahead. The streets were still busy with people heading out to the pubs, or making their way home from work.

A bus chugged past them. Lachlan glanced at the destination board above the driver's seat and saw it was going to Aberfoyle.

'Dad, can we go back to Aberfoyle soon? For a visit?'

'You missing wee Morag?'

Lachlan blushed, 'No. I just thought it'd be nice to visit Mum.' *But yes, I am missing wee Morag.*

'Sure son. Soon. Right, here we are.'

The main door of the station swung open and Lachlan gasped as the twisted face of Barry Turnbull emerged. He barged past them and headed back up the road, the way they'd come.

His father pointed at Barry as he hurried off and said, 'Was that?'

'Barry? Aye.'

Lachlan's blood ran cold. Barry hadn't even acknowledged

him. He'd charged out and kept his head down in much the same way Lachlan had when he emerged from the butcher's shop on Saturday.

Inside, it smelled of bleach, sweat, and cigarettes. The ceiling lights were far too bright. Lachlan blinked and screwed his eyes up as they approached the desk. From deep within the station, he could hear someone shouting and a door slamming with an echoing thud.

The policeman at the desk looked up. He was young with a trim little moustache. 'Can I help you?'

'Aye,' said his father, pointing back towards the front door. 'The lad that's just left, Barry Turnbull, we were coming to report him in relation to the murder at the river. I'm Sandy McCormack. I was in earlier. I'd forgotten we'd spotted him earlier in the day. The day of the murder that is.'

'Yes sir. That you might. You weren't the only ones though.'

'But he's walking away up the road there.'

'Correct. He was merely helping us with our enquiries. Turns out there are a lot of curtain twitchers up that way, and we've had three separate people through the door today pointing the finger at young Mr Turnbull.'

'We saw him hurrying down the road, about the time it all happened.'

'He kept looking back over his shoulder like he was running away from something!' Lachlan added.

The policeman stood up and looked over the counter at Lachlan.

'Not something, son. Somebody.'

'Eh?' said Lachlan's father.

'Can't really tell you any more at the moment sir, but we're following a very positive line of enquiry. Mr Turnbull was very helpful and we hope to bring this case to a close soon. Now, is there anything else I can help you with?'

'Eh, no. Suppose not.' His father patted the counter. 'We'll just be getting back up the road then.'

The policeman nodded, then looked at Lachlan. 'Is your laddie okay? That's some shiner he's got.'

'Aye he's not much of a fighter, are you son?'

Lachlan put his hand to his eye.

'And where did you get that? Must have been some punch,' said the policeman.

Lachlan pointed back towards the door and said, 'Barry Turnbull, sir.'

The policeman grinned and shook his head. 'Aye? Well I have to be honest, Mr Turnbull is usually in here in a less co-operative capacity, shall we say?' Then, to his father, 'Do you want to report it?'

His father looked at Lachlan's swollen cheek and blossoming black eye.

'No, I think he'll be fine. No point wasting your time on a daft scrap.'

The policeman smiled then looked again at Lachlan. 'Next time son,' he mimed a sharp right-jab. 'Punch the bastard back, okay?'

****

Lachlan spat toothpaste into the sink and looked in the mirror. His cheek was almost back to normal and his black eye had mostly cleared up.

It had been just over a week since the punch and he'd spent the evenings sparring with his father in the living room. *It'll toughen you up,* he'd said. *Take a swing at me.* Lachlan had thought it funny at first but by the end of the week he was beginning to enjoy it. He'd winded his father with a belly-punch on Friday night that sent him flopping into his chair and reaching for the whisky.

It was Sunday again, and he'd arranged to meet Gerry and Johnny down by the old bridge. He returned to his bedroom and hauled on his trousers and a T-shirt. It looked like a nice day, but he wrestled himself into a jumper anyway.

'I'm just heading next door to Moira's!' his father shouted from the hall.

His father had been through to see Moira a couple of times this weekend already. What on earth was he doing through there? Lachlan knew she lived alone, with her wee girl. He thought about it some more. Surely not? Was his father trying to get him a new mum and a wee sister? He certainly hoped not.

Outside, summer was definitely in the air. The overpowering smell of smoke from hundreds of coal fires had been replaced by the more pleasant aroma of cut grass and engine oil, as the few car owners on the scheme jacked-up their vehicles for some annual maintenance. The chill was gone, and there was at last some heat in the sun. He ran down his street and over the crossroads at the end. A few folk were out in their gardens, tending young hedges, chatting, hanging up washing. Somewhere he could hear the sound of a roller mower struggling over a lawn.

Gerry spotted him approach the bridge and shouted, 'Here he is, the Road Runner!'

'Meep meep!' called Johnny.

Lachlan laughed and said, 'Shut up, Foghorn Leghorn.'

Gerry and Johnny looked at each other in mock surprise as Lachlan ran up the cobbled surface to the crest of the bridge.

'Aye, very good Lachlan. Great comeback.' said Gerry, wiping his nose on his sleeve.

Lachlan stopped and put his hands on his knees, as he gathered his breath.

'So, what'll we do?' said Johnny, flipping the filter of a cigarette over the side of the bridge.

Lachlan looked down at the river below, then back upriver to where he'd spent the day fishing with his father just a week ago.

'We could go up to the new houses and break some windows?' suggested Gerry.

'Or build a den?' said Johnny.

Lachlan looked to the north bank of the river, where more new council houses were being built. The site would be empty today. Abandoned lorries and diggers for them to climb over; piles of bricks, timber and bags of cement everywhere - perfect for den-building. But he had another idea.

'What about I show you where we found the body?'

****

'We were fishing in there,' said Lachlan, pointing to the bank where he'd sat with his father. 'And the body was up here.'

They continued along the road. The river to their right, houses to their left. The day was growing warmer and Lachlan was tying his jumper around his waist when Johnny muttered, 'Oh shit,' and pushed him off the pavement and into the undergrowth.

'What the...' Lachlan managed before he tripped over Gerry's foot and fell face-first into the long grass.

'Sorry,' muttered Gerry, as he pulled Lachlan to his feet and ushered him towards the trees.

'Barry Turnbull,' said Johnny, nodding sideways while shoving Lachlan forward.

Lachlan peered up the street. Sure enough, Barry Turnbull was there, sitting cross-legged on the rise of the embankment. He hadn't seen them, or at least he hadn't appeared to, as he sat with his head hanging down - staring at the grass between his legs.

Johnny and Gerry positioned themselves in the cover of a tree and gestured for Lachlan to join them, but Lachlan couldn't take his eyes off Barry. What was he doing? He'd never seen him sit like this - he wasn't the contemplative type.

'What's up with him?' asked Lachlan.

'No idea,' said Johnny.

'Looks like he's pished himself,' offered Gerry.

Slowly, they made their way upriver - taking care not to stand on any fallen branches and create a crack that would alert Barry to their presence. The river flowed soundlessly beside them, and there was no traffic noise to cover their approach.

Soon they were level with him, lying in the long grass and the tree roots, looking at the back of his home-knitted blue jumper. He was barely twenty feet away. And from here, it was quite clear that he was crying. His shoulders jerked up and down and they could hear him sobbing and muttering to himself.

They looked at each other but said nothing. This was new territory. Barry continued to sob. They continued to watch.

'Shit,' whispered Gerry.

'What?' said Johnny.

Gerry's face was contorting. He squirmed. 'I'm going to sneeze.'

Lachlan shook his head, with a panicked expression.

Gerry's resolve gave way. He jerked upwards as he sneezed loudly, a gobbet of snot drooped from his nostrils.

Barry stood and turned to face them. They jumped to their feet, their brains frantically seeking the quickest escape route, but instead they froze.

Barry's face had been battered black and blue. His eyes puffed up; both his cheeks swollen and purple; his nose flattened against his face; his mouth hung open, the bottom lip twice its normal size; one of his ears stuck out even more than usual and there was blood all down the front of his jumper. Lots of blood. He turned and ran.

'Who the hell would be mental enough to do that to him?' said Johnny.

Gerry shook his head.

Lachlan eventually said, 'I've no idea, but I wouldn't want to meet him.'

****

'Hiya son, where have you been?' his father said, as he busied himself at the cooker frying some eggs.

'Just up at the river,' said Lachlan.

'Hope you were behaving?'

'Course!' said Lachlan, joining his father in the kitchenette. He ran the tap and washed his hands before continuing. 'Dad, we saw something really crazy. Barry Turnbull's been battered. He looked like he'd done ten rounds with Sugar Ray Robinson.'

'Well well well,' said his father, flipping the eggs over in the pan.

'Do you know something about it?'

'I've heard some things. These eggs are ready. Put a couple of plates out will you?'

Lachlan pulled two plates out of the draining rack and set them on the table.

'What sort of things?'

His father slipped the eggs onto the plates and they took their seats.

'Well, I just went for a wee walk up to the shops with Moira this afternoon. Thought I'd help her with her messages.'

'Uhuh,' said Lachlan. 'Dad, are you erm, going out with her?'

'No son, Jesus. No. Don't be daft. She's just good company, that's all.'

Lachlan took a mouthful of egg and studied his father. He seemed to be blushing.

His father continued. 'So aye, there was the usual bunch at the post office and the shops. The women, you know?'

Lachlan nodded.

'Anyway, somebody had heard from somebody else that there had been an arrest. For the murder.'

'Aye, who?'

'Well, you'll not know him, but he's known as Malky. He lives over there somewhere.' He pointed out the window. 'Have you heard about him?'

'I think I've heard folk saying *Big Malky'll get you* and things like that, but I don't know him.'

'Well, good. He's a nasty piece of work, involved in all sorts of stuff. Anyway, it turned out that he'd been doing a bit of business with another local character - Joe McLeish.'

'Business?' asked Lachlan, as he forked another piece of egg into his mouth.

'Aye. Buying and selling things that didn't belong to them, you understand?'

Lachlan nodded. 'So they were crooks?'

'Exactly. So Malky had fallen out with McLeish over money that he owed him, and this fall out had turned into a fight, and then it got even nastier. It was Joe McLeish we found in the river.'

'So Barry had nothing to do with it?'

'Nothing at all, apart from the fact he'd been walking past when it happened and he saw Malky and McLeish fighting.'

'And Malky saw him?'

'No, I don't think so. But somebody did.'

'When we saw him hurrying down the road?'

'Aye. Barry couldn't get away fast enough. He'd have known who Malky was, and wouldn't fancy getting involved, but the police went around the doors later that day and somebody else must've spotted Barry. That's why he was in the station last week.'

'Helping with our enquiries,' said Lachlan, remembering what the desk sergeant had said.

'Exactly. Or *singing like a canary,* as you could also put it. The police would have taken Barry in as a suspect - he'd been spotted in the area after all - but when they got him into the station he'd told them everything he'd seen.'

'Then they knew it was Malky?'

'They'd be well aware of Malky and his crowd. I expect they already had their suspicions but Barry just confirmed it all for them.'

'So then they arrested Malky?'

'Aye. One of the women at the shops said she'd seen him getting bundled into the back of a police car.'

'So who battered Barry? How did Malky know it was him who told the police?'

'That,' said his father, polishing off the last piece of egg, 'remains a mystery. But these guys have eyes everywhere. And Malky has four brothers. My money would be on one of them.'

'Wow,' said Lachlan. He stabbed the last piece of egg with his fork and held it to his mouth.

Nothing like this had ever happened in Aberfoyle.

****

The following Saturday Lachlan once again found himself in the butchers, buying some tripe. He hated the stuff but his dad seemed to like it. Two women in the queue in front of him had been talking animatedly about the possibility of rationing coming to an end, but that they couldn't bring themselves to vote Tory to bring this about.

Lachlan placed his order and handed over the ration book. While the butcher busied himself stamping the book Lachlan looked at the sparse amount of meat on display and thought that these people must have had a very good reason for not voting Tory. He'd picked up a growing tension from his father recently - the wireless was making him angrier and angrier. It looked like Scotland was split between Labour and the Tories and that Mr Atlee might be out of a job soon. This made his father reach for the whisky even more than usual. Lachlan couldn't understand why he didn't just turn the wireless off if it made him so unhappy.

'There you go son,' said the butcher, handing over a paper bundle of offal and the ration book. The cash register chimed and Lachlan took his change and stuck it in his pocket.

'Thanks,' he said. Then, 'Mister, are you Labour or a Tory?'

The butcher laughed and leant forward. 'Neither son. I'm neither.'

'Oh,' said Lachlan. 'Right… Well, what are you?'

'SNP son. Scotland's party.'

Lachlan had heard about them, his father got even angrier whenever they were mentioned on the wireless. He muttered a quick, 'Oh okay, bye then,' and left in a hurry.

Politics was so confusing, thought Lachlan. They all seemed to say one thing then do another thing. Then people got angry with them, and voted in the other ones again, who they'd been angry with the last time, as if this time they'd actually keep their promises. Adults were weird. And SNP folk were even weirder, according to his father. *Tartan bampots,* he called them, but the butcher had seemed nice enough.

Outside, it was a fine summer's day. The street was busy. Women with prams stopped to talk while their older children played on the road and groups of men hurried to the football, their coloured scarfs wrapped around their necks despite the heat. A coal lorry trundled past, two soot-blackened men in caps sat at the rear smoking cigarettes and swinging their legs over the tailboard. In the middle of all this, Lachlan spotted the familiar figure of Barry Turnbull walking towards him, hands buried in his pockets, his face still looking like the butcher's shop window.

Lachlan took a deep breath and walked on, slowing as Barry got closer.

'The fuck are you looking at?' said Barry as he approached.

Lachlan muttered, 'A grass?' and waited for the punch, but none came. Barry sneered and kept walking, but his swagger appeared to be gone.

Lachlan turned and watched him walk away. It looked like Barry Turnbull might have thrown his last punch.

On the downside, it did mean that he'd still be getting tripe for dinner.

****

As summer faded and the evening chill returned Lachlan spotted Mr Harper at the coal bunker one evening. He hadn't heard Lachlan approach and was helping himself to a shovelful of coal from the McCormack supply.

'Hey!' called Lachlan.

Mr Harper turned quickly, his mouth open. His cigarette hanging from his dry bottom lip. He looked at the shovel of coal in his hands then slowly tipped it back into Lachlan's bunker.

'Keep your hands off our coal Mr Harper. The more you steal from us, the more I steal from you.'

Mr Harper looked shocked. He straightened up. 'You thieving wee bastard!'

Lachlan tilted his head to one side. 'Did you think we wouldn't notice?'

'I should take my hand to your face you-'

He didn't get a chance to finish as Lachlan's father opened the front door and said, 'You'll what Frank? Batter a wee boy? If you want to have a go, have a go at me. Come on.'

His father stepped out and took a couple of quick steps towards Mr Harper, who quickly dropped the coal shovel and scurried towards his front door.

'We're watching you Frank. And we can hear you too. Any more threats to that woman up there and it'll be the police you're dealing with okay?'

Mr Harper's door slammed closed.

'I don't think he'll be nicking our coal any more son, do you?'

Lachlan laughed, 'No Dad.'

'Come on in, there's a letter for you.'

'A letter?'

'Aye.' His father went back inside and grabbed something from the kitchen. Lachlan followed and tried to snatch it from his hand.

'Who's it from?' said Lachlan.

His father looked at it, still holding it just out of Lachlan's reach. 'Well it's got a postmark from Aber-something. Aberdeen? Abertay? Can't quite make it out. It's a bit smudged.'

'Aberfoyle?!' beamed Lachlan. 'It's from Morag, come on, give me it.'

His father laughed as Lachlan made another leap for the letter, then handed it over.

Even the sight of Morag's handwriting set Lachlan's heart pounding. He hurried into the living room and jumped onto the settee.

Dear Lachlan

Thank you for your letter. It was nice to receive it and to hear about your new life in Stirling.

Your friends sound nice. I haven't really made any new friends since you left and there's an old couple in your house now. They sometimes get visits from their family from Glasgow. They have a wee boy. He's the same age as us, but he doesn't really play with me when he's here. I think he's a bit odd.

School is just the same. Mr Barclay is teaching us about the Battle of Hastings now. I asked him if we'd be getting lessons on the Battle of Bannockburn and he told me to stop asking silly questions!

I have some big news I suppose. My mum and dad have decided that they don't want to be married any more. I'm upset about it and I don't know what's going to happen yet but my dad said he was moving to Edinburgh to get a new job.

It feels like everyone just keeps leaving and it makes me sad but I think it's for the best as they weren't happy and this made me unhappy too.

I hope you are having a nice time and I would love to come and visit you in Stirling. I hope there are trees to climb? Is your house near the river? I sent you a message in a bottle, did you get it?

Anyway. Please write back.

Your friend

Morag

PS: of course I still have your flagstone. It's on my bedroom window ledge and reminds me of what a rubbish painter you are! (Joke!)

Lachlan had just started to read the letter again when his father shouted from the hallway, 'I'm just nipping through to see Moira.'

Over the dregs of the summer his relationship with their

neighbour had seemed to ease off while his love affair with the whisky bottle blossomed. During the flirtation, Lachlan had at least found out a bit more about her. Moira's husband had been killed while on overseas duty after the war. It was something to do with a new country in the Middle East for Jewish people to live in. It was all very complicated. Now it was all about Jews versus Arabs when they were still getting over the whole Allies versus Axis thing.

It seemed like the world just stumbled from one problem to another.

If only he could help his father with his own problems. It certainly didn't help that the dreaded Tories had just won the election. Mr Churchill was back and Mr Atlee lost his job. His big coat finally falling to the floor. They should have fixed that shoogly nail! His father had poured himself a whisky and muttered at the wireless as the news came in that Labour had won more votes than any other party in history, and had actually received almost a quarter of a million more votes than the Tories.

'So how did they lose?' Lachlan had asked.

'That's the way it works son,' said his father.

If that was the way it worked then it sounded like it didn't work very well, Lachlan thought.

Anyway, it looked like rationing might be coming to an end soon, which pleased him. If only they'd rationed whisky, his father might have spent a bit less of his wages on the stuff.

While his father was gone, Lachlan penned another letter to Morag, telling her all about his grisly discovery in the river. He hoped it made his life sound more interesting and exciting and as he sealed the envelope he was already looking forward to Morag's reply.

WEDNESDAY

Some of the residents were playing bowls on the lawn. Lachlan sat on a bench and watched while drumming his fingers on the flaking wooden arm. He could have joined in, he chose not to. He was content taking a walk around the grounds most days. It kept the blood flowing, for all that was worth.

It was another warm day and he sat in a white short-sleeved shirt, enjoying the heat on his skin. He heard a door bang shut and looked up to see Fraser, another resident, shuffling along the path.

Fraser was almost bent double. He'd certainly earned his nickname of Frazimodo. He paused after a few steps, winked, and patted the pocket of his dressing gown.

'Fraser,' said Lachlan.

'Lachlan,' said Fraser. Dropping to the bench he straightened himself up the best he could.

'How's life?' asked Lachlan.

'Better for this,' said Fraser, pulling an Irn Bru bottle from his pocket.

'You'll be getting us chucked out.'

'Chance would be a fine thing,' said Fraser, unscrewing the cap.

He took a fly swig, glancing around as he did so and handed the bottle to Lachlan.

Lachlan pretended to take a mouthful and grimaced. 'Jesus, what is it?'

'Whisky, vodka, wee bit of gin, some sherry and a handful of crushed up co-codamol.'

'A cocktail eh? Have you got a name for it?' asked Lachlan.

'A Coffin Dodger?' suggested Fraser and they both chuckled, the rickety bench rattling beneath them.

'There's that bloody bird again,' said Lachlan. The magpie hopped across the lawn, taking flight as a stray bowl almost hit it.

'Ach they all look the same, how do you know it's the same one?' asked Fraser, taking another glug.

Lachlan stared ahead, 'I just know.'

ALLOA 1964

'Lachie-Boy!'

Lachlan's eyes struggled to adjust to the gloom. The Highlander Bar was a windowless concrete box. From the outside, it had all the charm of a public toilet. Inside wasn't much different. There were no horse-brasses behind the bar. No fake beams or timber-clad nooks and crannies for conspiratorial pints or illicit liaisons. It was merely a charmless, rectangular, functional place. The only thing separating it from the town's public convenience was that here, the patrons were more concerned with liquids entering rather than exiting.

Through the fug of smoke he saw Johnny waving an empty glass from a corner table. For a Friday afternoon, it wasn't busy, but the dozen or so regulars smoked enough to ensure the air remained choked with a toxic mix of cheap cigar and Woodbine fumes. The only nod to jollity came from a transistor radio behind the bar, its small speaker shaking with the latest tune from The Beatles, or one of their impersonators.

Lachlan made his way across the sticky carpet to the bar.

'Aye?' asked Mandy, the barmaid.

Lachlan had been frequenting the Highlander with Johnny

since they'd moved to Alloa some three years previously, but his discourse with Mandy had never progressed beyond this simple transaction. She'd say 'Aye?' He'd say 'Two pints of Special please.' She'd pour two pints, usually in the cleanest glasses she could find but this depended on her mood, then she'd drop them on the drip tray which was almost always overflowing. Lachlan would say 'Thanks', hand over his money, wait for his change - always delivered without eye-contact - then return to his table.

Today was no different.

'The ice maiden's in a good mood I see,' said Lachlan.

'Isn't she always?' said Johnny. 'I'd still love to have a go at thawing her out though.'

'Aye well,' said Lachlan. 'Wouldn't we all?

It was true, Mandy had film-star looks. Maybe not Hollywood, but certainly worthy of a supporting role in an Ealing comedy. Quite unusual for a barmaid in one of Alloa's less salubrious drinking-holes. With her peroxide blonde hair, heavy mascara and the slash of red lipstick that usually adorned her pouting lips, she could have been making her fortune in swinging London. Instead, she was pulling pints in this place. A place that, to be fair, Lachlan and Johnny probably wouldn't be drinking in if she wasn't behind the bar. Her siren magnetism drawing them here, to be cast adrift on the rocks of inebriation.

'So, you all ready?' asked Johnny.

'The interview? Aye, sure. Wee sharpener here then I'll head over.'

'Just remember, don't mention football. If he brings it up, say you're an Alloa Athletic supporter.'

'Anything but Celtic?'

'Especially not Celtic,' laughed Johnny.

Luckily Lachlan had only a passing interest in football, so getting past this stage of the interview shouldn't cause him too many problems. He was aware of a shock result at the weekend though, Celtic had beaten Rangers 3-1. Their first league win against their city rivals in four seasons. It was hard to avoid news like that when you drank in the Highlander.

'Any other pointers?'

'Aye, don't come across as being too brainy, he doesn't like smart arses. You'll just be bottling lager, he's not after a historian.'

Lachlan took a swig of his Tartan Special. It was a rich brown, like he'd always thought beer should be, but lager was taking off. The world was changing in more ways than one. Men were growing their hair. Women were cutting theirs short. The old boys at the bar would always insist on a short back and sides and a brown ale, but there was no denying the power of the fizzy yellow stuff.

'Right, act dumb. What about experience?'

'You don't have any, doesn't matter.'

'I work in a petrol station.'

'Aye, pumping petrol. Good point. He'll like that. You're used to working with volatile liquids. Don't say it like that though, he'll think you're a prick.'

Lachlan sat back and drained his pint. The song had finished on the radio and the presenter's voice faded in and out briefly before being drowned in a screech of static.

'Christ almighty!' bawled one of the old guys at the bar.

'Sorry!' said Mandy. She dropped the damp rag she'd been cleaning glasses with and retuned the radio. Seconds later another song faded in. To Lachlan it sounded much like the last one but Mandy started nodding her head from side to side in time with the music. She glanced briefly at Lachlan and Johnny. Or did she glance at Lachlan? He wasn't sure.

She was a mystery to him, that much he was sure of. The only thing he knew about her was that earlier that year, she'd gone to Edinburgh for The Beatles concert at the ABC. And, legend had it, she'd gone backstage after the show. That's where the story ended but The Highlander's regulars liked to fill in the blanks with their lurid imaginations, some even resorted to mime which Lachlan just found distasteful.

'Another one? You've got time.' Johnny was already standing and lifting Lachlan's empty glass.

Lachlan glanced at his watch. 'Aye go on.'

Johnny breezed up and placed his order. He even got a half-smile from Mandy as she poured two more pints. Cocky bastard.

Johnny had remained a good friend throughout his school years. They still took the bus into Stirling occasionally to meet up with Gerry and some others, but Johnny and Lachlan had decided it was time to move on. Johnny had landed the job at the brewery and was tiring of the bus journey to and from work every day. On a drunken Saturday night in 1960 he declared his intention to leave home and make his way in the world. ('New York? London? Berlin?' they'd asked. 'Alloa!' he'd replied). Lachlan boldly claimed that he would follow as soon as he could find work. He'd started an apprenticeship at the coach-works, but living and working with his father was beginning to put even more strain on their relationship than his father's alcoholism.

And move to Alloa he did. Although a petrol pump attendant wasn't exactly a career choice that pleased his father, it paid just enough to cover the cost of his bedsit. And it was just a stop-gap. A stop-gap that had lasted three years, but now was the time to move on. A job at the brewery would pay more. He'd be able to sharpen up his image, maybe even buy a pair of those boots the Beatles wore, then he'd make his move on Mandy.

He just had to work out what to say first.

'There you go,' said Johnny as he placed another pint on the table. 'And hold on,' he jogged back to the bar and returned with two whiskies.

'Jesus Johnny I'm going for a job interview,' Lachlan laughed.

'In a brewery,' Johnny said. 'They're not going to smell it off you are they?'

****

Lachlan sat on a hard wooden chair outside William Sinclair's office. Mr Sinclair's secretary sat opposite, tapping away on her typewriter.

'You're fast,' said Lachlan, by way of conversation.

She looked at him over her glasses. Her hair was up in a tight bun that made her look older than she was. She smiled briefly and wound another sheet of paper into the machine.

The clock ticked loudly on the wall as they sat in silence. Sinclair's gruff voice rumbled from behind his office door and it sounded like the previous interview was nearing its end. The secretary started rattling the typewriter keys again.

'Has he had a lot?' asked Lachlan, pointing at the door.

The secretary stopped, sighed and said, 'A lot of what, sorry?'

'Folk? In? I mean… for interviews. Has there been a lot?'

She pulled her glasses down her nose and peered at Lachlan. 'Have you been drinking?'

'Me?' Lachlan bristled on the chair, shook his head wildly. 'No way. Ha! As if I'd-'

The door to the office swung open and a short red-haired man in a brown suit stepped out. He hurried past the secretary's desk, retrieved his coat from a hook, then was gone.

'Well, you're next,' she said to Lachlan.

'Cindy!' Mr Sinclair's voice boomed from within. 'Check the school he said he went to. I'm not convinced. Looked like a left-footer to me.'

'Yes Mr Sinclair,' she said. 'I've got Mr McCormack here for you now.'

'Aye, send him in.'

William Sinclair stood and eyed Lachlan up and down. Lachlan's only impression was of a hulking silhouette, framed by the bright window behind. He reached out a hand. 'Lachlan McCormack sir. Pleased to meet you.'

Sinclair leaned forward and took Lachlan's hand in a brief, firm grip. He eyed Lachlan momentarily, then released his hand just as quickly.

'Sit down,' he said.

Lachlan dropped a bit too sharply to the small chair positioned in front of Sinclair's imposing mahogany desk.

'Right, Lachlan McCormack. What school did you go to?'

'Stirling High,' Lachlan said, then cleared his throat.

Sinclair studied his notes. 'Got your leaving certificate I see. Why aren't you at university?'

Good question, Lachlan thought, as he remembered his coach-work days making excuses for his father's sudden absences after another liquid lunch. 'I started an apprenticeship instead, at my dad's work. The coach-works, in Stirling. Wasn't for me.'

Sinclair stood and grunted, stretching backwards with a bear-like hand on his shoulder. 'So you're a quitter?' He turned to look out the window.

Lachlan tried to gauge if Sinclair was joking, but the low winter sun was almost directly behind his head now. He was just a dark shape and a voice.

'No sir. I've worked three years at the petrol station.'

Sinclair turned, let out a low growl, and moved on.

'Primary?'

'Aberfoyle,' Lachlan offered.

'Aberfoyle to Stirling to Alloa. What brings you here?'

'Work. I feel it's important to develop -'

'Work?...' Sinclair interrupted, saying this slowly while studying Lachlan. 'Ever worked in a bottling plant?'

'I've spent three years filling cars. I think my skills are transferrable.'

Sinclair allowed himself a brief chuckle at this. Lachlan squinted into the light but still couldn't make out his face. The shadow eventually spoke. 'Good, good. Do you like football? Some result at the weekend eh?'

Lachlan remembered Johnny's words.

'Aye sir.' Then - and he was never sure if this was the alcohol talking - for good measure he added, 'Fenian bastards.'

Sinclair sat back in his chair and exhaled. Lachlan couldn't be sure, but he appeared to be smiling. After a moment, he leaned forward and extended a hand.

'Can you start Monday?'

Lachlan slumped, resting his cheek on the bus window, hoping the damp glass would cool him down and ease his hangover. Instead, the bus rattled over a pothole causing him to bang his already pounding skull. He rubbed a circle into the condensation and peered out. The River Forth was visible off to the left, making its slow winding journey through the fields.

A small girl of about three or four sat with her mother a few rows in front. She turned to face him, perhaps wondering why this man with the grey-pallor kept making groaning sounds. He stuck his tongue out and she quickly turned away.

Another bump in the road made Lachlan's stomach lurch. Those last double whiskies were definitely a mistake, but he had been celebrating after all. Johnny had insisted on a Saturday night at The Highlander. A couple of his colleagues from the petrol station had joined them, to wish him farewell and good luck by topping up his tank. If only they'd stopped before he'd reached the "Full" mark.

Mandy had been working, and the night had flown by in a blur of alcohol and good humour. He'd even managed a brief interaction with her, beyond the usual transaction of money for beer. He'd asked about a particular song on the radio. She was certainly enjoying it, shimmying behind the bar as she poured his pints. *'You really got me'*, she'd answered. He thought she'd meant she didn't know, but spotting his blank expression she added, '… by The Kinks. *You really got me* is the song.' And she'd laughed. The ice had cracked. He'd told her he was celebrating his new job at the brewery. She responded with a smile. His heart briefly fluttered in time with the song's guitar riff.

Tiny increments.

They were entering Stirling now, passing more new council houses. Smoke billowing from clustered chimneys and carried east towards Alloa. Everything seemed to head in that direction. The river. The smoke. Him. Travelling against this natural flow always felt like going back in time, and in a way that's what he was doing. Going back to visit his father on a Sunday afternoon. The promise of a decent meal, the papers, and a few hours dozing in front of a fire was a powerful magnet for him, and hundreds of other twenty-somethings with crippling hangovers across the country.

As the bus crossed the bridge over the river he rose and rang the bell. The little girl glanced up and stuck out her tongue.

'Morag! Don't be cheeky!' said her mother.

He smiled as he stepped from the bus. There was a name he hadn't heard in a while. Morag never did reply to his last letter. As he walked the familiar streets to his father's house he hoped her life had turned out okay after her parents' separation. Would she still be in Aberfoyle? He doubted it.

He felt a pang of homesickness as he pressed the doorbell, but couldn't hear a ring from inside so rattled the letterbox a few times.

After a moment, the door swung open and there was his father. The cigarette in his mouth sent a cloud of smoke over his face but his eyes still shone in welcome.

'Hiya son, in you come.'

'Hiya Dad.' Lachlan said with a smile, and followed his father into the warmth of the hallway where he hung his coat alongside his father's threadbare donkey jacket. 'Your doorbell's broken'.

'Aye I know. Nobody ever comes here anyway. Go through, I've got the fire going. Do you want a drink?'

'Jesus Dad, it's barely twelve o'clock. Have you started already?'

'Ach it's Sunday son. Come on, I haven't seen you for weeks.'

'Just a wee one then.'

Lachlan flopped to the settee. His father poured two half-full tumblers of whisky and took his chair by the fire.

'I said a wee one!'

'What's the matter? Got a hangover?'

Lachlan grimaced as he accepted the drink and recounted his news, and about the celebrations that followed.

'That's great son. Stick in at the brewery. You were wasting your time at that petrol station.'

'Aye, it's amazing how quickly the time goes when you're going nowhere.'

'Well you're going somewhere now.' His father leaned forwards and clinked glasses with Lachlan before draining half his glass.

'So how have you been? How's work?' asked Lachlan, taking a sip of his whisky.

'Same as ever. Still busy. Lots more buses on the road so more things to fix.'

'Seen much of Moira?'

His father fidgeted in his chair at the mention of her name. 'No,' he reached for his newspaper, folded it and shoved it back down the side of his chair. 'She's… with somebody now. Works in a bank in town.' He drained his glass and reached for the bottle.

'Ah well,' said Lachlan. 'Plenty more fish in the sea eh?' He felt uncomfortable discussing this with his father. It was meant to be the other way round wasn't it?

'I'm not bothered,' his father said while topping up his glass. 'I'm better off alone.' He offered the bottle to Lachlan.

'I'm fine Dad, I've barely touched this one.'

He watched as his father settled back into his chair. Not yet fifty but already looking sixty. Puffy cheeked with an explosion of broken veins around his nose. He still had the mop of black hair, slicked back with Brylcreem, but it was greying at the edges now. The war-hero of Lachlan's youth was gone and in his place, what? Just another middle-aged Scottish alcoholic? Was this pre-ordained? Lachlan thought about the previous night's excesses and came to the conclusion that, in a way, it was. What else was a man to do in this country of cold winters, disappointing summers and constant sporting, political, and emotional disappointment?

'Stick the telly on if you want,' said his father, indicating the living room's newest feature.

Lachlan rolled from the sofa and pushed the large button on the front. The unit clunked as it slowly came to life, the picture darting this way and that before settling to show a packed church in full song.

'There's no sound,' Lachlan said.

'Aye I turn it down most of the time. I just like the…' his father gestured at the screen.

'The company?' asked Lachlan.

His father took another drink. 'Try the other channels. Can't stand these Holy Wullies.'

Lachlan pressed the button marked 2. The screen filled with a blizzard of dots.

'Aye I don't get that, try 3.'

Another clunk and the picture warped to reveal a message saying: *Close down. Broadcast returns at 2.45pm.*

'Well that's that,' said Lachlan and switched the television off. The screen sizzled as it faded to a dot.

'Great eh?' said his father. 'Welcome to the space age. I'll go and put the steak pie on.' He threw the newspaper at Lachlan. 'You can educate yourself while I'm away.'

Lachlan lay on the sofa leafing through the newspaper. Most of the first half was taken up by the forthcoming general election. Could Harold Wilson's Labour win back power from the Tories? It was hardly surprising his father drank so much when his beloved Labour party had been out in the cold for the last thirteen years. Lachlan had received his polling card in Alloa. It was to be his first vote in a general election. He expected he'd vote Labour. It was the done thing.

He dropped the newspaper to the floor and stared at the fire. The coals burned brightly, filling the room with a dry heat. On top of the tiled mantelpiece sat a framed photo of the family, standing outside the house in Aberfoyle. His mother smiling into the sun. His father sneaking a fly cigarette. A seven-year old Lachlan peering at the camera with a hand over his eyes. Beside the photograph a brass carriage-clock ticked away the seconds. At least his father kept this wound, a sign that he wasn't completely lost to the bottle.

The fire snapped and a puff of smoke escaped into the room, floating upwards. He watched it gather by the ceiling light and drifted off to sleep.

****

Lachlan unlocked his front door, listening for signs of life.

Tony, a divorced bank clerk in his late thirties, was home. The separation obviously hadn't ended well as Tony had the demeanour of a man lost. The sound of a mournful jazz trumpet drifted from his room.

There was no sound from Mikey's room. Lachlan didn't know much about Mikey, other than he worked at the brewery. He hadn't seen him all weekend, so hadn't had the chance to let him know he'd be joining him tomorrow. Mikey was a dark-set wiry guy with a patchy beard. A few years older than Lachlan, and always seemed to be in a hurry. He was seldom home, which suited Lachlan and Tony just fine. It meant there was less competition for the toilet and the phone in the hall.

He opened the door to his bedsit and reached inside for the light switch. With a click, his room was bathed in the bulb's anaemic glow. His bed, unmade, sat underneath the solitary window. Along one wall were a couple of small yellowing kitchen cabinets with sliding glass doors. Underneath this, a tiny worktop with a cracked sink and a counter-top cooker with a single electric ring. Beneath this, a small refrigerator hummed. Against the opposite wall, a wooden chair, which doubled as a bedside table and a place to hang his towel. Beside this, his wardrobe - stuffed with more than clothes. The shelf above the rail also served as his bookshelf and was lined with paperbacks. Westerns, mostly, but he had a growing collection of *Galaxy Science Fiction* magazines. Living in this place, he needed the escape they offered.

Home sweet home, he thought as he hung his overcoat on a nail hammered into the back of the door. He kicked the door closed, filled the kettle, and stuck it on the cooker.

As he rinsed a mug for tea he heard the main door open and the voice of Mikey, chatting loudly. The conversation continued as Mikey's door opened and closed with a slam. The other participant didn't seem to be getting a word in but whatever they were talking about, Mikey seemed enthused by it.

The kettle whistled and Lachlan poured his tea. Picking up one of his science fiction magazines, he sat on the bed. The cover showed a bright red fire engine, its ladder extending into a pale blue sky where a silver craft floated. People were climbing the ladder to enter the craft, escaping from some earthbound terror. In the foreground a semi-clad blonde woman ran away from the scene. She looked a bit like Mandy.

From the hallway, Mikey's door opened again. He was still talking.

A small sheet of paper slipped under Lachlan's door, then a moment later the main door slammed shut and their voices faded down the stair.

He retrieved the note. It featured a poorly reproduced photo of a smiling man and the words: *On 15th October 1964, Vote Drysdale, Scottish National Party.*

So Mikey was a Nationalist? They were still regarded as a political sideshow around here, but maybe Mikey's almost permanent absence meant he was out campaigning most nights? Perhaps they were on the up? Who knows? Who cares? He scrunched up the leaflet and tossed it into the sink. Tomorrow Lachlan started his new job so he decided to get cleaned up. He drained the last of his tea, grabbed the towel from his chair and stepped into the hallway. Tony was changing 78s. He heard the crackle as the needle hit the surface of the record, then another syncopated beat kicked in, joined a second later by a meandering trumpet.

A cold draught blew through the open bathroom window. He pulled it closed and yanked the string on the small wall-mounted electric heater. It crackled into life, the smell of dust filling the room as the single bar sizzled with a dull orange glow.

With a shudder he turned the hot tap on the bath and closed the door. The slip-bolt was hanging by a single screw but the unspoken rule of the house was that if the door was closed, the bathroom was occupied.

When the bath was half-full, he slipped out of his clothes and lowered himself in, ignoring the clumps of hair and mould around the bath's edges. Once he'd settled, he lay and listened to Tony's music. It seemed very old-fashioned these days, to be listening to jazz trumpet as the world went crazy for the new sounds coming from Liverpool and London. It was a decent tune though. He tapped his fingers on the sides of the bath in time with the drums.

Without warning the volume suddenly increased as Tony's door flew open. A fraction of a second later the bathroom door swung against the bath with a thump as Tony charged in.

'Fuck's sake Tony! I'm having a bath!'

'Sorry Lachlan, can't hold it.' He wrestled with his belt and with horror Lachlan realised he intended to sit down.

'Christ man! Can it wait?'

But Tony was already in full swing. His normally dour face showed an expression of pure relief. The scattergun jazz drumbeats, now filling the whole flat, were joined by off-key and offbeat rattles from Tony's backside.

'Sorry Lachlan. Dodgy pie I think.'

Lachlan dipped his head, avoiding eye contact as Tony cleaned himself up. He grabbed a lump of Pears soap from the side of the bath, picked a pubic hair from it, considered washing his armpits but decided against it, raised his knees, and slid forward until his head and face were submerged.

****

They trudged into the cold night under the already darkening sky. Lachlan's first day had ended at last. Eight hours that felt like eighteen. In the morning he'd been trained on the various bottle-related tasks he was required to do: Cleaning them in a machine; Loading them into another machine; Taking full ones off yet another machine. Some respite came when he helped load the lorries in the yard. At least that got him out of the deafening noise of the bottling plant. Beer everywhere, and not a drop to drink. So they were heading for The Highlander.

'So how was it? Better than pumping petrol?' asked Johnny.

Lachlan raised his eyebrows, 'Marginally. Some racket in there though eh?'

'Aye you get used to it.'

'And the heat. I'm still sweating under here.'

'You get used to that too.'

'So how was your day? Must be easier when you're a foreman eh?'

Johnny lit a cigarette and blew a smoke ring into the cold air. 'Aye. Different types of grief though. Personal problems. All that shite. I mean look,' he indicated the crowds they were walking with. 'All these guys are heading out to get drunk now. Most of them can handle it, but one or two will go too far, take a sickie tomorrow, then I'm in the lurch. Or they'll show up with broken hands after a scrap, and need to get time off for the hospital.' He took another long drag of his cigarette. 'I sometimes wish I was still on the line. Much easier.'

'Much less money though.'

'Aye, there's that. How was your old man?'

'Fine. He does a mean steak pie. Still pouring whisky down his neck like there's no tomorrow though.'

Johnny flicked his cigarette into the gutter. 'Ach a man's got to have some pleasure in life.'

Ahead, The Highlander's door opened and the sound of raucous laughter spilled out as a small man in a black suit staggered off down the street, before raising a finger to the air and turning to head in the other direction. It was easy to lose yourself after a few hours in The Highlander.

Inside, it was already heaving with workers from the brewery and the bar was three deep as they jostled for position.

'Usual?' asked Johnny.

'Get me a lager,' said Lachlan. 'I've been watching the stuff clatter past all day. Probably time I started drinking it.'

Johnny muscled into the crowd and Lachlan stretched to his full height to get a better look behind the bar. He could see the greying flat-top of Grant the owner, leaning forward to take an order, but there was no sign of Mandy.

He stepped away from the crowd and looked for a seat. Most of the tables were taken but there were a couple of stools free near the door. Two men sat at the table, deep in conversation, with their backs to him. He pulled a stool out and sat down at the edge of the table.

'Lachlan, how's it going?'

'Mikey!' said Lachlan, realising he'd sat beside his flatmate. 'Sorry didn't recognise you. Aye good. Started at the brewery today, didn't see you though.'

'Big place,' Mikey smiled.

'Don't usually see you in here?'

'No,' Mikey nodded. 'We're leafleting in the area. This is Gus by the way.' He gestured at his colleague; a rangy fellow in a duffle coat that didn't quite fit.

'Hello,' said Lachlan, then, 'Aye, I got your leaflet last night. Thanks.'

Mikey studied him for a moment. 'And what do you think? Who are you voting for?'

Lachlan gritted his teeth. 'Hate to say it, but Labour.'

Mikey didn't look surprised, but asked, 'Uhuh, 'cos your dad voted Labour?'

Lachlan shrugged. 'Guess so.'

Gus took a mouthful of his pint, then said, 'You should consider the SNP. Labour have taken this place for granted for too long.'

Lachlan was spared having to think of a reply as Johnny returned with two pints and placed them on the table, spilling some foam as he did so.

'Ah shit, sorry. This stuff fizzes up like an ice cream float.'

'Cheers,' said Lachlan, then made the introductions.

'We're just heading anyway,' said Mikey, draining his pint. 'I'll maybe see you back at the flat Lachlan. Hey, what's up with Tony by the way?'

Lachlan lowered his drink. 'Christ, he's rotten isn't he?'

Mikey shook his head as he buttoned his coat. 'I thought one of you had died when I got in last night. Hope he's better. Not sure I can take another day of that. See you later.'

'Aye see you.' Lachlan waited a moment then nodded in their direction as they left. 'SNP.'

'Really?' said Johnny. 'A rare beast round here.' He lit another cigarette and looked at Lachlan. 'What? Are you considering it?'

Lachlan shrugged and took a mouthful of lager. He belched almost as soon as it hit his stomach. 'Oof, that's lively stuff eh?'

'Doesn't taste of anything either,' said Johnny. He lifted the glass to the light and watched the lines of tiny bubbles fizzing to the surface.

Lachlan took another mouthful, swirled it around his mouth then gulped it down with a grimace. He studied the glass, and noticed Johnny was doing the same.

'Pint of Special?' he asked.

Johnny nodded. 'Aye, I think so.'

Lachlan stood and scanned the bar, assessing the best spot to get served. 'Is Mandy not on?'

'Doesn't seem to be. Sorry, lover-boy,' Johnny said with a grin.

Lachlan edged up to the bar. 'Two pints of Special please.'

Grant grabbed two glasses and started pouring. 'Gave up on the lager?' He glanced towards their table where their mostly-full pints still sat.

'Aye, guess we're traditionalists,' said Lachlan. He shivered as a cold blast of air hit his back and Grant glanced towards the door.

'Hiya Grant,' said a familiar voice from behind.

Grant nodded a hello and Lachlan turned to see Mandy standing behind him. She unbuttoned her green coat with one hand while she removed a matching knitted bobble hat. Her blonde hair tumbled down and she shook it wildly, before brushing it from her face.

'Oh, hiya,' she said. 'How was your first day?'

She remembered! He realised she was staring at him, waiting for an answer.

'Good! It was good!'

'Good,' said Mandy. 'I'm glad.'

'Good!' said Lachlan, unnecessarily.

'There you go pal,' said Grant, placing the pints on the bar.

Lachlan fumbled for his cash, handed it over then turned back to Mandy. 'Are you working tonight?'

'No. Night off. Meeting some pals.'

'Great,' said Lachlan. Grant tapped him on the shoulder and handed him his change. 'Right, well. Pints. That's my pal.' He pointed at Johnny, who was watching the interaction with barely disguised glee.

'Aye I know,' said Mandy. 'Well, enjoy!' She flashed him a quick smile and stepped forward to take his place at the bar.

Lachlan felt like he was walking on clouds as he returned their table. Sticky, grubby clouds, but the best clouds the floor of The Highlander could offer.

'Fantastic display Lachlan. I hereby give up any claim to Mandy's nether-garments.' He patted Lachlan on the back. 'You, my boy, are in there.'

'Do you think so?' said Lachlan, staring at Mandy's back while sipping his pint. A foam moustache remained on his lip.

Johnny clinked his glass against Lachlan's. 'Think so? I know so. She could have gone anywhere there, she stood right behind you. What does that say?'

'That I was getting served and she's an experienced barmaid and knew Grant would return my change giving her a decent chance of being served next?'

Johnny scooped a mouthful of Special. 'No, it says she's got you' - he tapped Lachlan on the head - 'in her sights.'

Lachlan looked back at the bar. The Beatles were singing about holding hands on the radio. Mandy glanced over, flattened down some stray hair, and smiled.

After four hours of beer, whisky and awkward glances, the cry went up from Grant: 'Time gentlemen please! Do your talking while you're walking!' The radio was turned off, and all that remained was the clamour of drunk men and the laughter of Mandy and her friends, who'd spent the evening fighting off waves of advances from the regulars and were now draining their drinks and wrestling into their coats and scarves.

'Right, are we off?' said Lachlan. 'I've not even had my tea.'

'Aye, let me finish this,' slurred Johnny, draining his pint and knocking back his last whisky chaser.

Lachlan watched as Mandy pulled her hat on. She glanced over at him as she tucked her hair behind her ears.

He slugged the last of his whisky and felt a sudden rush. An odd feeling. Something approaching bravado. He felt energised as Mandy approached and nodded a farewell in their direction.

Play it cool, Lachlan, play it cool.

'Mandy!' Lachlan called just as she was about to leave.

She turned to him. One hand on the door. A cold blast entered the pub. 'Uhuh?'

'Would you... do you... is it okay if... could I... maybe...' he gulped in a lungful of Alloa's night air as it spilled into the warm interior. 'Do you want to go out sometime?'

She shrugged, and said, 'Aye okay. I'm working on Friday. Come in and see me.'

Dizzy and dumbstruck. He could think of nothing to say so just raised a hand and saluted in a weird confirmation of their agreement. Mandy offered an awkward smile in response and the door swung shut behind her.

A cheer went up from the remaining regulars. Lachlan turned to them and shrugged.

'Jesus Christ! Well done Bilko!' laughed Johnny. 'But what was the salute for?'

'I've no idea,' said Lachlan, his head still spinning. 'I panicked.'

****

The afternoon gloom was descending as he reached the end of the High Street. They'd arranged to meet on neutral ground, The Cardoon rather than The Highlander. It was also closer to the cinema, where they'd agreed to see The Beatles' *A Hard Day's Night*. Lachlan would have preferred *Dr Strangelove* but didn't think nuclear war was first-date material.

The town was still busy with shoppers, and passers-by seemed to regard him with suspicion. Maybe the fact that his trousers needed constant adjustment drew their attention, as he surreptitiously fumbled at his back-side and groin. He'd borrowed one of Tony's suits. Sartorially, it was a bit more beatnik than he was used to.

The general election loomed, and the lampposts were festooned with posters. The red and blue of Labour and the Conservatives fought for the prime head-height spot, but it looked like Mikey and his colleague had been out attaching their yellow SNP posters above both. Futile? He thought so. This was Labour country - always had been. The central belt and Fife held the bulk of the Scottish population. And the bulk of that population worked down the mines, or in factories, or mills. Labour was their party and it always would be. The lairds and the toffs of the Highlands and the Borders might send Conservative MPs to Westminster but the days when the Unionist Party or the National Liberal & Conservatives had some clout in Scotland's heartlands were long gone.

Still, like the big bands giving way to jazz, and jazz being edged out by rock and roll, and now rock and roll being sidelined by the new sounds coming from England, things changed. And to Lachlan, the SNP posters had an undeniably dangerous edge to them. For the first time it seemed like Scotland maybe had a music of its own.

His father wouldn't approve if Lachlan did take the plunge and mark his X against anything other than Labour, but he'd never know, would he?

The Cardoon was quiet when he arrived. Alloa Athletic were playing at home, so it'd be busy in a couple of hours, but for now, there were just a few afternoon drinkers at the bar. He bought a pint and took a seat by the window.

Twenty minutes later, he bought another pint and was just pocketing his change when Mandy hurried through the door.

'Sorry,' she said. 'Have you just got here?'

'Aye,' lied Lachlan. 'What can I get you?'

'Vodka and soda please.' Mandy looked Lachlan up and down and raised her eyebrows. 'You look different.'

'Aye, well, Saturday night eh?'

She slipped out of her green jacket. Underneath she was wearing a mini-dress with a rose-petal print and her usual black knee-length boots. Her hair was held in place with a wide, black ribbon that mirrored her long dark lashes, thick with mascara. She'd opted for pink lipstick, to match the rose-petals on her dress. She's gone to some effort, thought Lachlan, which pleased him, but also managed to make him more self-conscious.

'Is this your pint?' she said as they sat down, pointing to the empty glass on the table. 'I thought you just got here?'

'I did,' Lachlan said. 'At four o'clock.'

'Och, who shows up on time? Don't be so old fashioned.' She smiled briefly and took a cigarette from her handbag. 'Want one?' She offered the box to Lachlan.

He shook his head and took a large mouthful of his pint.

'Bit of a goody two-shoes aren't you?'

He considered this. He supposed he was, but he also supposed this wasn't the way to impress Mandy.

'Oh go on then. I was trying to give up,' he lied and took a cigarette.

She held out her lighter and he leaned in, puffing amateurishly. A cloud of smoke engulfed his eyeball which instantly started to water as he fought back the urge to cough. He took another large gulp of his pint. This was going well.

'So,' said Mandy slowly. 'I'm looking forward to this film. Did you know I saw The Beatles in Edinburgh?'

'I'd heard that aye. It's the talk of The Highlander.'

Mandy grinned. 'It was amazing.' Her eyes widened. 'Honestly. I've never known anything like it. Lassies were fainting and everything.'

Sounds bloody awful, thought Lachlan. 'Sounds amazing,' he said. He thought of asking Mandy about her legendary back-stage visit but decided against it and tried to steer the conversation away from The Beatles.

'So, are you from Alloa?' he asked.

'Aye, born and bred. You're not though are you? Don't remember you from school.'

'No, Aberfoyle when I was wee. Then Stirling after my mum died. Then here.'

Mandy took a drag on her cigarette. 'Sorry to hear that. About your mum.'

'Ach well. Years ago now. Your parents still around?'

'Oh aye,' said Mandy.

Lachlan nodded and took a mouthful of beer. He watched as Mandy sipped her vodka and examined her nails. She was a looker, that much was undeniable, but why did he feel so out of place?

'Are you alright, you seem a bit quiet?' she eventually asked.

'Quiet? No. I'm fine. I'm just a bit, well, I'm not used to this kind of thing.'

'What kind of thing? Going out with a lassie?'

He took a sip of his pint. A fire engine rumbled past. No bell ringing, just the rattle of the ladder and the clatter of the buckets hanging from its flanks.

'Suppose so,' he said.

'You've had girlfriends before though?'

'Oh aye, of course,' Lachlan lied, again. He'd lost his virginity at least, at a Stirling house party when he was eighteen with an accommodating girl called Hazel. Turned out she was very accommodating indeed, and had offered accommodation to half the boys on the scheme at one point or another. But girlfriends? No, he'd never actually been in a relationship for some reason. He'd never met anyone he wanted to be in a relationship with either.

He started toying with a beermat, drumming it off the table's edge.

'Anyone special?' Mandy asked, eyebrows raised.

The beermat fell to the floor and Lachlan stretched to pick it up. He dropped it back onto the table where it flipped over revealing a beer-stained saltire. He stared at it and was transported to the banks of the Forth in Aberfoyle, where thirteen years ago he'd given Morag his saltire stone and almost passed out when she'd kissed him.

'Aye there was one girl,' said Lachlan.

'Oh aye?' said Mandy. 'Do tell. Must have been recent, you're blushing.' She lit another cigarette.

'Ach, couple of years ago now. I'm over it,' he lied. Again.

****

The rain drummed angrily against Lachlan's bedroom window. Gusts of wind rattled the flaking frame. He opened one eye and checked his watch. 11:30am. His head beat in time with the torrent. The thin curtains were hanging open and shifting slightly in the draught. He hadn't closed them when he stumbled home after The Highlander, choosing instead to fumble out of Tony's suit and collapse into bed.

Despite his debilitating hangover, he managed a small smile at last night's reveries. It hadn't been a disaster at least. The film had been rubbish, but as last orders were called in The Highlander he'd exchanged numbers with Mandy on two halves of a torn beermat.

They'd parted at 1am. Mandy heading home to her parents, who as far as Lachlan remembered seemed to live in a fairly nice part of town. Once outside she'd offered her lips to him, swaying back and forth, and he'd pecked her on the cheek and said goodnight.

The perfect gentlemen, he thought as he rummaged in the fridge for breakfast. *Tiny increments.*

He retrieved a wrap of bacon he'd bought last weekend. Seemed edible. He threw the bacon into a small blackened frying pan and turned on the ring.

As the bacon sizzled and he spread margarine on a not-quite-stale slice of bread he recalled events in The Highlander. Johnny had shown up drunk with some of his football associates. They'd been at the game and had been drinking since 5pm. Lachlan at least had ninety minutes of The Beatles to give his liver and brain some respite.

He turned the bacon and looked at Tony's suit, draped haphazardly over the chair beside his bed. No sound from Tony's room yet. He'd return the suit later. Remembering Mandy's number, he left the cooker to retrieve the torn beermat from the pocket.

He pulled out the piece of card just as the phone rang in the hall. He placed it on the chair and waited a few rings. Nobody was going to answer it. Tony was still sleeping and Mikey had been locked in the bathroom for at least an hour, so he opened his door and picked up the handset from the small table in the cold, dark hallway.

'Hello?'

'Hello son, it's Dad.'

'Hello Dad, what's up?'

'Nothing son, nothing. Just calling to see if you're coming out today?'

He was slurring his words. Already drunk and it wasn't even noon.

Lachlan twisted the spiral cord around the index finger of his free hand.

'Oh, no Dad sorry. Had a bit of a late one last night and I'm not feeling too great.'

A pause, then, 'Not to worry. I just wanted to know if I needed to peel more tatties. How's the new job?'

'Good aye,' Lachlan said, untwisting his finger from the cord.

'I'm glad you got yourself sorted out,' said his father. 'Stick in there, that's a good place to work.'

'Aye, I will,' said Lachlan, now winding the cord around his ring finger. He looked back into his room, the bacon still sizzling away. A thin plume of smoke rose from the pan.

'Are you remembering it's the election this week?'

'Aye Dad, don't worry.'

'Your first vote. Don't forget.'

'As long as it's Labour?'

His father chuckled then coughed. It sounded like he was holding the receiver away from his mouth as he gathered himself. Lachlan heard him take a gulp, then the dunt of a glass being dropped to the table.

'Aye son. As long as it's Labour,' he eventually said.

He thought of telling his father about Mandy, but decided it could wait. Early days and all that. He looked back at the frying pan where the smoke was thickening.

'Look Dad, I've got some bacon on and it's burning. I'll give you a call next week okay?'

'Okay. That'd be good. I'd like to see you next week if you can make it.'

'Sure Dad will do. And I promise I'll vote. Up the workers eh?'

His father chuckled again, 'Aye. Up the workers son. Bye now.'

'Bye Dad.' He replaced the handset with a clunk.

The bacon was ruined. Blackened and charred, it would have to do.

From Tony's room, the first jazz record of the day spun into life. A solemn number which seemed to suit the weather. The rain continued to drum against the window and showed no signs of abating. Mikey emerged from the bathroom with a groan and his door slammed shut.

Lachlan's mouth was dry and full of burnt bacon. He needed a drink. He reached for the glass of water beside his bed and instead, picked up the torn piece of beermat with Mandy's number.

He unfolded it and smiled at her looped, stylish handwriting.

His smile disappeared as he read the words, "Mandy Sinclair, 21727".

****

'Your dad's my boss?' Lachlan said, stirring a sugar lump into his tea.

They sat in the small cafe below Lachlan's flat. Silver teapots and sugar lumps in little china bowls. Mandy fiddled with the edges of a lace doily on the table. The rain continued to batter down outside, bouncing off the pavement and running down the gutters.

'So what?' she asked, staring at Lachlan.

She was bleary-eyed. She'd called him that afternoon and suggested meeting for a cup of tea, just two hours after he'd burnt his bacon. He'd worried about calling her in case her father answered. He hadn't even known then that Sinclair *was* her father, but he hadn't wanted to take the risk.

'Why didn't you say?' asked Lachlan.

'Why should I?' she said. 'What difference does it make?'

He shrugged and took a mouthful of tea. 'I don't know. I just think he might hold it against me?'

Mandy nodded and said, 'He might, aye. Are you scared of him?'

Lachlan laughed. 'I don't even know him. I couldn't even make out his face at the interview. He was just this... this... intimidating shape.'

'Aye that's my dad,' laughed Mandy as she lit a cigarette.

He swirled the last of his tea around. He looked around at the other patrons; a few old women in headscarfs and raincoats, gossiping over scones.

The door dinged and a burly gent strode in. A damp, dusty smell in his wake, as if his overcoat had been hanging in an old hallway for months before he'd ventured out into this downpour.

'Hello Mary. Okay if I put a poster in the window?' he asked the thin woman behind the counter.

'Course you can Stan,' she said, then giggled at her unintended rhyme.

Lachlan watched as he pulled a poster from the folds of his jacket and stuck it to the window. It read: 'Let's GO with Labour'.

As he left, the man called back - to no-one in particular - 'Remember to vote Labour on Thursday folks.' And with that he was gone, pulling his collar around him as he headed off into the rain.

Mandy watched him through the window and muttered, 'Aye that'll be right.'

Lachlan placed his cup carefully into its saucer, sat back in his chair, and stretched his legs out under the table.

'You're not a Labour voter then?'

'Are you kidding? My dad would kill me!'

'Let me guess. Big house. Senior management. Funny handshake. He's a Tory?'

'Through and through,' said Mandy, with a single, firm nod of her head.

'So you are too?'

Mandy shrugged, 'Don't we all vote the way our parents do?'

Lachlan considered his dilemma, then took another sip of tea and said, with a sigh, 'Aye, I suppose we do.'

Mandy leaned forward, put her elbows on the table and cupped her face in her hands. 'Are you going to hold it against me?'

Lachlan smiled and shook his head.

Under the table, she moved her leg against his. He caught his breath and their eyes met. She held his gaze. Intensifying, like a cat about to pounce.

'Are you going to hold it against me?' she asked again.

Lachlan gulped. 'No. It's up to you who you vote for.'

Her shoulders dropped a fraction of an inch. She moved her other leg towards Lachlan's, trapping his leg between her own, then leaned forward a bit more. Her breath now warming Lachlan's face, which was already increasing in temperature as his cheeks reddened.

'Are. You. Going. To. Hold. It. Against. Me?' she tried again, slowly, with a suggestive pout.

Lachlan squirmed and shrugged.

'For fuck's sake Lachlan. Do you want to shag me?'

He was out of his seat in an instant. 'Can we get the bill please?' The fine china and silverware rattled on the table. The old ladies turned from their conversations and tutted as he scattered some coins onto the counter and left, fumbling an arm into a jacket that was inside out.

****

Election day arrived and Lachlan had slept late, his alarm clock unwound, was stuck at 2am. From his bed, he pulled the curtain aside. It was another grey day. The clouds blurring the tops of the chimney pots on the adjacent flats.

His foot caught something under the sheets. He reached down and pulled out a pair of Mandy's tights. They'd spent most evenings this week locked together in his single bed. Tony had been forced into increasing the volume on his record player to mask the noise of their love-making. Mikey had been out every night on the campaign trail, so was still oblivious to Lachlan's new-found role as the flat's resident love machine.

Ten minutes later, he emerged, bleary-eyed and unwashed, into the street and made his way to the brewery.

'Empties,' his foreman, Davie said by way of a welcome. 'Two hundred crates in the bay. And try to stay awake eh?'

'Aye boss. No problem.'

There was a small trolley for transporting the empty bottles to the washing machines. He stretched, loaded three crates onto the trolley, and trundled them along a narrow alleyway to the washers.

After an hour, he'd entered the trance-like state he'd become used to with such monotonous work, and his thoughts drifted back to Mandy. Her curves; her hair; her eyelashes; her breasts; all brought a smile to his face. But her smell (vodka and cigarettes) and her personality (cold and… dull?) meant it soon changed to a frown. He stopped suddenly. The top crate on the trolley fell forward and crashed to the ground, its contents smashed into a thousand pieces.

'Shite,' he muttered and headed back to the loading bay for a broom.

It had been niggling him. The sex had been okay, but was there anything else? It had been less than a week mind you. He hadn't really given her a chance.

He was dropping glass shards into a bin when a voice called 'Lachlan!' from the loading bay behind him. It was Davie. He gestured at Lachlan to return quickly.

'It was only one crate Davie, I've swept it up.'

Davie shook his head, 'Doesn't matter. Sinclair's wanting you in his office.'

Lachlan's blood ran cold. 'Did he say what for?'

'No,' Davie said. He looked at the stack of crates still to be moved. 'But you'll better get your arse in gear. You've still got all these to shift.'

Lachlan made his way along a high-level link corridor towards the administrative offices. He could see the river through the grime-stained windows. It cut back on itself in wide confused loops, heading south, then swooping north again. Deep enough now for ships, a cargo steamer was anchored at the small harbour, plumes of smoke puffing from its chimney.

Sinclair had found out. He knew he would. What was he going to say? He'd probably be sacked. He hadn't even lasted a fortnight. Maybe the petrol station would take him back? It was no less dull, to be honest, and at least he got some fresh air on the forecourt. He started to sweat as he reached the end of the corridor, his neck itching under his blue boiler suit.

He pushed open the double doors and entered the offices. The atmosphere suddenly changing from that of industry and toil to a far more agreeable perfumed quiet. A phone rang and a man in a sharp suit picked it up, speaking in hushed tones.

He reached Sinclair's office and took a deep breath. His secretary was busy typing at her desk, Lachlan was about to say he'd been called for but she stood and smiled awkwardly. 'Go straight in Lachlan.'

He pushed open the door. 'Mr Sinclair sir, I'm -'

'Sit down Lachlan,' Sinclair said. He'd been looking out the window and turned to face Lachlan. In a more favourable light, he realised his boss didn't appear as intimidating as he'd first thought. He was ruddy-cheeked, and red-nosed. Still built like a tank, with a military haircut, but he seemed more agreeable today.

Lachlan took a chair and steeled himself.

'There's no easy way to say this, I'm afraid,' Sinclair said. He filled his chest and straightened his back. He held his breath momentarily, and looked Lachlan straight in the eye.

Here it comes, Lachlan thought.

'I'm afraid your father's dead son.'

****

Lachlan stood in the hall and dialled his Aunt Jean's number. Eventually, she answered. She sounded small and distant.

'Hello?'

'Hello Jean. It's Lachlan.' His voice seemed to echo around the empty flat.

'Oh hello,' she paused and sniffed. 'Did your work tell you why I called?'

'Aye,' Lachlan managed, trying hard to keep himself together. He looked up at the ceiling. Cobwebs hung around the light fitting, dancing in the heat from the bulb. He blinked rapidly and took a deep breath.

'I'm so sorry Lachlan. It must be such a shock to you.'

'What… what happened?'

Jean took a couple of sharp breaths then said, 'It was all very sudden. A heart attack.'

'At home?' Lachlan wondered who'd found him.

'No. And here's the funny part. Well, it's not funny, but you know what I mean. He was voting. During his tea break. Collapsed at the polling station just after he'd cast his vote. Local MP grabbed him on the stairs as he fell.'

It was little consolation, but Lachlan was somehow glad his father had died doing something he cared about.

'I'll take care of everything okay?' said Jean. 'I'll get in touch with his work and all his old friends. Your gran knows, she'll get the train down from Inverness. I just hope you'll be okay? You're still young Lachlan. Too young to have lost both your parents.'

He hadn't seen his gran for a couple of years. She was his only remaining grandparent. His mother's parents had passed away when Lachlan was still in nappies, and his father's dad was killed in the first war. Funerals and weddings, the only things that brought families back together.

'Thanks Auntie Jean.'

'The funeral's on Tuesday. He'll be buried beside your Mum in Aberfoyle. We're booked for 2pm.'

Booked? How strange it was that appointments had to be made for things like this. It was all just part of the system. Forms to be filled. Registrars to be notified. Another life rubber-stamped as "Completed".

'Okay, I'll see you on Tuesday,' he said. He realised he'd tangled his finger in the phone cord and started unwinding it as he said goodbye. He studied the white ridges in his flesh, turning pink as the blood flowed back and tried not to think of his father's body, lying in a coffin somewhere in Stirling. Stagnant blood gathering at his back.

Silence overwhelmed him. He poured himself a whisky, gulped it down in one stinging shot and sat on his bed. He poured another. Then another. The fumes, for a while at least, seemed to evaporate the tears before they had a chance to form.

As darkness fell, he walked to the polling station in a drunken haze. He looked at the ballot paper. Labour, Conservative, or Scottish National Party were the choices. He thought of Mikey and Gus, and the butcher in Stirling. The only SNP people he'd ever met. He thought of Scotland, but most of all he thought of his father. He placed the pencil in the box beside Labour and stopped. He was about to mark his cross but then had a thought: Labour would win here anyway. His father deserved to be noticed. Some sort of tribute. He left all three boxes blank, and wrote in the margin:

Sandy McCormack. February 12th 1915 - October 15th 1964.

As he walked home, he wondered if he'd done the right thing. He really didn't care who won the election, it seldom made any difference. But it pleased him that someone out there, even if it was just some volunteer at the count, would briefly notice his father's name as they added it to the pile of spoiled ballots.

'Vauxhall Viva Eric?' asked Lachlan.

'Aye. A wee cracker eh?' Eric beamed. Jean's husband was a small man with burgeoning nasal hair that made it look as if a moustache was trying to hide up his nose.

Lachlan stole another heart-stopping glance at the hearse in front. The coffin was like a piece of furniture out for delivery. His father was in there, yet he wasn't. His father was in his head, and in his memories. That's what he had to keep telling himself as they made the short trip to Aberfoyle.

'Nice day Lachlan isn't it?' asked Jean from the back seat, placing a hand on his shoulder.

Lachlan took his eyes off the coffin for a moment and looked around at the passing fields. A frost lay in some of the hollows, but the sun shone brightly and the birds still sang. As they entered Aberfoyle, he spotted a magpie hopping around on the verge. On a nearby fencepost another pecked at the wood then cocked its head towards them.

'Aye,' he said. 'It is.'

In the darkness of the church, among the furniture polish smells and the sniffles from the assembled mourners Lachlan forced his eyes wide and stared upwards, grief like a fire burning at his brain. He stood between Mandy and Jean in the front row.

He glanced back over his shoulder. The sunlight blazed through the open doors but he estimated about a hundred silhouetted heads. A decent turnout. He'd no idea his father had been so popular.

Jean smiled at him. 'He'd be happy with this,' she said.

'Who are all these people?' Lachlan managed, his voice breaking. The minister was heading for the pulpit and a hush slowly descended on the church.

'He had a lot of friends,' Jean whispered. 'Some of his army pals; men from the coach-works; the slate mine; he was well-liked.' She stopped as the minister cleared his throat and began.

Lachlan listened to Whistling Willie the minister, who must have been well into his eighties, recount his father's life. He knew Willie didn't know his father. Jean would have given him a scribbled page of notes. Dates, family names, and places he'd worked.

The ceremony ended with a chorus of "Abide with me" - Lachlan had no idea if his father even liked this hymn. It seemed like the boilerplate option for a Scottish funeral. He sang along as best he could, staring at the coffin throughout.

He remembered his mother's funeral, in the same church, with the same minister. The difference being that his father had been by his side. Now his father would be joining his mother in a small patch of earth, in a small corner of Scotland, forever.

This gave him some comfort. If his father had left a piece of himself behind in the war, he'd left even more behind when Lachlan's mother had died. Almost as if he was fading out of existence. Evaporating in a haze of whisky fumes. The angel's share. Tiny increments. He stared at the roof as his eyes began to water and the hymn came to an end.

Lachlan stared at his shoes as he followed the coffin out into the sunlight. Mandy by his side. Jean, Eric and his Gran following behind.

He watched as his father was loaded back into the hearse for the short journey to the graveyard. The crowd from the church gathered around. Lachlan didn't recognise anyone but Jean was saying hello to several men while Eric shuffled his feet beside her.

'Come here,' said his gran as she hugged him.

Lachlan's chin rested on the top of his gran's head and he breathed in her flowery scent. He hadn't seen her for years. She stepped back and dabbed her eyes with a tissue.

'And who's this bonnie lassie?' she said, taking both Mandy's hands.

'This is Mandy. Mandy, this is my gran.'

'Hello,' said Mandy.

'I can't see your eyes dear. Take those glasses off.'

Mandy removed her sunglasses.

'There, that's better. Lovely eyes. Too much makeup though.'

Mandy and Lachlan both laughed, 'Aye okay gran. How are you anyway?'

'I'm as well as I can be Lachlan. You're the man of the family now. I hope he's treating you right dear?' She turned to Mandy again.

Lachlan noticed that the funeral directors were ready to leave. His gran was now questioning Mandy on Lachlan's hair and whether it was suitable for a boy. Jean had spotted the hearse readying to depart too and was finishing her conversation with a man Lachlan thought he recognised but couldn't place. She glanced at Lachlan and her face lit up momentarily, looking just beyond his shoulder.

'Hello Lachlan.' A woman's voice from behind him. He turned and squinted into the sunlight. His heart leapt as his eyes found their focus.

He gasped. 'Morag?'

'Yup.' Morag tipped her head quickly to one side, a strand of hair falling over her face. She brushed it aside and smiled.

'Lachlan we need to go now,' Mandy called as she was bustled to the car by his gran. The crowd was quickly dispersing and the hearse's engine rumbled to life.

'Jesus. I can't believe it. Look at you. All grown up!' Morag wore a black cardigan over a dark blue dress. Her hair still had a messy charm, but was now cut into a shoulder-length bob. He was glad to see there was still a sprinkle of freckles over her nose.

'Lachlan,' Mandy called again, eyeing Morag as she did so.

'Aye, give me a minute. I'll see you in the car.'

'I'm so sorry about your dad,' said Morag, placing a hand on Lachlan's arm.

'Thanks,' he said. Her touch seemed to spread a warmth throughout his arm and beyond. A healing balm. 'How did you know?'

'My dad. That was him talking to your Auntie there.'

'The slate mine. Of course. Are you coming to the graveyard? Or later? There's a thing in Stirling for him. Sandwiches and platitudes. Be good to catch up.'

'I can't sorry. I need to get back to Edinburgh. I just wanted to show my respect. And to see you. To say hello.' She waved at her father who waited by the gates of the church, swinging his car keys in his hand.

The hearse slowly pulled away and Eric revved his engine briefly to remind Lachlan it was time to leave.

'I need to go,' said Lachlan. 'Why didn't you write to me?'

Morag smiled again, and looked at her shoes. 'I… I don't know. I just thought you needed to move on. Jesus, that was thirteen years ago Lachlan. You seemed to have settled in Stirling. I sent you a message in a bottle. Did you not get it?' she laughed.

'No. No I didn't.' Eric's car horn gave a quick blast. 'Only thing I found in the river was that dead body.'

'Aye that sounded horrible. What a cheery letter that was,' said Morag. 'Look, you'd better go. It was nice to see you again Lachlan.' She took his hand and clasped it between her own. 'You take care of yourself now.'

Mandy was staring out of the rear window, gesturing for him to hurry up.

He sighed. Morag released his hand and took a few steps backwards, towards her waiting father.

'So you're in Edinburgh now?' asked Lachlan. He didn't want her to go.

'Uhuh, after my folks separated. I went with my dad. Still there.'

'Lachlan!' Mandy shouted from the car window, 'We need to go!'

Morag glanced at Mandy. 'Sorry! Old friends,' she called, and turned back to Lachlan, 'Bye then!' She turned and hurried back to her father who had climbed into a faded green Rover with a missing hubcap.

He didn't want to admit it, but on the day he was burying his father, his world suddenly felt a lot brighter.

****

The bowling club was rammed with his father's workmates and acquaintances. Lachlan lifted a sausage roll from a table at the window and perused the room.

Jean and Mandy sat in the corner. He'd hoped they'd be locked in conversation but they both sat, staring straight ahead at the increasingly drunk crowd, fidgeting with their drinks.

'Well, at least your dad went out doing something he loved,' said Eric, swaying slightly as he approached.

'Voting Labour?' Lachlan smiled and nodded. 'I suppose so. It's a shame he couldn't stick around to see that they'd won eh?'

His father had spent the last thirteen years complaining about the Tories, but at last Labour had scraped home with a slim majority and Harold Wilson was the new Prime Minister.

'Made a difference though,' said Eric. 'His vote I mean.'

'Eh? They weigh the Labour vote around here Eric. They can't lose.'

'Aye, but without the Scottish seats this time the Tories would have won.'

'Really?' said Lachlan as Johnny returned from the bar with two pints.

'First time since the war,' said Eric. 'Usually doesn't matter what way we vote up here. We get who we're given. But this time, for once, Scotland helped Labour scrape over the line.'

'He'd have been pleased with that,' said Lachlan.

Johnny muttered, 'Politics, I'll leave you lads to it.' He handed Lachlan a pint and wandered off into the crowd.

Eric studied Lachlan for a moment, his eyes darting behind his thick lenses. 'Do you not think that's a bit, well, undemocratic? That we usually have so little influence?'

Lachlan took a mouthful of beer and shrugged. 'I suppose it is.'

Eric leaned closer and said to Lachlan, 'That's why I stopped voting for them.' He glanced around, as if this was dangerous news, or he'd been admitting he preferred the company of sheep to women.

Lachlan noticed Johnny had joined Jean and Mandy's table. He was at least getting the conversation going and they both seemed delighted at the distraction.

He looked back at Eric, 'Are you… what?'

Eric tapped his nose.

'SNP?' whispered Lachlan.

'Aye.' Eric grinned. 'And we're on the rise. Ten percent of the vote here. Twelve percent out your way.'

Lachlan thought of Mikey's efforts in Alloa. 'That's never going to get you elected though is it?'

Eric took a mouthful of whisky and said, 'Mighty oaks from little acorns grow.'

Tiny increments, thought Lachlan.

'Anyway, here's to your father. A good Labour man, Sandy McCormack.' Eric held up his whisky and Lachlan dinked it with his pint. 'And I think you'd better go and speak to that girlfriend of yours.'

Lachlan looked over at their table. Johnny had Mandy in hysterics. She never laughed like that with him. What was his secret? She flicked her hair away from her face and sipped vodka through a straw, still chuckling at his joke.

He patted Eric on the shoulder and looked for another sausage roll, but all that was left on the table was an empty bottle of Bells. He stared out at the perfect lawn, its colour draining as the light faded from the day. Beyond the bowling club wall, between the houses, he could just see a small stretch of river.

She'd sent him a message in a bottle. Her words probably drifted past here twelve or thirteen years ago on their way to the sea. He drained the last of his pint and wondered what they might have said.

****

Winter passed, like winters do in Scotland, by slowly retreating to somewhere beyond the hills, but staying close enough to laugh at the efforts of Summer.

For Lachlan, it was a winter to forget. It had begun with the loss of his father and hadn't improved much as darkness took its grip. Christmas had come and gone. They'd drank themselves stupid in The Highlander on Christmas Eve. It had been festive enough. Johnny was putting on the charm as usual, even Tony joined Mikey in a rare foray out of the flat, but Lachlan and Mandy were pulling apart like one of the cheap Christmas crackers Grant had scattered around the pub.

Now Spring was here, and there was still an hour or two of sunlight after he'd walked home from the brewery, but he didn't feel warmed by it - if anything his heart was still stuck in the depths of that cold, dark winter. He felt frozen, and Mandy was doing little to help with the thaw.

Today was the day. It had to be.

The hall was quiet as he dialled Mandy's number. After a few rings, the familiar voice of William Sinclair answered.

'Hello?'

'Hello, is Mandy there?'

'That you Lachlan? Hold on…' he said. Word had got to him about his staff member's liaison with his daughter. To Lachlan's surprise there had been no bollocking, just a wry smile and a convincing threat of death if Lachlan ever did anything to hurt her.

'Hello?' Mandy cleared her throat, as if she'd been sleeping.

'Fancy a walk?' said Lachlan, twisting the cord around his fingers.

'Sounds romantic,' she said.

'Be good to clear our heads. And the sun's out.'

'Aye okay. I'll see you in a bit.'

The line went dead and Lachlan dropped the handset towards the floor. He watched it swing round and round while the spiral cord untangled itself from his fingers. Rubbing the white flesh, he watched as the blood slowly returned.

****

They walked past the brewery and onto a single track road heading nowhere. The air was still and the sky was a washed-out blue. Sparrows chirped among the hedgerows. Eventually, after leaving the road and trudging through some undergrowth, they came to the river.

They stopped at the north end of a large teardrop-shaped grassy expanse. A cargo ship was docked at the harbour, with another at anchor. It was hard to imagine this was the same river Lachlan had paddled in as a child.

Mandy picked a dandelion from the bank. 'What time is it?' she said, absently.

'It's time we had a talk,' said Lachlan. The words felt like they'd come from somewhere else. But he'd said them now and there was no going back.

'We do.' Mandy pulled her legs up to her chin and looked at Lachlan, unblinking. This was a statement, not a question.

'We do?' he asked. He placed his fingers at either side of his nose and took a deep breath. 'You see that farmhouse out there?' He pointed to a grey building on The Inch, a small island in the middle of this great sweep of the river.

'The Inch Farm? What about it?' asked Mandy.

'See how the river splits and flows all around it?'

Mandy nodded. 'Are you getting weird on me Lachlan?'

He managed a brief smile then said, 'It's how I feel.' His head dropped and he picked at a piece of fluff on his jumper.

Mandy looked back towards the farm. A few russet cows stood in the field, trapped on every side by the water. 'Like a farmhouse?'

'Like a farmhouse on an island,' Lachlan said slowly. He pointed towards the river. 'Everything flows Mandy. Everything flows except us. We're stuck. I'm stuck. You're stuck. We're going nowhere.'

'Right,' said Mandy. She leaned back on her elbows and looked away. 'So what are you saying?'

Lachlan looked at the back of her head. Her blonde hair tied up in a high ponytail exposing a mole on her shoulder. She was beautiful, but why could he only see her flaws? He pictured Morag and knew why. He imagined her message in a bottle bobbing its way past here when they were children. Of course he'd missed it in Stirling. The only thing they'd hauled out the river there was the bloodied body of Joe McLeish.

'I suppose I'm saying that I think we've drifted apart.' He waited for a response. She remained still. After a moment she picked another clump of grass and tossed it into the river. She sat up again and turned to face him.

'Okay,' she said. Her brow furrowed. She looked down at the grass. 'Well, there's not much I can say to that is there?'

He reached for her arm but she recoiled at his touch. 'You can say whatever you like Mandy. It's not like we've got much in common is it?'

She rose to her feet and wiped grass off her jeans. She held Lachlan's gaze. 'No. No we don't. We've got fuck all in common. You're right. Good-bye. And good fucking riddance.' She threw a handful of damp grass in his face, turned, and walked back the way they'd come.

He watched her go. After she'd put some distance between them he saw her shoulders jerk and her head fall forwards. Her hands went to her face. At the harbour, the cargo ship's horn blasted as it prepared to leave the dock.

He lay back on the grass and watched the clouds drift east in the pale blue sky.

****

The door creaked behind him, breaking the hush of the library. The smell of old books mixed with a blend of hair oil and musky perfume hit him as his eyes adjusted to the dusty interior.

He headed for the table where they laid out today's newspapers, took a chair, and scanned some of the stories. A new offshore pirate radio station, Radio Scotland, was said to be launching that year. It hoped to emulate the success of Radio Caroline in the south. Anything to break the archaic monotony of the BBC could only be a good thing.

The United States had launched the first atomic-powered spaceship into orbit. The race into space was hotting up and after the world being on the brink of destruction a few years ago with events in Cuba, Lachlan was more at ease. It was time he ventured forth too. The countdown had begun. Ignition sequence started.

He flipped to the vacancies pages and began reading. Factory workers - he'd had enough of that. Bank Clerks - no thanks. Salesmen - he'd be hopeless.

He thought of his career to date. Filling cars with petrol and watching travellers come and go from a weed-strewn patch of forecourt. Everyone moving while he remained rooted to the pump. And then the brewery. Hundreds of bottles rattling past him every day. Being stacked; filled; loaded; shipped; returned; washed; stacked; filled; loaded; and so on, and so on, and so on. Six months of that and he'd had enough of the world passing him by.

There, in a large panel, was the advert that would set him on his way.

The Institute of Geological Sciences seeks administrative staff.

I'd hate to work in an office. This came back to him, from where? From that day with Morag when they'd discussed their futures at the river's source and swirled a stick in the water to set it free. He wasn't so sure now. He'd had his fill of manual work, literally.

He looked for the address on the advert. *Please apply in writing to IGS, Grange Terrace, Edinburgh.*

We have lift off.

THURSDAY

Lachlan closed his eyes and breathed deeply, taking in the smell of diesel as a bus departed the hospital car park. He blinked, a piece of grit had lodged in one eye. He picked it out with a fingernail that was badly needing cut. He wondered if it ever would be.

'Everything okay?' asked Ali, the home's driver and general dogsbody.

'Dirt in my eye,' said Lachlan as he climbed into the passenger seat. 'Can you get the air-con on? It's roasting in here.'

He opened the newspaper and turned to the back page. The familiar sight of a Scotland player on his haunches with his head in his hands after another disastrous international performance. The same old story.

As they accelerated onto the dual carriageway that would take them back to North Berwick a magpie skipped onto the grass verge, casting them a questioning glance. He didn't even try to look for its partner.

The doctor had said: *I'll let you know as soon as I can.*

Fucking cancer. Hello, come in. I've been expecting you.

They hit a pothole and Lachlan let out a groan.

'Sorry,' muttered Ali. 'These roads are a disgrace.'

Soon, the land dropped away and the Firth of Forth appeared, a deep blue blanket to their left. In its midst, a tanker sailed west, to be filled at the oil and gas plants upriver. Heading in the other direction was another, much lower in the water, already burdened with oil, heading out to sea, and who knows where.

EDINBURGH 1974

'Throw it all out.' Lachlan's boss, Mrs Hutchison, pointed to a pile of boxes in the corner. She pushed her glasses up her nose and returned to the paperwork on her desk.

'All of it?' asked Lachlan, rubbing his chin.

She shrugged. 'Name change. Bin it.'

He sighed. 'Sure thing chief,' and hefted the first box of stationery onto his shoulder.

'And when you're done, can you distribute the post?'

'Yup. So why the name change?'

She turned in her chair and tipped her head forward, catching Lachlan in her owl-like stare. 'Civil Service Lachlan. I'm just surprised it's the first change since you've been here. Ten years isn't it?'

'Nine,' said Lachlan, as he pulled the office door open with his foot.

Nine years. Hard to believe. *Tick tock,* he thought as he approached the large entrance hall. I'm not working in an office, he'd convinced himself, remembering the promise he'd made back in Aberfoyle, *I'm working in a rather grand converted Victorian mansion in*

Edinburgh's leafy Southside.

Whatever gets you through the day.

He pushed the main doors open and dumped the box at the front of the building.

'Christ, you get the short straw again?' said Jack, his colleague of the last five years, as he puffed rapidly on a cigarette.

'Perfect Peter chuck you out again?'

'Aye, says I'm giving him cancer. Twat.'

'You're too similar, that's the problem.'

Jack hoisted his middle finger and took a last drag of his cigarette. 'So what are we now?' He gestured towards the box of redundant stationery.

'*British Geological Survey,* apparently. And there's twenty boxes of these old letterheads to get chucked. When you're finished enjoying your break you could give me a hand.'

Jack blew a smoke ring into the summer air. They were shaded here at the front of the building, but all was warm and still. 'I could. But you know me and Hutchy. She's still giving me the cold shoulder after Friday night.'

Lachlan recalled their payday night out as he re-entered the building. 'Aye she was fairly pished wasn't she? Thought you were in there too.'

'No amount of alcohol, Lachlan, could make me warm to her advances.'

The tiled floor of the vestibule had a scattering of mail, and the welcome sight of the new 1974 Phone Book. Lachlan scooped it all up and returned to Mrs Hutchison's office.

'Here you go. Various letters. Some bills. The usual.'

She didn't lift her head. 'Be a star Lachlan and do the rounds. You can chuck the rest of this crap later.'

'Okay,' he thumbed through the pile. 'These are for you,' he said as he dropped a pile of bills on her desk. 'The rest are for the tank-tops upstairs.'

In the hallway he checked the remaining letters, all addressed to individual geologists who operated in the rarefied atmosphere of the first floor. It wasn't often he had reason to venture upstairs, the admin staff were strictly downstairs people. He climbed the grand staircase, running his hand up the walnut bannister to the half-landing where squares of sunlight brightened the stair's worn brown carpet.

At the top, he knocked and entered the first room. Once a sitting room, it now housed half a dozen scientists, who smoked so much the fine cornicing was forever lost in a cloud.

'There's the mail,' Lachlan said, to nobody in particular, and placed the letters on a table by the door.

'Anything for me?' Alan Ferguson, a short barrel of a man asked, raising his head from the maps he was studying. He swept a strand of his long brown hair away from his face.

'There is Alan, aye. Here, looks important,' Lachlan took an envelope from the pile. The UK Government's crest sat above the small address window.

Alan took the envelope with a nod, as if he'd been expecting it, and said 'Thanks. Anything else like this arrives, bring it straight up okay?'

'Will do,' said Lachlan as he retreated to the cleaner air of the landing.

After half an hour of lugging redundant stationery, Lachlan finally returned to his office with a coffee. Jack and Peter were typing up some paperwork that would mean as much to them as it did to Lachlan: Nothing. They'd all signed the Official Secrets Act; Nine years ago for Lachlan. Five for Jack. (Peter had been here since time began), but it seemed pointless, as the majority of the admin staff had no idea what the paperwork they dealt with even meant. Stats on soil samples; rock density; earthquakes. It all sounded interesting but the reality of it was excruciatingly dull.

'Thanks for making us one,' said Peter.

'Kettle's in the usual place,' said Lachlan as he sat down with the new phonebook.

He took a sip of coffee and flipped the pages until he reached Paterson, then scanned further until he reached the Ms.

Paterson, M. 76 Easter Road... He'd tried that one in 1968.

Paterson, M. 253 Ferry Road... An old man. As he'd discovered in 1972.

Then he saw one that made him pause mid-sip. He lowered his mug, picked up his freshly-sharpened pencil, and carefully underlined a new entry in the listing.

Paterson, M. 57 McDonald Road... Could it be Morag? His heart thumped.

Peter rose to his feet with a grunt. 'Coffee then Jack?'

Jack pulled a sheet of paper from his typewriter and dropped it to his desk. 'Aye, I'm away for a shit. Enjoying your book there?' he said as he passed Lachlan's desk.

Lachlan snorted and watched them leave.

Alone now, he reached for the phone; a standard issue two-tone grey, civil service device with years of muck and crumbs gathered in the mouth-piece, and dialled the number.

He listened to the ringing tone at the other end of the line. Was it in Morag's flat? She'd probably be at work anyway. Assuming she had a job, that is. He pictured some bohemian apartment, full of books and music. On an old fireplace sat his flagstone, front and centre, to remind her of him. The phone kept ringing. He was about to hang up when the sound of a baby crying tumbled from the receiver.

'Hello?' A woman's voice. Flustered, but Scottish, and youngish (she'd be 33 now, same age as Lachlan).

'Morag?' said Lachlan, his heart pounding, a sweat on his brow.

'Eh? Who?'

'Oh sorry, I was looking for Morag.'

'Wrong number, sorry.'

Lachlan pressed the black switch on the receiver's cradle and the line went dead.

He sat back in his chair, looked at the pile of paperwork he had to get through and buried his face in his hands. He was between girlfriends. Again. Since moving to Edinburgh he'd endured a smattering of awkward relationships featuring infidelity (on their part, unsurprisingly), and ending in mutual loathing, or indifference. One of these years, he thought, the phonebook would bring her back into his life.

His phone rang, just as the office door swung open and Peter barged in with two coffees.

'You going to answer that?'

'Aye,' said Lachlan with a sigh. Most likely it would be Hutchison with some other menial task.

'Hello?'

'Lachlan?' A voice from the past.

'Johnny?'

'The very same. How's things? Just calling to say I'm in town this weekend and it'd be good to catch up.'

'Aye sure. Fine here. Bored out my tits of course, but other than that all good. You?'

Johnny paused for a moment, 'Lots to talk about Lachlan. I'll see you Saturday. One o'clock? Milne's?'

'Sounds like a plan.'

'Right, got to run. The wee fella's off school sick.'

'Oh, right. No problem. See you Saturday.'

Johnny, a blast from the past right enough. He'd seen him off-and-on for the first few years after he'd left Alloa. The fact he'd started dating Mandy didn't even bother him. In fact, he was happy for both of them. And they had a wee boy together, Billy, named after Mandy's dad. Johnny, despite being the first to escape Stirling, seemed to have settled in Alloa, and why not? He was moving up the corporate ladder at the brewery, and was now married to the boss's daughter.

He wound another sheet into his typewriter. It was always easier to get through the slog of the nine-to-five when he had something to look forward to at the weekend.

****

He checked his watch as he approached the basement that housed Milne's Bar. A crowd of well-oiled gents were climbing the stairs singing "*Yabba dabba doo we support the boys in blue*" - Scotland had breezed through qualification for the World Cup for the first time in sixteen years and spirits were high. Aye bring on Yugoslavia, and

Zaire. Easy. Easy. And Brazil. Let's not forget Brazil.

Inside, the sun illuminated the tables by the windows where a few shoppers sat smoking and drinking by the unlit fireplace. He checked behind, into the snug known as the "Little Kremlin" after it had housed years of debate, both political and poetic, by Scotland's 20th century literati. In the corner sat the familiar curly-topped figure of Johnny, nursing a pint.

'Lachie-boy!' Johnny stood and grabbed Lachlan by the shoulders. 'What'll it be?'

'Pint of whatever you're having,' said Lachlan. 'How's life?'

Johnny glanced towards the ceiling for a moment. 'Interesting, Lachlan. Interesting. Have a read of my paper and I'll get the drinks in.'

The paper didn't make for pleasant reading. Labour's new minority government under Harold Wilson may have wished they'd lost the election that year, given the state of the nation. The news seemed mostly concerned with events in Northern Ireland; Direct rule had been imposed on the province. The IRA were bombing England, while the UVF were bombing Dublin. Meanwhile, this spilled back into Scotland's Irish diaspora. He groaned at a photo of an Orange Walk in Glasgow. Scottish identity had enough problems of its own. This was confirmed in Edinburgh's tourist shop windows, where tartan dolls fought for shelf space with tartan rugs and tartan tins of shortbread. An image seemingly forced upon Scotland. An identity for the tourists that bore little relation to the modern nation.

'Right! How's the Institute of Geography or wherever the hell it is you work?' Johnny thunked a pint on the table.

'The British Geological Survey, I'll have you know,' said Lachlan in a high-and-mighty tone. 'We've just changed our name.'

'Why?'

Lachlan shrugged, 'Makes us more British I suppose. More united. God Save the fucking Queen and all that.'

Johnny took a mouthful of ale. 'Must be boring as fuck though?'

Lachlan supped at his pint. 'Aye. But I get to sit on my arse all day. And you know me.'

Johnny laughed, 'You'll better watch yourself, that's quite the gut you're growing there.'

Lachlan looked down at his expanding middle. Years of fried food had taken its toll. He patted his stomach and said, 'You're right. I do get off my arse occasionally though. We've started getting these big fucking maps in. About twelve feet long some of them. Part of my exciting job is rolling them up on the floor and fitting them into cardboard tubes.'

'That sounds very satisfying. What kind of maps?' Johnny asked while lighting a cigarette.

'North Sea mostly. None of my business. I just log the details and file them. Anyway,' he continued in a hushed tone, 'I've signed the Official Secrets Act so if I tell you any more I'll have to kill you.'

Johnny put his hands up. 'I've heard enough. And I can't blame you. That Civil Service pension will be nice to have after a hard life rolling things up for the government.'

'Exactly. Anyway, how's things with you? How's the wee fella? And…' Lachlan trailed off and took a mouthful of beer.

'And Mandy? She's fine. The wee fella's fine. He's not doing too well at school mind you. Gets himself in bother a lot, but I…' Johnny paused and stared into his pint. 'I love the wee bastard anyway.'

'I should hope so,' Lachlan said, patting Johnny on the shoulder.

'Look man, you know I'm okay with it all. With you and Mandy and all that. It was never an issue. You always got on better with her anyway, and I was lost in Alloa. I had to get out.'

Johnny nodded and drained his pint. 'Aye I know.'

'So how's the brewery?'

'Folk will always want beer Lachlan,' Johnny grinned, waggling his empty glass.

'Aye. Very subtle. Same again?'

****

They'd barely noticed the pub growing busy around them as the shoppers drifted away and the evening crowd moved in. They'd moved onto half-pints with whisky chasers. Accelerating, or stumbling, towards the finish line, like all good Scottish drinkers.

'See if there was a World Cup of fucking this?' Johnny said, his head bobbing slowly back and forth as he pointed at the whisky glass he was about to drain. 'We'd be booking the open-top bus.'

'Aye,' Lachlan agreed, nodding furiously. 'We'd struggle against the Germans mind you. But we'd wipe the floor with every other bastard.'

'Another?' said Johnny patting his pockets for money.

'Be rude not to,' said Lachlan as he threw the whisky back.

Johnny wobbled towards the bar and Lachlan studied the crowd. It was standing room only now and the noise was deafening. Most of the talk seemed to be about the forthcoming tournament in Germany. Jimmy Johnstone, Denis Law, Billy Bremner, Gordon McQueen, Joe Jordan and Kenny Dalglish. How could they fail with such a squad? Zaire? Easy! Yugoslavia? Easy! Even the

Brazilians weren't to be feared. We were going to do it. If England could win it, so could we. Easy!

It wasn't all football talk though. Two men at the next table seemed to be deep into a more weighty discussion. A ginger haired guy with bushy sideburns was hammering the table with one hand to make his point.

'Doubled the vote. Doubled! In four years. How is that not progress?'

'It's still fucking pointless,' said his friend. 'Seven SNP MPs. What can they do? Nothing.'

'The same as fifty Labour MPs then? There's got to be more point to Scotland than propping up an occasional Labour majority.'

Lachlan leaned in. 'I'm with you pal,' he slurred, pointing to the sideburn guy. 'All the way!' he declared drunkenly.

The man laughed and shook Lachlan's hand. 'Finn. Nice to meet a fellow patriot.'

'Lachlan,' said Lachlan. 'I wouldn't go that far. I'm just saying it's good to see Scotland getting a wee bit confidence. We need it.'

'We do, and it's growing. Are you a member?' said Finn.

'Me?' said Lachlan, 'Oh no, Christ, I'm not that keen. I'm an armchair supporter.'

'Well you should consider it. This government can't last. We'll be voting again soon and we need all the help we can get. Here...' He reached into his pocket, pulled out a card and slipped it towards Lachlan on the table. 'Give me a shout if you want to get involved.'

'Cheers. Aye, I will,' said Lachlan as he pocketed the card. He'd never seen himself as much of a political activist. He'd seen what it had done to his father. Sometimes it was better not to care.

'There you go,' Johnny said as he sloshed beer over the table. 'Shite. Sorry.'

A chorus of *"Yabba dabba doo we support the boys in blue"* started up again in the crowd and soon half the pub was singing along as Lachlan knocked back his whisky before starting on the fresh beer. He joined in the song, but noticed Johnny was focused instead on lighting another cigarette.

'Sing you miserable bastard!'

Johnny took a drag with a stony-faced stare.

Lachlan trailed off after a half-hearted *and it's easy, easy* - 'What's up with you?' he asked. The jollity of the surroundings didn't seem to be rubbing off on Johnny.

'Lachlan, I need to talk to you. Seriously.'

Lachlan studied him for a moment, wondering if this was a joke, but Johnny seemed nervous. He puffed rapidly on his cigarette before leaning forward on his elbows.

'What is it? You in trouble?'

Johnny paused again, took a last long drag and thumbed the stub into the McEwan's ashtray. He slid this to one side and gestured for Lachlan to lean forward. Whatever he had to say, it was obvious that Lachlan needed to hear it.

'It's not easy this, Lachlan, but I need to tell you.' He took a sup of his beer and wiped his mouth. 'Me and Mandy were thinking it'd be good for Billy to have a wee brother or sister.'

'Aye?' Little Billy was what, eight or nine? He'd never really thought about it, just assumed they were happy with one.

'And, well. We've been trying but…' he shrugged. 'Nothing.'

'Right,' said Lachlan slowly. So there had been complications after the first? Mandy could no longer have children? That must have been it. 'I'm sorry to hear that Johnny. At least you've got Billy though eh? One's better than none surely?'

'Well that's the thing,' said Johnny as he lit another cigarette. He blew smoke towards Lachlan. 'We've had tests, and it's not Mandy that's the problem.'

'Eh?' said Lachlan.

'It's me.'

'You?' Lachlan felt the ground shake beneath his feet and it wasn't the stomping, chanting crowd causing it.

'I'm shooting blanks Lachlan.'

'Fuck,' said Lachlan.

'And you know what that means?' said Johnny. He seemed calmer now, as if a great weight had been lifted from his shoulders.

Lachlan looked at the table. Flakes of the veneer had been chipped away after years of abuse. He raised his eyes to meet Johnny's but couldn't say anything. He waited.

'Billy's yours.'

Lachlan felt like he was slipping down a helter-skelter. He grasped for the sides, for something to hang onto. Across the pub, a pint glass smashed and a cheer went up.

'But how? Are you sure?'

'She was pregnant when you left her Lachlan. She was going to tell you that day by the river, but you fucking dumped her instead. And look at him. He's the fucking spitting image of you. The older he gets, the more obvious it becomes.'

'Oh fuck,' said Lachlan. He buried his face in his hands. 'I'm sorry Johnny. I really am.' He peered between his fingers. 'Why didn't she say? She could have told me that day.'

It was Johnny's turn to fidget in his seat. He drained his beer and took another drag of his cigarette. 'She didn't know whose it was.'

Lachlan sat back. 'You mean you were already shagging her?'

Johnny grinned awkwardly. 'I guess we're both a pair of bastards eh?'

Lachlan ran his hand through his hair and shook his head. 'Fuck. So what now?'

Johnny placed both hands on the table, 'How about another pint? It's your round.'

Lachlan gathered himself and attempted to put his thoughts in order. He was a father. With responsibilities. He'd missed the first eight years of his son's life. His son's mother had been two-timing him with his best friend, who his son now viewed as his father. There was only one thing for it.

'Double whisky?'

****

The office clock crawled towards the oasis of lunchtime like a dying man in a desert. Lachlan propped his head up on his hands and watched the minute-hand drop.

'Pint?' said Jack, to the room.

Peter puffed out his cheeks, shuffled a pile of documents, and shook his head while casting a disapproving glance at Jack.

Lachlan opened his desk drawer and retrieved his wallet. 'Maybe. Stuff to do first though.'

Half an hour later, Lachlan joined Jack in The Old Bell. They still had enough time for a quick pint. It'd make the afternoon drag even more but the temptation to dull his senses before returning to the office was too great.

Jack slipped a beer towards him and raised his glass. The bar was empty save for a middle-aged man leafing through a newspaper by the window and a solitary, bored, barman.

'Get your business done then?' asked Jack.

'All sorted,' said Lachlan.

As he'd filled out the paperwork in the bank he was sure it was the right thing to do. Johnny and Mandy weren't ready to tell Billy just yet, but they would, eventually. How would a child accept the news that the man he'd called Daddy all his life wasn't his father? And would he accept Lachlan? He'd have to face up to it at some point in the not-too-distant future. The least he could do was put some money away for him. He'd declined the offer of a blue piggy-bank and a furry gonk with the bank's logo emblazoned on the side, as his child wouldn't know anything about the account until he was eighteen.

Lachlan supped his pint, and surveyed a basket of cheese rolls, temptingly placed alongside the drip-tray. They looked a day or two past their best but he nodded to the barman as he helped himself to one and dropped some coins on the bar.

'Seen that?' Jack asked, nodding towards a poster on the wall. It showed an illustration of an American eagle atop a shield featuring a hybrid Union Jack and Stars & Stripes. In bold stencilled lettering the title proclaimed *The Cheviot, the Stag & the Black Black Oil* - a local theatre group production. Lachlan considered the flags for a moment, remembering his flagstone collection. Now lined up along the mantelpiece in his shared flat in the city's West End as a reminder of home. He took a bite of the roll and briefly thought of the missing flagstone, and its missing owner.

'What about it?' Lachlan asked, through a mouthful of cheese.

'Sounds like the kind of thing you'd like. Very anti-English.'

Lachlan spluttered. 'I'm not anti-English. Where'd you get that idea?'

'All that nationalist stuff you've been coming out with. That last works night out, you and Alan the geologist were like a right pair of William Wallaces. Hutchie was appalled.'

'Having a bit of interest in Scotland's history doesn't make you anti-English for fuck's sake.'

Jack seemed taken aback. 'Aye okay, keep your hair on. Come on, sup up, we'll better get back.'

'I'm appalled that you'd think that,' said Lachlan before shoving the remains of the roll in his mouth and draining his pint. It was true. Lachlan didn't hate anyone. He wasn't too keen on certain politicians but that was more down to them being utter arseholes than the country of their birth.

He glanced back at the poster. It looked interesting. Close to his flat, and the production still had a week to run.

****

They arrived back at the office just as the postman was leaving. Lachlan stood in the hallway and thumbed through the mail. There was another letter for Alan Ferguson. Again with the UK Government crest, but this time featuring a red-stamped "CONFIDENTIAL".

He was just about to head up the stairs when Alan came bounding down two at a time.

'Anything for me in the second post?'

'Sure thing Alan. Top secret too. You're going up in the world.'

Alan took the envelope. Instead of returning to his office, he tore it open and scanned the contents. His face seemed to darken the more he read. He swept his hair back over his shoulder and frowned.

'Everything okay?' asked Lachlan.

Alan leaned on the bannister. 'Hard to say Lachlan. Hard to say.'

'Oh,' said Lachlan, unsure of what to say. It was confidential, after all.

'Lachlan could you pull the last half dozen surveys from the store for me?'

'Sure, I'll bring them up.'

Lachlan ducked through the windowless print room where the smell of chemicals always caught his throat. Simon, "the map guy" seemed immune to the stench as he pulled a huge sheet from the printer and lay it on a large table to dry.

In the tube store beyond, he exhaled and took a deep breath of the slightly more pleasant air. He turned on the overhead lights and headed for the end of the racks as the room flickered into view. Row-upon-row of neatly stacked cardboard tubes. Each one stuffed with sheet-upon-sheet of tightly rolled acetate and paper maps. He pulled out the last six tubes and stacked them against the wall.

'Made a mistake?' asked Simon as Lachlan negotiated the tubes through the print room. Usually once the surveys were stacked, they were left there. It was unusual to see them heading back out of the store.

'Nah. Alan's wanting them.'

Simon nodded. 'Interesting…'

'How?' asked Lachlan, adjusting the tubes under one arm as they threatened to escape his grip.

'Oh, well…' Simon glanced around, conspiratorially. 'Just been printing a lot of stuff lately. All focused on one area.'

'Uhuh?' asked Lachlan. Had there been a concentration of earthquakes perhaps? One of the BGS's jobs was to monitor these, wherever they happened in the world.

Simon tapped his nose, 'Very close to home. Let's put it that way.'

'Where?' asked Lachlan. 'Edinburgh? Is Arthur's Seat about to blow?'

'No. But the North Sea looks like it's about to explode. All over the news.'

'Oil?' said Lachlan. They'd been internally branded the Hydrocarbons Research Unit recently - and the majority of the work did seem to concern surveys of seemingly blank areas of the North Sea. The cross-sections of the sub-sea geology that accompanied the maps meant nothing to Lachlan, it was just varying concentrations of black squiggles as far as he was concerned.

Simon nodded. 'Alan's been consulting with the government on a report, but it's not been made public yet.'

'Why?' asked Lachlan.

Simon shrugged, 'Dunno. Probably don't want to overplay it. No idea why though, the country could do with some good news. The economy's in the toilet.'

Lachlan decided he'd need to get drunk with Alan again as soon as possible.

****

The night was still warm as they marched, in a slight zig-zag, towards the venue. The last two hours in the pub had seen them consume around eight hours worth of alcohol. A double-decker bus shuddered towards Princes Street, the driver struggling with the gears. The road opened up into two wide, airy crescents and they side-stepped into the small gardens that separated the main thoroughfare from the residents of the apartments at either side.

'So, do you think you'll be getting any more top secret letters?' asked Lachlan.

'No, that's all done. Over and dusted. Done and dusted, I should say,' slurred Alan.

'So what was it all about? Must have been interesting? You were away at the Scottish Office a lot weren't you?'

'I was Lachlan, I was. Doing my bit for Queen and country,' he saluted and shook his head.

'That country being…'

'The United Kingdom Lachlan. What else? We are servants of Her Majesty after all.'

The throaty growl of a V8 engine echoed off the Georgian facades as a racing-green Triumph Stag sped past, heading towards Haymarket. The top was down, and the driver had his arm casually thrown around the shoulder of the young woman in the passenger seat. She leaned across and pushed his floppy blonde fringe aside as she rose from her seat to kiss him.

Alan gestured towards the sports car as it pulled up to the kerb. 'And all for those fuckers.'

'Eh?'

'Cars. Oil. And the rich bastards who'll profit most from it.'

Lachlan looked at the car. Just a pair of young lovers with a bit of spare cash, as far as he could see. 'I guess they've been finding lots of it, but surely that's great for us?'

'For who? For Scotland? You'd think so wouldn't you.'

'It's not?' Lachlan slowed as they approached the crowd milling around the door of the church hall, occupying the ground floor of a Georgian townhouse. The driver of the Stag swung his door closed with a clunk, and quickly kissed his passenger. He seemed to be keeping one eye on the crowd as he did so. She broke from his embrace and headed back towards Lachlan and Alan. The driver watched her go, then fixed his hair and headed towards the venue.

Alan stopped, and looked around. They waited for the Stag's passenger to pass. She was in her early twenties. A tangle of wild red hair hung at either side of her large brown-tinted sunglasses. Alan watched her go then gripped Lachlan by the shoulders and said, 'Lachlan, you don't know the half of it, and it's better that you don't, but I'll tell you this much.' He paused, glanced around, then lowered his voice. 'I've been working with a professor called McCrone, on a document about the value of Scotland's oil. The letter I received the other day was telling me the report is to be buried. It'll never see the light of day. If any word of it gets out…' He dragged a finger across his throat.

'Why the secrecy?'

'Why do you think?'

They watched as two girls with saltires wrapped around their shoulders ran by, on their way to the show. Alan looked at the flags, then looked at Lachlan, and Lachlan thought he understood.

****

The interior of the hall had the smell of neglect that seemed to be present in all Church of Scotland establishments. Rows of plastic chairs filled the room and as they edged into their seats a wild-haired gent at the side of the hall started playing a lively reel on his fiddle.

The murmur of the crowd grew as the hall filled. The fiddler increased the tempo, his fingers dancing over the neck of the instrument. Lachlan spotted the Stag driver a few rows ahead and wondered why he wasn't being joined by his attractive companion. Maybe she wasn't a theatre type? Truth be told, neither was he. Or Alan. He took a sideways glance at his colleague as he necked another mouthful of whisky from his hip-flask.

'Remember. Mum's the word,' said Alan.

Lachlan nodded. 'You didn't tell me anything Alan, so I've got nothing to go to the papers with. Don't worry.'

Alan laughed just as the lights went down. The fiddler ended his reel and a hush fell on the crowd.

Under a single spotlight an actor who looked more like a rock star took to the stage. He introduced the performance and said something about the story *having a beginning, a middle, but as yet, no end*. Lachlan glanced around at the crowd. A mix of old and young, male and female. He recognised a man sitting near the front as the SNP guy, Finn, he'd spoken to in Milne's the night Johnny had dropped his bombshell. Edinburgh may have been Scotland's capital city, but it really was more like a village sometimes.

The show began with a piece on the Highland Clearances. The brutal treatment Scotland's crofting communities received in the pursuit of profit by their landlords, newly emboldened by the Act of Union. This culminated with the forced evictions and burning of the crofters' homes. And all because sheep were more profitable. The audience fell silent as a woman's voice read out the names of those dispossessed, beaten, or killed in the skirmishes. All women, as the men had been forced south to earn a wage, or enlisted in the British army.

Lachlan turned to the voice, at the side of the stage. Still in darkness as the amateur lighting engineer struggled with the equipment. A moment later, she was caught in a blinding light that stopped her like a rabbit in headlights. She held a hand over her face, shading her eyes and grimaced towards the engineer. 'Are you sure that's bright enough!?'

The audience laughed nervously. The engineer shouted, 'Sorry!' as the light faded to a normal level and the woman returned to the script.

Lachlan didn't hear a word of it though. He stared at her, bathed in white light and bedecked in a red tartan dress. She finished reading the list and the audience fell silent. The first actor returned to the stage and moved the story onwards but Lachlan was still staring at the woman. She dropped the list to the floor at the side of the stage and raised her head, scanning the audience. When she spotted someone she knew a smile flashed across her face that confirmed what Lachlan had been hoping.

It was a smile like no other.

It was Morag.

****

Applause rang through the hall and Lachlan stood with the rest of the crowd. The cast held hands and took a final bow before disappearing into the wings.

Alan stirred and looked around as if unsure of his whereabouts. 'Is it finished?'

'Aye,' said Lachlan. 'I'm going to try to speak to someone backstage. Will you be alright getting home?'

Alan stood like a baby elephant taking its first steps. He grabbed for the back of the chair in front and it slipped away from him with a screech. Lachlan grabbed him before he hit the floor.

'Need a hand there?'

The Stag driver had spotted Lachlan's predicament and stepped over to help.

'Thanks. He's had a few.' Lachlan said, as they hoisted Alan upright.

'I'm fine, look.' Alan, now that he was awake, took a few steps towards the aisle. He turned with a flourish, said, 'I'll see you on Monday Lachlan,' then staggered off. Lachlan wondered if he'd even remember the conversation they'd had earlier.

'Thanks for that,' Lachlan said.

The Stag driver flicked his fringe to one side. He looked about the same age as Lachlan, but Lachlan doubted if he'd been brought up in a Stirling council house. 'Not a problem. I'm Josh, by the way.'

'Lachlan,' said Lachlan, shaking his hand. 'Well, really appreciate that. I was just going to…' He pointed towards the stage.

'Oh, do you know someone in the cast? I'm heading back too. Come on.'

Josh opened a side door and ushered Lachlan into a dimly-lit corridor. Laughter spilled from a room at the end where the cast had assembled. A champagne cork popped.

Lachlan watched as Josh entered the room with an easy confidence that he couldn't help but admire. He shuffled in after him and looked for Morag. There were around thirty cast, crew and hangers-on crammed into what appeared to be a small dining room lined with melamine-topped tables. The mood was buoyant, and it seemed to lift even more with the arrival of Josh.

Lachlan edged along the wall and watched as Josh headed directly to the centre of the room, and straight into Morag's arms.

****

Lachlan had almost finished the bottle of beer he'd lifted from a table near the door. Almost invisible, as the party continued around him, he watched as Josh busied himself making a joint and Morag turned to speak to another cast member. She hadn't spotted him yet. She probably wouldn't recognise him anyway, would she? It had been ten years since they'd met briefly at his father's funeral and he'd filled out a bit, in all directions. His hair was long now, tucked behind his ears and hiding the back of his shirt collar. Morag was unmistakeable. It wasn't just her smile, but the whole way she carried herself. Her brown hair sat loosely on her shoulders, hanging down on either side of her face in loose curls.

'Hello, are you from the church?' a girl appeared at Lachlan's side and he jumped at the intrusion. One of the crew? He didn't recognise her from the stage. She was short, wore round glasses, and her figure was completely hidden in a psychedelic pattered dress that flapped like a circus tent in the wind.

'Oh, no. I'm just here to…' Lachlan trailed off. 'I just wanted to say hello to someone.'

'Oh really? Who? I'm Shiela, the costume designer, I know all these reprobates.'

Lachlan's skin prickled as he considered his next move. He took a swig of beer and nodded towards Morag. 'She's an old friend.'

'Ah, the lovely Morag. I might have guessed,' she laughed. Then, without warning, called 'Ms Paterson! Someone to see you!'

Lachlan felt his face flush. He took another mouthful of beer and wiped the sweat from his brow as Morag touched her colleague on the arm and headed towards them, looking quizzically at Lachlan, who was slowly sinking towards the skirting boards.

'Darling Morag,' said Sheila. 'This is…' she turned to Lachlan, who had straightened up and was busy trying not to be sick. 'Sorry, I didn't get your name?'

'Lachlan?!' said Morag, her mouth falling open.

'Yup,' said Lachlan, grinning. 'Hello stranger.'

'Oh my god,' said Morag, and Lachlan was delighted to see that smile crack her face in two. She looked like she was about to cry. He wasn't sure if this was a good thing or a bad thing but he did realise he was staring at her like a hypnotised chicken. 'So how the hell are you Lachlan McCormack?'

I feel like I'm floating on a cloud. And also a bit sick. He gulped. 'Fine. You know. Doing away.'

'Well I'll leave you to it. Your man's finished his work there Morag. I feel a celebratory spliff is in order,' said Sheila and she floated off into the crowd, her dress eventually catching her up as she reached the middle of the room.

Morag did an excited little dance, hopping from foot to foot in a way that Lachlan found painfully endearing. 'I can't believe it's you. It's been ages. I haven't seen you since…' Her face darkened as she remembered their last meeting.

'My dad's funeral. Aye. Ten years. Time flies eh?'

'Och Lachlan I'm so sorry,' she touched his arm and he felt his blood rush in a million different directions. 'Are you okay now? Where are you living? You're not still in Alloa are you?'

'No, just around the corner actually. Working in town now.'

'In an office?' asked Morag with a squint smile. 'Remember we said we'd never work in an office?'

Oh my fucking god she remembers a conversation we had in 1951. 'Afraid so,' he laughed. 'At least you followed your dream eh?'

She looked towards the ceiling and danced her head quickly from side-to-side. 'Sort of,' she said. 'This isn't a full-time thing. Just a hobby really. I work in a nursery. Part-time. And in a bar. Also part-time. And the rest of the time, I'm a part-time actor.'

'Well I thought you were great,' said Lachlan. 'Almost as good as a proper actor.'

'Cheeky git!' laughed Morag. 'Hey, come and meet my friends.' She grabbed his hand but he pulled her back.

'Och no. You know me. Not a fan of crowds. I've met your, erm…' He nodded towards Josh who was blowing a pungent smoke ring into the air through half-shut eyes.

'My boyfriend?' said Morag. She smiled, but it was a brief flash of a smile, then turned back to Lachlan. 'Do you not remember him?'

'Eh? No? He wasn't with you at the funeral was he?'

'No,' said Morag. 'Long before that.'

Lachlan was lost. He shrugged and shook his head. 'Is he famous?'

Morag laughed again, 'Only in these circles I'm afraid. He's from Aberfoyle.' She gazed at Lachlan quizzically, gauging if he was any closer to identifying her lover.

He looked at Josh again. He pictured their classroom and the occupants of every desk came drifting back to him. None of them matched the easy-going, effortlessly confident, irritatingly handsome figure that sat in the centre of the room surrounded by adoring thespians. 'Nope. I give up.'

'Remember the day we walked to the river's source? The day

after…' Morag grimaced.

'My mum had her stroke? Aye. Can you stop going on about my dead parents please?' Lachlan shook his head in mock outrage.

'Yes, sorry. Remember the car?'

Lachlan pictured that day, twenty-four years ago. He did remember the black car speeding past them on the road, such an unusual sight in those days. Then it came back to him. The blonde boy in the back seat who shyly waved as the car drove off.

'Fuck! The laird's son?'

Morag nodded. 'The very same. Marcus Joshua Dalrymple-Brown to give him his kennel name.'

Dirty Fucking Cheating-Bastard more like. 'Well there you go. Imagine that?' he gulped, trying hard to conceal his disappointment. 'So how did you two meet?'

Morag took Lachlan's beer, 'Mind if I take a swig? I've left mine over there.' She didn't wait for an answer. She wiped her mouth and handed the bottle back to Lachlan. 'Oh you know what a small place Edinburgh is. I was out with friends one night. He was there. We got talking. I said *I think my mum used to wipe your bum*. And that was that.'

'I thought your mum worked in their kitchen?'

'She did, aye. But never let the truth get in the way of a good chat-up line Lachlan.' She smiled again. 'What about you? You've grown up to be quite the hippy.' She flicked at Lachlan's collar-length hair. 'Are you still with… sorry I didn't know her name. The girl at the…'

'The funeral?! Fuck's sake Morag. I'm trying to move on from these things.'

'Sorry Lachlan,' her eyes sparkled in the fluorescent strip-light.

She furrowed her brow, cleared her throat theatrically and said in a mock-serious voice, 'What was her name?'

'Mandy. Her name was Mandy. And no. I'm not with her anymore.' Lachlan considered this. He wasn't with Mandy, that much was correct, but he couldn't deny the connection was still there in the form of an eight-year-old boy.

'That's a pity. She seemed nice. And there's no-one else? Come on Lachlan. A big handsome boy like you…'

Lachlan thought of the disappointingly sparse hit parade of his Edinburgh conquests and shrugged. 'Not really.' He held Morag's gaze and wondered if he looked too much like a puppy begging for a biscuit.

'Oh well. I've got lots of friends. I'll sort you out. Don't you worry.' With the last three words she poked Lachlan below the shoulder with pointed fingers. 'You should come into the pub when I'm working. Cafe Royal. I'm there most Saturdays.'

'Hey, you've met my girlfriend then?' Josh appeared by their side, blowing a cloud of smoke into Lachlan's face.

'Aye. Old friends,' said Lachlan. He felt his head spin. 'Fancy that eh? Small world!'

Josh handed Lachlan the joint and nodded slowly.

'Lachlan's from Aberfoyle too,' said Morag. 'We were at school together.'

'Well well,' said Josh. He leaned forward and grabbed Morag in an embrace, tilting her backwards and kissing her deeply. She fidgeted her way free and straightened up.

'Easy tiger,' she said. Lachlan took a long puff of the joint and instantly regretted it.

'Sorry, you know how this stuff makes me randy,' said Josh.

He leered at Lachlan looking for approval but Lachlan was concentrating hard on the fact he could no longer feel his legs and his head was filling with white noise. He felt his stomach churn as an evening's worth of beer and whisky fought with the new herbal addition to his bloodstream.

'I think I'm going to go,' said Lachlan. 'Morag. Great to see you. And Josh.' He handed Josh the joint and barged from the room.

In the corridor, he spotted an emergency exit, lit from above by a dim yellow bulb. It opened into the outside cellar area. The coolness helped, but it wasn't enough. He bent over a pile of black bin bags and threw up. He leaned against the damp stone of the walls and wiped his mouth.

Tiny increments, he thought. Then threw up again.

****

Lachlan took his time as he approached The Cafe Royal, for two reasons: He wanted to think carefully about his tactics, and he didn't want to work up a sweat.

The streets were full of dejected drunks in Scotland tops, spilling from bars with an air of not-unexpected misery. Bottles were kicked into the gutters. A young guy sat on the steps of the art gallery, his head in his hands.

Cruelly, the group had ended with Brazil, Yugoslavia and Scotland all on the same points after Scotland's 1-1 draw that afternoon, but Yugoslavia's nine-goal hammering of Zaire put them above Scotland on goal difference. Brazil and Yugoslavia would continue the party in Germany, while Scotland and Zaire would be heading home.

At least Zaire is a proper fucking country he thought as he dodged through the crowds.

His shadow stretched out in front, leading him on. He glanced into a darkened shop window at his reflection. Denim jacket, jeans, black shirt, and baseball boots. Maybe he should have dressed smarter? He didn't think so. He winced at the memory of the borrowed suit he wore to his first date with Mandy. This was who he was. Morag knew that. She'd appreciate his lack of effort, he was sure of it.

He paused before taking the steps down to the barroom floor. The high-ceilinged, tiled interior of the old Victorian pub meant everything was amplified, creating a cacophony of Saturday night sound. He scanned the island bar and there, serving a man with a half-undone tie, was Morag. Smartly dressed in a white shirt with her hair tied back in a ponytail. She moved effortlessly behind the bar, grabbing three pint glasses from the gantry and dropping them expertly beneath the taps.

There was a sudden draught as the door swung open behind him. He took a quick step forward to let the newcomer enter. 'Excuse me,' came a voice from over his shoulder.

'Sorry,' Lachlan said and turned to the voice. If tonight had looked like a tough draw for Lachlan, it just got worse as Josh barged into the bar, all confidence and bluster.

'You again!' said Josh patting Lachlan on the shoulder. 'And what brings you here?' he asked with a raised eyebrow.

Lachlan's defence held firm. 'Came to see Morag. You?'

Josh rocked back slightly, shocked at Lachlan's honesty. 'Same. Get me a pint will you? I'm bursting for a piss.'

With that, Josh forced his way through the crowd.

Fuck. A tactical change was needed, and quick. He shoved through to the bar and pulled a five pound note from his jeans.

Morag had delivered the three pints to tie-man and was counting his change from the till.

'Morag!' called Lachlan.

She turned and her face lit up, this time without the need of a spotlight. She rushed the change over to the other side of the bar. Within moments, she was with him.

'Hello. Still alive then?' she grinned. Lachlan's heart rate quickened.

'What? Oh, last night. Aye, sorry about that. Had to make a sharp exit.'

'You're looking well, anyway.'

'I should hope so. I've been in my bed all day.' This wasn't exactly an incisive through-ball. He tried again. 'So are you. Looking, you know, well, I mean.'

Morag looked at Lachlan, her cheekbones twitched and a faint hint of red appeared among the freckles. 'Thanks. Well, what can I get you?'

'Right, erm, pint of lager for me. And whatever your boyfriend drinks.'

'Eh? Josh? Are you with him?'

'He's in the toilet. And no, I'm not. He just arrived at the same time.'

'Oh,' said Morag and her face seemed to darken, just for a moment.

'So have you been together long?' asked Lachlan as Morag poured a Guinness for Josh.

She shrugged, 'Six months or so, I think.'

'It's great to see you again Morag. Really.'

She looked down at the Guinness as it finished pouring, and Lachlan could tell by her eyes that she was forcing back a grin.

'What are you two old bores talking about?' boomed Josh as he returned from the toilet and edged in beside Lachlan at the bar.

'Oh, nothing,' said Morag.

'School,' said Lachlan, at the same time.

Josh looked at them both then pulled a packet of cigarettes from his jacket. He offered it to Lachlan, 'Smoke?'

'Nah,' said Lachlan.

'Right, well, love to chat, and hello darling,' Morag smiled at Josh. Lachlan thought it looked forced. 'But I need to work. I'll let you two get to know each other.' She turned to the crowd and nodded towards an elderly gent who pointed his pipe towards the whisky optic with a grunt.

Josh clinked his pint against Lachlan's and blew smoke into the air. 'Cheers Lachlan. She's quite a catch isn't she?'

'She's an old friend Josh. A very old friend.' Lachlan took a lengthy draw at his pint.

Josh tapped some ash onto the floor. Lachlan was aware Josh seemed to be studying him. 'Well any friend of Morag's is a friend of mine. Let's get pissed. Terrible result today eh?'

Lachlan shook his head, 'Nothing worse. Coming that close then getting it taken away from you. There's always next time eh? We'll do better in '78.'

'Argentina I believe?' said Josh.

Lachlan nodded and supped at his pint. He hadn't been expecting Josh to be so damn, *normal*. He stared at a tiled mural of George Stephenson on the wall. Beneath was a quote from the famous engineer. He mouthed the words, *'There is no limit to the speed if the works could be made to stand.'*

Josh turned to look at the mural. 'Stephenson's rocket?'

Lachlan nodded, 'That wasn't him. That was his son Robert. George, there,' He waved at the bearded figure immortalised in porcelain, 'Was his father.'

'Okay,' said Josh, confused. 'And?'

'Nothing. Just thinking about my dad, that's all. He was an engineer. Funny how life pans out isn't it?'

'I suppose it is,' said Josh as he stubbed his cigarette into an ashtray. 'Are you getting weird on me Lachlan?' He chuckled, 'Don't get weird on me. I barely know you.'

Lachlan looked at this chiselled adonis and couldn't find it in himself to dislike him. Despite his easy life, his wealth, his looks, his charm, and the fact he was going out with the woman he'd fucking loved all his life, Lachlan found himself warming to him. This wasn't how the evening was meant to go.

'You boys getting to know each other?' Morag appeared at their end of the bar, sipping a glass of lemonade through a straw.

'Lachlan's getting weird on me Morag. I need your help,' Josh said with a grin aimed squarely at Lachlan.

'Ha, sorry,' Lachlan flustered. 'I didn't mean to. Just saw that mural there and thought of my dad. No more weirdness, I promise.'

Josh placed a hand on Lachlan's shoulder. 'I'm joking. Morag told me about you two growing up together. It's cool.'

'Josh's dad's going to be an MP isn't he Josh?' Morag said with a playful air.

Josh seemed to shrink on his barstool. He puffed on his cigarette and nodded towards the ceiling. 'Possibly. We'll see.' He shot a silencing glance at Morag.

Lachlan watched the pair of them. To break the silence he said, 'What party?'

Josh grimaced. 'What do you think?'

'Tories?' laughed Lachlan.

'Got it in one,' said Josh.

'There's probably going to be another election,' said Morag. 'Daft really. We've just had one.'

'Aye, Wilson's trying to run the country with a minority. It was never going to last,' said Lachlan.

'I take it you're a Labour man Lachlan,' asked Josh.

Lachlan shrugged, 'I try to keep that kind of thing to myself to be honest.'

'Hey, I'm not knocking it,' said Josh. 'At least you're not a nationalist like mad Morag here.'

'Hey you!' laughed Morag.

Lachlan wasn't surprised she'd ended up supporting the SNP. He remembered her rebellious ways at primary school and wondered if she'd kept his saltire flagstone. He finished his pint and placed the empty glass on the bar.

'I'm leaning that way, to be honest.'

****

'Listen, I'm telling you. This is huge,' said Lachlan, stabbing the bar with his finger.

Outside, darkness had fallen and the Cafe Royal crowd had begun drifting home. Morag was busy drying glasses while the other staff cleared tables and swept around the remaining drinkers.

'Huge like bring-down-the-government huge?' Josh leaned closer.

Lachlan shrugged. 'We'll never know.'

'This sounds like it should be news. I've got pals at the papers you know. We could make a few quid here.' Josh patted his pockets, looking for his cigarettes. Lachlan slid the packet along the bar to him. 'Oh, ta.'

'He won't talk.'

'The little goblin fellow from last night?' said Josh as he tried to flip a cigarette into his mouth and missed.

Lachlan tried not to laugh, 'That's harsh. Alan's a nice guy. We're civil servants though Josh. Official Secrets Act and all that.' He wagged his finger. 'Anyway, Alan doesn't know. He only consulted on it. All he knows is that whatever the report says, it'll never be seen by the public.'

'And what do you think it says?' Josh was now repeatedly failing to spark a match. Lachlan reached over and turned the matchbox around the right way. 'Oh, ta.' The match sparked to life.

'The surveys we get don't tell us where the oil is, but the potential for discoveries is huge. The surveys just tell the oil companies where to look. Saves them drilling holes everywhere. Otherwise the sea would drain away.'

'Would it?' said Josh with a start.

Lachlan chuckled, 'No you fucking idiot. Anyway, that's all I know. Put two and two together, what do you get?'

'Lots of fucking oil?' said Josh.

Lachlan raised his whisky and downed it in one. 'Another?' he asked.

'You're a devil Lachlan, I like you,' Josh said, then 'Shit, what time is it?'

Lachlan checked his watch. It had stopped at 8.30pm. 'Dunno, sorry.' He leaned forward on the bar, 'Morag! What time is it?'

'Time you two were sobering up,' laughed Morag. 'Half eleven. Another two whiskies?'

Lachlan gave her a thumbs up as Josh slipped from his stool and headed for a pay-phone mounted near the door. Lachlan watched him pat his pockets for change. He winked at Lachlan then turned his back to him.

'There you go,' said Morag as she slipped two more whiskies towards Lachlan. She glanced across at Josh.

'You okay?' asked Lachlan.

'Aye,' said Morag. She leaned on the bar, taking her attention from Josh and focusing on Lachlan. 'Nice to get a minute with my old pal. We'll need to catch up properly. Here…' She slipped a piece of paper with a phone number on it. 'Call me.'

Lachlan pocketed the note and tried not to smile too much, but he could tell by Morag's expanding grin that he'd failed miserably. 'Thanks. I will.'

In the dying minutes of injury time, he thought he might have just nabbed a winner.

****

The journey to Alloa had passed in a blur. Lachlan had made two phone calls that morning. One arranging to meet Morag the following Saturday in Princes Street Gardens. *As friends obviously*, she'd said. *Tiny increments*, he'd thought. The second to Johnny, asking if he'd be up for a visitor.

Johnny's front garden was small but well tended. Laid to gravel on either side of a path that led to a large timber front door guarded on either side by carefully trimmed conifers.

He reached for the iron ring and knocked twice. He looked back at his flatmate's car, borrowed for the day - the engine ticking away as it cooled. Beyond this were the trees that lined the park. Johnny's house was a fine old merchant's villa. He appeared to have done very well for himself.

Marrying the boss's daughter could do that to a man, he supposed.

He heard a clunk as a deadbolt was slipped back. The door opened inwards without a whisper and there, in all her splendour, was Mandy. He'd hoped Johnny might have answered, but at least this gave them a moment alone. She offered a tight-mouthed smile. 'Hello.'

'Hi Mandy,' said Lachlan. She didn't appear to be inviting him in. 'I take it Johnny told you I was coming?'

She nodded, 'He did. Sorry. In you come.'

Lachlan paused on the step for a moment, 'Look Mandy, I'm sorry. I'm sorry about leaving you like that.'

Mandy sighed, 'That was years ago Lachlan. Things have changed. I obviously had some news for you that day, but you kind of took the wind out of my sails.' She glanced down at the tiled floor.

'You should have said,' Lachlan lowered his head, trying to regain eye contact.

'Maybe I should, but here we are.' She shrugged. Then, after another moment's silence, added, 'And well. Things were complicated.'

Lachlan nodded and chewed the inside of his cheek. 'You were shagging my best mate I suppose.'

Mandy snorted and a faint smile appeared on her face. She was still beautiful. Motherhood agreed with her. Lachlan thought of saying this but decided against it. 'Aye there was that.' She changed the subject. 'What's that?' and pointed at the parcel under Lachlan's arm.

'Oh, wee present for…' Lachlan still struggled to say his name.

'Billy?' said Mandy. 'You shouldn't have.'

From the back of the house, Lachlan heard a door slam. A draught blew down the hallway. 'Is that Lachie-boy?' called Johnny from within.

'Come in Lachlan,' she said, suddenly putting on the genial host act. 'No hard feelings eh?'

She turned and walked back to the kitchen. 'I'll let you boys catch up, I'll get the tea on.'

You boys, thought Lachlan and his stomach clenched. The last time he'd seen Billy, he was in nappies. He also hadn't known then that the toddler who smelled like shit and had a constant line of green snot approaching his upper lip was his flesh and blood.

'Found it alright then?' said Johnny as he entered the hall. He closed the kitchen door and ushered Lachlan into the living room.

'Aye, not many houses like this here are there?' joked Lachlan. He looked up at the cornicing, and the large sofa occupying the bay window. A TV stood on a wheeled stand by the fireplace. In the centre of the floor was an elaborate rug, covered in Matchbox cars.

Johnny opened a sideboard and pulled out a couple of heavy-based glasses and a crystal decanter. 'Whisky?' he asked, not waiting for an answer.

'Just a wee one,' Lachlan said as Johnny poured two generous measures.

'Cheers,' said Johnny, clinking glasses. 'Come on, sit down.'

Lachlan dropped to one end of the sofa and Johnny took the other. There was another armchair in the room but it was so far away that any conversation would have required shouting.

'The wee lad's out the back, still trying to do the Joe Jordan goal.'

'I didn't see it,' said Lachlan, 'Any good?'

'Flicked it up from a cross and battered it in on the volley. A cracker.'

'Not enough though,' said Lachlan sipping at the smooth whisky.

Johnny nodded slowly. 'Nah. There's always Argentina. We'll do better next time.'

'Ever the optimist,' laughed Lachlan.

'Always the pessimist,' Johnny chuckled. 'So, are you okay with this? Meeting him, I mean.'

Lachlan sat up. The small talk hadn't lasted, now they were onto the real business of the day. 'Aye. If you are.'

Johnny took a drink. 'As long as you're not going to get possessive, or anything like that. He's a good few years away from knowing the truth, and he's… well, you know he's getting in bother at school. We don't want anything else to get in the way.'

'It won't Johnny. I promise. I just feel like I need to see him. Since you told me, it's been eating away at me. I've set up a savings account for him.'

Johnny shook his head, 'You didn't need to do that. We're not short of cash for fuck's sake.' He made a vague gesture that took in the whole house and its grounds.

Lachlan looked up at the chandelier and said, 'I know that. It's for him though, not you. I can just hand the money over when he's eighteen or something. He can do what he likes with it.'

'If it helps clear your conscience, I suppose,' said Johnny as he drained his whisky.

Lachlan spluttered, 'What? You were the one that was doing the dirty with my girlfriend Johnny, let's not forget that.'

'Well, aye,' said Johnny. 'Want another one?' He held up his empty glass.

'Fuck it. Aye, go on.'

'I loved her. You didn't,' Johnny said.

'And you still do?' asked Lachlan.

Johnny said nothing as he poured two more measures. The clock on the wall ticked loudly and Lachlan sank back into the folds of the sofa.

Johnny was just about to sit when the door to the living room swung open and in barged Billy. He glanced at Lachlan and stopped in his tracks. 'Who's he?'

Lachlan took a large mouthful and said, 'I'm your dad's pal, Lachlan. Pleased to meet you.' He stood and offered a hand.

Billy grinned, as if unused to such formalities and shook Lachlan's hand. There was no doubting that Lachlan was his father. He had the same mouth, ears, nose, hair. It was like looking down a time-tunnel into the past. 'So your dad was telling me you're the next Joe Jordan?'

Billy grinned and wiped his nose. 'Aye,' he turned to Johnny. 'I did it Dad, and you didn't see it. Flicked it up and volleyed it, like he did. Right into the net.'

'Well done son, I'm sure you'll be able to do it again,' said Johnny.

'Took me all fucking morning, I doubt it,' Billy spluttered.

'Hey! What have I told you about using language like that? Lachlan works for the government. He'll put you in jail.'

'Will you mister? Can you do that?' asked Billy, wide-eyed.

Lachlan grinned, 'Oh aye. I'm what you call an Executive Officer,' he delivered the job title in a voice he hoped suggested gravitas.

'What's that mean?' asked Billy.

'It means I can execute people.'

'Really?'

'Really,' said Lachlan with a scowl. 'But you're in luck. I'm off duty today, so I brought you a present instead.'

'Is he winding me up Dad?'

Johnny shrugged. Lachlan tossed the parcel towards Billy. He caught it and ripped it open.

'Scotland away strip!' he beamed.

'So you'll be even more like Joe Jordan. I thought you might already have the home strip.' He looked at Johnny, who nodded.

'Thanks mister,' he wrestled himself into the top and ran out of the room, slamming the door behind him.

Lachlan sat back and for a moment they sat in silence. Billy seemed happy here, that was all that mattered, and Lachlan felt no paternal pangs, or at least none he was aware of.

'Well?' said Johnny.

'That's a fine wee boy you've got there,' said Lachlan.

Johnny offered his tumbler to Lachlan. A simple clink of glasses, and no more needed to be said.

'Dinner's ready!' called Mandy from the kitchen.

'You hungry?' asked Johnny.

'Always,' said Lachlan. They rose together and drained the last of their whiskies.

'After you,' said Lachlan at the living room door.

'Yes, you were,' said Johnny with a wink.

Lachlan shook his head but couldn't keep the smile from his face. 'You're an absolute bastard Johnny.'

****

Dinner had been pleasant enough. Lots of small talk about the brewery and the Geological Survey and living in Edinburgh and *was Lachlan seeing anyone* and *yes he was*, sort of. Or at least he hoped to be. He hadn't gone into too many details.

'There, done,' said Billy, tipping his plate towards Mandy.

'Ok, off you go and play,' she said.

She seemed to have taken to motherhood. The Mandy of old had gone, replaced by a slightly defrosted version. She'd kept her figure, he noticed, carefully, and her hair had returned to a dirty blonde, free now of the peroxide she'd poured on it in the 60s.

'Cup of tea?' she asked as she rose from her seat. She gathered the plates into a pile. 'You're on the dishes.'

'Yes dear,' said Johnny. 'Think we'll have something stronger. Another whisky Lachlan?'

'I can't Johnny, got to drive back.'

'Oh give it a rest, one more won't hurt,' Johnny said as he opened a cupboard. Inside was a healthy selection of whiskies, vodka, rum, and something wrapped in wicker that looked like it had been brought back from somewhere foreign and hot.

'Twist my arm why don't you. Okay, one more. For the road, as they say.'

'Good man. Right let's see…' Johnny scanned the cupboard's contents and pulled out a bottle with a label Lachlan didn't recognise. 'This is nice stuff.' He pulled the cork and poured two glasses, leaving the bottle on the bunker.

'Thought you'd be taking it easy after last night,' said Mandy as she dried her hands on a towel.

Johnny mumbled something under his breath, then added, 'Do you want one?'

Mandy appeared shocked, 'Thanks for asking dear, but no.' She shook the towel and hung it on a rail. 'I'll leave you boys to it. Lachlan, you can dry.'

'Aye no problem Mandy. Thanks for dinner, it was lovely.' He sat back and patted his belly.

Mandy glanced at Lachlan's swollen gut, and left the room.

Lachlan watched the closed door for a moment, feeling the atmosphere change, then took a sip of the whisky. It was was even smoother than the one in the living room. 'Christ that's nice, what is it?' He glanced towards the bottle, leaning back in his chair for a better look at the label. He couldn't make it out, but was that a set of compasses embossed in gold?

'Oh just a wee present,' said Johnny. 'From some friends.'

Lachlan swept some crumbs into his hand, then dropped them back on the table in a neat pile. 'So you were steaming last night? Where'd you watch the game? The Highlander? Do they even have a telly?'

Johnny laughed, 'Christ no. My Highlander days are over. Haven't been there in years. I was in a…' he paused. 'A club.'

Lachlan knew where this was going. 'A private member's club?'

'Something like that aye,' said Johnny.

Lachlan took another mouthful of the whisky. It lit a pleasant fire in his belly. He narrowed his eyes and looked at Johnny, 'Are you a mason?'

Johnny bristled in his chair, wiped his mouth and chin with one hand, then said, 'What do you think?'

Lachlan made a quizzical face. 'Well, Mandy's dad is, and you seem to be climbing the corporate ladder fairly quickly, so I'd hazard a guess that, aye, you've joined the funny handshake brigade.'

Johnny laughed, 'Guilty as charged.' He knocked the last of his whisky back then grabbed the bottle from the bunker. He placed it squarely between them so Lachlan could read the label.

'Grand Master Mason's Choice,' Lachlan said, turning the bottle with one hand. 'Well, when the whisky's this good I can't blame you I suppose.'

Johnny shrugged, 'Just sort of fell into it to be honest. Mandy's dad can be quite persuasive.'

'Quite fucking terrifying too, as far as I remember,' Lachlan said.

'Aye there's that,' Johnny placed both hands on the table, palms up. 'Look, don't hate me for it Lachlan. It's just the way it is.'

Lachlan looked around the well-appointed kitchen and out at the expanse of lawn where Billy was busy commentating on his own footballing prowess. Johnny was living the high life, that was clear, and Lachlan couldn't find it in himself to hold it against him. He had nothing he wanted.

It's Scotland, he thought, *it's just the way it is.*

****

The path through Princes Street Gardens was dappled with spots of sunlight filtering through the trees. There wasn't a breath of wind down here, between the ancient rock of the castle and the New Town's shops, and Lachlan was feeling similarly breathless.

'Do you want a cone?' he asked as they passed an ice cream van, parked beside the fountain.

'A Ninety-Nine if you can stretch to it,' said Morag. 'Are you okay? You're not saying much?'

This was true. They'd batted some pleasantries back and forth as they'd walked, but without the crutch of alcohol Lachlan felt somewhat off-balance.

'I'm fine,' he said after he'd placed his order. 'I'm just aware that, well, it's been a long time eh? We've a lot to catch up on. A lot to tell each other?'

'Well I've pretty much filled you in. It's your turn.'

Lachlan fumbled for change as their cones were placed in a little wire holder on the counter. Morag had summarised the intervening years. Her parents divorce; Her mum's move to Glasgow; and her new life in Edinburgh with her dad. He still lived here, tending to his allotment somewhere out in the suburbs, and she'd moved into her flat in Leith a few years back, after five years sharing with some actors and artists.

They took a bench, Lachlan first checking for spillages, suspicious stains, and pigeon shit. Morag didn't bother. She leaned back, stretched her legs out and crossed them at the ankles. 'Go on then.'

Lachlan took a bite of his flake and watched an elderly couple walk past hand-in-hand. He was suddenly aware of the birdsong all around. The trees were full of blackbirds singing, pigeons cooing, and magpies chattering. This really was a little piece of paradise in the city centre.

Here goes. He felt sick.

'Okay, well. Stirling you know about.'

'The body?' asked Morag, licking her cone.

'Aye. Pretty horrible really, but in a way, it was a good thing, because,' he paused. 'Well, I think I said in my letter that I was getting bullied.'

'Poor wee thing,' said Morag, sticking out her bottom lip.

Lachlan squirmed, aware that his cheeks were reddening. 'Anyway, he stopped bullying me after he got a kicking. He stopped bullying altogether in fact. Not just me.'

'Every cloud,' said Morag as she inspected her cone - choosing where to attack it next.

'So, my dad kept drinking and I just kept busy with my hobbies, you know - history books and painting.' He paused, 'Have you still got my flagstone?'

Morag raised her eyebrows. '*Your* flagstone? The Saltire? I seem to remember it was a present.'

'Aye of course it was. Anyway doesn't matter. I just-'

'I still have it Lachlan. On my fireplace.'

Lachlan gulped at the thought of his remaining collection, and a gap he'd absent-mindedly created in the middle of them just a week ago. Would they be reunited? He tried hard to conceal a smile.

Their eyes locked for a moment before Morag took what Lachlan perceived as a provocative lick of her ice cream and said, 'Alloa?'

'Alloa,' repeated Lachlan, in at attempt to recalibrate the conversation. 'Yes. Well, I moved there after working beside my dad for a bit. Worked at a petrol station, then got a job at the brewery.'

'So what about your girlfriend? Brigitte Bardot?'

Lachlan recalled his father's funeral, when Morag and Mandy had briefly met. Morag turning to go, and him climbing back into the car with Mandy, but feeling like he just wanted to run to Morag's father's battered old Rover with the missing hubcap.

'Yes, well,' Lachlan finished his cone and wiped his hands clean. A slight breeze blew through the gardens causing sunlight to dance momentarily across Morag's face. 'Mandy. Let's talk about Mandy.' He sat back and placed his hands on his knees. 'Mandy was a barmaid that we all fancied. Well, most of us. Well, aye, all of us I suppose. Even the old guys in the pub. She was very popular.'

'Yet she chose you?' said Morag. 'Joking!' she patted Lachlan on the knee. 'Go on.'

'Well, aye, she did and we went out for a bit. Turned out she was my boss's daughter. It was all a bit messy.'

'Never dip your pen in the company ink,' said Morag waggling her finger.

'She wasn't company ink, as such. Anyway, after my dad's funeral, things started going a bit downhill.'

'Why was that?' asked Morag. Lachlan knew why, and he suspected Morag did too.

'We just sort of drifted apart. And I didn't feel much connection to Alloa anymore.'

'*Much* connection?' Morag asked. Damn she was perceptive.

Lachlan took a deep breath, 'But there have been a few developments, recently.'

Her eyes seemed to bore a hole in him, searching for elaboration. 'Uhuh?'

'Yes,' Lachlan said, with the realisation that he'd come this far and there was no stopping now. 'Well, here's how it is.' He paused and cleared his throat. 'I find myself in the unexpected position of, erm, well…' He trailed off and tried again. 'I've discovered that I've unwillingly taken on the role of… no. I'm what you call a, umm, how can I put this?'

'In words?' suggested Morag.

Lachlan thought that this was certainly the correct answer. He had the feeling Morag was right about most things.

He took a deep breath. Then said, 'I'm a father.'

The tree above them suddenly emptied of birds. A hundred wings beat their way into the blue sky. A single white dollop of bird shit landed on the path in front of them.

'A father!?' Morag yelped.

Lachlan slumped forward, somewhat relieved to have finally delivered the news. He stole a sideways glance at Morag. Did she look disappointed? Crestfallen? No. She was beaming. He looked her in the eyes. There was something there, behind the smile. Perhaps just a hint that she was playing a role.

'Yes,' he sighed. 'To a wee boy called Billy.'

'How old is he?' asked Morag. She'd moved along the bench marginally. Lachlan could feel the heat from her body and had to fidget with his collar to cool himself down.

'Eight.'

Morag's eyes danced as she counted backwards. 'And when did you leave Alloa?'

'Nine years ago,' Lachlan said. 'So, he's Mandy's, yes.' He searched Morag's face for a response but either she was genuinely non-plussed by this, or she was a better actor than he thought.

'Gosh,' said Morag. She swept her hair back behind her ears and looked down at the pavement where a pigeon was pecking at the remains of a discarded cigarette.

'But, and here's where it gets complicated, I didn't know he was mine until the other week.'

Morag stood up and to Lachlan's surprise, grabbed his hand. 'Come on, let's walk some more, you can tell me all about it.'

****

The Scott Monument towered above them. A blackened gothic rocket ship preparing to launch Sir Walter's statue into orbit. Lachlan peered up at the pinnacle, glad that he'd reached the end of his story.

'And you and Johnny are okay with it all?' asked Morag.

He shrugged, 'Aye. Weird though it seems. From his point of view, he loves the wee guy, and has done for years. Why wouldn't he? He thought Billy was his flesh and blood up until recently. Mandy's happy, because otherwise, if she'd stuck with Johnny they would never have had kids. And me? I'm just pleased for both of them.'

Morag looked at Lachlan and smiled. 'Well, it's all worked out beautifully hasn't it?'

Lachlan puffed out his cheeks. 'Suppose so.' They were nearing the end of the gardens, and getting perilously close to the Cafe Royal where Morag would soon be starting her shift. They still had an hour to kill though and Lachlan didn't want the afternoon to end. He glanced upwards. 'Fancy a climb?'

Morag followed his eyes, 'The monument? I've never been up there in all the years I've lived here. Why not?'

They ducked into the tiny entrance hallway and paid the admission fee.

'Two hundred and eighty seven steps. Two hundred feet high.

And six inches, if you care about the finer details,' said the sweating lump of an attendant.

'After you,' said Lachlan, allowing Morag to enter the cool stone staircase first.

They soon emerged onto the first viewing platform. Morag first, Lachlan wheezing behind her.

'Oh this is fab!' Morag said grabbing the ramparts and leaning over. 'We're not high enough though. Come on.'

Lachlan looked over the edge and felt dizzy, then looked upwards at the remaining structure still towering above them. 'Aye, slowly though eh? I'm struggling.'

The steps to the second platform were narrower and ran in a tighter spiral. They met a procession of Japanese tourists on their way down and pressed themselves against the outer wall to let them pass. Morag smiled at each passing tourist while Lachlan pretended to find some interesting graffiti on the wall. Eventually, the staircase ahead cleared and they pressed on.

'Wow,' said Morag as she stepped onto the second level. 'This is more like it.' They edged around the platform quickly taking in the panoramic views over the city, but Morag still didn't seem satisfied. She looked up towards the pointed peak. A black dart jabbing into the azure sky. 'Nearly there. How's your lungs?'

Lachlan groaned. 'Fine. Go on then.' They ducked into the final tiny doorway and climbed the single-file spiral that leaned ever-inwards as they neared the summit. Eventually, exhausted and dizzy, they stepped out onto the small platform at the peak of the tower. A cool breeze blew Morag's hair over her face. When she cleared it away she was smiling her familiar ear-to-ear smile.

'What?' panted Lachlan. He was incapable of anything more erudite at this stage.

Morag looked north, over the New Town towards the green fields of distant Fife. Above the rooftops the Firth of Forth sparkled in the sun - as blue as the sky above.

'Our river,' said Morag.

He grasped the stone balustrade and looked out over the city towards the Forth. It was *their* river! The river they'd splashed about in as children. Morag in her wellies, her fishing net over her shoulder. The day they'd parted, when she'd kissed him and he felt like he was at the centre of the universe. *It was their river.* And here they stood, together again at last, gazing out towards this body of water, born where they were born. The tiny river that had matured into an estuary and now made its slow and steady way to the sea.

'I've been meaning to ask you something,' Lachlan said.

'Uhuh?' said Morag, turning slightly towards him.

'What was in the *message in a bottle* you sent me?'

Morag's eyes twinkled. 'That would be telling.' She moved closer, he could feel her heat against his leg.

A wave of nausea swept upwards from his feet - a combination of utter exhaustion, unexpected vertigo, and all-too-familiar gut-wrenching nerves. *Now is the time,* he thought, *don't blow it.*

Morag tipped her head to one side, and ran a hand down his arm.

Lachlan gulped. Then did nothing.

The moment passed and they stared out at the river and the rooftops, side-by-side, but still apart.

'We'll better get down then,' said Morag after some time, with an air of disappointment. 'Shame, it's nice up here.'

Lachlan managed a laugh, but his eyes remained on his baseball boots. Two hundred feet didn't sound like a lot, but from up here, he may as well have been orbiting the Earth in a rocket with failing engines. Had he screwed up possibly the most important moment of his life? He was overcome with a sudden gloom.

Hello darkness my old friend. His internal jukebox never let him down.

'Aye, let's go,' he said.

Morag edged past him as he straightened up. There was barely room to move up here and for a moment their bodies were pressed together. 'I'll lead the way,' she said, locking eyes with him for a moment.

Lachlan gestured towards the doorway that would take them back down to earth.

'After you,' he said then screamed a silent scream at the sky.

As they descended, they heard footsteps on the stairs ahead.

'Coming down!' called Morag.

There was a grunt of acknowledgement and the sound of footsteps receding.

Morag reached the exit first and stepped quickly out onto the mid-level platform where a sweating middle-aged man wearing National Health glasses and, given the weather, an unnecessary yellow tartan scarf waited to ascend. Lachlan followed and nodded at the man. 'Alright?'

The man nodded. Lachlan stepped aside and let him into the stairs.

'This any better for you?' asked Morag, spreading her hands out towards the view. The clock on the North British Hotel showed that they didn't have much time left. Arthur's Seat, Edinburgh's little bit of the Highlands, sat imperiously to the south-east, a dozen tiny stick-like figures atop the summit.

'I think I need a drink of water, can we just get down?'

Morag rolled her eyes, 'Aye okay. I need to start work in twenty minutes anyway. What are you up to tonight?'

Lachlan hadn't made any plans. He hadn't really thought beyond this afternoon, if he was honest. 'Nothing,' he said, truthfully. *I'll spend all night beating myself up in total torment*, he thought to himself, also truthfully.

They entered the final staircase and made their way back down to ground level. With each step he knew his time was running out. Maybe they could reschedule? He wanted to tell Morag about her cheating boy-friend. Or did he? He had to confess, despite himself, he had enjoyed Josh's company the previous weekend. Maybe he should just ask her? *Morag, I've been thinking about you almost every day since we were re-united at my father's funeral, and I think…* What? That he loved her? That would be crazy. She'd run a mile.

Tiny increments, he reminded himself. *Tiny increments.*

They emerged into the late afternoon crowd ambling through the gardens. Some hurried with bags of shopping, trying to catch their trains or buses; some drifted like branches in a stream, meandering this way and that, just enjoying the sunshine and the views; some were intertwined, arms locked in easy familiarity. Lachlan and Morag remained apart as they turned towards the garden's gates.

Morag edged them towards the side of the path and stepped onto the grass, separating them from the flow of people.

'Okay,' she said, checking her watch. 'I need to get to work now.'

He glanced up at the clock tower. 'Yeah, you do.'

'You're just an office boy Lachlan. All those steps must have killed you. Look,' she chewed the inside of her cheek, then furrowed her brow. 'Why don't you come into the pub again tonight?'

Lachlan tried to keep his cool. 'Aye, could do. Will your… will Josh be there?'

Her shoulders slumped and she shook her head. 'Josh and me are finished.'

He felt himself straighten up. Like he was a half-deflated inflatable and someone had switched on the air-pump. He tried to look disappointed. 'Oh… I'm sorry.'

She flashed a smile then looked away, 'Well, he wasn't exactly what you'd call faithful.'

'You knew?'

Morag turned her head slightly, 'What do you mean? You mean *you* knew?'

Lachlan, always right in there with his size ten feet. 'No, well, yes, I mean I wasn't sure, but I did see him with someone before your show that night.'

Morag lowered her head, 'Yeah, well. That'd be one of them, probably. There were others. He wasn't even smart enough to hide it from me. All his little phone calls from the pub, like I was an idiot.'

'You're not an idiot,' said Lachlan, trying not to sound too pathetic but failing.

'Well you are,' laughed Morag.

He grinned and while thinking of a response heard a scream, followed by an almighty thump

Suddenly, he was aware that all eyes were on him and Morag. He looked quickly around, a woman was staring at them with her hand over her mouth. Or was she? No, she was staring past them. He looked beyond Morag, who looked similarly confused, and ten feet behind her shoulder, lying on the grass in a twisted heap, was a middle-aged man. His National Health glasses still on his face, but skewed and broken.

Slowly, a yellow tartan scarf floated to the ground beside him.

Lachlan grabbed Morag just as she turned but it was too late, she'd seen the wrecked body. He turned her towards him and she buried her head in his shoulder.

He walked backwards, leading her away from the scene as a crowd gathered. Shoppers stopped at the railings separating the gardens from Princes Street, staring in disbelief. A man in a white shirt hurried through the crowd. 'I'm a doctor,' he called. 'It's not a doctor he needs, it's a hearse,' muttered an old woman.

Why that man had chosen this fine summer afternoon to end his life, Lachlan would never know, but he was suddenly struck with the thought that he was probably the last person to speak to him. Poor bastard. He couldn't help himself and looked back towards the crumpled body. The doctor was feeling for a pulse and shaking his head, which seemed unnecessary given the guy had just fallen two hundred feet onto the hard, unyielding earth.

Morag kept her head pushed firmly into Lachlan's shoulder as they backed away from the gathering crowd. He leaned back against a tree and she looked up, slowly, her eyes wet with tears. At that moment, in her eyes, he sensed something. It was as if the intervening years had disappeared and they were still nine-year-olds, awkwardly kissing on the banks of the river.

'It said *I miss you*,' said Morag.

'Eh?'

'The message in a bottle,' she glanced down. 'Sent in 1951, lost in the post I guess.'

This time, it was Lachlan who initiated the kiss. He touched her chin, pointing her face upwards. Morag parted her lips slightly as he kissed her, and he knew at that moment, as death visited him once more, that they were finally together.

FRIDAY

'Chapping,' said Fraser, frowning at his dominos.

Lachlan placed a double-five on the table.

'Fifty five eh?' wheezed Bob, an ex-miner with lung and identity problems. 'You hate that eh?'

'Fuck off Bob,' said Lachlan. He was referring to the 55/45 independence referendum result. Nearly four years ago now, but Bob still saw himself as being on the winning side. Lachlan looked at Bob's pock-marked face, his bloated body gurgled with every breath. Nobody visited Bob. His loyalism didn't seem to have brought much reward.

'Grandad!'

Lachlan sat up at the familiar voice.

'Phoebe!' He pushed himself out of his chair. 'Sorry gents, I was winning anyway.'

In the hallway, his daughter was chatting to Stella. They parted with a smile.

'Hello,' said Lachlan. 'This is a nice surprise.'

'Just thought we'd pop in. How are you?'

Back in his room he told her all about his week, but not the news he'd been given at the hospital.

She walked to the window and wiped some dust from the leaves of the pink and yellow begonia. Outside, the sun was creeping over the lawn.

'Any word on getting moved upstairs?'

He pondered this as Phoebe bounced and giggled on the bed. *Yes actually, but from the doctor, and not the upstairs you're thinking about.*

'Nothing yet,' he said. He'd asked several months back to be moved to a room with a better view but it was really dependent on which resident was wheeled out next by the undertakers.

'Oh well, I'm sure you'll hear soon. Listen, I'm off on Monday so we're taking you out. Anything you fancy doing?'

He stepped to the window and thought for a moment, then turned the begonia so the newest flowers faced the light. 'Can we go to the beach?'

LEiTH, 1979

'Three hundred for you, three hundred for me,' said Morag, dumping a pile of leaflets on the coffee table next to Lachlan's slippered feet.

'Three hundred?!' He lowered his newspaper. 'I bet I've got all the tenements?'

'Sure do sucker. It'll do you good.' She nodded at Lachlan's stomach, where their cat Winnie snoozed.

He sat up and grabbed a leaflet, dislodging Winnie, who fired a disgusted glance at him before sloping under the table. It featured a vivid blue saltire, the word YES, and the message 'Vote Positively'. He scanned through the remaining text. All bark, no bite. Self respect. The future of Scotland is in our hands.

'Very good,' he said. 'Cup of tea first?'

'Go on then.' Morag flopped onto the settee. 'And be a dear and stick a wash on too.' She picked up the discarded newspaper and flicked it open.

Lachlan left the tiny living room, followed by Winnie mooching for something to eat. He stepped into the even smaller kitchen, found an open can of Kit-e-Kat, and forked some into her bowl. He flicked the switch on the kettle and clicked on the radio cassette player on the window ledge. Beside this was a pile of letters and bills, weighed down with a perfectly smooth round pebble, painted with the saltire. His flagstone. Now *their* flagstone.

Outside the window, their neighbours - an elderly couple called Tom and Moira walked up the path. He waved and Moira waved back. Tom didn't. He never did. Lachlan suspected that Tom didn't trust the young nationalists next door. He was a Labour man, through and through, and even though some of the Labour party's Scottish representatives were backing a Yes vote in the forthcoming referendum, he'd said he wasn't comfortable with it. He reminded Lachlan of his father. Some things never changed.

The radio DJ announced the new number one and he turned it up. The opening riff of Blondie's *Heart of Glass* filled the kitchen and after a few beats, Lachlan joined in with Debbie Harry's falsetto.

'WASHING!' yelled Morag from the living room.

'Oh aye, sorry. Kettle's on,' he called back. He returned to the hall and side-stepped into their minuscule bedroom. When these colony flats were built, how did families manage to live in them? Were the people of Leith shorter in the 19th Century?

He bundled up some washing and returned to the kitchen where he stuffed it into their shiny new washing machine. No more launderettes for the McCormack-Paterson household, they were moving up in the world.

'Hey did you read this?' Morag called from the living room as Lachlan dropped the teabags into the bin.

'What?' he said, returning with the tea.

'The polls have slipped again. Shows the power the bloody papers have. We were at sixty-three percent last year. Now we're at fifty-four.'

'Oh dear,' he said. 'Still a win surely?'

'Not with that Labour amendment it's not.' Morag blew on her tea.

'Oh aye, the forty percent thing?'

'Bloody disgrace,' Morag muttered, placing her mug on the table and balling her fists. 'Even if we win, we'll lose. They're effectively counting the dead against us, do you realise that? Dead folk that are still on the electoral register. And non-voters. How can we compete against that?'

Lachlan's head swirled with the arithmetic and failed to come to a solution. All he knew was that a Labour MP had tabled an amendment stating that forty percent of the entire electorate had to back the proposed Scottish Assembly for it to pass. So, non-voters, and the recently deceased, would all be counted against them. Dirty tricks, but only what he'd come to expect. 'We can only do our best, I suppose. So sup up and let's get out with these leaflets.'

****

An icy chill met them as Lachlan pulled the front door closed. The ground still packed with snow that showed no sign of shifting. They paused for a moment while Morag handed Lachlan a list of flat numbers. 'These are yours. Easter Road, first twelve doors on either side.'

'All tenements?'

'Mostly. It'll do you good. Should only take an hour or two.'

'And you'll be doing the colonies and the main road? All the nice ground-level easy stuff I suppose?'

Morag smiled her smile and nodded. 'Exactly, now off you go. If you're good I'll buy you a pint in the Percy afterwards.'

'Deal,' said Lachlan.

They parted with a kiss and he made his way slowly towards Easter Road, his feet skittering over the ice. A bitter wind howled down the gully of tenements as he approached the first doorway and a few drops of snow started falling from the cold February sky. Some of the door's flaking red paint came away in his hand. Inside, the stairwell was cold and dark with a faint smell of urine and rotting food.

He climbed to the top floor and pulled out the first leaflet. Always safer to work your way down from the top, as it limited the chance of being confronted by an objectionable tenant. You were out the main door before they'd had time to see what had been dropped through their letterbox.

Six leaflets were delivered without incident, but as he dropped the seventh through a letterbox on the first floor he heard a click from within and the door swung open. The smell of alcohol hit him first. A woman of indeterminate age stood leaning on the doorframe.

'What's this?' she croaked in a voice that suggested she was a sixty-a-day smoker.

'Leaflet,' said Lachlan. Was there any point explaining?

'What's it about?'

'Devolution,' he offered. 'The referendum on a Scottish Assembly?'

'Never fucking heard of it. Politics is it?'

'Aye you could say that,' said Lachlan with a sigh.

'What party?' she eyed Lachlan up and down in a way that made his neck itch.

'No party. It's a vote to bring more powers to Scotland.'

She barked, emitting a throaty laugh. 'And what fucking use is that?'

'Well,' Lachlan took a deep breath. 'Read the leaflet and you'll see.' He backed away, pulling another leaflet from his satchel. The woman remained leaning on her door frame.

'Do you fancy a drink?' she asked.

'Eh? No thanks. Lots to do sorry.'

'Come on. Nice guy like you,' she tossed her matted hair aside in a manner she possibly thought seductive. 'I've just opened a bottle of voddy, come on in.'

'Bye!' Lachlan said as he scurried down the stairs for the exit.

'Your loss,' she cackled from above.

He stepped outside into the beginning of a blizzard and shook his head, she wasn't even going to vote, which was as good as a 'no' vote.

Across the road, the lights from the Persevere bar shone bright in the gloom of the afternoon.

****

'She what?!' laughed Morag, spluttering into her drink.

'Invited me in!' said Lachlan. 'And I don't think it was because she wanted to discuss devolution.'

'You wee devil!' Morag's eyes were alight with mischief, sparkling in the low light of the pub.

Outside, the blizzard had taken hold and the snow was blowing horizontally. Inside, all was warmth, good cheer, and reasonably priced beer. Hibernian's match had been postponed and the place was packed with supporters enjoying a Saturday afternoon free of one of their team's usually erratic, often disappointing but, just occasionally, brilliant performances.

Lachlan and Morag had squeezed into a table along the wall and sat side-by-side on the leather bench, beneath timber panels and a tiled mural depicting 19th Century golfers on Leith Links. This had become their home-from-home since they'd moved here four years previously.

'I wouldn't have done anything,' said Lachlan, supping his beer.

'And you're such a gigolo too. Shut up you idiot I know you wouldn't have done anything. Anyway, did you get all the leaflets delivered?'

'Aye, although I dumped the last hundred in the train station.'

Morag looked towards the windows, where the remains of Leith's once grand railway station were barely visible through the snow. 'You'll better not have.'

'Of course I didn't. All delivered, for all the good it'll do.'

'Now now,' said Morag, tapping the table with her finger. 'What's that thing you always say? *Tiny increments?*'

'Aye,' Lachlan flipped a beermat on the table.

'This is just one battle in a long war. We can't give up the fight.'

'I won't,' he said, flipping the beermat again.

'Good, because I'm getting another six hundred leaflets next weekend.'

'Oh for fuck's sake,' Lachlan said, dropping the beermat on the floor. 'Can't we do normal things? Like normal couples?'

'Of course we can. We've got our wee road trip tomorrow remember? Will the car be okay?'

He looked out at the snow, which showed no sign of abating. 'It'll be fine. It's the roads I'm worried about.'

'Well stop worrying. A bit of positive thinking wouldn't go amiss.'

'Suppose not. I'm positively thinking I fancy another pint though, do you?'

Morag eyed the throng at the bar. 'No, you have one though. Get me an orange juice.'

'Boring,' said Lachlan as he edged past the table.

Morag threw a beermat at him, hitting his arse. 'Early start tomorrow pal.'

****

'Take a left here,' said Morag.

'Eh? But we're nearly there,' said Lachlan, as he lifted his foot from the accelerator.

'Wee detour,' she said.

He tapped the brakes gently and slowed for the junction. The road was clear of snow, but there was a crystalline sheen on everything today. The sky was clear, and the low winter sun dazzled him briefly as he turned off the main road to Aberfoyle.

'This is the loch road,' said Lachlan. 'If you think I'm going swimming you've another thing coming.'

Morag chuckled, 'I've got my costume, did you not bring your trunks?'

The road was narrower here, with snow piled in large drifts at either side. They'd set off from Edinburgh at ten, his hangover not too bad from the previous night and the roads were quiet. Sunday morning in the not-quite Scottish Highlands was still a time for either church or a lie-in. They'd planned a visit to Lachlan's parents' shared grave, in Aberfoyle's little cemetery, but Morag's unannounced diversion had taken him by surprise.

'Is it the island?' Lachlan asked. In all the years they'd lived in Aberfoyle, he'd never once set foot on Loch Inchmahome's little island sanctuary - the ruined priory there was a tourists' favourite.

'Might be,' said Morag. 'A little pilgrimage, if you like.'

Lachlan glimpsed the loch through the trees to his right, dazzling in the sunlight as he carefully negotiated the narrow road. He looked at Morag as she squinted through the trees.

'The ferry only runs in the summer,' he said as they approached the small car-park. 'See,' he pointed ahead. 'The car park's empty. No ferry.'

Morag shielded her eyes from the sun and stared towards the loch just as they passed a gap in the trees. Her face lit up. 'Ha! We won't need the ferry, look!'

Out on the loch, halfway to the island, was a bizarre sight. A group of men, some hunched over, some slowly drifting - furiously scrubbing the surface of the loch with brooms.

It was frozen solid.

'Wow,' said Lachlan as he parked and yanked the handbrake.

They stared out towards the island nestled in the centre of the loch. The entire surface was marked out with what appeared to be dozens of clusters of concentric circles. As well as the first group of men, they spotted another few dotted around - their breath rising in clouds.

'Crazy eh?' said Morag.

'Curling? Aye, always seemed a bit of a niche sport to me,' said

Lachlan. 'Come on,' he opened his door and was hit by the bitterly cold air. It froze the breath in his lungs. He pulled the door closed again. The car had warmed up nicely on their journey, and it'd be a shame to waste all that heat.

'Saw it on the news this week,' Morag said. 'The Bonspiel. Think you were in the toilet.'

'The bon what?' asked Lachlan with a hint of annoyance. It was true though, he was pretty regular and she had a point - he usually did miss a chunk of the news every night as he locked himself away in their microscopic WC.

'The Grand Match. Only happens when the ice is eight inches thick. Hasn't been one since 1963. There were thousands of curlers here on Wednesday. North versus South.'

A cheer went up from the lake. Hands were shaken and hip flasks were removed from jacket pockets.

'So you want to walk to the island?' asked Lachlan.

'Aye,' said Morag. 'It'll be fun.'

Lachlan considered his definition of 'fun' and a series of images came to mind: Watching Doctor Who; Drinking in The Percy; Snuggling in with Morag and Winnie in front of a roaring fire; Eating chips; Staring into space.

Sliding across a frozen lake in sub-zero temperatures featured pretty low on the list.

'Are you sure?'

'Damn right,' said Morag as she opened the door and climbed out. 'Come on.'

They held hands as they crunched across the frozen ground to the shoreline. As they stepped onto the loch Morag released Lachlan's grip and lunged forwards.

'Wheeeeee!' she yelled as she performed a rudimentary figure-eight on the ice.

'Careful!' said Lachlan as he struggled to keep his feet. 'Jesus this is slippy.'

'It'll make the crossing all the quicker. Come on, slow-coach.' And with that, she slipped into an easy rhythm, her flat shoes gliding effortlessly across the surface.

After a few moments Lachlan found some semblance of balance, and set off in pursuit with a series of short, shuffling steps.

'Hurry up, Bambi,' she called as she turned to face him.

'You're putting me off,' he laughed. His arms cartwheeled in an attempt at keeping his balance. 'And you know what happened to Bambi's mum?!' he said, just as his legs shot out behind him and he landed face first on the ice.

'Och, come here,' Morag said as she slipped alongside Lachlan's prone figure. He raised his face and was dismayed to spot a circle of blood on the ice. 'Oh shit,' Morag laughed, 'Are you alright?' She spun him onto his back then sat him up. He spat blood onto the crystallised surface.

'Ouch,' he said, tentatively touching his nose.

She squatted beside him and lifted his head. Lachlan stared into her green eyes, her pupils reduced to pin-pricks by the sun reflecting off the ice. 'You're okay. It's not broken. You just took a dunt.'

'Here!' a voice called. They turned to see one of the curlers slip towards them, trailing a sledge. 'You can use this. Just leave it on the shore when you're done.'

'Oh thank you,' said Morag, standing up and squinting at the approaching figure.

Lachlan placed a hand over his eyes and watched the man approach. It was reassuring to see the ice bear up to such a load, as their good samaritan wasn't exactly skinny.

'Jesus… Morag? Morag Paterson?' the man said as he slid to a halt.

Lachlan watched as Morag narrowed her eyes. The glare from the surface turned everything into silhouettes and he struggled to make out any detail on the man's face.

'Oh my god. Michael? Michael McLeod?' said Morag, clasping a hand over her mouth. 'Lachlan, it's Michael! From school.'

'Lachlan?!' said Michael with a smile. 'Well well. I always knew you two would end up together.'

Morag laughed. 'Took us a wee while though, eh Lachlan?'

'Twenty-three years, or thereabouts,' said Lachlan as he finally struggled to his feet. 'How the hell are you Michael? Still in Aberfoyle?'

'Oh aye. I'll never move,' said Michael. 'Why would I, with all this?' He opened his arms to take in the loch, the island, the clear blue sky and the snow-capped hills.

It really was beautiful on a day like today. Even when your trousers were soaking, your nose bleeding and you'd cracked a tooth on the ice.

****

'Beat you!' Morag called from the island's shore.

Lachlan gave one last shove and glided face-first towards the narrow beach where the sledge crunched onto the stony surface. He disembarked carefully and looked back at the distance they'd covered. Michael gave them a wave from halfway back to the shore.

'Well, we made it,' said Lachlan, checking his nose for blood.

'We did. Now come on. Something to show you,' said Morag as she grabbed his hand and led him towards the ruined priory.

They emerged from the trees and found themselves alone among the stone ruins. The crumbling windowless walls still stood, but the roof was long gone. She led him through the priory, and eventually stopped, looking at the ground.

'Here,' she said. She took a few steps to one side then stopped and scraped at the snow with her shoe. 'Give me a hand to clear this.'

'Aye okay, what it is? A secret passage?' He shovelled the snow aside with his feet and a stone edge was revealed.

'Gotcha!' said Morag as she dropped to her knees and swept the remaining snow aside with both hands.

Lachlan joined in, and soon they'd uncovered a stone slab, set into the ground. A grave marker.

It read: *Robert Bontine Cunninghame Graham of Gartmore. 1852 - 1936.* Underneath this was a strange symbol, like a letter T with a circle over its centre.

Morag stood and dusted snow from her hands. 'Don Roberto!' she exclaimed, with a smile.

'Don who?' asked Lachlan. 'Is he a relative?'

'You could say he's a relative of all of us Lachlan. This great man was the first president of the SNP, in 1934.'

'Oh,' said Lachlan. He looked around at the deserted ruins, the trees heavy with snow, and the far shore beyond the glittering loch. 'Well I'm glad we came all this way.'

'Not just that Lachlan. He also founded the Scottish Labour party with Keir Hardie and was the first socialist MP at Westminster. He started Scotland's whole journey to Home Rule.'

'Some guy,' said Lachlan, staring at the stone slab. 'What's the weird symbol for?'

'That was his cattle brand, from when he was a rancher in Argentina. That's where the *Don Roberto* thing comes from.'

Lachlan laughed and shook his head. 'Jesus. Anything else?'

'Well, he was an author. And he went treasure hunting in Morocco. In disguise, of course. Oh and he married a Chilean poet called Gabriella, who he met in Paris. Only she wasn't Chilean, she was from Yorkshire, and her name was Carrie. And look…' Morag dropped to her knees beside Lachlan and scraped away more snow. 'This is her grave. He dug it with his own hands.'

'Right,' said Lachlan. Years of monotony at the Civil Service suddenly weighed heavily on his shoulders. 'That's some life eh?'

Morag turned towards him and took his hands. 'It's the only way to live a life. This guy didn't stop for a minute. Would you dig my grave for me? With your own hands?'

'Of course I would,' said Lachlan, truthfully.

They hugged, locked together among the ruins, over the graves of two of Scotland's great adventurers. Snowflakes drifted around them, dancing slowly in the still air. As they kissed the snow began to swirl, like they were in their own little snow-globe.

After a while, Morag said, 'I didn't just bring you here to visit dead people.'

'You brought a picnic too?' Lachlan asked, hopefully.

She grinned. 'Sort of.'

'Sort of? Where is it then?'

'It's in here.' She patted her belly.

'You've already eaten it?'

Morag rolled her eyes and said, 'It's a bun.'

'A bun?'

'In the oven.'

Lachlan's head spun as a million snowflakes twirled around them. 'You… you're pregnant?'

There it was again: the smile that could melt a frozen lake.

The smile that said Yes.

****

'I'm taking the sledge this time,' said Morag as she blew a snowflake from her nose.

'Only fair,' he said. 'You're sledging for two now.' He eyed the icy expanse. They'd remained on the island for an hour after Morag's news, keeping each other warm in the ruins. They'd decided if it was a girl, she was to be called Gabriella, and if it was a boy, Robert. She was two months gone. The baby would be born in September.

Across the ice, Michael and his friends had finished their game and were heading back to shore.

Morag positioned herself on the sledge and waddled it onto the loch. 'Give me a shove then,' she said, glancing over her shoulder.

Lachlan placed his hands on her back. With a gentle push, she was off, giggling, onto the ice.

A gloom settled around them as they left the island. The sun disappeared behind some rapidly advancing clouds and the loch's surface was being dusted with another fresh fall of snow. Slowly at first, but gathering pace.

Lachlan eventually found a rhythm that worked, after landing on his backside twice, but Morag seemed to be having a great time. She weaved this way and that, pushing herself along with her feet then sticking them in the air and gliding for twenty or thirty feet at a time.

'Come on!' she cried as she neared Michael and his friends.

A sudden gust of wind nearly knocked Lachlan off his feet, then the snow really began to fall. Within seconds, Morag and the rest were reduced to dark smudges in the blizzard. After another minute they were gone. He stopped, squinting into the driving snow. A dark band ahead must have been the trees lining the shore. He shuffled onward, picking up the pace. The dark shapes grew bolder and through a gap in the gusting snowstorm he could make out the shoreline. There was no sign of Morag and the others though.

'Morag!' he called out.

No answer. His voice was whipped away by the wind. With a sigh of relief, he eventually stumbled the last few steps onto the pebbled shore and looked around. Where was the car park?

'Morag?!' he called again. Still nothing.

He trudged through the trees, the snow now driving into his side. Despite the conditions, he was surprised that he felt warm. Too warm.

Ahead, he could make out two figures, facing him.

'Morag?' he called again, with one hand shielding his eyes.

The figures didn't move. He stepped forward cautiously. Why weren't they answering? One of the figures seemed to raise a hand towards him and he suddenly felt more warmth wash over him.

'Mum?' he asked.

The figure seemed to nod, and clasp its hands to its chest. The other opened its arms towards Lachlan. A plume of smoke rising from its hand.

'Dad?'

Then everything went black.

****

Burning. Itching. Flickering light. The smell of wet hair. The crackle of a fire. He opened his eyes.

'Hello,' said Morag. Her hair was tied up on top of her head, and she was wearing an oversized Arran jumper. In her hands she cupped a mug of something hot. She blew on the rising cloud of steam and smiled. 'How are you feeling?'

'Where am I? What happened?'

'We're in Michael's house. Well,' she glanced towards the door and lowered her voice, 'his mum's house. And you fainted.'

'I fainted?'

'Appears so. Combination of you being chronically unfit and exerting yourself in somewhat adverse conditions, I'd say. We found you lying on the beach once the snow eased off. You had me worried sick you bloody idiot. I thought you'd fallen through the ice.'

He sat up and looked around. They were on a cracked leather settee in a small living room furnished with flimsy wooden furniture and surrounded by a terrifying collection of porcelain dolls. A fire crackled in the hearth.

'Jesus. Sorry. I don't know what happened. Got lost in the storm and then…' The apparitions on the shore came back to him.

'What?' asked Morag.

Lachlan shook off the memory. 'Oh nothing. I was shouting on you, did you not hear?'

'Nope. The wind was howling. Anyway, how do you feel? How many fingers am I holding up?' Morag said, presenting her middle finger.

'Cheeky,' said Lachlan. 'What's in the mug? Can I get some?'

'Soup. Home-made Scotch Broth. Here.'

Lachlan took a drink and felt his insides creak as he began to thaw.

'How long have I been out for?'

'Nearly an hour,' said Morag. 'You've been talking though. Muttering gibberish mostly, so I knew you weren't dead.'

'Well that's reassuring,' said Lachlan. He passed the soup back to Morag.

'We'll need to stay here tonight,' she said. 'The roads are all blocked.'

The door swung open and Michael stepped in, carrying a bottle of whisky.

'Lachlan, you're back in the land of the living!'

'Aye, I think so. Thanks Michael, for, you know…'

'Saving your life? No problem. Wee whisky to celebrate?'

Lachlan looked at this lumbering giant, who he hadn't seen since 1950. Other than his girth, he didn't appear to have grown in any other way. He was still that nine year old boy, now in an adult body. Living with his mother, yet seemingly quite happy with his lot.

'Sure Michael, why not?'

****

Lachlan hopped over the slush-filled gutter and through the school gates where Morag waited, hands tucked into her coat pocket and a woollen bobble hat pulled down tight over her ears. Her face a sickly yellow in the glow of the street lights.

It had been a busy few days. They'd driven back to Edinburgh after a night in Michael's spare room, and made it as far as Corstorphine before a plume of smoke belching from the rear of the car told Lachlan his Hillman Imp's days were numbered. They'd waited by a row of shops next to a pile of uncollected rubbish for the recovery driver, shivering in the cold morning air. Idle chit-chat in the cab revealed that the driver would be voting Yes. Whereas Michael, who'd resisted change all his life, would be voting No.

We're no further forward, Lachlan had said to Morag as they were deposited back in Leith. More leafleting followed, and the car was eventually freed from the garage with a hefty repair bill.

'Come on, it's starting,' she said, grabbing his hand and dragging him through the empty playground.

Lachlan hopped up the steps to the main entrance where a notice stuck to the glass proclaimed: *Yes or No? Public meeting. 7:30pm*

They hurried into the hall, set out with around two hundred plastic chairs. At least a hundred of them were empty. On the stage, four men sat at a table, shuffling notes. Lachlan recognised them from the TV. MPs from Labour, the Conservatives and the SNP. At the edge sat a man with a ginger beard, sipping a glass of water as the audience settled into their seats.

Morag took off her coat and looked around the hall. 'I was hoping this would be busier.'

'Saturday. The Generation Game's on,' said Lachlan. 'Daft time to have it.'

A hush fell over the audience as the man with the beard stood and addressed the hall.

'Good evening and thank you for coming to our debate tonight. My name's Finn Cowan and I'm sure you all know our guests. If you could keep any questions until the end, that'd be great. Okay, without further ado. Our first speaker…'

Lachlan whispered, 'Finn Cowan! I met him years ago in Milne's. About the same time we got together. He was at your play too.'

Morag nodded, 'Small world eh?'

The first speaker was the Conservative MP, who, to jeers from the audience, presented a doom-laden view of Scotland's prospects should it have the temerity to vote for devolution.

'Everyone in here's a Yes voter by the sound of it,' Lachlan muttered.

'I noticed that,' said Morag. 'It's the folk sitting in front of their TVs that need to be here.'

As the Conservative MP summed up with a warning that, with a Yes vote, Scottish MPs would be banned from voting on matters reserved to Westminster which would turn them into second class parliamentarians, a couple at the end of their row clapped enthusiastically. The audience turned and glowered at them. Lachlan shifted to get a better look. A tight-mouthed pair with heavily lined foreheads. The cartoon image of the presbyterian Scottish unionist had become a cliche, but these two did little to counter that.

Next up, the Labour MP attempted to deliver a more balanced summation of the situation, but still recommended that people think very long and hard about their decision, and preferably vote No, just to be on the safe side.

'Radical as ever,' groaned Lachlan.

Last to speak was the SNP MP who stood to cheers and whose every word was met with thunderous applause from the audience. Opportunity. Hope. Progress. All of which Lachlan thought were as far-fetched in their optimism as the claims from the rest were in their pessimism. He suspected the truth lay somewhere in the middle. His opponents sneered, shook their heads, and smiled at each other in their new-found camaraderie, only sitting up in their seats when he started talking about Scotland's oil, which had them casting nervous glances across the crowd.

Lachlan remembered his colleague Alan, and his contribution to the 1974 report that would never see the light of day. The bureaucracy had become too much for Alan and he'd left the BGS a few years back with plans to travel the world. Lachlan had no idea if he'd made it any further than the bottom of his next bottle of whisky.

Despite the positivity of the SNP MP's speech, he ended on his only negative point; a dire threat about Scotland's prospects under a Conservative government, which was looking increasingly likely thanks to their new leader's growing popularity in England. Even the mention of Margaret Thatcher's name sent a shiver down Lachlan's spine.

'Rubbish!' jeered the man at the end of their row. 'She's just what this country needs!' yelled his wife. The audience turned on them again and laughed in light-hearted dismissal of their interjection. The couple bristled. The woman pulled a pair of gloves from her handbag and stabbed her hands into them.

Enjoyable though it all was, Lachlan looked at the rows of vacant seats behind them, and each empty plastic chair seemed to applaud the couple as they stormed from the hall.

The cross-examination part of the debate began, and Lachlan

found himself drifting off. It was two against one. The chairman attempted neutrality but his leanings were obvious as he leapt to the defence of the SNP MP repeatedly. The Conservative MP was the most vociferous in his attack on the notion of devolution; the Labour man again tried to appease the audience by telling them they were all wrong.

When Finn opened the debate to the floor and sought questions from the audience, it was the Conservative's turn to retreat to his corner as a barrage of hostile blows were landed from the crowd. The Labour man smiled benignly throughout.

'This is a waste of time,' whispered Lachlan.

Morag glanced sideways at him and blew sharply from her nostrils, which he took as agreement.

He looked around the hall for a distraction. It was decorated with painted flags of all nations, hung from string all along the walls and above the stage. Taking pride of place in the centre spot above the stage was the Union Flag. He craned his neck and eventually found a saltire, tucked away at the back of the hall. It was hardly surprising the country felt the way it did when they were still drumming the same message into their primary school children: Know your place.

He was fidgeting with his shoelace when he heard the words he'd been waiting for. The evening was over. Thanks for coming. Thanks to our guests. And please remember to vote.

He doubted very much that the empty chairs would heed the message.

****

The ringing alarm roused Lachlan from a dream where he'd been running at impossible speeds across a sun-drenched plain, taking huge, effortless strides.

'Kettle,' muttered Morag, as she pulled the blankets away. He groaned, reached for the glass of water he kept beside the bed and felt the familiar furry warmth of Winnie as she ducked her head into his glass. It was a race to get the first drink in the morning, and the cat usually won.

He stretched as he shuffled into the kitchen then clicked the radio on.

'*...but despite Yes achieving 51.6% of the vote, this only represented 33.9% of the electorate. So as a result of the government's forty-percent amendment, the proposal for a Scottish Assembly has failed and the Act has been repealed. In other news-*'

His permanently low expectations had prepared him for this news. He sighed, clicked the radio off, switched on the kettle, and dropped four slices of Mother's Pride under the grill. The telephone rang. He stepped into the hall and grabbed the mustard coloured handset. The gruff voice of Finn Cowan barked a hello. They'd hung around after the meeting and exchanged numbers, with a promise to keep up the campaign should they fall short.

'You heard?' said Finn.

'Aye,' said Lachlan. 'No surprise. How are you taking it?'

'Fucking raging,' said Finn. 'We won the vote too. Just need to regroup in time and start again. Anyway, fuck it all, I'm going fishing.'

'Fishing?'

'Aye, my old man's got a boat out at Cockenzie. Going to spend some time clearing my head. You should come out sometime. You and Morag.'

'That sounds great Finn. I'll call you.'

'Right Lachlan. Onwards and sideways.'

He replaced the handset and returned to the kitchen. 'Did you hear the radio?' he called through to the bedroom in passing.

Morag appeared at the door, her hair a tangled mess and tears in her eyes. 'Aye. I was expecting it. But doesn't make it any easier.'

'Come here,' said Lachlan and Morag buried herself in his arms.

'Cheating bastards,' she said. 'It's so unfair.'

They stood there in silence, keeping each other warm while the kettle boiled beside them and the grill ticked to life.

'Chin up love,' said Lachlan eventually. 'We did our best. And Finn's invited us fishing.'

The kettle wobbled slightly as it reached the boil then clicked itself off.

'It's not over Lachlan. Folk will see sense eventually.'

Tiny increments, thought Lachlan, as he reached for the teabags. 'I really can't be arsed going to work today,' he groaned as he filled the mugs.

'Life goes on pal,' said Morag. She rubbed her eyes. 'Me neither. But kids need educating and you need to do that stuff you do with maps.'

He handed her a mug of steaming tea. 'Hey, I don't get my hands dirty with the maps anymore. I've got to do a salary review across the whole Hydrocarbons Unit. Think they're looking to cut costs.'

'Watch you don't put yourself out of a job,' said Morag. 'Although you could always retrain to be a teacher. It's all the rage.'

Lachlan pulled the grill out, checked the toast, and slipped it back under the heat. 'Nah. I'd be hopeless. Anyway I'm a lifer at the BGS now.'

'There's more to life than a civil service pension Lachlan,' said Morag as she sipped her tea. 'You need to be a bit more *Don*

Roberto. Where's your sense of adventure?'

He leaned back on the kitchen bunker and folded his arms. 'I spent twenty-three years on a quest to find you again. I hunted high and low. I fought off the advances of Lords-to-be. And I didn't give up…' He reached for the window ledge and grabbed his saltire flagstone, '…until I'd found the treasure.'

'X marked the spot?' said Morag, through her smile.

'Ex-actly,' said Lachlan. He tossed the stone up and caught it in one hand.

Morag nodded towards the grill. 'Your toast's burning.'

There was a clatter from the hall as the morning newspaper dropped through the letterbox.

'Ah!' said Morag as she hurried off to retrieve it.

He kicked the living room door open with one foot and delivered a plate of hot toast, smeared with melting margarine, to the coffee table. Morag had her head buried in the paper.

'Come on, eat up. You're eating for two now remember,' he said, poking the newspaper.

'Aye, thanks,' Morag said absently as she reached for a slice. 'Two million, three hundred and eighty seven thousand, five hundred and seventy two. That's bloody shocking.'

'What's that? Turnout?' said Lachlan through a mouthful of toast.

'Aye. The biggest decision we've ever had to make, and nearly a million and a half couldn't be bothered. It makes me so angry!' She lowered the paper to her knees.

'Well, the two at the end there. That's us. At least we can see our impact.'

'Great. But all those lazy bastards sitting on their backsides counted against us. How can we win against a system that's permanently rigged?'

Lachlan reached for another piece of toast. 'We just have to keep going. Like you said. Keep up the fight.'

'We won the vote though, that's what stinks. Anyway, better get ready for work.' She drank the last of her tea and headed for the bathroom.

Lachlan sat back, picked up the paper and flicked through the rest of the news. Callaghan's minority Labour government was reeling and still relied on the support of the Liberals, the Ulster Unionists and Plaid Cymru's MPs, as well as the SNP's eleven members at Westminster. Surely this would now be unsustainable? The Winter of Discontent showed no signs of a thaw. There seemed to be a permanent grey cloud of despondency over the UK, and despite Scotland's proposed Assembly offering a beacon of light, a way out of the darkness, not enough of his countrymen had grasped it.

Winnie shoved the door open, jumped up onto his lap and nudged the paper aside, looking for affection.

'I wonder if your namesake will still have a job in the summer?' said Lachlan, rubbing her chin.

****

Sometimes, just sometimes, the sun did shine on Easter Road stadium, and that Saturday afternoon at the end of March it blazed down. Hibs were beating Celtic after a headed goal from a corner in the third minute and the terraces were bouncing. A mere thirteen minutes later a goalkeeping error gifted them a second.

'Glad I came through for this,' yelled Johnny into Lachlan's ear.

'Two up against Celtic with a quarter of an hour gone? Aye. Plenty time yet though.'

Johnny laughed, 'You've not changed a bit. Thought hooking up with Morag might've put a smile on your face.'

Lachlan grinned, 'It has. But it helps to keep one foot on the ground.'

Johnny had called that week to suggest they meet up for the Hibs match. A tough game against the green half of Glasgow, who were racing towards the title in a tussle with city rivals Rangers.

According to Johnny, Billy had been hearing rumours, and Johnny felt he was ready for the truth. The source of the rumours was unclear but Lachlan had imagined Mandy saying something in a fit of spite. Either that or word had just got around, as it always does in a small town.

Billy had moped along behind them as they headed to Easter Road from Waverley Station. Now a sullen teenager. He stood beside Johnny and regarded the game with cold disinterest.

'So when's the baby due?' asked Johnny.

'September,' Lachlan said. 'We're planning to move house soon. Need another bedroom. How's things in Alloa? Mandy doing alright?'

Johnny looked away momentarily then sighed, 'Aye, she's fine. We're fine. You know how it is?'

'So, you think Billy will be alright about this?' Lachlan said, quietly.

Johnny shrugged, 'I'll be honest Lachlan, I've no fucking idea. I can't get through to him these days. He's been expelled from school twice. We've had the police at the door more times than I care to remember.'

'Jesus. Do you think this news will help him?'

The ref's whistle blew for a foul and a boo went up from the crowd.

'It can't make him any fucking worse.'

As the first half neared its end, Johnny nudged Lachlan. 'Half time. I think we tell him then.'

'You sure?' asked Lachlan. He gulped and felt his mouth dry up. 'I'll meet you at the pie stand. I need a drink.'

As Lachlan edged through the crowd and down the steps the whistle blew for half-time. He hurried for the pie counter where he bought a cup of scalding Bovril and shuffled to one side to await his friend and his son. His son? HIS son. He still struggled with the concept, but he didn't have long to think about it as he spotted Billy muscle his way through the mass of bodies.

After ten minutes idle chit-chat about the game Johnny glanced at Lachlan, who shrugged in a way he hoped said *go for it*.

'So, Billy,' said Johnny.

Billy blew on his drink. 'What?'

Johnny continued, 'Well, it's just that you're thirteen now and there's something you need to know.'

Billy rolled his eyes and said, 'That this prick's my dad?'

Lachlan gasped, spraying Bovril over Johnny's shirt. 'You knew?'

'Course I knew,' said Billy. 'I'm not daft. Your wee visit. The Scotland strip. The way my mum is around you. The way you look like an older, decrepit version of me.' He shrugged. 'I couldn't give a shit.'

Johnny looked at Lachlan. Lachlan looked at Billy. Billy looked at both of them and shrugged. The crowds began to disperse as the second half approached.

'Look Billy, I didn't know,' said Lachlan. 'For years I mean.

Neither did your dad.' He pointed at Johnny to make his point clearer. Johnny was busy mopping Bovril from his shirt.

Billy forced a weak smile, 'You want the truth? I'd rather have neither of you for a dad.'

'Well, like it or not, you do,' said Lachlan. Despite the abuse, he couldn't help but admire Billy's headstrong nature, and could only assume he'd inherited this from Mandy. 'You have both of us.'

Billy puffed his cheeks and leaned back against the wall.

'Morecambe and Wise? Fuck's sake. Lucky me.'

****

There was a faint warmth in the air but summer still seemed like a long way away. They stood together in the street, scanning the properties on offer in the estate agent's window. Morag suggested going inside but Lachlan thought this showed too much commitment, and he didn't trust estate agents one bit, or rather he didn't trust his own ability to walk out again without landing them both in horrific debt.

Financial concerns weren't the only thing bothering him. As he'd feared, the Conservatives had won the election at the beginning of the month and Margaret Thatcher was the new Prime Minister. The SNP had been reduced to two MPs, their vote share plummeting to seventeen per-cent with both Labour and the Conservatives making gains in Scotland at their expense. Once again, the Scottish vote had no impact on who formed the government. England could elect a Conservative government, and sometimes, England could elect a Labour government. Scotland stood by, wringing its cap, knowing its place, just watching the revolving door at Westminster turn once again and taking the government it was given.

'That looks nice,' said Morag, pointing to a sandstone property in Willowbrae.

'An upper villa? No use for prams. Also, I can think of twenty thousand reasons why we can't afford that, and each one of them's a pound.'

'Good point,' said Morag. She hunkered down to check the bottom row of properties, while Lachlan scanned the top. Condensation ran down the glass as the interior warmed up. Inside, a grey-haired man in a sober suit sat on the edge of a desk, laughing with a younger woman. He glanced towards Lachlan and gestured towards the door. Lachlan pretended not to notice.

'Ach there's nothing,' grumbled Morag as she rose to her feet. 'Come on, we're not in any rush. We've got months yet.' She patted her belly. The baby was only just starting to show, but Lachlan considered this to be like blowing up a balloon. The first bit was the hardest, then once you'd got over the initial resistance, it would swell rapidly. He didn't want to be moving house at that stage.

He leaned toward the glass trying to get a better look at the last property in the row but it was shrouded in condensation. Without warning, the suited gent appeared on the other side of the glass with a cloth and wiped the window clean from the inside. Lachlan pretended he hadn't been looking at that particular property at all, and waited for the man to retreat again before stealing a glance.

'Oh,' he said.

'What?' said Morag.

'Look at that. Two bedrooms. Portobello. Sea views. Looks right over the Forth.'

'No garden though. It's a flat.'

'We wouldn't need a garden. It's ground floor, and the beach is right outside the door.'

'It's a bit of a dump.'

'Hence the price. And it's nothing a lick of paint wouldn't fix,' said Lachlan, in an uncharacteristic moment of positivity.

They looked at each other, and without saying a word they both knew this was where they'd be bringing up their child.

****

As it turned out, it needed a bit more than a lick of paint. It also needed new floorboards; a full rewire; the drains rodded; a new living room window; the bedroom ceiling plastered; and a battery for the doorbell. It seemed though that, at last, they could call it home.

Lachlan straightened the nameplate on the door and popped in the second screw, making sure it was level. He wiped the brass clean and stepped back into the common stair.

'Should have been *Paterson McCormack*,' said Morag.

'Nah. *McCormack Paterson* sounds better. Like a legal firm.'

He put an arm around Morag's shoulder, and placed his free hand on her belly.

'Come on,' said Morag, breaking away. 'It's too hot in here, let's go for a walk on the beach.'

Outside, the sun was still high in the sky. They walked the short path to the promenade and joined the early evening crowds taking the sea air, which at this time of night seemed to consist mostly of vinegar from the beachside chippies and, if the wind changed, the whiff of the sewage works upriver.

'Chips?' asked Lachlan.

'Why not?' said Morag.

They strolled to the chip shop and left a few minutes later with a large parcel smothered in salt and Edinburgh's uniquely vinegary brown sauce. Hopping onto the wall separating the beach from the promenade, they sat with their legs dangling over the sand, overlooking the Firth of Forth.

'Our wee river,' said Morag. She popped a chip in her mouth and threw another onto the beach where it was snapped up by a gull. Within moments, a dozen squawking birds had descended.

'Aye, and look at it. All grown up.' Lachlan tossed another chip for the birds to fight over.

The Forth was calm today, a waveless glassy blue. Portobello faced the distant mouth of the estuary, where the river met the sea. To their right, the coastline of East Lothian. The twin towers of Cockenzie Power Station dispensing thin plumes of smoke into the early evening sky. To their left, Fife was almost lost across the water in the haze.

'Hard to imagine it's the same river,' said Morag.

Lachlan looked upriver, to where it narrowed at Queensferry allowing road and rail to cross. Beyond that the coasts were closer still. At Alloa it meandered this way and that. He remembered the day at the brewery, his father's demise. Stirling, and the river-bloated corpse. The river sped up the further back his thoughts took him, and he recalled its youthful gurgle below them as they climbed a tree on its bank. The day his mother collapsed. The day he'd been set adrift.

'Penny?' said Morag. She leaned forward for a better look at Lachlan's face.

'For my thoughts?' he said. 'Ach just being sentimental. Chip?'

'Ow,' she gasped, with her hand on her stomach.

'What?' asked Lachlan. The squawking gulls were edging closer. He threw the remaining chips far onto the sand and they turned and flapped off in a white flurry.

'Nothing, just a twinge. The wee one's enjoying the chips I think.'

A gang of kids charged past on the promenade and barged into the amusement arcade behind them. The bleeps, bloops and ringing bells of the machines spilled out as the door slowly swung closed.

'Fancy a flutter?' asked Lachlan.

The darkness took a bit of getting used to, and even once their eyes had adjusted there was still the fog of cigarette smoke to contend with. The clack-clack-clack of one-armed bandits mixed with the laughter of the children and the bleeps from the newly installed Space Invader machines. Lachlan loved these - it seemed like the future promised in the his *Galaxy Science Fiction* magazines was finally here.

'I'm going to have a wee shot of this,' he said as he pulled ten pence from his pocket.

'I'll get some change and play the penny falls. I'll see you in five minutes.'

Lachlan stabbed the *1 Player* button and began defending Earth from alien attack. He ducked behind the barricades and popped back and forth, firing rapidly upwards and taking out a column of invaders each time. The flying saucer appeared with a blooping siren and made its way across the top of the screen. He slipped across, pausing once to allow an invader's bomb to explode harmlessly in front of him, and positioned himself to fire on the saucer. A brief pause, then he stabbed the fire button. Missed. He cursed and hauled the joystick to the right, firing again and again but the saucer had escaped. No bonus. He couldn't believe he'd missed - he must have perfected an almost ninety-nine percent hit rate on the saucers. The invaders reached the edge of the screen and dropped closer. He slipped to the left and was about to start firing when a fast bomb from a low-level invader hit his ship before he could take evasive action.

'Bollocks,' he muttered as his second life flashed into existence on the screen. He glanced along the rows of machines and saw Morag turning from the change booth with a paper cup of pennies.

The invaders were speeding up now. He blasted two more columns before ducking behind a shelter to avoid another flurry of bombs but the barricade was already weakened and a bomb snuck through and destroyed him in a fizzle of pixels.

'Crap,' he sighed. His final life flickered onto the screen.

There were three invaders left now, zipping along the screen and dropping closer and closer. He picked off one with a single shot. The remaining two accelerated. He blasted three, four, five shots and took one out which left the last invader racing towards him. He hammered the fire button as it wiped out his barricades. One more row, this was his last chance.

He missed.

The invader ploughed into his ship and the words GAME OVER flashed up on the screen.

Then he heard the scream.

****

The strip lights shone with a blinding intensity. Porters rattled past with gurneys and Lachlan's head was beginning to pound.

He stood, scraping the plastic chair across the floor and stepped quickly to the nurses station for the tenth time that hour.

'Any news?'

'I'm afraid not Mr McCormack. We'll let you know as soon as you can go in.'

He walked off down the corridor. At the exit he stepped outside into the night, still oppressively warm and humid. It had only been a few hours since they'd stepped out for a walk on the beach, but in those few hours, his world had been turned on its head. There was still a faint hint of blue in the sky. It gave him hope.

'You okay son?' An elderly man with a haunted appearance stood by the entrance, smoking a cigarette and fidgeting in his dressing gown pocket.

'Not sure yet.'

The man pulled out a hip flask. He passed it to Lachlan. 'Here, there's nothing a wee dram can't help.'

Lachlan looked at the man. He had a ghostly appearance. Sunken eyes, below which his skin hung down in a manner that seemed to scream defeat.

'Thanks,' he said. He took a generous gulp without enquiring on the contents.

Whisky. Luckily. He let the warmth sink into his stomach and thought of his father, then he took another drink.

'Finish it if you want son. I've got another full bottle coming tomorrow.'

Lachlan drained the flask in a series of stinging gulps. His eyes watered as he handed it back. 'Thanks. I'm Lachlan,' he said, offering his hand.

'Lachlan,' said the man. A smile crept over his face, his eyes now twinkling. 'Well well.'

'Sorry?' asked Lachlan. The man's hand was cold, and dry. He released his grip.

'Lachlan,' the man said again. 'That's my name too. Unusual to meet another Lachlan.'

'What are you in for?' Lachlan asked.

Old Lachlan chuckled. 'Bad behaviour, you might say.'

'It's a hospital, not a prison.'

The old man was silent for a moment, then said, 'Well I've been given life without parole. I'm not coming out. Tell me how that's different?'

Lachlan stared ahead, towards the Meadows - an expanse of greenery on the southern edge of Edinburgh's city centre, breathing life into the choking air. In the distance, a siren blared as another ambulance made its way towards the infirmary.

'You make your own choices I suppose,' Lachlan said eventually. 'If you don't want to be here, you can walk away. Go enjoy whatever time you have left. Have you got family?'

Old Lachlan grunted, and puffed on his cigarette. 'Two children. This one,' he held up his cigarette. 'And this one,' he patted the empty hip flask in his pocket. 'And one wife. Who, as you put it, walked away.'

It would appear that his companion had been undertaking a prolonged suicide for some time.

Tiny increments.

The door behind him swung open. 'Mr McCormack, you can go in and see her now.' The nurse smiled a faint smile. A smile of professionalism. A smile of compassion. And a smile that made Lachlan's heart sink.

They'd called her Gabriella, after *Don Roberto's* wife. Gabriella never really existed either.

The weeks that followed the miscarriage were dark and initially without hope but slowly, Morag returned to him. Lachlan had suggested she get back into acting, and she'd taken a small role in a local production. They'd secured a venue during the Festival Fringe, which took Lachlan some time to find as it was in a back room of a forgotten council building somewhere in the Old Town.

He entered the room. Ten rows of empty seats faced a stage that barely rose above the ground. He was ten minutes early, but how many people would show up to a 6pm performance of a domestic comedy drama that was, as the local paper said, *'short on laughs'*?

As it turned out, the answer was nine. The show began. Morag flashed a quick smile at Lachlan, who'd sat front and centre. After five minutes two people got up and left, scraping their chairs along the floor as they did so. Lachlan watched as Morag glanced in their direction. Her shoulders slumped and she stumbled on her lines.

His heart ached. He sat up and laughed a bit too loudly at the scene that followed. Morag played the role of a wife who'd discovered her husband cheating with the au pair. The au pair turned out to be a Russian spy. The husband wasn't the diplomat she thought he was. A case of mistaken identity, with hilarious consequences.

Only it wasn't hilarious. And the consequences were fairly inconsequential.

After an hour, it ended to a smattering of polite applause. Morag and the other cast members took a bow, slipped through a side door and Lachlan returned to the entrance. He had plans for the evening, which he hoped were better received.

Somewhere, a cheer went up as a street performer swallowed a sword, or rode a unicycle, or juggled something you wouldn't expect to be juggled. Lachlan stuck his hands in his pockets and leaned against the wall. The Festival was the best, and the worst, time to live in this city. He was torn between the undeniably infectious desire to join in the fun, and wishing all these bastards would fuck off back to Oxfordshire. He settled on an aloof disinterest.

'Okay handsome? Where are you taking me?'

Morag appeared at his side, shaking her hair out of the ponytail it had been in for the performance. Behind her, Patrick - her stage-husband, and Joyce - the au pair, lit cigarettes in a manner that suggested their on-stage affair had benefited from a method approach.

'Dinner first,' said Lachlan.

'Ooh, nice,' said Morag. She turned to her colleagues and waved farewell. 'Same time tomorrow?'

Patrick frowned and said, 'Afraid so. Maybe we'll fill three rows? Adieu mon ami.'

Morag took Lachlan's arm and they headed up a cobbled alleyway towards the High Street. She leaned her head on his shoulder as they walked.

'Thanks for coming.'

'Eh? Don't be daft. That reviewer didn't know what he was talking about.'

'I think he did Lachlan. It's shite isn't it?'

Lachlan looked at Morag, her smile had been absent for weeks now, and he'd do anything to spark it back to life but he couldn't lie to her. 'Aye. It is a bit.'

She snorted, and for a fleeting moment her face brightened.

'So what's the occasion?'

'Nothing,' lied Lachlan. 'Just thought it'd be nice. Up town. Nice night. Celebrate your return to the stage and all that. And here we are…'

He pushed open a door and ushered her in. They were met within seconds by an officious Maître d' - a thin man in wire-rimmed spectacles who led them through the tables to a window seat, overlooking the Royal Mile. The restaurant was almost full, a gentle buzz of quiet conversation filled the air. Lachlan fidgeted with his pocket as he took his seat.

Morag noticed his awkwardness. 'What's that?'

'What's what?'

'In your pocket.'

'Car keys,' said Lachlan. 'Thought I'd lost them.'

An hour later, after Cullen Skink (Lachlan), Scallops (Morag), a 12oz steak that had him wishing he'd brought some scales (Lachlan) and Salmon (Morag) they were nibbling on cheese and draining their second bottle of red.

Morag tipped her glass back and licked her lips. 'God I needed that.' She placed it down, clunking it against the edge of her plate which raised some eyebrows at the neighbouring table. 'Sorry,' she said in a stage whisper. The couple looked away and started fidgeting with their cutlery.

'Are you alright there?' said Lachlan.

'Think I'm a wee bit drunk,' Morag said, looking around.

'Good. Because I was thinking of saying something.'

'What's that then?'

'Well. I think we should try again. For a kid.'

Morag leaned forward onto her elbows and brought her hands to her face. She nodded slowly. 'It still hurts Lachlan. Losing Gabriella like that.'

'I know. But we're not getting any younger. Christ, we'll be forty in a couple of years.'

'No no no,' said Morag, waggling her finger. 'You do not discuss a lady's age. Isn't that right?' she turned to the couple at the next table, who made a point of ignoring her.

'Come on Morag. We can't give up.'

She nodded, and took his hands across the table. She still looked like she was on the verge of tears.

Lachlan wondered if tonight was the night. Morag was drunk. He wasn't drunk enough. He excused himself, went to the toilet, and paused at the bar on the way back. 'Double whisky please.' Morag had her back to him and was staring out the window.

'Certainly sir, I'll bring it over.'

'No, I'll drink it here thanks.'

The barman raised an eyebrow, placed a glass on the bar and poured a double. Lachlan knocked it back in one.

Outside, they wandered through the festival crowds on the darkening Royal Mile. Lachlan's stomach was in knots as he tried to assess Morag's mood. The fresh air helped, and she appeared more sober but her face still seemed cloaked. Like it was shrouded in a damp mist.

They wandered down to the New Town, and onto St Andrew Square where they could see the Firth of Forth and the orange streetlights of Fife, way across the water.

'There's our river,' he said.

Morag stared into the distance with damp eyes but said nothing.

'It's still going Morag. It keeps flowing.'

She returned her eyes to Lachlan and a faint smile found her lips.

'I know Lachlan. All the way to the sea.'

'We're still flowing aren't we?'

Morag sighed, and nodded. 'Of course we are.' She grabbed his arm as they meandered back to Princes Street where the Scott Monument loomed large above them.

'Our first kiss, remember?' said Lachlan. He was momentarily distracted as a flash lit up the night sky followed by a bang. The Military Tattoo fireworks marking the end of the evening's performance had begun.

He took a deep breath, reached into his pocket, and dropped to one knee. She hadn't noticed, she was busy watching the show.

'Morag?' he said.

'What?' she replied absently. Her face still impassive as she looked to the heavens.

Lachlan held the box up. Like a magician preparing to pull a rabbit from a hat. Morag looked around and her mouth fell open.

'Will you marry me?'

Her eyes sparkled as a rocket exploded in the night sky. She stared at Lachlan and there it was, absent for months, but back with a bang.

That firework smile.

SATURDAY

In the lounge, Bob wobbled on a chair as he struggled to attach some Union Jack bunting to the wall.

'That's upside down,' said Lachlan as he walked towards the table where the residents were enjoying their weekly 'arts and crafts' activity.

'Eh?' said Bob.

'Your flags. They're upside down.'

'Does it matter?' said Bob.

'Not to me it doesn't, but it should to you. What's it for anyway?'

'MP's coming for a visit.'

Lachlan grunted and took a seat. He pulled the saltire flagstone from his pocket and picked up a paintbrush.

He watched the TV news as he waited for the paint to dry. Footage of crumbling buildings and screaming mothers. Bodies of children pulled from the rubble in the latest Middle East war zone. Back in the studio a stony-faced Etonian explained to the host and to the nation how this was anyone's fault but their own.

'Lachlan! Phone!' Stella called from the hallway. He tapped the flag-stone. The paint was dry. It was as good as new.

'Mr McCormack? Doctor Blair. Just to say your results should be back on Monday. Bit of a delay I'm afraid.'

'Oh,' said Lachlan. 'Okay.' He steadied himself against the wall. Outside in the car park, he spotted that bloody magpie again, bouncing over the roof of a car.

'Didn't want you waiting around today, that's all.'

'I'm not going anywhere doctor.'

'Well I'll give you a call on Monday.'

Lachlan hung up and returned to the lounge where Bob was busy turning the flags around.

'Those are upside down,' he said.

'What!?' said Bob.

'Aye sorry. You were right the first time.'

'Fuck it,' said Bob. 'They'll do.' He stepped from the chair with a grunt and started a coughing fit that seemed to have no end.

'That's the spirit,' said Lachlan.

JOPPA, 2003

Someone once told him that moving to the suburbs was just preparation for death. Lachlan tended to agree. At sixty-two, he was beginning to feel Father Time's hand on his shoulder. And increasingly, the doctor's finger up his arse.

The new millennium had started with a bang. Grace, their daughter, turned twenty on the day the 20th Century died. They'd celebrated with a barbecue in the small back garden of their comfortable bungalow in Edinburgh's Joppa, the capital's last stand before the regional border.

Morag had been pregnant with Grace at their wedding. A registry office affair in Edinburgh's Victoria Street attended by a few close friends and Morag's father. He'd drained a bottle of single malt, danced once with his daughter, then collapsed in a corner, but not before professing his love for everyone in attendance, even Lachlan. It had been a day to remember. Unfortunately, due to the amount of single malt Lachlan had also consumed, remembering it was difficult.

Now he sat in his armchair, where, if he craned his neck, he could just make out a sliver of sea. The estuary a steely grey under a sky that threatened rain. Another Scottish spring full of promise.

The news was on, and it made for equally grim viewing.

'Fucking idiots,' he grumbled at the TV, where the western leaders shook hands as they colluded to send thousands to an early grave in Iraq.

Morag lowered her book and tutted. 'Millions of us marched against this. And for what?'

'So those arseholes could boost their egos by ignoring us,' said Lachlan.

Morag grabbed the remote and stabbed the *off* button. For a moment, the hum of the boiler in the hall cupboard and the ticking of the clock on the fireplace were the only sounds. She dropped her book to the settee. 'I was thinking we should probably do something with Grace's room. Now she's away.'

'Uhuh,' said Lachlan. 'We should probably leave it for a bit. Just in case.'

'In case what? She's gone Lachlan. Your wee lassie won't be coming back. She's got her own life now.'

He hated thinking about this, but it was true. Grace had completed her medical training and started full-time at the Western General. Where had the last twenty-three years gone? They'd sold the flat in Portobello and moved along the coast when she was three, thinking they'd like to add a wee brother or sister to the mix, but a sibling never came. They'd rattled around in this three-bed bungalow for twenty years. Grace had the advantage of having both a bedroom and a playroom growing up, but the spare room served as a reminder not only of the absence of a younger sibling, but also of the big sister she never had.

He clicked the TV back on. Footage of fighter jets taking off. Maps. The presenter on his feet. This meant war.

'Things can only get better,' he said. 'Remember that?'

'Aye,' said Morag. 'The only election win we've celebrated in a lifetime of voting and look where it got us.'

'It was meant to be a new beginning, not more of the same old shite.' Lachlan stood and pulled a bottle of Glenfiddich from the bookshelf. 'Want one?'

'Too early for me. Have you nothing better to do? What about your fishing trip with Finn tomorrow? Get ready for that.'

'Suppose I should,' muttered Lachlan. He returned the bottle to the shelf and sloped off through the empty house and into the garden.

The shed stood at the bottom corner, underneath a neighbour's tree that was in dire need of pruning. Brushing aside the cobwebs he pulled his fishing rod from the wall then located his tackle box. The hooks rusting but still usable, not that he'd be needing them. He kept a waterproof jacket bundled up somewhere but couldn't see it in the gloom. Grabbing an old cloth, he wiped dirt from the window and smiled as he spotted his saltire flagstone, sitting on the ledge.

From a dusty Wellington boot, he retrieved a hidden bottle of Grouse, drank straight from the bottle, and wiped the dust from the stone's surface with his thumb. The paint faded but the brush marks still visible after fifty-three years.

****

'Bit of a swell today Lachlan. Hope you'll be alright,' said Finn from the deck of his fishing boat.

The twin chimneys of Cockenzie power station loomed large

overhead, lit by the morning sun as it rose over the distant mouth of the estuary. Lachlan threw his bag and rod onto the deck and stepped aboard.

'I'll be fine,' he said. 'Where are we headed?'

'Thought we could take her out towards the rock. The tide's with us.'

'Great. I've packed the essentials,' Lachlan pointed to his bag. 'Highland Park, and a few cans of Export to get us going.'

'Brilliant,' laughed Finn. 'You won't be needing the fishing rod.'

'That's for Morag's benefit,' Lachlan chuckled.

Finn started the engine and manoeuvred the small blue boat away from the harbour. As soon as it was beyond the breakwater he opened the throttle and the little vessel lurched forward into the Forth estuary. Lachlan cracked open two cans of Export and handed one to Finn.

'So,' shouted Finn over his shoulder. 'How's life now Grace has gone?'

Lachlan took a swig of his beer and looked back at the receding coast-line. 'Quiet, Finn. Much like when your Ian left home. I remember at the time you said you were struggling with the silence.'

'You'll learn to savour it though. Is Morag okay?'

'You know Morag. She'll find something else to occupy her time. She can't sit still for long.'

A fat grey seal lounged on a nearby rock. It regarded them with disinterest as they passed.

'Some life eh?' said Lachlan. He took another drink and watched the seal as the seal watched him.

'He probably thinks the same about you,' laughed Finn. 'How's that pension working out?'

Lachlan had, after almost a lifetime of the civil service, taken early retirement. His state pension would start too in a few years, but for now, he was doing fine. 'Great aye. Especially now Grace is away.'

Finn crunched his can and tossed it into a box that was meant for the boat's catch. Lachlan handed him another, then drained his own and dropped it into the box. It already had the makings of a successful trip.

'And what about your other family?' asked Finn.

Lachlan narrowed his eyes and watched a gull swoop overhead. 'I try not to think about them much, to be honest.'

'Well you were a grandfather at forty one. Can't say I blame you.'

Lachlan shook his head. 'Billy. Fucking idiot. A father at sixteen.'

Finn eased off the throttle and pointed the boat towards the Bass Rock. 'And how is your grandson?'

'Mark? I've only met him twice. He'll be twenty one now. Last time I spoke to Johnny he was thinking of joining the army. He seems like a good lad. Got his head screwed on. More than his father does anyway.'

The boat rose and fell as it spluttered onwards, towards the North Sea, a fine spray blowing over the deck. Finn nudged the wheel to starboard. 'Big tanker coming in.'

Lachlan peered ahead. A tanker, empty and high in the water, was powering up the estuary towards them.

'Here for our oil,' muttered Finn. 'It'll go away again slow and full, and we'll see nothing for it.'

'Aye, the only country on Earth to discover oil and get poorer,' sighed Lachlan.

'Here, I was reading a thing the other day about this new

Freedom of Information Act.'

'Aye?'

'It's one of the few good things those arseholes have done. Means the public have a right to access government information. I was thinking about that report you always used to talk about.'

'Oh aye,' said Lachlan. 'Wonder what happened to old Alan. He was quite bitter about it all back in the 70s.'

'Well, here's the thing. I'm still active with the SNP, and I've been making noises to the top brass about pursuing it.'

The peace was shattered as the approaching tanker blasted its horn five times. Finn jerked the wheel further to the right. 'Fuck's sake, we're nowhere near you pal.' He stood up and waved, shaking his head as he sat back down.

'Do you think you'll get anywhere?' asked Lachlan.

Finn shrugged. 'Scotland's getting a bit more recognition than the Tories ever gave us. We need to start getting the truth out of these bastards.'

Lachlan shook his head. 'Good luck with that. Like the weapons of mass destruction old Saddam's got hidden?'

Finn laughed, 'Never underestimate the government's ability to take us for a bunch of fucking mugs.'

Lachlan watched the tanker, its orange bow ploughing through the waves. 'It's impossible Finn. Remember '79? Nobody cared enough then, and I doubt they do now.'

'Three quarters of the country wanted a parliament.' Finn peered towards the distant rock. 'That's progress.'

Tiny increments, thought Lachlan as the boat bobbed in the receding tanker's wake.

The sun was overhead now, casting a faint warmth onto the deck where Lachlan lay. The air filled with the squawking of gulls and gannets as the boat approached the Bass Rock, the Firth of Forth's great sentinel.

'Land ahoy,' called Finn.

Lachlan sat up and studied the rock. Covered in thousands of gannets, and the shite of thousands of gannets, it shone a bright white in the sun. Waves lapped against a small pier at the bottom of the 100m cliffs.

'You're not going to attempt to dock here are you,' asked Lachlan.

'Why not?' said Finn. 'I'm a man of the sea. Plus, I'm very drunk and full of confidence.'

'Oh Christ,' said Lachlan. He lay back down.

'Right you bastard. Let's be having you.'

Lachlan felt the thrum of the engine through the deck as Finn gunned the boat towards the pier.

'Easy… Easy…' Finn said. The waves rocked them up and down as he approached. Lachlan remained on the deck staring at the sky.

'Are you allowed to do this?' he asked.

'No fucking idea,' said Finn. 'It's privately owned. One of the original *parcel o' rogues* I think.'

Lachlan wasn't surprised. The landed gentry in Scotland had done very well out of signing their country's sovereignty away in 1707.

'Didn't he plant the *Act of Union* beech trees in North Berwick too?'

'Aye. A right old lickspittle,' said Finn as he cut the throttle.

'Nearly there. Oh, and those trees are nearly all dead now by the way. Think of it that way. Once the last tree dies, maybe the union will go with it, and we can get back to being a normal country.'

'Superstitious bollocks,' laughed Lachlan.

'We'll see,' said Finn. 'Right, shut up. This is the tricky bit.'

Lachlan closed his eyes. The boat lurched as a wave crashed into them. Finn swore under his breath. He gunned the throttle again briefly, then turned sharply to one side.

After a few moments, there was a thump as the boat hit the dock.

'Ding doun Tantallon. Mak a bridge tae the Bass!' sang Finn, triumphantly.

'Eh?' Lachlan sat up. Finn had scrambled onto the dock to tie up the boat.

'It means *to do something impossible,* Lachlan,' said Finn. 'Come on, up you get. We've got your Highland Park to get through.'

A sign warned that the owners took no responsibility for any mishaps that befell visitors to the island. Lachlan looked up at the crumbling walls of the old castle prison, and the newer lighthouse within.

The ruins offered little shelter, as they had no roof, but also because they were occupied by a hundred or so gannets. Finn sat with his back to the crumbling wall and pulled out his hip flask. 'If we sit still, they'll stop swooping around so much.'

Lachlan mumbled and dropped to his side. After a minute, the birds appeared to settle.

'See?' said Finn. 'You've just got to adapt to the environment. Like the Scottish aristocracy when they performed their treachery. Sit still, don't rock the boat, and you'll be rewarded.'

'Aye, but they were gifted fortunes and highland estates. We're just avoiding being shat on.'

'Isn't that the Scottish way?' laughed Finn as he passed the flask.

Lachlan took a swig and stared back at the coast. North Berwick snuggled comfortably in this pleasant corner of East Lothian - a wealthy town of commuters. Here they could enjoy the country life and the seaside, while still only being half an hour from the capital.

Lachlan wondered if it was time to move out of the city, to somewhere smaller and more manageable.

He passed the flask back to Finn and watched two columns of smoke dance into the blue sky from the distant power station.

'How do you like living in Cockenzie?' Lachlan asked.

Finn shrugged, 'I like living by the water. How do you like living in Joppa?'

'Much the same,' said Lachlan. He swigged at the whisky, his head swirling as much as the waves below. He tried to study the thistle motif on the hip-flask but struggled to focus. He handed it back to Finn and lay back, drunk on this prison rock.

****

They stood together on the shore. Their towels hanging over the last timber groyne on Portobello beach.

He'd forgotten their anniversary. Again. Morag had woken him with the news that she had plans, and he knew resistance was futile. Twenty-three years of marriage meant *silver plate* and her take on this was that they'd go swimming in the Forth, their own piece of silver plate, just a few hundred yards from home. It did look particularly silvery today, Lachlan had to admit. A fine spring day with just a light haze meant the sun imparted a metallic sheen to the river.

'Well Lachlan. Here we go. It struck me the other day that as much as we love our river, other than paddling at Aberfoyle, we've never set foot in the bloody thing. It's ridiculous.'

'It's not ridiculous. It's sensible. There's a reason folk don't swim in it.'

'And what's that?'

'Well, other than the temperature, there's Seafield sewage works just up there.' This was true. With a prevailing wind the smell of the entire population of Edinburgh's bowel movements sometimes wafted their way.

'Don't be such a bloody feartie. Remember all those years ago at Don Roberto's grave? Where's your sense of adventure?'

Lachlan looked down at his feet in the sand. A good six inches of his ankles and lower leg were visible where the wetsuit stopped short. 'You might have got me one that fitted,' he grumbled.

'It's Shirley's husband's,' Morag said looking down at his feet and trying not to laugh. She'd borrowed the wetsuits from a friend. 'He's a lot shorter than you.'

'Obviously,' said Lachlan. 'So. Happy Anniversary then dear. What do we do now?'

Morag pecked him on the cheek. 'Happy Anniversary mon cherie. Now, we swim.'

She grabbed his hand and lunged forward, submerging them both in the Firth of Forth's icy waters.

'Jesus Christ!' spluttered Lachlan.

'There you go,' said Morag. 'Come on. Let's go deeper.'

She turned and took a few strokes, keeping her head above the surface. Lachlan reluctantly followed, making swimming motions but keeping his feet tip-toeing on the sand below.

After a few seconds Morag stopped swimming and bobbed on the surface. 'Oh, my feet can still reach the bottom,' she said. She seemed disappointed.

'That's not a bad thing,' said Lachlan. 'We're in our bloody sixties. I don't want us to die out here.' He grimaced as some seaweed tangled around his ankles. At least he hoped it was seaweed.

Morag looked skywards. 'You and your bloody obsession with death. Will you try living a bit for goodness sake?'

'I'm not obsessed with death,' said Lachlan.

Morag flashed her smile and shook her head. 'No Lachlan. Of course you're not. *Let's go to Paris on honeymoon* you said. Lovely, I thought. Then we spent a week touring cemeteries and the bloody catacombs. You were in your element. Thousands of skulls in those tunnels. I've never seen you happier. I've still got that picture of you holding up some poor sod's thigh bone like it's a bloody trophy.'

'That was a great day,' recalled Lachlan. 'You liked it too, don't forget.'

'It was interesting but it's your fascination with your own mortality that gets me. You spent ages staring into those empty eye sockets like you were trying to communicate with them. Like they were sending you messages from beyond the grave.'

'Maybe they were,' said Lachlan, as he bobbed on the surface.

A wave lapped at Morag's chin. She spat out some water and wiped her mouth. 'And the cemeteries. Montparnasse? I thought we'd never leave.'

'It was peaceful.'

'It was, aye, but you might have taken me up the Eiffel Tower or something. But no. Let's go look for dead celebrities. Jean-Paul bloody Sartre's lipstick-covered grave.'

'I wasn't just looking for celebrities,' Lachlan chuckled at his attempts to impress Morag. 'I was just as taken by the family tombs. Remember? *Famille Beauvert?* And all that? Generations together for eternity. The ordinary folk in there had more impact in death than they probably had in life. They could have been clerks, or florists, or died young, but when their names are carved in marble, they're there forever. It makes a mark. It did on me anyway.'

'So you'll be wanting a fancy grave then? Something that'll make a bit of an impact?'

'Aye,' said Lachlan, treading water. 'I do. A bloody great pyramid.'

'What about Don Roberto? He just had a slab in the ground. It's what you do when you're here that matters Lachlan. Nobody gives a toss about you when you're dead.'

'Well I gave a toss about those folk in Paris.'

'Aye, but you're weird. Anyway, I thought you wanted cremated. To let your atoms blow free and be transported away on the feathers of birds and all that stuff?'

'I do aye.'

'But you want a headstone too?'

Lachlan pondered this for a moment. 'Aye. Can you do a half and half?'

Morag swam towards him and they kissed as they bobbed together in the silvery waters.

'Twenty-three years, Lachlan. I expect another twenty-three at least before we have to start thinking about that.'

He squeezed his Volvo estate into a parking space then glanced up at Grace's flat. It was a Sunday in August. Overcast but muggy.

He should have called, but then she'd have been able to palm him off with an excuse. So he'd fabricated a reason to visit. He'd found a box of CDs under her bed. All that Oasis and Blur stuff she used to blast from her bedroom. He thought she'd appreciate it if he delivered them. Nothing odd about that, he was just passing. Why? Why would he be in Polwarth?

He switched off the engine and the car spluttered a few times before going quiet. That was it. There was a car parts shop around the corner. He was up here to get something for the car. Perfect.

He pressed the button beside 'McCormack' and smiled at Grace's looped handwriting. She'd made a smiley face from the O. Eventually, from the intercom, 'Hello?'

'Hello Grace. It's Dad.'

'Dad? What are you doing here?'

'You're meant to say *come up*, and press the bloody button to let me in.'

'Okay, sorry.' There was a buzz and the door clicked open. Lachlan entered the cool, dark stairwell. He glanced at the doors on the ground floor. All fairly well kept, he was pleased to note, with proper brass nameplates. Grace's flat was on the top floor. It would be wouldn't it? He looked up at the roof cupola bathing the interior in a milky light and started climbing.

On the first landing, he heard a door grind shut further up. That door needs a wee bit of adjustment, he thought. Take a plane to the bottom. Or stick a sheet of sandpaper under it and open and close it a few times. These young folk, they had no idea.

He paused by a door on the second landing. A battered plywood panel with a dent where it had been kicked. There was no name on it. The letter-box was taped shut with dried out strips of sellotape. Bloody idiot. Gaffa tape would be more effective and would last longer. He shook his head.

A young man, about thirty, with sandy tousled hair hurried by. He stared at his shoes as he edged past Lachlan.

'Hello,' said Lachlan. The man mumbled a reply and jogged down the stairs.

No bloody manners either, he thought as he continued his climb.

He reached Grace's door, took a breath, and knocked twice. A blue door, with the nameplate he'd had made for her at the locksmith place in Portobello. *G. McCormack*. His wee girl. All grown up.

'Just a minute,' she called from inside.

He leaned towards the door and heard her fussing about. She was tidying up for him, bless her.

After a moment the door opened with a grinding noise that sounded familiar.

'Hiya, come in,' said Grace. She smiled, bleary eyed. Her hair tied up in a ponytail, she looked half asleep. It was nearly noon for goodness sake.

'Hi darling. I brought some of your things.' He held the cardboard box up, like an offering to the gods, as he stepped into the small hallway. The living room door was open and Grace ushered him through. 'I was just in the area and, well, thought you might want these back.'

Grace looked sceptical but smiled and said, 'Coffee?'

'Aye that'd be nice. So how's things?' He dropped to the settee, inspecting every corner of the room. The window had been pulled open and the curtains flapped in a gentle breeze.

'Oh fine. Day off today, you're lucky I'm in. I've been working the last few Sundays.'

'I thought I'd just take a chance. I'm going to that wee car specialist around the corner.'

'I know the one. Are there no car specialists in Joppa or Portobello? Maybe Leith?' she smiled as she poured milk into two mugs.

Lachlan fidgeted, 'Probably. But this guy knows his stuff. There's a problem with the Volvo. It's running on, you know?'

'No Dad, I've got no idea what that means, but I hope you get it fixed. How's Mum?'

'She's grand. Daft as a brush.'

'What's she planning now? Munro bagging? Trekking the Andes?'

'She's into the anti-war stuff. We've got the internet now too. She's never off the bloody thing.'

Grace chuckled, 'Aye she's a handful. She'll keep you on your toes Dad.' She handed him his coffee. A *lion rampant* mug she'd taken from home. 'So how are you keeping?'

He shrugged, 'Same as always. You know me.'

Grace leaned forward and furrowed her brow. 'Your nose is a wee bit red there. You still knocking back the whisky?'

Lachlan bristled and sat back, 'Och, no more than usual. Nothing for you to worry about.'

Grace drank some coffee and placed her mug on a side table. 'It's just, Dad, I see this every day now at the hospital. It's a killer. Just take it easy, please?'

'Aye, don't you worry about me,' he said. Then, changing the subject, 'Your front door needs a bit of sandpaper. It's rubbing on the threshold. Do you want me to fix that for you?'

'Oh, thanks. Hadn't really noticed. Trust you though.'

Lachlan looked around the room. They both sat on the single sofa. She had a tall shelf overflowing with books, and her TV on a little table. The original cast iron fireplace sat in the centre, unused. At the back of the room was her kitchenette. A few cupboards, a fridge and a cooker. It reminded Lachlan of his Alloa days, although this was a step up from his little bedsit.

'Maybe all the doors in the stair do it. I heard another door grinding when I came up. Young guy, about thirty. Do you know him?' He studied her response. She glanced downwards, fiddled with her earring and shook her head.

'No, don't think so.'

That was all Lachlan needed to know. He took a drink of coffee and felt it swirl in his stomach. He had to let her grow up. She was twenty-three after all. A woman. Entitled to do whatever the hell she pleased with whoever the hell she liked. But it didn't make it any easier for him.

'Anyway,' he patted the box on the table. 'The Blurs. The Oasis. The Spiral Carpets. They're all in there.'

Grace grinned. 'Inspiral, Dad.'

'Eh?'

'Inspiral Carpets,' I thought you'd remember that. I played it enough. *This is how it feels to be lonely?* Remember?'

'Oh aye, of course.' He stood and paced across the living room. On the fireplace was a family picture, taken in the garden of their Joppa bungalow ten years ago. It reminded him of the photo of him with his mother and father outside their Aberfoyle cottage all those decades ago.

'You're not though are you?' he asked.

'I'm not what?'

'Lonely?'

Grace looked up at him and smiled. 'No Dad, please stop worrying about me. I'm not.'

'Right. Good. It's just that…' he trailed off. He knew the guy in the stairwell had made a sharp exit from his daughter's flat, but was that any of his business? He continued, 'So do you have a boyfriend?'

'Dad! For God's sake.' She laughed and shook her head, her mouth hanging open. 'What if I did?'

'Nothing. I'm just asking. There are a lot of idiots out there, you know that. Drugs and stuff.'

'Jesus Dad I'm not twelve.'

'No but to me you are. To me you're no different to when you were born. You'll always be my wee baby.'

Grace stood and gave him a hug. 'You big sap. Stop worrying about me. Maybe you should get yourself a hobby? An interest, like Mum. Something to fill your days. Other than drinking whisky.'

He rubbed his head, sweeping his greying hair back. 'You're right. I still see Finn. We go fishing sometimes.'

'That's nice. What about Johnny? You heard from him? Why don't you take a wee trip out to Alloa?'

He sat down again and fidgeted with a cushion. 'Aye. I might. It's complicated at the moment though. I don't think Johnny and Mandy are getting on too well. And that Billy's an idiot.'

'Hey, he's my half-brother. Things no better between you?'

'Nah, not really. I tried my best. I do feel responsible for him. Gave him all that money when he turned eighteen and he…' He paused, trying to think of a more appropriate phrase than the one he was about to use.

'Pissed it against a wall?' said Grace.

'Exactly. He's my son though, can't get away from that. Christ, he'll be forty in a few years. Never worked a day in his life either.'

'Well, what with your money and the Sinclair millions, he'll manage.'

'I wouldn't be so sure. As far as I know Mandy's pretty much disowned him.'

Grace finished her coffee and clunked the mug on the table. 'And how's Mark?'

Lachlan blew an exasperated sigh, 'My grandson?' He laughed a weary laugh. 'He's joined the army, apparently.'

'Jesus. Is he old enough?'

'He's twenty now. Old enough to serve Queen and bloody country.'

'I always liked him. He seemed nice,' Grace said, glancing at the clock.

'Sorry, do you need to be somewhere?'

'No. Not at all. Just thinking about lunch. Do you fancy going out for something? Pub around the corner does a nice Sunday carvery. You can get your car things later.'

'Car things?' asked Lachlan, momentarily forgetting his little subterfuge. 'Oh aye! Of course.'

Grace smiled and grabbed her coat. 'Come on, before they run out of Yorkshire Puddings.'

****

A train trundled across the rail bridge overhead. The screech of metal on metal as it accelerated north towards Fife. A cold wind blew in off the Forth but the pub's heating was up full and Lachlan and Johnny had already discarded their jackets and were close to removing their jumpers. Johnny had called Lachlan to South Queensferry to impart the not-unexpected news that after almost forty years of marriage, he and Mandy were splitting up.

'Spain?' said Lachlan.

'Aye,' said Johnny with a smile. 'Can get apartments out there for fuck all. They're springing up everywhere. I've been to a few events, local things. I'm paying the deposit next week.'

'On a house you've never seen?'

'I've seen pictures,' said Johnny, taking another mouthful of beer.

'Right,' said Lachlan, drumming his fingers on the table. 'And?'

'And it looks bloody marvellous. Golf course. Pub. Swimming pool. And the shop sells all English stuff.'

'English stuff?'

'Aye. Ketchup, digestive biscuits, sliced white bread...'

'No Scottish stuff then?'

'Same thing isn't it?'

Lachlan laughed. 'And here's me thinking you were a proud Scotsman. What about the pub?'

'What about it?'

'Well, what's it called? Do they sell Special?'

'I think it's called the Red Lion.'

Lachlan spluttered into his pint. 'Sounds great Johnny. Really it does. So when do you move?'

'Don't pish on my chips Lachlan. I've got a second wind here. I feel re-born. Time to grab the bull by the horns.' Johnny grabbed Lachlan's shoulders and shook him, spilling his pint.

Lachlan wiped his sleeve dry. 'You'll be able to do that at the local bullfight. Or do they just play cricket there?'

'Fuck off. Anyway, I'll be moving as soon as it's ready.'

'Ready?'

'Aye well, it's not been built yet.'

Lachlan could barely contain his laughter. 'You're buying a house that hasn't even been built yet? Based on a drawing? What about the shops and the pub?'

'Aye, they're getting built too. Listen, this company, they've built these things all over Spain. Showed us pictures and a video of other developments. It's the high life pal. You're just bloody jealous.'

'Aye, maybe you're right,' Lachlan lied. 'We've been thinking of moving too actually. Now that Grace is away. We don't need all the space, and it's a pain in the arse having a front and back garden to look after.'

'Come to Spain, it'll be just like old times.'

'That's what worries me. We're thinking of somewhere along the coast a wee bit.'

'Fuck's sake Lachlan. We're in the EU, you can live anywhere you like. They'll pay your pension over there. Hospitals are better, and it's all free. Why the hell would you want to see out your days in this shithole?'

Lachlan pondered this for a moment and it struck him that he could never see himself moving away from Scotland. Not just Scotland, he doubted he'd ever move away from the Firth of Forth. They were tied to this one constant in their lives, him and Morag. He was sure they'd end their days overlooking its waters and the sea beyond.

'So, how's Billy?' asked Lachlan, changing the subject.

Johnny sighed. 'Apart from *well known to the local constabulary?*'

'Still getting in bother?'

Johnny shook his head. 'Nothing major. A bit too quick with his fists after a few pints. He's got a bit of a reputation and some folk think they'll have a go at knocking him down a peg. Never works. They're always the ones that end up on the pavement.'

Lachlan laughed, 'Where the hell did he get that from?'

Johnny shrugged, 'I know. I'm a lover, not a fighter. And you, well you're what? Neither?'

Lachlan sipped his pint. 'I'm more of a drinker. Suppose he's got that from me. What about the wee lad, Mark?'

Johnny looked out the window. The boat from Inchcolm Island had just docked and day trippers were disembarking and heading towards the pub. 'What can I say? He's a good lad, what I've seen of him. Mandy's fond of him. I think having an arsehole for a father has done him some good, in a way. He probably vowed that he didn't want to turn out like his old man.'

'So he joined the army?'

'Well he wasn't exactly academically gifted, put it that way.'

'Could he not have got a job at the brewery?'

'He did. Briefly. Wasn't for him, and I think he wanted to put as much distance between him and his father as he could.'

'What about his mother?'

'She's dead. A few years back. Couldn't cope with Billy and started on the heroin.'

'Jesus,' Lachlan wiped his brow. 'Poor lassie.'

'They had an on-off thing for years. She was messed up. Best thing young Mark could do was sign up and get himself away from the pair of them to be honest.'

Lachlan drained the last of his beer. 'I feel bad. I've not seen him for years.'

'Don't feel bad about it. You did what you could for Billy. We both did. It was his job to look after Mark, not yours.'

'So where's he based?'

'Royal Scots. In Edinburgh, for now, but he's off to Iraq soon. Helping get rid of Saddam.'

Lachlan sighed. 'Fuck all to do with it. It's all about the bloody oil. It always is. Look out there.' He pointed to a tanker berthed at the gas distribution plant beyond the bridge. 'It's what makes the world go round. And they don't care whose blood is spilled to get their hands on it.'

'Well nobody's going to invade us Lachlan. I wouldn't worry.'

'We were invaded years ago Johnny. Actually, we weren't, we were blackmailed. Actually that's bollocks too. Just a few of us were. And I use *us* in the loosest possible sense.'

'Aye, the parcel o' rogues Lachlan. Heard it a million times.'

'And you'll hear it a million more, believe me.'

Johnny laughed and raised his empty glass, 'Whisky please Brave-heart. Oh, and get me one of those Spanish lagers. I saw bottles in the fridge. I need to start getting used to them.'

'I'm sure they'll have Tennents in that pub that hasn't been built yet.'

'*Vamos!*' Johnny cried.

'What?' asked Lachlan.

'It means *go*, in Spanish. I think.'

'*Tolla thon,*' said Lachlan, picking up their glasses.

'What's that?'

'It means *no problem* in Gaelic.'

Johnny smiled and sat back in the booth. Lachlan headed for the bar and chuckled to himself. It was true, Johnny was becoming a bit of an arsehole.

****

The whisky glowed a rich amber in the flickering light. Lachlan sniffed it, rolled it around the glass, then knocked it back. He threw another log on the fire and watched the flames wrap around it, crackling and spitting. He rose and placed the glass on the fireplace, listening to the voices next door. Morag was telling Grace's boyfriend, Gavin all about Grace's first attempts at cooking, when she'd proudly battered the bedroom door open and presented her dozing parents with two raw eggs cracked over some buttered bread. Gavin laughed politely.

What a boring prick, thought Lachlan. As he'd suspected, the floppy haired grunter from the stairwell that day was Grace's boyfriend. They'd been introduced to him a few months previously, and this was the big one - Christmas Day at the parents. Did Grace deserve better? Damn right she did. He poured another whisky and downed it in one before rejoining the party.

'So, Gavin. Tell me about your work,' he exclaimed, slurring slightly as he closed the door behind him. Morag cast him a suspicious eye. Bing Crosby crooned *White Christmas* from the little CD player on the sideboard.

'There's not much to tell really. It's a bank.' Gavin shrugged, playing with his cutlery.

'Oh come on Gavin,' said Grace. 'It's important. Stop putting yourself down.'

Lachlan could see the despair in Grace's eyes.

'Well, I write programs, procedures, that sort of thing. Pretty boring really.'

Lachlan stared at him. Gavin stared at the table.

Morag chipped in, 'Right, who's for pudding? Brandy sauce?'

'Lovely Mum, I'll give you a hand clearing this away,' said Grace.

'Thanks,' said Lachlan, smiling at his daughter. 'Stack them up and I'll wash them later.'

Once they were out of the room Lachlan reached for a bottle on the sideboard.

'Whisky?' he asked.

Gavin looked terrified. 'Oh no. No thanks. I don't-'

Lachlan poured two glasses and placed one in front of Gavin with a clunk.

'Oh well just this one then.' He nervously picked up the glass.

Lachlan held his up, 'Cheers.'

'Cheers,' Gavin said and took a delicate sip. He winced.

'So what's your plans with my daughter then?'

'Eh? Oh, well. We're, well, I don't know really. You'd have to ask her that.'

'I'm asking you,' said Lachlan.

Gavin grabbed at the tablecloth and twisted it in his fingers. 'We're going out I suppose. That's all.'

Lachlan grunted. 'And is she happy? That's the most important thing to me, that she's happy. Is she happy?'

Gavin shrugged and smiled awkwardly. 'I think so,' he offered with an expression that pleaded for leniency.

'Hmm.' Lachlan poured himself another whisky and held the bottle towards Gavin, who placed his hands over the top of his glass.

'Not for me thanks, one's enough.'

Lachlan sat back in his chair. He sipped at the whisky and watched Gavin squirm. From the kitchen he heard Grace and Morag laugh together. 'Let's just be straight here, if you do anything to hurt her I'll break your neck. Understand?'

Gavin looked like he was about to faint. 'I do. I won't. I promise.' He lifted his whisky and threw back a sizeable mouthful. He grimaced and shook his head, as his eyes started watering.

The door opened and the sound of Morag clattering around in the kitchen filled the small dining room. Grace looked at them both as she placed the Christmas pudding on the table. 'You boys getting along?' Her eyes darted between them in turn. Bing was just finishing his song, wishing that all their Christmases would be white.

'Smashing,' said Lachlan, smiling, 'eh Gavin?'

Gavin blinked, clearing the whisky tears from his eyes. He gulped. 'Great yeah.'

****

'It's bloody Arthur Scargill. How can you not know that?' Lachlan cried.

'Lachlan!' Morag yelped. 'Stop being so bloody rude.' The Trivial

Pursuit board balanced on a footstool between them all. 'I'm sorry Gavin, he gets like this on the whisky.'

'That's okay. Politics isn't my strongpoint,' Gavin muttered, glancing at Lachlan whose face was glowing red in the firelight.

'What is your bloody strongpoint then?' muttered Lachlan.

'Dad, can you calm down a bit?' laughed Grace. 'It's just a game.'

'Ignore him Gavin,' Morag said. 'I'm sure if there was a category on computer programming you'd be winning eh?'

Lachlan watched Gavin smile, then frown, as if he was unsure if Morag was taking the piss.

'I'm sorry,' said Lachlan, while he poured himself another drink. 'It's a generation thing. We grew up with the Tories. We had strikes and riots and hardship and the worst you've had to suffer was the fallout from the Britpop wars. Who's better, Oasis or Blur?'

'There's no need to shout Dad, we're in the same room,' Grace giggled.

'Right whose turn is it? Grace? Roll the dice,' said Morag in an attempt at moving things on.

Grace tossed the dice on the board. She perused her options for a moment before nudging her piece. 'Sport and Leisure pie!'

Morag pulled a question from the box and angled it towards the light from the fire. 'What was broken at Oxford England on May 6th 1954?'

Lachlan knew the answer but his thoughts seemed to have stopped linking up. He took another mouthful of whisky. He didn't even feel it going down, his insides were so scorched after a day of the stuff. He felt the effects instantly though, as the room took a sudden lurch, like a ship in a storm.

'The four minute mile?' said Grace.

'Correct. Orange pie for you. Right happiness, your turn.' Morag shoved the dice towards Lachlan.

Lachlan tried to pick it up but was struggling to focus. His fingers clutched at fresh air as three or four dice wobbled around in his vision. He shifted forward on the chair, muttering to himself, and grabbed for the dice. Again he missed.

He stared at the footstool in front of him. Why were they playing Trivial Pursuit on three different boards? He heard Morag say something but it sounded muffled and far away. He turned towards Grace, a trail of fairy lights on the tree smeared like a dripping rainbow. Gavin was looking at him. What was he looking at? Wee arsehole. Grace was looking at him too. She was saying something. What was she saying? Morag stood up and stepped towards him. His darling Morag. He lifted his head to smile and collapsed forwards from his chair, spilling the board and its contents. The last thing he saw before he passed out was the blue piece - Gavin's? - as it arced through the air and landed in the fire.

****

He was swimming in a golden sea. Flames licked the horizon. He was thirsty. So, so thirsty. Ahead, a shape bobbed on the surface - an orange inflatable life-raft with a glowing canopy. He swam towards it.

He tried to call out but his throat was raw. He gasped and lunged forward through the waves. His eyes stinging. His stomach churning.

'Come on!' A voice called from the raft. 'You can make it.'

Through the canopy, Lachlan could see a figure reaching out. A hand in the gloom. He grabbed for it as a wave sent him under again.

Beneath the surface all was light. The floor of the ocean was visible far below, covered in blue linoleum. There were no fish in this ocean, and he realised he could breathe. It was so bright - where was the light coming from? He twisted to face the surface where a hundred strip lights were floating in regular rows, lighting up the water. He turned again to face the floor. The linoleum was beginning to peel away and a blackness seeped out, like ink or smoke. It shrouded the ocean floor and drifted upwards towards him, performing a terrible, twisting dance. The smoke reached out for him and he kicked at it, dispersing it in a cloud of light. He kicked again and fought back to the surface. His feet turned to ice. He looked back and the blackness was beginning to wrap itself around his leg. With another push his face broke back into the darkness of night. The flames were closer now, yards from the life-raft. He reached up, the outstretched hand was still there.

'Come on! I've got you son!'

'Dad?' Lachlan managed a feeble gasp. His father's hand grabbed him and hauled him up.

'Dad?' he rasped. But he was alone. The raft bobbed gently. The darkness in the sea below seemed to dissipate. It was turning blue. He looked outside and saw the flames dying away. Flickering out, one by one.

****

Lachlan strode along the promenade, leaning into the wind.

Did you know, that walking a mile is as good for you as running a mile? The old TV advert came back to him. Gavin Hastings the rugby player wasn't it? That line had stuck with him and as his legs had grown weary with the years he'd repeated it to himself regularly, especially when he was overtaken by joggers.

He'd been sober for two months and this walk was part of his morning routine. Rain or shine, Monday to Friday, he could be seen powering along the promenade and back again - the recovering alcoholic - alongside the joggers, dog-walkers and cyclists, young mums and old... what? They were mothers too probably, but now grandmothers, roped into babysitting duties. He'd spent Boxing Day in hospital, after getting his stomach pumped. He'd tried to blame Morag for putting too much brandy in the Christmas pudding, but the doctor had taken him aside and told him that he'd been lucky to survive. A wake up call? Like father, like son? He didn't want to join his father just yet.

A sharp drizzle blew in from the grey Forth and stung his cheek. He pulled his collar up and squinted into the distance. Halfway there. It was good to have purpose. Good to take his mind off what his body was still craving.

Christmas seemed like a lifetime ago. But he hoped it was another life. Another Lachlan.

Morag had plans for them later; a drive into East Lothian. She'd suddenly seen the appeal of moving out of the city, and he wondered how much *distance from the nearest pub* would be a factor in the house-hunt.

Christ he needed a drink.

One good thing had come out of Lachlan's antics at Christmas - Grace had realised that Gavin wasn't the man for her. Not because of Lachlan's low-opinion of him, but because of the inescapable fact that he was unbearably dull.

A break in the clouds scudding overhead momentarily brightened the promenade. It darkened again in seconds as another wave of rain blew in from the Forth.

Just one drink, that would do.

He thought of their little lost girl, Gabriella as he passed the Amusement Arcade where Morag had miscarried all those years ago. Her existence snuffed out among the vinegar smells and dirty copper pennies. Grace came along soon after, but there was a fragility to having an only child. It made him worry more. They'd have been great sisters, but then maybe Grace wouldn't have happened? Was life a rollercoaster? There were ups and downs, but sometimes it did feel like it was on a set path - destined to follow the rails until the end of the ride, where you nudge the newly-loaded carriage of your offspring on their own identical journey. His father had died at 49, so Lachlan already felt like he was on bonus time.

The smirr was all-encompassing now. He looked to his right, the beach barely visible. The horizon lost. The river nowhere to be seen. He was alone in the grey.

He quickened his pace, patting his pocket. He had a few notes. That'd be enough. Just enough to get through today. Just enough to take the edge off.

At the end of the promenade a little pub occupied the ground floor of a tenement building. Warm and welcoming, an orange glow from the window shone like a lighthouse in the gloom.

He turned and headed for home.

****

The front door swung open as he approached. Morag stood there, saying nothing. A worried look on her face.

Lachlan smiled and stepped into the hall, fumbling out of his soaked jacket as he did so.

'Hello,' he said. 'What's up?'

She helped him with his jacket, shook it outside, then hung it on the coat stand while he slipped off his shoes. 'Come in and get dry,' she said.

'Bloody soaked,' he muttered.

'Aye, you certainly are,' said Morag. 'What a morning.'

He looked down at his damp socks. 'I think I knocked a minute off my time there. It's getting easier.'

'That's good Lachlan. Listen, you'd better sit down. Come in to the living room.'

She touched Lachlan gently on the shoulder in passing.

The fire he'd set before heading out for his walk was crackling away. He glanced at the log basket and noticed Morag had used most of them up.

'I'll better get more logs in,' he said.

Morag sat in her chair by the window. The glass clouded with condensation, her face similarly unreadable.

'Sit down Lachlan,' she gestured at the settee.

'I'm soaked through. Probably better get out of these clothes first,' he said, taking a step back towards the hall.

'Just sit down,' she said.

A sudden coldness ran through him. Had she thought he'd slipped off the wagon? He'd been tempted, but hadn't succumbed.

He sat on the edge of the settee and opened his arms, palms upwards. 'Morag, what's this about? I haven't touched a drop, I swear.'

She took a deep breath. 'It's not that Lachlan. I trust you.'

'Eh? What is it then?'

'There was a phone call, not long after you left.'

Lachlan's mouth dried up. He nodded.

'It was Johnny,' Morag continued. 'They got word this morning that young Mark was killed.'

He put his head in his hands. His grandson barely out of school and recruited into the British Army outside a shopping centre in Stirling. He felt numb. And now needed a drink more than ever. He let out a long sigh and fell back into the sofa.

'What happened?' he managed, eventually.

'An I.E.D. A homemade bomb. Him and his pals, all dead. They didn't stand a chance. The floor of the jeep they were in was torn to pieces.' Her eyes started watering. 'I'm sorry Lachlan.'

He stared into the fire. A log shifted and spat, sending a glowing ember up the chimney.

'He only joined up to get away from that idiot father of his,' said Lachlan - his voice breaking. 'How the hell can the British Army send boys out there so badly equipped they can be killed by a homemade fucking bomb?'

Morag hugged him. 'I know love. I know.'

Outside, the rain had turned to hail. The frozen pellets blasting the window in the strengthening wind.

****

The afternoon passed in a blur. A coffin draped in the Union Flag. The sound of the Last Post played on a solitary trumpet. A cold wind blowing from the north over the graveyard in Alloa.

Morag and Grace had been by Lachlan's side throughout and now they were making the short walk to the function room at the masonic lodge where a 'Celebration of Mark's life' was being held.

There hadn't been the usual family line-up after the service. Probably for the best given that Johnny wasn't talking to Mandy, and Billy was talking to neither of them. The last thing they needed was a stream of platitudes from people they hadn't seen in years.

Lachlan had watched Billy during the burial. He'd struggled to maintain his tough-guy persona. His shoulders jerked at one point as he stifled a sob. Johnny stood impassively by his side, his eyes masked behind a pair of sunglasses. Mandy completed the symmetry, her hair now cut into a short, grey bob. He was surprised to see that Mandy's father was still alive. Now well into his eighties, William Sinclair still cut an imposing figure, albeit a slightly more stooped version of the one that had terrified Lachlan all those years ago.

'Remember Dad, no drinking,' said Grace as they followed the crowd of mourners into the hall.

'Don't worry,' he said with a smile. 'We won't be here long. Just enough time to pay our respects. What are you having?'

Lachlan stepped towards the bar, already busy with people who seemed far too young to be making up the crowd at a funeral. Mostly Mark's friends and colleagues, by the looks of things. Army haircuts, wiry builds, yet looking like they'd barely started shaving. He spotted Johnny at the far end of the room. Mandy stood nearby but they had their backs to each other. There was no sign of Billy.

'Excuse me.' A tap on his shoulder. Lachlan turned to face a young woman with blonde-streaked hair and thick-rimmed glasses. Her eyes red with tears. 'Are you Lachlan?'

Lachlan nodded.

'I'm Sandi. Mark's girlfriend. You're his grandad then?'

He nodded again. 'I'm so sorry.' He placed a hand on her shoulder. 'It's a terrible, terrible thing.'

Sandi's eyes dropped to the floor. 'He talked about you a lot.'

Lachlan was surprised by this. Mark had been a child the last time he'd seen him. Before life, the miles between, and alcohol got in the way. 'He did?'

'Aye, you were his only granddad really. And it's not like his own dad was there for him. I think it's why he joined the army. He needed a family. He needed to feel like he belonged somewhere you know?'

Lachlan sighed. All he could say was sorry. Sandi said, 'Just thought I'd let you know,' and walked back into the crowd.

****

'Another one? Are you sure? We should probably be going,' said Lachlan, checking his watch.

'One for the road,' said Morag. 'And get one for Mandy, I'll take it over.'

Lachlan grumbled and stood up. They'd managed to find a table in the corner. Johnny had been boring them for an hour about his impending move to Spain. Morag being Morag, had hit it off with Mandy earlier and she was looking for an excuse to extract herself from Johnny's conversation.

Grace had left after her first drink for some pressing appointment in Edinburgh. *Is it a boy?* Morag had asked. By Grace's bashful grin he could tell that it was.

'What about you Signor? What are you having?' he asked Johnny.

'My shout Lachlan, sit yourself back down.'

'Well, if you insist. I'll have another lemonade.'

'No problem. *No hay problema. Tolla thon,*' exclaimed Johnny as he headed for the bar.

Lachlan chuckled to himself. *Arsehole.* Would Johnny still be using the one Gaelic phrase he'd taught him on the Costa, and would he ever learn what it actually meant?

This would definitely be the last drink, so Lachlan thought he'd better start preparing his bladder for the journey home.

He eased through the crowd towards the toilets. A stainless steel urinal down one wall, with two cubicles opposite. One door was locked and as he unzipped he heard the toilet flush behind him. The strip light in the ceiling flickered as the door slammed back against the cubicle wall.

His pee drummed against the stainless steel and he glanced sideways at the sinks. Whoever had emerged from the cubicle wasn't washing their hands. He glanced back over his shoulder to see the stooped figure of William Sinclair, glowering at him.

'You?' he croaked, raising a bony finger.

'Mr Sinclair?' said Lachlan, shaking himself dry. 'How are you? Terrible thing to have happened to such a young lad isn't it?'

'Terrible?!' said Sinclair, stepping forward. 'I'll tell you what's terrible. Shagging my daughter then fucking off and leaving her with the baby, that's what's terrible.' He pulled himself to his full height, which Lachlan estimated to be around five foot eight given shrinkage over the decades.

'Aye well. Water under the bridge now surely?' said Lachlan as he stepped towards the sinks.

'You think?' said Sinclair, shuffling towards him. 'There's

something I've been meaning to give you for years son and you're getting it now.'

'What's that?' asked Lachlan as he washed his hands.

'This,' said Sinclair with a wheeze. Lachlan turned in time to see the old man pulling a fist back, his arm shaking. He swung at Lachlan, who had the presence of mind to dodge before landing a punch square on Sinclair's jaw, sending his false teeth clattering across the toilet floor.

'Shite, sorry,' said Lachlan as the old man crumpled to the tiles. He tried to help him up. Sinclair was yelling something, but without his teeth, it was just coming out as gurgles and spit.

'Here, sit down.' He dragged Sinclair into the cubicle he'd just exited and kicked the seat down. Sinclair flopped, his head resting against the toilet roll holder, and promptly started snoring.

Lachlan straightened his jacket and checked the floor. He retrieved Sinclair's teeth from a puddle under the urinal, thought about washing them, then decided against it and sat them on the old man's lap.

Back in the hall Johnny was placing their drinks on the table. Morag was standing with Mandy, laughing. She spotted Lachlan by the toilet door, then saw the new drinks and stepped over to retrieve them from Johnny. Lachlan shook his head wildly. No time for that. We need to get the hell out of here.

'Hiya Dad,' came an unfamiliar voice. He assumed they were talking to somebody else.

'I said hiya Dad!' said the voice again. He felt a hand on his shoulder pulling him backwards. He turned and there was Billy. Now nearly forty. Ruddy-faced with cropped hair and a scar the length of a pint glass down one cheek. 'Long time no see eh?'

'Billy? Jesus. Where have you been? We were just leaving.'

'Not before you have a drink with me. Come on.'

Lachlan stumbled as Billy's firm hand steered him towards the bar. 'It's good to see you Billy. And I'm sorry for your loss.'

Billy gave the briefest of nods to the barman that suggested he was familiar with his order.

'Aye thanks. I just got here. Had to go and sort some stuff out. Not very good at these things.'

'No,' Lachlan glanced back towards the toilet door. 'Me neither really.'

'Like father like son eh?' said Billy with a hint of a smile. 'So, what's been happening with you?'

I've just battered your Grandad in the toilet. 'Oh you know, this and that.'

'I never did say thanks for the money did I?' said Billy, which caught Lachlan off-guard.

'Er, no. You don't need to,' said Lachlan. 'Christ, that was years ago.'

The barman placed two shot glasses in front of them.

'Well I want to,' said Billy. 'You've been a shite dad but I've been a shite son and I want to put that behind us. And that prick,' he gestured towards Johnny, 'can go fuck himself. He was never good enough for my mum.'

'And I was?' asked Lachlan.

'Were you fuck,' said Billy. 'You were as big an arsehole. But you're my fucking dad and there's nothing we can do about it, so here's to leaving it in the past eh? I'm a changed man these days.'

'Aye?' said Lachlan.

'Sure am. I'm heading up north. A mate got me a job on the rigs so I'll be staying out of trouble. I'll never land another punch, unless the cunt deserves it.'

'Right,' said Lachlan. 'Well that's good to hear. What's this then?' he indicated at the glass, 'because I don't really drink-'

'Jagermeister,' said Billy. 'Get it down your fucking throat.'

'Right,' said Lachlan, again. He sniffed the contents. 'Ooft!' he recoiled. 'That's got a kick eh?'

'Aye, goes down like juice.'

'Not for me Billy, thanks though. We'll need to be heading. I'm driving.' Lachlan's eyes darted between Morag's wine glass and the toilet door. 'I'm glad we met though. And, well, thanks.'

'For what,' said Billy.

'For calling me Dad,' said Lachlan.

'You are my dad,' said Billy. 'What else am I meant to call you?'

Lachlan had a feeling he was about to find out, as a young guy placed an empty pint glass beside them and headed for the toilet door.

Morag caught Lachlan's eye. She touched Mandy on the shoulder, drained her wine and headed through the crowd towards the bar.

'Hiya love,' said Lachlan hurriedly. 'Billy, this is Morag, my wife.'

'I know who you are,' said Morag with a smile. 'Lovely to see you two catch up.'

'Father and son reunion,' said Lachlan. 'But we should probably be going now eh?'

'Oh there's no rush, let's make the most of this awful day. What are you having to drink Billy?'

Oh Christ, thought Lachlan as he looked for an escape route.

'I'm just going to…' he edged away, leaving Morag and Billy at the bar. They were locked in conversation, they wouldn't notice if he just slipped out for a bit.

'Hey, are you wanting this lemonade or not?' said Johnny as he appeared at his side holding Lachlan's drink.

'Aye, thanks,' said Lachlan, grabbing the glass from Johnny. At that, the toilet door swung inwards and a polished shoe appeared, jamming it open. The young guy had William Sinclair's arm wrapped around his shoulder and was hauling him back into the fray. The geriatric stared wildly around the room as Lachlan ducked behind Johnny.

'Dad?!' screamed Mandy from across the room. 'Oh my God what happened?' Lachlan gulped as she hurried to her bruised and battered father.

All eyes were on the old man now who was spluttering incoherently as he scanned the room.

'What is it Dad? I can't understand? Where's your teeth?'

The young guy reached into his pocket and pulled out the piss-soaked dentures. With a shaking hand Sinclair grabbed them and shoved them back into his slavering mouth. He bared his newly re-installed teeth just as he spotted Lachlan duck behind Johnny's shoulder.

'That bugger… Oh Jesus!' With a look of horror, he wrenched his false teeth from his mouth and spat on the floor. His tongue hanging loose, his already creased face contorting even more.

Lachlan stepped forward, holding out his lemonade. 'Here, drink this.'

Sinclair grabbed it and downed it in one, half the contents spilling down his chin, then glared at Lachlan and offered another stream of incomprehensible spit-soaked gibberish.

'I think he needs to sit down. Do you want to sit down Mr Sinclair? Did you bump your head? Those toilet doors are lethal eh?' Lachlan said, taking hold of the old man and edging him towards the bench seats surrounding the hall.

'Thanks Lachlan,' said Mandy as she cast a withering glance in Johnny's direction. 'Just as well you're here.'

'Aye well. Happy to help,' said Lachlan. As he edged the fidgeting Sinclair down, he managed to grab the teeth from his hand and quickly pocket them. Sinclair snarled. Mandy sat down beside him and started dabbing blood from under his nose with a napkin.

'Did the door hit you in the face?' she said.

'Schflllkkknn bllleeshhhh fllllrrrrrpppp,' said Sinclair, pointing a finger at Lachlan, like a duelling pistol.

Lachlan stepped away and headed back to the toilet. The crowd was beginning to turn back to their conversations.

Lachlan waited for a moment in the gents. Nobody followed him in so he quickly dropped Sinclair's teeth down the toilet and yanked the flush lever.

Nothing.

'Fuck sake,' he muttered and cranked the handle again.

Still nothing.

With a groan, he rolled up his sleeve, reached into the bowl, and grabbed the teeth. As he stood, shaking them dry, the door swung open.

'What are you doing with my grandad's teeth?' said Billy.

'Washing them,' said Lachlan. He punched the button on the drier and held the dripping teeth in the hot air. 'He dropped them. Can't be too careful with germs and stuff. Especially at his age.'

'Aye,' said Billy as he unzipped at the urinal. 'Thanks. He's a miserable old bastard though. Never liked him. He never liked me either.'

'Well he's still your grandfather son. Whether you like him or not.'

Billy grunted. 'Your wife's nice. She's invited me to yours for tea.'

'Has she? Aye, of course. You're welcome I mean. I should have done it myself.'

Billy zipped up and turned around. 'Here, give me those.'

Lachlan looked at the teeth in his hand. 'Eh? These?' He handed them over. There was no getting away from it now, he'd have to face the music. If he could grab Morag quickly they might be able to escape before Sinclair was gifted the power of speech again.

Billy took the dentures and dropped them to the floor where he crushed them under his heel. 'I'm sick of that old prick's bullshit. And today's not the day for it.' He kicked the fragments under the cubicle door.

Under the flickering fluorescent light, Lachlan felt like he was seeing his son for the first time.

****

Lachlan stood in the doorway as Morag paused at the kitchen sink taking in the view from the small panelled window.

'I love it,' she said, her back to him.

Lachlan knew then that this would be their new home. A one-bedroom cottage on the edge of a tiny hamlet, a few miles outside Haddington. No pubs within walking distance. Just tree-lined fields of grain as far as the eye could see, literally. Haddington - the 'Hidden Toun' - nestled in a dip in the East Lothian countryside, as if shy, minding its own business. Keeping its head below the parapet. Exactly what Morag wanted and exactly what Lachlan needed.

'It's perfect,' she said, turning to face him.

He joined her at the sink and peered through the glass. 'Nice views I suppose,' he said, eventually.

'You suppose?'

He scanned the fields, all the way to the horizon where a line of trees kept the main road hidden from sight. The sky above them seemed huge. The fields in either direction rolled gently up and down, golden in the autumn sunlight.

'It's pretty remote, wouldn't you say?'

Morag grabbed his hands. 'Exactly. What better way to enjoy our retirement? Look at the garden - we can grow our own veg. We can take walks over the fields.' She paused for a moment. 'And listen...' she said, raising a finger.

'What? I don't hear anything?' said Lachlan.

Morag smiled. 'Peace, perfect peace. No buses. No kids charging up and down. It's got everything.'

Lachlan thought about their bungalow in Joppa. It wasn't exactly the Bronx. And the kids who ran up and down the street were all pretty decent. He was quite keen on the regular bus service too, but he'd known Morag long enough to know that resistance was futile. He tried one last throw of the dice.

'It doesn't have everything though, does it?'

Morag frowned. 'Eh? A decent bedroom; an oak-beamed lounge with an open fire; this kitchen is fantastic. What are you on about?'

Lachlan moved towards the window and peered this way and that.

'The river. We're miles from the water.' His breath steamed up the glass. He started cleaning it with the cuff of his jumper.

When the squeaking stopped, Morag said, 'It's not that far away. Come on Lachlan. It'll be fun.'

He took a deep breath and conceded defeat. She was probably right, as usual.

****

As the days shrank into winter they'd slowly prepared for the move. Lachlan was on first-name terms with the staff at the recycling centre after jettisoning a lifetime of flotsam and jetsam into the skips. They sat now, in their living room, surrounded by boxes containing what remained. Tomorrow, the lorry would be here at 9am and they'd lock the door on the place they'd called home for over twenty years.

The doorbell rang.

Lachlan grunted, put down his tea and stepped into the darkening hall.

He opened the door to a hooded figure in a black cloak. A scythe was thrust towards him.

'Jesus Christ!' cried Lachlan.

'No, I'm the Grim Reaper,' said the figure. 'Trick or treat?'

Lachlan remembered the date, 'Oh aye. Aren't you a bit small to be the grim reaper?'

'I'm only nine,' said the figure. 'Have you got any sweeties?'

Lachlan raked around the kitchen but all the cupboards were empty. Everything was packed away in boxes. He opened the lid of one and peered inside. The smell of spices and vinegar, but nothing sweet. He pulled out a packet, tipped out a couple of small brightly wrapped squares and returned to the front door.

'Here you go.'

Lachlan dropped two silver cubes into the Grim Reaper's expectant hand.

'Oxo cubes?' said death.

'It's all we've got I'm afraid,' said Lachlan as he closed the door.

He returned to his chair to the sound of their wheelie bin being tipped over.

'I take it he wasn't happy?' muttered Morag, not looking up from her book.

'Hmm,' said Lachlan as he picked up his tea.

The doorbell rang again.

'Oh for fuck's sake,' said Lachlan. 'It's your turn.'

Morag pretended not to hear.

With a groan, Lachlan stepped into the hall and opened the door to a small, rotund figure. His mask was fantastic, as he genuinely looked like an eighty year old Hobbit. The figure peered up at Lachlan from behind thick-lensed glasses that made his eyes appear huge. He swept a hand across his head. An unnecessary gesture, Lachlan thought, as the mask made him quite bald.

'Go on then,' said Lachlan. 'Have you got a joke or something? A poem? We've no sweeties so you'll have to make do with condiments. Who are you meant to be anyway?'

The figure's face contorted, confused. Christ that was a good mask. 'Lachlan McCormack?'

'Aye,' said Lachlan.

The face creased into a smile, the eyes seemed to grow even larger. 'It's Alan. Alan Ferguson.' He held out a hand.

Lachlan shook his hand out of politeness while he racked his brain, then remembered his old hirsute colleague from the British Geological Survey. 'Alan!? Goodness! What happened to your hair!'

'Aha,' chuckled Alan. 'It went the same way as my eyesight, I'm afraid. To buggery. Can I come in?'

'Of course, in you come. I haven't seen you since God knows when. Late seventies?'

'That would be right,' said Alan. 'I took a few years out, travelled the world. Ended up in Argentina working for an oil firm. Then we went to bloody war with them and I had to get out.' He stepped into the living room.

'Morag, this is Alan, from the BGS. The last time I saw him Scotland still had a manufacturing industry.'

After two cups of tea and a catch-up on the intervening decades, Alan stood and walked to the window. He cleared his throat, 'I suspect you'll like my next bit of news.'

'Uhuh?' said Lachlan.

'Remember that report I was helping out with, back in the early seventies?'

'The McCrone Report?' said Lachlan.

Alan nodded, 'Well, when I got wind that the government would finally be releasing it, I started moving in certain circles. The same circles as you. That's how I found out where you lived.'

'The SNP?' Morag asked.

'Indeed,' said Alan. 'I met your friend Finn at a conference and he said you'd be very interested in what's been buried all these years, so to speak. Literally and figuratively.'

Lachlan nodded. 'Go on.'

'Well we now have the report I slogged away on thanks to this new Freedom of Information Act. Although you won't be feeling particularly grateful towards any Westminster governments once you read the contents.' He pulled a bundle of folded A4 from inside his jacket.

An hour later, Lachlan was still pacing up and down the living room.

'Fucking unbelievable,' he said, for the tenth time.

'Thirty years we waited for this. I only provided stats. I wasn't expecting the wording to be quite so, well, damning, towards the government,' said Alan.

Lachlan flipped a page of the report and shook his head, reading the contents out loud. *'It must be concluded therefore that revenues and large balance of payments gains would indeed accrue to a Scottish Government in the event of independence…'* He ran a finger over the paragraph and continued. *'The country would tend to be in chronic surplus to a quite embarrassing degree and its currency would become the hardest in Europe with the exception perhaps of the Norwegian kroner… Scottish banks could expect to find themselves inundated with speculative inflow of foreign funds.'*

'No wonder they wanted to keep it quiet,' said Morag. 'The bastards.'

'Bastards,' agreed Alan.

'Bastards,' Lachlan muttered. '1974 wasn't it? How was the SNP doing back then?'

'Great,' said Morag. 'Thirty percent of the vote. Our best ever. If this report had come out it would have been curtains for the United Kingdom.'

'And instead we got Thatcher and the destruction of our industries.'

'All part of the grand plan, it seems,' said Alan.

Lachlan flipped the page. *'Scotland's economic problems would disappear and it would become the Kuwait of the Western world.'*

'It's McCrone's comments that irk me the most,' said Alan. 'About, *taking the wind out of the SNP's sails.*'

'Well that certainly worked,' said Morag. 'We got our parliament and we've been stuck with Labour making an arse of things ever since.'

'Maybe not for long,' said Lachlan looking out the window.

Tiny increments, he thought, as the Grim Reaper trudged back down the street with a bulging bag of sweets.

SUNDAY

Outside, the sky was a pale blue with high wispy clouds. Most of the staff were in the garden preparing tables for the afternoon's barbecue. His phone buzzed to life on his bedside cabinet.

'Lachlan? It's Johnny.'

'The wanderer! How are you?'

'Good. Yourself?'

He tipped his medication onto the bed. 'Oh, surviving. You know. How's sunny Spain?'

'Well, there's the thing. Not as appealing as it used to be.'

'Brexit? Aye well you made your bed eh?'

'What?'

'With your No vote in 2014. Could have avoided all this.'

Johnny muttered a few things that were lost in the rumble of passing traffic.

'The noise there's terrible. Where are you?'

'I'm in Edinburgh.'

'Eh? Have they ran out of HP Sauce in your wee British supermarket or something?'

'I'm house-hunting, actually. Healthcare's all up-in-the-air now. Lots of us are selling up. While I'm here I thought I'd come and see you. Is tomorrow okay?'

'Aye, that'd be good. Grace is bringing wee Phoebe over though. Are you okay with an ice cream and a coffee?'

'That's fine. Might have a wee surprise for you.'

'I love surprises. What is it? You've joined the SNP?'

'Ha! No. *Tolla thon,* old pal. It'll be good to see you.'

'Arsehole!' chuckled Lachlan.

'What?' said Johnny.

'I said *I've got to go*. I'll see you tomorrow.'

Outside, the barbecue flamed to life. He watched the smoke rise into the summer air, like a signal from a hilltop beacon. He had been expecting the worst yesterday. Now he had to wait until tomorrow to hear it.

He turned the begonia to the sun and pressed his face against the glass to catch a glimpse of the river, but it was already obscured by smoke.

HADDiNGTON 2014

Lachlan dragged the rake through the soil. When he heard the click of a stone he reached down to discard it, straightening up with a sigh. *Seventy three. How did that happen?* Autumn would bring their ninth harvest in the cottage. The first few years had been disappointing, but he'd finally got the hang of it. Spacing the seeds. Getting the soil just right. Tiny increments.

'Don't forget to water them,' said Morag from her deckchair.

Lachlan shuffled towards the outside tap and attached the hose.

'Those'll make lovely soup in the winter,' she said.

'Aye,' said Lachlan as he returned to the vegetable patch with the hose. He looked at Morag, sitting in the sun, fiddling with her new mobile phone. He couldn't resist it, and turned the hose on her.

She shrieked, and sat up, spluttering. 'Hey! Watch my phone!'

Lachlan chuckled, 'You're never off that bloody thing. What's so fascinating?'

'I'm speaking to the North Berwick Yes campaign people. They're asking if I can do a shift on the stall tomorrow.'

Once upon a time, Lachlan may have had to check the calendar, but recently it had been fairly blank. The only entries being related to Morag's increasing involvement in the Scottish independence campaign. 'Aye, we can pop in on Grace while we're there.'

'Perfect,' said Morag as she settled back into her chair.

He turned off the hose and looked up at a few starlings darting over the trees in a flawless blue sky. There was a calmness about this place. It had taken a while getting used to, but he was beginning to feel like he was settling in at last.

'Buggers!' muttered Morag.

Lachlan glanced back at her, she was sitting forward on her chair, flicking a finger over the screen of her phone. Since she'd got the thing Lachlan had found her increasingly detached. He'd managed without one all these years, there was no point in getting one now. If anyone needed him, they had their home number.

'What?' he muttered, untangling a knot in the hose.

'They've deleted all my comments!'

'Who has?'

'*Better bloody Together.* I was only pointing out a few things to some folk on their Facebook page. Was having quite a pleasant conversation with a woman from Tranent. She was coming round to the idea, now it looks like she's a head-case and she's been talking to herself.'

'You must have rattled them,' he said.

'You know they've pulled out of the debate at the Town Hall too?'

'Here we go again eh?' said Lachlan, remembering their involvement in the 1979 referendum.

Morag sighed. 'It's going to be even harder this time. We've a mountain to climb.'

Two thousand and fourteen, Scotland's date with destiny. The opinion polls still put the No vote way ahead, but the momentum was all with the Yes campaign. Anything could happen, although the relentless onslaught from the media made it incredible that the Yes vote was gaining any ground at all. The big money was all behind a No vote. Banks threatened to leave. Staff were told their jobs would be on the line. Pensions wouldn't be paid. Scotland would find itself out of the EU. They lined up to spread doom and gloom about Scotland's prospects on a daily basis.

And the report Alan Ferguson had brought to Lachlan had been all but forgotten. Discredited as an anachronism, ancient history, an irrelevance. Unlike a document signed by a handful of Scottish lairds three-hundred years ago, which somehow remained relevant and binding.

****

'Did you tell them we were coming?' asked Lachlan as they parked outside Grace's house. They'd done their stint on the Yes stand in the town centre, handing out badges to people already wearing badges. Lachlan's confidence was through the floor, but Morag remained hopeful.

A snippet of Greensleeves chimed from the hall as he pressed the door-bell; a legacy from the previous owner that they'd never got around to changing.

'I didn't,' said Morag. 'We'll just nip in for a cup of tea.'

Through the glass Lachlan saw the outline of Grace approach the door. It swung open and Baxter, their dog, scrambled from the kitchen yelping and barking. A friendly wee Highland Terrier, constantly wound like a spring.

'Hello love,' said Morag.

'Mum, Dad, hiya. In you come. Wasn't expecting you. Get down you!' she pushed Baxter away with one leg.

'We were on the stand in town, just thought we'd pop in. How's everything?'

'Great,' said Grace. She ushered them into the living room where her husband Richard was slouched on the sofa playing a football game on their enormous television.

'Oh, hello,' he said sheepishly as he dropped the controller.

'Who's winning?' said Lachlan, nodding at the television.

'I am,' said Richard. 'It's okay. I'll just switch it off. Sorry.'

'Are you not a bit old for that son?' asked Lachlan.

'Lachlan!' yelped Morag.

Lachlan chuckled to himself and dropped to the sofa. 'Stick the kettle on then.'

'I'll do it,' said Richard, glad to be extracting himself from the situation.

Grace smiled at Richard as he passed and touched his hand. Lachlan was glad his daughter had found someone who made her happy. That was all he could ask for. Richard had a decent job at some insurance firm in Edinburgh, and seemed well-liked by his colleagues. They had a good circle of friends and Grace seemed to be blooming. He'd spent decades worrying about her but she'd grown into herself and slowly he'd been able to let her go. He looked at Morag who seemed to be lost in similar thoughts.

'So how did it go today?' Grace asked, as she switched the television off.

'Hmm,' said Morag. 'Same as usual I suppose. Like banging your head off a brick wall.'

Grace glanced towards the kitchen and closed the door. 'I know what you mean. I'm still struggling with him.' She nodded towards the kitchen where Richard was clattering around making tea.

'He's still a No then?' asked Lachlan.

'Uhuh,' said Grace. 'It's his work. They've said if it's a Yes vote they'll all be out of a job.'

'Jesus Christ,' said Lachlan, shaking his head. 'And he believes them?'

Grace shrugged. 'It's hard for him Dad. He's been there for years. His colleagues are mostly voting No too. They just don't want to rock the boat. Small 'c' conservatives. Actually, some of them are big 'C' ones too.'

'Aye and I know what that stands for,' Lachlan chuckled,

'Don't be rude,' snapped Morag.

'What about the hospital?' Lachlan asked. 'Surely you lot have your heads screwed on?'

'Oh aye,' said Grace. 'We're all voting Yes. Well the nurses are anyway. And most of the doctors.'

'The Scottish NHS is performing miracles with the buttons they get. Imagine how good it could be with proper funding?'

Grace threw her hands up. 'What can you do? Anyway, let's not cause a fuss eh?'

At that, Baxter bounced into the room, closely followed by Richard with a tray of tea.

'There you go. Milk and one,' Richard said, handing a mug to Morag. 'And milk and none.' He passed a Scottish Rugby Union mug to Lachlan.

'I'm sweet enough,' said Lachlan. He took a sip and placed the mug on a side-table. 'So why are you such a shiter Richard?'

Grace and Morag spluttered in unison.

Richard put his mug down carefully, 'Eh? Sorry?'

'Voting no. A young man like you.' He gestured at the saltire on his mug. 'You should be proud of your country.'

'Jesus Dad, see when I said *let's not cause a fuss?*' said Grace.

'I'm not causing a fuss. I just want to hear it from him.' He turned to Richard who glanced at Grace and shifted awkwardly in his seat.

'Erm. Well, I am proud of my country. And I've been struggling with it to be honest.'

'So what is it? Don't tell me - you don't like the First Minister? Is that it? He'll be gone soon enough anyway.'

'Nah, I know that.'

'So why aren't you willing to stand up? What about *we can still rise now, and be that nation again?*' He tapped the mug.

'Well it's just that. Things are... well... we're not really wanting to rock the boat too much,' Richard said slowly. He didn't seem irritated by Lachlan's questions. If anything, there seemed to be a glint in his eye.

Morag sat back and watched the exchange quietly, as if she'd reached some conclusion that still evaded Lachlan.

'Grace has a good job. You've got a good job. Don't believe the shite about moving out of Scotland. Watch as your board of directors get bloody knighthoods or cushy wee advisory positions at Westminster. That's how it works.'

'Aye maybe,' said Richard. He was looking directly at Grace now, who grinned and took a sip of her tea.

'Dad,' she said. Lachlan turned to her.

'I know love, I'm sorry. I'm just trying to work out why your man's being so cagey about this.'

'I think what Richard's saying is that he doesn't want to risk any uncertainty at the moment. Especially with his job. As, well, he might be the only one earning soon.' She smiled at Richard who visibly relaxed.

'Eh?' said Lachlan. Morag's face creased into a smile and she grabbed Grace's hand.

'Are you saying what I think you're saying?' Morag said.

'Yes, Mum.' She smiled at Morag, then at Lachlan. 'We're having a baby.'

Morag squeaked with delight. Lachlan felt the room spin. They were going to be grandparents. Granny Morag and Grandad Lachlan. Well well.

'Come here you,' Lachlan said, hugging Grace. He grabbed Richard's hand. 'Well done son. I'm sorry I'm such an arse.'

Richard shrugged. 'I hope I can be as big an arse as you some day too.'

****

They woke early on the 18th of September and had a quick breakfast of toast and coffee. Morag flicked the radio on but Lachlan snapped it off again just as the presenter asked for listeners to call in with their polling day stories.

'I can't take any more of that,' he grumbled, stirring sugar into Morag's mug.

The previous week, an opinion poll had put Yes ahead for the first time in the campaign. 52% to 48%. It looked like the union of 1707 was on the brink of collapse. A union that barely anyone had wanted at the time, on either side of the border, but one that had become a red, white and blue comfort blanket for many.

During the intervening week they'd suffered an onslaught of pro-UK propaganda. The leaders of all the UK parties had cobbled together "The Vow" promising a raft of new powers for Scotland. A national paper dutifully knocked up a front-page that laughably presented the political leaders' empty promises on parchment to lend it more gravitas. Lachlan wondered if a ten-bob newspaper's graphics department may just have dealt independence a killer blow.

The previous evening, the BBC had broadcast uninterrupted coverage of a former PM's "Stronger Together" speech. In front of an invited audience, he paced like a caged bear banging his fist and terrifying Scotland's OAPs over fabricated risks to their pensions. None of it was countered or questioned. They'd gotten used to that during the campaign, but it didn't mean it ever stopped leaving a sour taste in the mouth.

Despite the one-sided media; the hostile interviews; the loaded television audiences; the propaganda-masquerading-as-reportage on the nightly news; the pleading celebrities and the doom-laden billboards and TV advertising. Despite all this, or perhaps because of it, support for independence had only grown. It was as if the union and its defenders were holed up in a mighty castle, but their powder was damp. The battering ram of independence was buckling the doors. All it would take was one almighty push.

And Lachlan no longer had the energy for it.

He sipped his coffee while Morag fiddled with the Yes badge on her lapel.

'Today's the day,' she smiled.

He nodded and smiled back. It was all he could do. All his

life he'd prepared for the worst, and today was no different. He saw little point in getting his hopes up and he worried Morag's optimism would lead to her being crushed. He knew how much this meant to her, and how much she'd put into it. Not just over the campaign, but over their entire life.

He liked to think he'd awakened the fire on that winter's day in 1951, when he'd gifted her his saltire stone on the banks of the river, but he knew it was already burning within her.

As if reading each other's thoughts, they both glanced at the window ledge above the kitchen sink, where the stone now sat.

Morag looked back at him, her eyes glittering in the morning sunlight. 'That wasn't yesterday was it?'

Lachlan reached forward and took her hands. 'It feels like it was.'

She nodded. They shared the silence.

'Can you feel that?' she asked.

Lachlan looked around, he couldn't feel anything. He shook his head.

Morag took a deep breath. 'It's hard to describe… This stillness… It's like the country's holding its breath.'

Lachlan puffed out his cheeks. 'I suppose it is. Only one way to find out I suppose. Shall we?'

Morag drained her tea and scooped up their polling cards from the table.

'Aye.'

****

Lachlan had gone to bed as soon as the first result came in.

Clackmannanshire had voted No. The region was regarded as "Scotland in miniature" by some pundits as it represented the national demographic fairly accurately.

He recalled his days living there, in Alloa. His days at the brewery. His nights in The Highlander. Mandy.

Fifty years ago.

He'd felt the weight of all those years as he'd said goodnight to Morag and climbed into bed. She'd insisted on staying up. Her confidence almost broke his heart.

Now, he rubbed his eyes and pushed one curtain back with his foot. It looked like a dreich, grey, mournful day. He turned to face Morag and was surprised to see she was staring back at him. Wide awake. Her eyes red and bloodshot.

'We lost,' she said.

He felt something give way inside his gut. Like the death of buried hope. It left an emptiness. A void. A nothingness so great it seemed to take a physical form. For the first time in years, he craved a drink.

'Shite,' he groaned. 'By much?'

'Fifty-five to forty-five,' Morag said, her voice croaky. Her shoulders jerked as she started sobbing.

'Come here,' Lachlan said, and pulled her close. He buried his face in her grey hair and breathed deeply. 'I told you not to get your hopes up.'

She cleared her throat and said, 'I know. I'm just a silly old bat. It's just so hard to believe. All those Yes windows. All that work. Years of it, for what?'

Morag had always clapped with glee when they'd driven past another house with a Yes poster in the window. She'd keep count every time they were out. 'Fourteen Yes windows and not a single No. We're going to win this Lachlan!' she'd said one day. Lachlan hadn't replied. He was too busy quickly estimating how many blank windows they'd passed. Like the empty chairs in 1979.

'For what?' he said. 'Well we did very well to get up to forty-five. Look at it that way. Considering what we were up against, that's pretty good.'

'Aye another glorious failure for Scotland,' Morag said, breaking from his embrace and sitting up against the headboard. 'I'm scunnered Lachlan. What other country on Earth would vote against its own independence?'

He climbed out of bed, pulled the curtains open and surveyed the fields beyond their garden. Not a breath of wind moved the trees or rustled the hedgerows. It was as if a guilty silence had descended on the nation. A greyness cloaked everything.

Overnight, Scotland had become a black and white country.

****

'So I said I'd maybe go and visit her. What do you think? Hold it steady man!' Morag yelped from the top of the stepladder. Lachlan looked up at her backside, now wrapped in sensible cords, and recalled that day on Fairy Hill all those years ago when he'd helped her up the wishing tree. Nothing had changed, other than her backside was a bit larger. He considered her question. Her friend Shirley had been in touch. She was now living at the peace camp at Faslane nuclear submarine base on the west coast. Another missed opportunity that the No vote had denied them - freeing Scotland of the UK's nuclear arsenal. Shirley had decided to keep fighting the fight. As had so many of their companions after the disappointment of last year.

'Sorry,' he said, and pushed the basket forward with his foot. It was already half full of plums. 'Aye I suppose so. How long would you be away for?'

'Oh not long. You can drive me up there. I'll stay for a week or two. She has her own caravan. Here,' she said handing down another clump.

Lachlan took the plums and placed them in the basket. He looked back at the box of potatoes they'd already harvested, and all the carrots waiting to be picked.

It would be a busy day.

'This is the best year yet,' he said as Morag stretched to reach more fruit.

'Aye it's a cracker,' she said. 'Amazing what living in a country with a lot of rain and occasional hot sun can do eh?'

'It certainly is,' said Lachlan. He knew what was coming.

'It's almost like we're actually capable of producing things, and growing things, and creating things.'

'Of course we are,' said Lachlan.

'Tell that to those BASTARDS OVER THERE then,' Morag yelled. Lachlan glanced over at the next cottage. Not an immediate neighbour, as there was a strip of farmland in-between, but their closest neighbours, who had proudly voted No, as Lachlan had found out later on referendum day. They didn't want to risk their pensions, apparently. Lachlan had pondered if they'd ever considered their grandchildren's right to a pension, but he'd suspected they hadn't. Either that or they had nothing but blind faith in the United Kingdom's ability to provide one. A faith he sometimes wished he shared.

'Now now,' he said. 'Matt's alright.'

'He's a wanker, Lachlan. A selfish, narrow-minded, wanker. Look at their bloody stupid car.'

Lachlan considered the gleaming white Range Rover parked alongside the cottage. He'd always thought it looked quite nice.

'Yes dear. Any more plums up there?' said Lachlan, trying to change the subject.

Morag stood on her tip toes and popped her head between branches. 'Oh yes, there's a few crackers. Hang on.' She reached to one side and the ladder wobbled. Lachlan tightened his grip.

'Jesus, be careful up there.'

'I'm always careful,' said Morag just as her foot slipped and the ladder shot to one side.

Lachlan didn't have time to think. Morag landed on top of him in an instant. She let out a scream as a branch tore at her arm on the way down. Winded, and flattened by the woman he loved, Lachlan tried to speak but could only manage a wheeze.

She rolled off him and looked at her arm, and then at Lachlan. 'Sorry. Are you okay?' she said.

He cricked his neck from side to side and wiggled his arms and legs. Everything appeared to be working. 'I think so. Are you? Let me see that arm.'

Morag held her forearm up, a line of blood ran down from a deep scratch but it was nothing a bit of antiseptic and a few plasters wouldn't fix. 'I'll live,' she said.

****

The dust on the mantelpiece lay thick over the saltire stone. Lachlan took it down and wiped it clean on his trousers. But this only served to remind him that his trousers weren't particularly clean either. He brushed the dust from his thigh and hunkered down to throw another log on the fire.

'Lovely,' he smiled as he settled back into his chair.

There was a knock at the door.

'Oh for fuck's sake,' he muttered as he forced himself back to his feet.

Outside the living room, the cold air of the hall hit him. How long had he been in there? Hours? It was getting dark outside.

'Dad! Open the door!' Grace's voice from the front step.

'Hello my wee princess,' he said as he kicked aside a pile of unopened mail and pulled the door open.

'Hi Dad. You took your time. It's freezing out here.'

'Sorry. Come away in. How's the…' Lachlan gestured at Grace's large bump. 'Not long now eh?'

'A few weeks. That's why I'm here. I've got you a present. Are you missing Mum?'

'Of course,' said Lachlan. She'd been up at the peace camp for three weeks, four days, and a couple of hours. Not that he was counting.

Grace lowered herself to the sofa and dug in her handbag. 'It's like a bloody hothouse in here Dad,' she said, squinting at the blazing fire.

'Aye. I'll open a window. I hadn't noticed,' said Lachlan. He jerked at the small window overlooking the fields. After a few tugs, it groaned upwards and a blast of cold air entered the room.

'That's better,' said Grace. 'Right, here you go.' She handed

Lachlan a small paper bag. 'It's a mobile phone.'

'Oh,' said Lachlan. 'That's lovely. Thank you.'

'You'll need it,' said Grace. 'For when, you know…' She patted her belly.

'Of course,' said Lachlan. 'What do I do with it?'

Grace took it from him and switched it on. He watched as the screen lit up with a crystal-clear picture of a crashing wave.

'There you go,' she said, handing it back. She glanced at the clock above the fireplace.

Lachlan turned it over in his hands. 'It's a tiny wee thing eh? I remember when we had to go out into the hall to make a phone call. Your granny and grandad didn't have a phone in the house at all for years. This is… super. Thanks. Can you change the picture though?'

'On the screen? Uhuh, what would you rather have?'

Lachlan reached up to the mantlepiece and brought down a picture of the three of them on holiday in Spain, when Grace was twelve. The waiter had asked if they wanted a photo. It seemed like a lifetime ago. All those years bringing up their wee girl had passed in a blur. The early years, with the sleepless nights. The primary school years with the parties and performances. The high school years, with the door-slamming and the tears. It was as if they'd been on fast-forward throughout those two decades. He wiped dust from the glass covering the photo. There was Morag with her wide smile, Lachlan with his awkward grimace, and Grace somewhere in-between.

'Can you put this on it?'

'Sure,' said Grace. She took the photo and the phone and tapped at the screen.

'There you go,' she handed the phone back and held onto the photo frame for a moment longer, smiling at the memory.

Lachlan grinned at the screen. 'That's amazing. You'll need to show me how to use it, but I'll put the kettle on first.' He placed the phone on the side-table and shuffled forward in his chair.

Grace looked at the clock again and raised a finger. 'Wait,' she said.

'Eh?'

Lachlan jumped as the phone exploded to life beside him. It played an irritating ditty as it jiggled its way across the table.

'Answer it then!' said Grace, laughing. 'Press the green thing on the screen.'

Lachlan stabbed at the screen then held the phone to his ear. 'Haddington 829414?'

Grace stifled a laugh as Lachlan shifted the phone to hear better.

'Morag? Oh hello love. How are you? Why didn't you phone the house number?'

Morag's voice came clearly from the handset. 'Just wanted to test your new toy Lachlan. You've joined the 21st century with the rest of us at last. How's Grace doing?' She laughed a throaty laugh that turned into a cough.

'Aye she's fine. Looks great,' he beamed at Grace. 'Are you okay? That's a terrible cough.'

'Och I'm fine. Just a bit of a cold. I'm coming home on Friday so you'll better get the hoover out.'

Lachlan's face split into a smile. 'I'll do that, don't worry. Although the place probably doesn't need hoovering, does it Grace?' he winked. Grace kicked a discarded Jaffa Cake box along the carpet towards the door and gave him a thumbs up.

'Great, well Shirley's son-in-law's bringing me back so you don't need to come and get me. Just make sure the house is clean.'

'I'll do that. I've…' he looked at Grace momentarily.

'What?' said Morag.

'I've missed you, that's all.'

'Och Lachlan. I've missed you too.'

'Have you got into any bother?'

'No more than usual. Lay down in front of a convoy of nuclear weapons, but a policeman dragged me away. Really nice guy called Alistair from Glasgow. I knitted his wee baby a *Bairns not Bombs* hat. He was delighted.'

'That's nice dear,' said Lachlan. There she goes, making pals everywhere. 'Well I'm away to put the kettle on for Grace. She's drinking for two after all.' He listened as Morag started coughing again, as clear as if she was in the same room. 'You'll better get yourself wrapped up in something warm by the sound of things. Is there heating in that caravan?'

'Paraffin,' said Morag. 'And about a dozen quilts. I'm fine. Looking forward to coming home though. We need to get everything sorted for Christmas, and for the wee one coming along.'

'Aye, we do' said Lachlan.

'And put fresh sheets on the bed. I'm looking forward to a decent sleep.'

'Will do,' said Lachlan. Then, 'Er, where are the clean sheets?'

Morag chuckled. 'The cupboard in the hall.'

'Smashing, I'll do that. See you soon love.'

'What do you think?' asked Grace, after he'd stabbed the red button to hang up.

'Aye it's a great wee thing. Clear as a bell. I'll stick the kettle on. Do me a favour and chuck another log on the fire.'

'Don't bother with the tea Dad, I've got stuff to do. You need to get this bloody mess tidied up though. I'll pop round again tomorrow and give you a hand.'

Lachlan glanced at the detritus of a month of bachelor living. Pizza boxes, newspapers, and at least four Jaffa Cake boxes littered the floor.

After she'd left, he pulled fresh sheets from the hall cupboard. At the bottom, something caught his eye. A bottle of Macallan they'd won at a raffle. Morag had stashed it away, planning to gift it to someone but had forgotten all about it. He pulled it out and sniffed the contents, that old familiar smell. Eleven years sober, he thought as he replaced the cork. But just one wouldn't hurt would it? It'd prove that he was no longer a slave to it. Plus, he was celebrating Morag's return.

He grabbed a glass from the kitchen and returned to his armchair.

****

It was the smell that woke him. A choking, chemical stench that stung his eyes. He threw the covers back and stumbled into the hall. His vision seemed blurred. There was a popping noise from the living room and he threw the door open to see the rug, curtains, and sofa merrily ablaze.

Fuck.

He pulled the door closed and stood frozen for a moment while he tried to force his brain into action.

Phone 999.

The landline phone was in the living room.

His new mobile? What had he done with it? He remembered sitting it on the bedside table before dozily crawling into bed, after falling asleep in front of the fire.

He stabbed it to life and called the fire brigade as he hurried out the front door.

He heard a crack. Something had collapsed in the cottage. The glass in the living room window shattered and flames started licking around the frame. Smoke was belching out all over, drifting up into the clear moonlight.

He stood, dumbstruck, and watched as their house burnt down. His head was pounding. He had little recollection of the second half of that bottle of Macallan.

Some time later the sound of sirens joined the creaks, cracks and thwumps of the cottage collapsing. He looked up at the moon, shining benignly down on him, indifferent to the chaos below and raised himself from the grass verge where he'd been sitting.

The trees were suddenly lit a flashing blue and the rattle of chains and ladders shook him back to his senses as the fire engine approached. A group of firemen jumped out as the engine came to a halt with a hiss of air-brakes.

'Anyone inside?' one of them called.

He shook his head, then the world started to spin.

The next thing he knew, he was inside the fire engine, wrapped in an aluminium foil blanket.

More sirens.

An ambulance stopped alongside and a woman climbed out

from the passenger side. She was about Grace's age. Jesus, Grace. She could be having her baby any time now and here he was, drunk again and causing fucking havoc.

'Lachlan, is it?' she asked through the window.

He nodded, then passed out again.

****

'You've got a visitor.' An unknown voice. The smell of bleach. Shit. Mince and tatties. A hand on his shoulder.

Lachlan opened his eyes and blinked. Too bright. A strip-light with mirrored panels shone above him. This wasn't his bed. The sheets were too clean for a start.

'Hello Lachlan,' said Morag, from the bedside.

What the hell had happened? He'd had the most terrible dream. His mouth was sandpaper dry and his head throbbed.

'Morag. You're home,' he said.

'If you can call it that,' said Morag. She placed a hand on his brow. 'How are you?' Her face was serious. Stern. No trace of a smile.

'I'm… why am I in hospital? I had the most terrible… oh Jesus…' Flashbacks of the previous evening hammered at his skull. 'Did…' His mouth fell open and he stared at Morag.

'Did you burn the house down? Aye you did. Honestly Lachlan, the things you'll do to avoid a bit of hoovering.'

He snorted, then the enormity of it hit home.

'Oh,' he said and stared ahead. He couldn't look at her. He didn't deserve her forgiveness.

'*Oh?!*' said Morag. 'I'll bloody *Oh* you. We're bloody homeless. A week before Christmas! We've lost everything! What the hell happened?'

He sank back under the sheets and groaned.

'I'm sorry,' he said, and stole a glance at Morag who he thought was doing a fine job of not sticking a pillow over his head and holding it there until he'd ran out of platitudes. 'I've no idea. I had a fire going and fell asleep.'

'Are you drinking again?' she asked.

'No!' he lied. 'Not a drop, I promise.' He couldn't tell her, it'd break her heart. At that moment he vowed that he was finished. Although he'd also made that vow over ten years ago.

She let out a sigh.

They sat in silence for a bit. Lachlan's eyes were beginning to water as his brain was flooded with memories of everything he'd lost in the fire. But those things were just that, *things*. Stuff they'd accumulated over the years. None of it mattered.

'We've still got each other,' he said, reaching for Morag's hand.

Morag jerked her hand away. 'And I'm meant to be grateful for that am I?'

'The insurance will pay for it, surely?'

She coughed into a tissue. When she'd cleared her throat, she nodded and said. 'I suppose.'

'You didn't like living there anyway,' said Lachlan. 'Admit it, you missed the river.'

Morag forced a smile back down but her eyes glinted in the strip lights.

'True, but burning the bloody house down was a bit much. There are easier ways to move house Lachlan.'

He reached for Morag's hand again, and this time she took it. Her hand felt cold and damp.

'What am in here for anyway?' he said.

'Apart from having nowhere to live? Smoke inhalation,' said Morag. 'But you'll be pleased to know you'll live. Which is just as well because I'm going to kill you.'

****

They could smell the wreckage long before they could see it.

The cold winter air trapped the smell of smoke, weighing it down like a shroud over the corpse of their home.

Lachlan pulled up on the grass verge and looked at Morag, her eyes spilling tears.

'Lachlan, what have you done?' She stared at him and shook her head.

She walked at funereal pace up the path to the front door, or rather the hole in the blackened wall where the front door used to be. Lachlan shuffled along behind her. He'd spent two nights in hospital and the flames had long since died. Now all that remained was the stench of smoke and the skeletal remains of the things that wouldn't burn. A charred roof beam hung at an angle, pointing at Lachlan like an accusatory finger.

Morag clasped her hand to her mouth and let out a sob that ripped through him as violently as the fire had ripped through their home. He placed a hand on her back. She shrugged it off and stepped into what used to be their hall.

Their home was open to the sky now. Most of the roof timbers burnt away. They crunched over roof slates and stopped where the hallway opened up. Straight ahead into the kitchen, left to their bedroom, and right into the living room.

Morag looked into the rubble and started coughing.

'Are you okay?' asked Lachlan. 'That cough's not getting any better.'

'I'm fine,' said Morag.

She stood and turned to face him.

'How could you?' she said. Her shoulders slumped. Her eyes pleading for an answer but expecting none.

'I…' Lachlan said then looked away. 'I don't know,' he said to the wall. 'It's not like I meant it. I'm sorry Morag! For fuck's sake. I'm sorry! What else can I say?'

She crunched through the debris in the living room. Nothing but the springs of Lachlan's armchair remained. He looked for signs of the whisky bottle but it had melted away along with his desire to ever drink again. The wooden surround of the fireplace had been lost in the flames but the tiled hearth remained. Morag leant down, then stood clutching a brass-framed picture. The photo of the three of them that Grace had replicated on his phone screen.

He stepped forward and placed a hand on her shoulder. This time she didn't jerk away. She leaned into him and held the photo up. 'Happier times eh?'

He wiped ash from the surface. The glass had been lost but the picture had remarkably survived. Charred around the edges, but otherwise intact.

He clutched her close. 'Aye. And we'll have happy times again. A fresh start. I was thinking we should move back to the river anyway. Get a place nearer Grace, for when the baby comes.'

Morag looked up. 'That'd be nice.'

'Assuming the insurance pays out of course,' said Lachlan, ruining the moment.

Morag looked away. She stopped suddenly and said, 'Oh my God!'

'What?' asked Lachlan as she reached down and plucked something from the rubble.

'Ha!' she said, holding up a perfectly round smooth pebble with the Scottish flag painted on it. Faded and grubby, but unmistakeable. Their flagstone.

'Well well,' said Lachlan. 'That's a good sign.'

'Hmm,' said Morag. She turned her head at the sound of an approaching car. 'And here's the insurance inspector. Let me do the talking.' She jabbed him in the chest.

'Of course. I'll play dumb.'

'Should be pretty easy for you then,' said Morag. 'Oh Jesus, I shouldn't laugh,' she clutched at her chest as a gurgling cough rattled through her. 'Right here he is. Mum's the word.'

Lachlan watched her stride confidently back into the hall and wondered what he'd ever do without her.

****

The posters on the wall offered little in the way of Christmas cheer. 'Have you had your flu jab?'; 'Wash your hands'; 'Depression - don't suffer in silence'. There was even one illustrating the correct way to cough. Christ, he'd been coughing wrong all his life apparently. Morag's cough had brought them to the doctor though, their house hunt would have to wait. Anyway, they were enjoying living in Grace's spare bedroom. It's not like they had any belongings to clutter the place.

'Wild swimming?' said Lachlan, his hands on his knees.

'Aye. A wee bit,' said Morag. 'It wasn't all waving placards and singing.'

He looked at his seventy-three year old wife and said, 'Don't forget lying down in front of nuclear convoys. When are you going to grow up?'

Morag grinned a mischievous grin. 'Never.'

'You're seventy-three years old Morag.'

'Aye but I'm still eighteen in here,' she tapped her head.

'Mrs McCormack?' A young doctor in a corduroy skirt appeared at the side of the waiting room.

'Keep out of trouble,' Morag said to Lachlan, and she followed the doctor down the corridor.

The snow gathered on the windows as darkness fell. He watched the flakes settle then looked around the waiting room. A young mother in a red coat bounced a snot-choked toddler on her knee. A man about Lachlan's age sat with his head buried in a newspaper. One of the ones that screamed on a daily basis about how terrible things were in Scotland.

He heard a door squeak open and sat up, expecting Morag to appear. She'd been in there for ages now. Instead, the doctor returned.

'Mr McCormack?'

'Yes?' he said. 'Is everything alright?'

The doctor nodded back down the corridor, 'Come with me please. Just want a wee chat.'

Lachlan entered the consulting room moments after the doctor, to see Morag sniffling into a hankie. She smiled at Lachlan, but the smile didn't seem to reach her eyes.

'Take a seat,' said the doctor. 'Your wife's going to need to attend hospital for some checks. Purely precautionary. Are you able to take her?'

'Of course,' said Lachlan. 'When?'

'Now, if you can. She may have some fluid on her lungs. The hospital will be able to confirm this, and if so, they'll be able to treat her. But I wouldn't want to send her home again without getting it checked. I'll call ahead, so they're expecting you.'

'It's just a cold surely?'

'Possibly,' said the doctor. 'But, sorry to be blunt, at your age it's better to be safe than sorry.'

They made their way through the hush of the surgery and back to the car. The snow continued to fall, settling quietly on the roof and clinging to their coats as Lachlan fumbled for his keys.

'Christ, it's getting heavier,' said Lachlan. 'I'll turn the heating up.'

Morag nodded and coughed into a hankie. 'Oh this is horrible! Come on driver, sooner we get to the hospital the sooner we get back to Grace's. Have you got your mobile? I think my battery's dead.'

Lachlan patted his coat pocket. 'Aye, it's in here, don't worry. If Grace calls it'll start playing *Scotland The Brave* and vibrating like a supercharged pacemaker.'

'Good,' said Morag. He glanced across and was pleased to see her smile return. 'Poor girl's fit to burst.'

The headlights of East Lothian's commuters flashed past, returning from their jobs in Edinburgh. Their side of the dual carriageway was mostly clear, with just the occasional red glow of tail-lights.

Lachlan flicked the indicator and pulled into the fast lane.

****

'Merry Christmas!' yelled the fat hospital porter in the Santa suit.

Lachlan grunted and thought, *is it?* He looked at Morag, lying in the hospital bed where she'd been for three days now. Oxygen mask stuck to her face and a plastic tube delivering god-knows-what into her arm. He turned to the guy who'd drawn the short-straw and said, 'Merry Christmas to you too Santa.'

'You look like a good boy,' he winked. 'Here you go!'

Lachlan took the small parcel and sat it on the bedside cabinet. A packet of shortbread. Merry fucking Christmas.

They'd decided to keep her in for observation. Her blood pressure was worryingly low, and she was showing an increased heart-rate. The hospital had confirmed that there may have been some *restrictions on her lung capacity* but were hoping this was viral and were treating her with antibiotics.

He looked up at the clock. Visiting time was almost over and soon he'd be back at Grace's. Lachlan just wanted her home. Or rather, *looking* for a home.

Morag removed the mask again and grabbed Lachlan's hand. 'How's the wee one?' she said. Staring at Lachlan under a furrowed brow.

'Eh? What wee one?'

'Grace's baby?'

'Love, Grace hasn't had the baby yet,' he smiled and shook his head. 'What kind of drugs are they giving you?'

Morag looked away slowly and gave a slight nod. 'Of course she hasn't. Sorry. I'm just… oh I don't know.' Her eyes glistened, damp in the cold hospital lights.

Lachlan squeezed her hand and mopped her brow with a tissue. He dabbed at the corners of her eyes where tears were starting to form. 'Come on love. You're going to be fine.'

She replaced the oxygen mask and it misted up within seconds. Closing her eyes, a calmness returned to her face.

As the minutes disappeared and the clock ticked towards 8pm he felt a familiar twinge in his gut. Around him, the scrape of chairs as other visitors ended hushed conversations with their loved-ones.

He stood and kissed Morag gently on the forehead. 'Bye love.' A tiny smile formed at the corner of her lips through the fogged plastic of the mask.

****

'Dad! Wake up!'

Lachlan hadn't been sleeping.

'What is it?' he said. It was 2am but already his old bones were aching from underuse and he'd been noticing a growing pain in his stomach ever since burning down the house.

'I think the baby's coming,' said Grace. She flicked the light on and Lachlan blinked at the sudden brightness. Grace stood, calm as ever, with her coat on and a thick red scarf wrapped around her neck. 'We're away to the hospital. We'll call you as soon as there's news.'

Lachlan smiled and hugged her. 'You'll be fine. Do you want me to come with you?'

The toilet flushed and Richard flapped out, patting his pockets and pulling his coat from the hooks in the hall.

'No point,' said Grace. 'You could be sitting around for ages. Listen out for your phone. Are you ready Richard?'

'Yup,' Richard said, as he pulled on his jacket and held up his car keys.

Lachlan watched from the window as Richard reversed out the drive and spun away towards the dual carriageway. It was a half-hour drive to the maternity unit at Edinburgh Royal Infirmary. By dawn he could be a grandfather.

Sod it, he thought. Baxter yapped at his ankles as he threw on yesterday's clothes and grabbed his car keys.

In the distance he spotted a pair of tail-lights. That had to be them. The A1 was mostly deserted at this time of the morning, just the occasional supermarket delivery lorry rumbling through the night.

The snow hadn't lasted. It seldom did here. The warmth of the estuary's water kept the temperatures marginally higher throughout the winter. Just a few lonely patches of white remained on verges that hadn't been touched by the sun. He pulled out to overtake a lorry and flicked the wipers as the spray from the truck splattered his windscreen. He pulled the lever to blast some screen wash but heard only the whine of the motor. Empty.

The wiper scraped back and forth, smearing the gritty spray across his field of vision so he eased off on the accelerator and pulled back into the slow lane.

'Bloody typical,' he muttered.

Another empty bottle. The story of his life.

****

An hour later, with his windscreen almost opaque with smeared grit, he arrived at the hospital's maternity ward.

'Grace McCormack. My daughter. Came in a wee while ago.'

The nurse checked some notes. 'She's fine. The midwife's just doing some tests but all's well. You can go in and see her soon.'

'Okay,' said Lachlan. 'Thanks. I don't think she'll want me disturbing her though. I just wanted to be here, you know, in case.'

The nurse nodded and smiled with tired eyes. Lachlan took a seat in a corner, as far from the other occupants of the room as possible.

He closed his eyes and stretched out his legs. They were going to be grandparents. They were moving back to the river. To the river's end, no less. Where the river meets the sea. Everything was working out just fine. It was time to take it easy. Morag would have to realise her days of wild swimming and protest were behind her. It was time to finally settle and just enjoy the time they had left. He pictured them together in a flat by the sea. The sun shining. The waves *shhhing* at the shore.

'Hey,' a hand on his shoulder. He opened his eyes and was surprised to see the room in daylight. Richard's face came into focus.

'How's Grace?' Lachlan said with difficulty. His tongue stuck to the roof of his dry mouth.

'Fine,' said Richard. 'She's fine. The baby's being an awkward wee bugger though. Doesn't want to come out.'

'Heh,' laughed Lachlan. 'Wonder where she gets that from?'

Richard grinned. 'Aye. Could be a while yet though.'

Lachlan checked his watch. 9am. 'Jesus I've been asleep for hours.'

'You might want to get something to eat, if you're staying.'

'Might as well,' said Lachlan. 'No point heading up and down the road again. I'll go see Morag while I'm here.'

'Visiting's not until 3pm,' said Richard.

'Ach bollocks to that,' Lachlan said with a dismissive wave. 'You pay too much attention to the rules.'

'Probably. Anyway, I'll better get back.'

'I'll see you in a wee while. I'll tell Morag she's going to be a granny. She'll be over the moon.'

Lachlan stretched and yawned. A milky light outside filtered into the waiting room. The sun was there, behind thin clouds, just waiting to break through.

He slowed as he approached Morag's ward. The door was locked so he washed his hands with the sanitiser spray and waited. After a minute there was a ding from the lifts and a porter appeared, wheeling a patient on a bed. Lachlan leaned back against the wall to let them pass. The door was buzzed open, and he snuck in behind the new arrival.

Morag was fast asleep. He pulled the curtain around her bed, shifted her uneaten breakfast to one side, and kissed her forehead.

'Morning dear,' he whispered.

She opened her eyes and they immediately creased with the smile buried under her oxygen mask. She reached up to pull it aside.

'Morning Lachlan, what are you doing here?'

'Grace is having the baby,' he said, smiling. 'They woke me up in the middle of the night so I followed them in. Felt useless sitting out there on my own.'

'You could have started on decorating the kitchen,' said Morag. 'That's still needing done.'

Lachlan's brow furrowed. She had been going on about getting their kitchen painted for a while now, but that was before he removed the need for it by destroying the house, kitchen included.

'The kitchen?' he said. 'It's gone Morag. Don't you remember?'

Morag narrowed her eyes and looked at the ceiling. 'Of course it is. Sorry.' Her voice tiny, like it was coming from the far end of a long tunnel.

'How are you feeling?' asked Lachlan. He placed a hand on her brow. It was slick with sweat.

She tried a smile but grimaced at some pain from within. 'I'm fine Lachlan. When do they think the baby will arrive?'

'Soon,' said Lachlan.

'Do they know what they're having?' she asked.

'No. Well if they do, they're not saying.'

There was a terrible wheezing noise from Morag's chest as she tried to sit up. 'Oh hell,' she said, banging at her lungs. She settled back into the pillow. 'Do you remember our first kiss?' she asked.

'By the riverbank? Of course I do. It felt like a bomb had gone off.'

Morag replaced the mask for a moment and took a few breaths. Then she slipped it aside and said, 'Kiss me again. The way you did that day.'

'Nervously?' he laughed. 'It was you doing all the kissing as far as I remember. I just stood there.'

Morag managed a chuckle. 'Come here.'

He leaned over and she stretched up to kiss him on the lips. As she withdrew another rasping wheeze escaped her chest.

'You're still the man for me Lachlan. Even though you burnt our house down and you can be a bit useless.'

'Thanks, I think,' he said.

They sat in silence for a moment, listening to the noises of the ward beyond the curtain. A doctor spoke to an elderly lady opposite, telling her about the operation she'd be having that afternoon. It was brisk and business-like. Not a second to spare, not a wasted word. The doctor said goodbye and the ward fell silent. Just the occasional beep from a monitor and the murmur of the nurses outside.

'I need to tell you something,' said Morag.

'Uhuh?' said Lachlan.

There was a buzz from Lachlan's coat pocket.

He pulled out his phone. The screen was illuminated with a green balloon and the words: 'It's a GIRL. Phoebe Morag. Born 9:34am. 7lb 8oz. All's well!!! G&R xxxx'

He held it towards her. She removed the mask, mouthed the words, and her face broke into the smile he'd missed so much. Seventy-three years of laughter lines crinkled all over her ageing skin.

Tears ran down Lachlan's cheeks as he said, 'How does it feel Granny?'

'Wonderful,' she said. She was crying herself now. 'Just wonderful.'

'What was it you wanted to tell me?' asked Lachlan, wiping his tears.

'Och nothing. Just that I love you, you old fool. Go and see Grace. Go on!'

He kissed her again. 'I'll see you soon.'

'Aye you will Lachlan. Soon enough.'

'Are you sure about this Dad?' asked Grace, head cocked.

'Aye, I'm sure,' said Lachlan.

'So where's Mum?'

'I'll go and get her. You sort the wee one in her car seat.'

Ten minutes later they were driving west along the coast road. The sun had disappeared behind hazy clouds but it remained warm. It had been a decent summer, all things considered. Little Phoebe had turned out to be everything they'd hoped for. A happy, healthy baby who had just discovered her wide, welcoming smile.

Lachlan turned from the passenger seat to check her. Strapped in and gurgling happily at the world as it sped past her window. Morag sat in the other rear seat. Lachlan smiled at them both and turned to Grace.

'Enjoy it while it lasts Grace,' he said.

'What? Don't get all maudlin on me again Dad.'

'Childhood I mean. The bairn. Enjoy it.' He looked out at the World War 2 tank defence blocks littering the shore on this stretch of East Lothian's coastline. Crumbling concrete cubes with moss gathering on their flanks.

'I will Dad, don't worry.'

'It's just that…' he rolled the window down for some air. 'Childhood doesn't end you know. There's not a day in the future when they suddenly don't want to play with you and you can just accept that they've grown up. It doesn't end. It just sort of fades away.'

Grace slowed for a corner and dropped a gear. 'Okay. You could say that about any age though. Some folk are middle-aged at thirty.

It's all blurred lines. Shades of grey. Look at you, you've never really grown up have you?'

Lachlan managed a smile. 'No. Me and your Mum. The eternal teenagers.'

'And that's how it should be,' said Grace. 'What's that thing you always said? *Tiny increments?*'

'Aye,' said Lachlan. 'My dad said that one day and it always stuck with me. Change happens slowly. Not everything's a revolution.'

They came to a stretch of road with uninterrupted views over the Forth. 'Look at all the boats,' said Grace.

It was overcast now, there was a washed-out look to everything, but spots of colour were dotted throughout the estuary. Little blue fishing boats. White-sailed yachts. Even the local rowing clubs were out there in kayaks and dinghies.

He checked his watch. 'They're early. Didn't realise there'd be such competition for a spot.'

'I'm sure you'll be fine. What time did you say you'd meet Finn?'

'In fifteen minutes. Can you drop me down at the harbour?'

'No problem.'

Phoebe let out a yelp and a chuckle. Grace checked in the rear view mirror. 'You talking to your Granny, Feebs?' She smiled at Lachlan who sighed and rubbed at his tired eyes.

'We loved this river Grace,' said Lachlan.

'I know Dad.'

'Could I ask you something?'

'Something maudlin?'

'A wee bit, maybe.' He cleared his throat. 'Could you put me and your mum's name on a bench when we're gone? Looking out at the river.'

'Jesus Dad. Okay. Stop it, you'll make me cry.'

Ten minutes later they pulled up at Cockenzie harbour. A photographer was setting up a tripod with an expensive looking camera, and a crowd was gathering. Grace crouched in her seat to look up at the two giant chimneys towering above them. 'It'll be weird without these things.'

'It'll be great,' said Lachlan. 'Ugly buggers.'

'They're such a… don't know… an icon.'

'Aye, the *Sentinels of the Forth* or some such rubbish that the papers only came up with last week. They're a blight on the landscape and I'll be glad to see the back of them.'

'Well. Different strokes I suppose,' said Grace. 'Right. You take it easy out there, okay? Be careful.'

Lachlan spotted Finn on the deck of his boat and waved. 'I will, don't worry.'

'You're absolutely sure this is what you want to do? With Mum I mean.' She glanced into the back seat.

Lachlan turned around and smiled. 'Aye. It's what she wanted.'

He reached back and lifted the silver urn.

****

Finn powered up the engine and the little boat chugged its way out of the harbour. 'This is the busiest I've ever seen it,' he said from the cabin.

Lachlan leaned back. 'A fine turnout for the final goodbye.'

Finn looked back at the urn. 'You're ready for it though?'

'I meant the chimneys, but aye, I think so,' said Lachlan. 'I'll keep a wee bit of her though. I can't...' he trailed off.

There were more boats arriving from Edinburgh and Fife's harbours now, all heading for the waters by the derelict power station, all facing the same way like a nautical drive-in movie theatre.

Along the shore to Musselburgh and beyond crowds were gathering. 'It's certainly brought people together I'll say that much.'

Finn laughed. 'Aye. Much like the election this year eh?'

Lachlan knew it wouldn't be long before Finn started on politics. 'Some result. Where do they go from here though?'

The election that year had seen the SNP take 56 of Scotland's 59 seats. One Labour, one Tory, and one LibDem remained, and they'd survived on wafer-thin majorities. A natural backlash of the nation's Yes vote consolidating around the only major party actually registered in Scotland.

'Onwards and, hopefully, upwards,' said Finn.

'Maybe,' said Lachlan. 'Things go in cycles though don't they? The youth are on our side but who knows what the next generation will want?'

Finn dropped the revs and the boat slowed giving them a fine view of Cockenzie's twin chimneys, soon to be reduced to rubble. 'EU referendum will be interesting.'

'Think we'd be daft enough to vote Leave?'

'Never underestimate the stupidity of the general public Lachlan. It's the reason we're not preparing for independence now.'

Lachlan watched a yacht as it turned, its sails luffing in the wind. 'How's your boy?' he asked.

'Ian's fine. The bairn's fine. Their new house is smashing. Up on the hill at Willowbrae. Looks out over the Forth.'

'Lucky bugger,' said Lachlan. He lifted the urn and cradled it in his hands. 'That's all Morag wanted. To end her days looking out at this river.'

He looked towards the bridges and beyond, where the river narrowed then meandered across flat fields where ancient battles raged, before narrowing again, rushing quickly over rocks and boulders where a little boy and a little girl had splashed about in the shallows fishing for sticklebacks all those years ago.

A klaxon blared, and a hush descended as three thousand souls held their breath. A moment later, a massive cloud of brown dust emerged from the base of the chimneys, followed a second later by the almighty thwump of the explosion.

Several thousand people gasped at once as the chimneys fell towards each other with a synchronised grace. The two blackened tops kissed each other briefly before crumpling to the ground in an enormous cloud of bricks and dust.

'Would you look at that!' said Finn.

Just for a moment, the dust cloud formed the shape of a person. The head created by the point where the chimney tops had met, the body by the crumpling stacks, with two arms of dust dangling by its sides, created by the falling peaks.

The ghost of the power station hung in the air for a few seconds before it was engulfed by a rising cloud of rubble, smoke and ash.

Lachlan stood, open mouthed. 'That was Morag.'

Finn wiped something from his eye. 'It could have been.'

'I'm telling you. It even looked like her.'

'I don't recall Morag being quite as stoory as that but aye. Maybe she's sending you a message?'

Lachlan looked confused. 'What would that be?'

'Don't you dare chuck me in the water?' said Finn.

'Or, *go ahead and chuck me in the water?'* said Lachlan.

'So what's it going to be?'

'I'll chuck her in the water,' said Lachlan. 'Most of her anyway. She could end up in Venezuela. Or Timbuktu.'

'Any particular spot in mind?' asked Finn.

'Could you give me a lift home? It'd be nice to give her a head start, where the river meets the sea.'

'North Berwick it is,' said Finn as he increased the throttle and turned to the east.

Lachlan moved to the back of the boat. The sun was trying to break through the haze but the river remained cloaked in grey. There was a brightness though. The coastline of East Lothian still felt like a home, of sorts, even though he was now *in* a home.

It had been Grace's idea and he had to admit she was right. The Seaview in North Berwick did offer a sea view, just, and he was learning to tolerate the other residents. He couldn't stay at Grace's, not with the baby, and after Morag's death in February it seemed like the right time to move on.

How he'd suffered in the spring. The final week in the hospital side-room; the *Hospital Use Only* nightgown; the Sodium Chloride drip - its quiet trickle Morag's only source of sustenance; the syringe pump at her back, locked away in a plastic box, easing her into the dark with drips of morphine. Tiny increments. The itching; the cramps; his quiet tears as pneumonia took her away.

As Morag's coffin sank into the crematorium's furnace he felt his future disappear with it. It wasn't so much that the ink had faded on the remaining chapters of his life, leaving blank pages to be filled with a new story, but rather that they'd been torn out completely, leaving ragged stumps hanging from a broken spine. Back at Grace's that evening, his howls of grief could be heard across the rooftops.

He clutched the urn to his chest, lay on the bench seat, and let the rhythm of the swell rock him to sleep.

After a while Finn called from the cabin.

He woke with a start. The fine houses of North Berwick were off to his right; the Bass Rock up ahead; and beyond - the North Sea, Europe, and the world.

'Perfect,' he said, stretching some life into his bones.

Finn killed the engine.

Lachlan leaned on the side of the boat and unscrewed the urn's cap. He may have been saying goodbye to Morag's powdered remains but she would live forever in his head, and in his heart, and in the heads and hearts of everyone she'd met on her journey.

'Goodbye my love,' he said as he tipped the urn over the side. A cloud of ash, dust, and crushed bone fragments spilled into the sea. Some blowing back onto his arms, like a last embrace.

Checking that a small amount of ash remained at the base of the urn he replaced the lid and held it briefly to his lips. As he lowered it again a beam of sunlight caught its curved body.

It flashed, just for a second, like a smile.

MONDAY

The dying waves grasped for the shore and retreated with a *shhhhhhhh*. The vast river finally ending its journey as it joined the unforgiving North Sea, where Morag's remains had long since mixed with the seaweed and the shipwrecks, and spread beyond the estuary mouth, becoming part of the world. He stepped forward, sinking into the wet sand.

He stared ahead while the grey waters regarded him with a cold indifference.

Phoebe appeared at his side, carrying her bucket and spade.

With a grunt, he picked her up and swept her hair from her face. Three oyster catchers landed on the beach twenty yards away, pecking at shell-fish coming in with the tide. Or were they magpies? He wasn't sure.

'You see this?' He pointed at the sea beyond the Bass Rock.

'Uhuh,' said Phoebe narrowing her eyes.

'Well this is the sea. And it can take you anywhere in the world. Anywhere you like. Venezuela, Canada, Iceland, or Timbuktu.'

'Timbuktu?' said Phoebe.

'Aye,' said Lachlan. 'And don't let anyone tell you otherwise.'

'Okay Grandad,' she said. Her nose was running.

'Here I've got a wee present for you.' He lowered her to the beach and reached into his pocket.

Phoebe looked expectantly at Lachlan's hand as he opened it in front of her.

She reached for his saltire pebble and took it with a smile. 'That's pretty.'

'Now I want you to keep that and give it to your grandchildren when you're a big girl okay? Promise me?'

'Promise,' said Phoebe.

Grace trudged towards them over the sand, carrying two ice cream cones from the van on the esplanade. She walked like Morag. He saw Morag everywhere, in everything.

'Enjoying your paddle?' said Grace as she handed Phoebe a cone.

'Och!' Phoebe yelped as her ice cream fell in the sand.

'Phoebe!' sighed Grace.

'Want another one,' said Phoebe. Her lip quivering.

'Okay,' said Grace. 'Come with me. You okay Dad? Do you want one?'

'No thanks,' said Lachlan. 'I'll stay here for a bit.'

He watched them walk back over the beach. A few families were enjoying picnics, brightly coloured wind-breakers staked into the sand. Barbecue smoke rising into the air. The faint chatter and whoops of children over the constant tearing noise of the sea.

He remembered his father, on the banks of Loch Ard, when he'd picked up that pebble all those years ago, and his mother. How different might his life had been if she'd lived? Maybe he'd still be in Aberfoyle? Married to Morag? Probably not. She was always going to head for the city.

His thoughts drifted downriver from Aberfoyle to Stirling and the body in the river. Would Barry Turnbull have bullied him throughout his school years if they hadn't made that grisly discovery? Maybe he'd have fought back, eventually. Become the man his father wanted him to be. He'd managed the drinking part, until it nearly killed him, but he'd never been good with his fists.

And his father, the rock he'd been anchored to, crumbling in a sea of whisky. The chains rotting away over the years before his final act. Another vote in a democracy that couldn't give a damn.

Unchained, he'd made it to Edinburgh. The capital city that could have been. Morag had fallen into his arms as another life ended. Another time-line complete. He scanned the horizon, looking for a sign. Anything. Something to say Morag was there and she was waiting for him.

He took a few steps into the water. It lapped against his knees, soaking the bottom of his trousers. Had his withered old legs come to the end of their journey?

What if Gabriella had lived? Would they have had Grace? And if they hadn't had Grace, wee Phoebe wouldn't be here. He peered back towards the esplanade where they sat on a bench beside the ice cream van. Grace gave him a wave.

And young Mark. Killed in the desert for nothing. Buried under a flag he'd grown to detest. He'd brought Billy back into his life but at what cost?

Lachlan's heart was heavy. An unbearable ballast. His three score years and ten had been and gone. He'd got to where he wanted to be; where the river meets the sea. And like the river, he got here by following the path of least resistance.

Now was the time for action. To do something, rather than wait for something to be done. He took another step. He closed his eyes tight as the freezing water lapped around his waist.

Someone shouted 'DAD!' from the beach. A family, together, enjoying their day. It was time for Lachlan to let his family get on with their own lives. And time for him to be reunited with his childhood sweetheart, his first kiss, his lover, his wife. His everything.

His phone rang.

He pulled it from his shirt pocket and read the screen - *Doc Blair*.

Did he need to hear the news? He decided he didn't and returned the phone to his pocket.

'I'm coming Morag,' he said. The tears running freely down his cheeks now, joining the waves. He glanced along the shore. The oyster catchers had been joined by a fourth, their squawks filling the air as they fought over food. They seemed fatter than oyster catchers though. They couldn't have been magpies? Could they?

'Lachie-Boy!' a familiar voice called from the beach.

Lachlan stared at the sea and took another half step forward. The chill of the water reached his gut where it masked the throbbing pain he'd been suffering for months. There was a sudden splashing behind him.

'DAD! What the fuck?'

He turned to see a face he recognised. Older than he remembered, but different. Kinder. The scowl was gone.

'Billy?' he said.

'Aye. Come on.' Billy grabbed Lachlan around the waist. 'You're in too deep. What the hell are you doing?'

Lachlan looked down at the water swirling around his midriff. 'I'm just... paddling son. Why are you here?'

Billy jerked a thumb over his shoulder where Johnny stood at the edge of the beach.

'Sorry we're late,' shouted Johnny. 'You didn't tell me we were going swimming.'

As Billy edged Lachlan back towards the sand he wiped the tears from his father's face. Grace and Phoebe were hurrying towards them.

'Wee surprise for you,' said Johnny, indicating Billy.

'Certainly is,' said Lachlan, shocked back into the present. 'How are you son? Still on the rigs?'

'Aye,' said Billy. 'Two weeks off though. Was down in Alloa seeing Mum and she said old Señor Fannybaws was over from Spain. Thought I'd come out with him. How are you doing? Sorry to hear about Morag.'

Lachlan looked at his bare feet and his soaked trousers, then towards the waves as they continued to shush onto the shingle. 'Thanks son. I miss her.'

His phone started ringing again. He ignored it.

'You going to get that?' asked Johnny.

Grace arrived, out of breath, 'Dad, answer your phone.' Phoebe smiled at Billy, wiped ice cream from her face, and said 'Who are you?'

Billy laughed. 'I'm your Uncle Billy. You must be Phoebe?'

Grace pulled the phone from Lachlan's pocket and read the screen. 'It's the doctor.' She pressed the answer button and handed it back to Lachlan.

Lachlan took it with a sigh. The sound of the sea made it difficult to hear what was being said.

'Doctor Blair?'

'Yes… Calling with your results… Tried the home but they said you were out…'

'Sorry doctor I can hardly hear you. I'm at the beach.' Lachlan held a hand up to Grace, Johnny and Billy and stepped away, pressing the phone tight against his ear.

'Good news,' the doctor continued.

'Really?' said Lachlan. Phoebe had taken the flagstone from her pocket and was showing it to Billy, who was kneeling on the sand. Grace was complementing Johnny on his suntan. Johnny grinned like an idiot.

'Well, as you know, you do have cancer of the bowel. But the good news is it's operable. So with surgery we should be able to get it out.'

'I'm not dying?'

'We're all dying, Mr McCormack. 'It's just that some are approaching their final destination faster than others. Hopefully we'll be able to move you into the slow lane.'

He didn't know what to say. He stood, his trousers dripping onto the sand, watching his son, his daughter, his grand-daughter, and his best friend smile and laugh on a sunny summer's day in Scotland. Grace gave him a lop-sided smile. As if she could see the weight lifting from his shoulders, like he'd just dropped a bag of bricks.

'Good news?' asked Grace.

'Aye,' said Lachlan. 'Good news.'

'I was coming to tell you some more good news. I got a call from the home when we were eating our ice cream.'

'Oh aye?' said Lachlan. He didn't think he'd ever had two pieces of good news on the same day before. Or the same year, for that matter.

'Bob's dead. So you can move into his room tomorrow. You'll get your sea view.'

Lachlan thought of the begonia on his window ledge. Morag's remaining ashes had gone into the soil. She'd have her sea view again at last.

The sun swept across the beach, turning everything golden, and he smiled.

'Can I get a present Uncle Billy?' said Phoebe.

Billy laughed. 'Of course. We'll go to the shops.'

'Don't need to. Look.' Phoebe held out the flagstone. The blue of the saltire as vivid as the blue of the sky. 'Grandad made me this. Make me something.'

Lachlan looked at Phoebe, proudly holding up the pebble he'd plucked from a distant riverbank nearly eight decades before. That little pebble had taken some journey. But this wasn't the journey's end.

This is where it began.

Craig Smith lives on the edge (of Edinburgh) with his wife and children. In a former life he was a musician with a couple of NME *Singles of the Week* to his name. In this life, his spare bass gathers dust in a corner while his Fender Precision left to begin a new life in Marseilles. His debut novel *The Mile* (Pilrig Press) was published to much acclaim in 2013. An alumni of the Faber Academy, he continues to write about Scotland, Scottishness, and Scots, and hopes one day he might live in a normal country. Preferably Scotland.